The Children at the Bottom of the Gardden

Jonathan Butcher

Published in Great Britain in 2018 by Jonathan Butcher & Matthew Cash, Burdizzo Books Walsall, UK.

Also by Jonathan Butcher:

Flash Fear (editor/contributor)

The Chocolateman (a short story)

What Good Girls Do

Demon Thingy – Book One

Visions from the Void (editor/contributor)

Acknowledgements

This book was a long time coming. Eternal thanks to everyone, past and present, who has ever encouraged me in my writing or who helped inspire the story you now hold in your hands. These include but are not limited to: Mum and Dad, Sian, Mrs Lamb, Naeem, Matty-Bob Cash, Em Dehaney, Justin Park, Duncan Ralston, Jim "The Don" Mcleod, Duncan Bradshaw, Chad Clark, Chris Hall, Mignon Garret, Shapeshift Dan, Dan Billing, Chris Rollason, Hal Duncan, Isis, Aborym, Dodheimsgard, DJ Krush, Locust Toybox, Wednesday 13, Irvine Welsh.

Welcome ... yes yes yes.

PROLOGUE
"The People Game"

Thomas

Thomas has already played, like, a zillion of the children's dumb games, and they stopped being fun a long time ago.

From his kitchen doorway, the Gardden looks like nothing more than an overgrown hotch-potch of long grass, weeds, shrubbery and gnarled branches. Bugs zoom and fizz through the ragged-haggardy trees, which stretch up and over him to scrape the farmhouse roof. Tottering on the doorstep, Thomas drums his fingers against the 'Monster Munch' t-shirt that barely hides his gut, while with the other hand he grips a plastic bag that's heavy with glistening dead flesh. At 25 he's probably an ickle bit old to be playing such silly games but, sadly, it's not up to him.

He rubs his wiry beard, frowning. He'd gotten it right, hadn't he? He'd remembered everything, so there's no reason to be afraid.

The sun licks the back of his neck when he hops down onto the soil, but after a few steps into the trees he feels like he's been gobbled up by shadows. The rest of the world seems super-far away as he pulls leaves and dried twigs aside like a rainforest explorer, repeating to himself the items that the children had challenged him to remember.

"Three rashers of bacon, 200 grams of minced lamb, five Cumberland sausages - no, four Cumberlands - 150 grams of liver ..."

That's today's weirdy-weird game.

After a minute or so, he comes to a tangle of lifeless wooden arms. He drops the bag of butcher's shop meat and, wheezing, hunkers down to kneel before the rotten elm tree. Pressing his cheek against the bare ground, as if he's listening for a stampede, he sings gently, "Helloooo... are you dooooown there?"

At first there's nothing - no birds whistle, no breeze blows - but Thomas understands. It's just another game. He huffs with aggravation, raising dust from the bone-stony dirt.

"Look, I got the stuff, so I won, okay? Stop messing around."

And from nowhere in particular, there's a giggle.

"Who's that?" Thomas asks.

The laughter rises into a squeak.

"Hello, Benny," Thomas says, ending playtime. He scans the trees for the little boy.

A young voice, which seems to come from the air around him, replies, "Aww, no fun, Fatty-Tom-Tom. How did you know it was me?"

Thomas ignores the question. "Why don't you all just come out? Where's Simon?"

A pause. Another chuckle. "Are you sure you want to speak with him, Mr Fat-Fat? After all, *you got it wrong!*"

"No I didn't," Thomas counters, plonking his round backside down and sitting cross-legged. "I counted them perfect."

"You got it wrong!" Benny's voice mocks, circling Thomas's ears. "You got it wrong! You got it wrong!"

"No I *didn't!*" Thomas shouts. Peeved, he wrenches packages from the bag, tearing the plastic to reveal strips and splodges of meat. "Look," he says. "Three bacon rashers, five Cumberlands, no, I mean four Cumberlands, an, um ..."

Another voice interrupts him, high-pitched but stern like a parent.

Simon.

"Pay attention, Thomas. You forgot the list, you got it wrong, and that's just the way it is."

Thomas closes his mouth, staring at the plastic-wrapped meat scattered in front of the elm tree. He'd been *so sure* he'd won.

Still out of sight, but like a voice inside Thomas's head, Simon says, "It's okay. Don't worry about The Meat Game right now - there's something much bigger we're gonna have to play, soon."

Suddenly, they're with him. To Thomas's right stands Hanna, a blonde girl of five with curls that make Thomas think of cooked spaghetti and a blue dress that sparkles like starshine. To Thomas's left appears Benny, a tubby, mean-faced boy of a similar age to Hanna, wearing a mucky green shirt with two missing buttons and a baseball cap that reads, "Dinoman". Lastly, with a crunch-snap, something emerges from the centre of the elm tree: a pale, bodiless face with eyes like black beetles. This third and last kid is Simon, and even without arms and legs, even as just a face poking out of a tree trunk, Thomas has to do *exactly* as Simon tells him.

"Why are you trying to frighten me today?" Thomas asks, staring at the meat again to avoid Simon's black eyeballs. "Why can't you just look like *you*, like normal?"

"Because you're going to leave us," Simon says.

Thomas scrunches up his face. He's definitely considered running away before, but he'd never do it. He wouldn't dare.

"You're going to disappear, and that's why we're gonna have to play The People Game."

"That's ... that's not true," Thomas says, daring a peek at Simon's face. It's not smiling or glaring – it's just straight, and maybe an ickle bit sad.

"Pretty soon, Thomas, a bunch of people are going to

come here, to our home."

Thomas glances at Hanna and then at Benny. Normally they'd be grinning or fooling around but today they're just standing there, watching him with faces as blank as Simon's.

"Look, I don't know what you're talking about," Thomas says. "I'm not going anywhere."

"Maybe you can change things after all," Simon replies. "Maybe *you'll* win The People Game."

Scratching his head, Thomas shrugs. "I really don't understand."

"You will." Simon smiles at last. "But anyway, enough about that. You lost The Meat Game, didn't you? So now you've got to pay a forfeit."

"Yay!" Hanna yells, and Benny starts to dance gleefully.

"Okaaaaaaay," Thomas moans, though Simon's words have made him feel ooky. "What do I have to do?"

Benny stops dancing and Hanna falls quiet. They look excited. A pukey, horrid thought makes Thomas's guts plunge.

Please don't let the forfeit be the suitcase...

Instead of the suitcase, though, Simon says, "You have to eat it. Eat it all up, right now."

Thomas looks at the raw pink mishmash spilling from the plastic. "What ... the meat?"

"Yes," Simon agrees. "Every last bit."

A chorus of cackles fills the Gardden, and little Hanna squeals, "You're really thick, Thomas! Thick as dog shit!"

At her words, the Gardden begins to *change*.

Thomas focuses on the meat. He doesn't want to see the great trees stirring, like the brown fingers of an awakening giant. He doesn't want to see the creeping shapes, the grasping vines, and the twisting, twirling, terrible shadows.

Most of all, he doesn't want to see the Gardden's eyes.

"Ha ha, Fatty-Tom-Tom!"

"Eat the meat, you fat thicko!"

"NOW, THOMAS," Simon blasts. "RIGHT NOW!"

With their clamour rattling his eardrums and with the tree branches flexing and flailing, Thomas rips open a package and fingers a clammy, uncooked sausage. The children hoot when he raises it to his lips. It feels awful on his tongue but he chews and takes it down, trying to ignore the laughter and the writhing trees and the huge black eyes of the Gardden. He wants to tell himself that the sausage is a cake and that it's delicious, but the very first mouthful has him dry heaving.

He mustn't stop, though.

When he moves on to the chewy, bloody mince, pushing away thoughts of The People Game and the children's cackles and the freakish storm of branches, Thomas tries to calm himself with a single chanted thought.

It's okay, at least it's not the suitcase ... it's okay, at least it's not the suitcase ... it's okay, at least it's not the suitcase ...

PART ONE
Summer Days

CHAPTER 1
"He's just a kid and he'll be trouble"

Ray

Ray told himself to ignore the two cold, grey eyes boring into his back. For God's sake: he was 20-years-old and had tougher friends in higher places.

Sipping vintage *Veuve Cliquot*, he and his boss Henry Borders stood alone in the night-time shadow of the wine bar's balcony. Three storeys above one of Seadon's exclusive drinking districts, the ocean air drifted through Ray's thin purple dreadlocks and Henry's tattered, middle-aged hairline. Ray could almost taste the gushing testosterone and booze-loosened holes of the crowd below, and their presence made his groin ache. Beyond the luridly dressed tourists and the neon glamour of the bars lay the distant black tide, shimmering with the city of Seadon's lights and the white pallor of the waxing moon.

"Fackin' beautiful," Henry said, spitting his words past a fat Cohiba cigar. "You know what that ocean means to me?"

The bar's glow played across Ray's half-empty champagne flute. "What?"

Henry leaned tipsily against the wooden frame of the balcony, his rough face carved into a scheming grin. Clutching a glass in one hand and a champagne bottle in the other, he replied, "It means money." He gestured towards the road's criss-crossing bustle. "These fackers come 'ere from their shit'oles up north, and they're drunk before they've even hit the bottle. An' you know what gets 'em pissed?"

With one black-varnished nail, Ray fingered the studs of his leather dog collar. "Beer?" he suggested, smirking.

As usual, Henry failed to notice Ray's obtuseness. "Nope. What gets 'em drunk is that big, blue, foamin' slag over there. Visitors look at that sea, an' they think, *I want everythin' this place has to offer. An' that's where we come in.*"

Ray considered the words: the emphasised 'we', as if they were a team.

"This city's mine, Raymond-son," Henry said, and squeezed Ray's youthful shoulders. "But one day, I want it to be *yours.*"

Henry's nickname of Raymond-son, spoken like the Japanese honorific Raymond-san, was just one of several titles Ray went by. 'Ray' in his own head, 'Raymond' to his mother, and in the city's gloriously degenerate Goth scene, his old pals had crossed 'Ray' with 'Satan', and made 'Ratan'.

Henry released Ray, who risked a glance behind him, hoping that those blank grey eyes had found someone else to follow. But through the balcony's sliding doors, between the mingling forms of the stylish revellers, Ray saw that Percy Locker, a dainty-faced gorilla of a man, still stared. Their eyes met and Ray forced a smile, but Percy's near-feminine features did not alter.

"I'll be leaving Seadon soon though, Henry," Ray said uncomfortably, turning back to the street. "I feel like I ..."

"Nah," Henry said, refilling Ray's glass. "You'll change your mind about that, son. Wiv all this booze, cooze, an' more besides? No place like home, is there?"

Ray let the question hang. The decadent lifestyle he was becoming accustomed to certainly had its perks, but he was hungry for the turn of a page. When people grew tired of having lived in the same, dead-end city their whole lives, they travelled, didn't they? They tried something different, they journeyed somewhere new and they saw what they could see.

Besides, Ray's newfound circumstances were by no means risk-free.

"I don't think Percy likes me," Ray said.

"Don't let him hear ya call him that, son," Henry warned, spiked shadows dancing on his rough face. "He's 'Locker' to you, an' Percy Locker don't like no one at all. But he'll get used to ya, don't worry."

Ray watched the crowds below, zeroing in on an attractive couple. She had a serpentine tattoo across her cleavage and he had alluring, asymmetrical lip piercings. If Ray drank any more, he'd risk breaking one of his rules. "I should be off, Henry."

Henry chuckled. "You sure, son? There's still champagne to drink, birds to bang, white lines to hoof..."

Ray smiled, nodding. "I know, but I think I need an earlyish night."

Henry made a show of looking at his chunky gold watch, raised his eyes, then grunted, "Alright, son - back to ya crypt. I'll see you at the shop tomorrow."

Ray needed to get away from the evening's drinking and the temptation to delay things any longer. He'd had it with Seadon, their whore of a city, and had set himself a few important rules to observe while preparing to leave. He'd avoid class A drugs, because they were too easily available. He'd abstain from sex, because his cock had a brain of its own. And, most importantly, he'd do his best to stay on *everyone's* good side.

LOCKER

SAT HUNCHED AND ALONE ON A BAR STOOL, PERCY LOCKER EYEBALLED THE SMARMY GOTH CUNT. AS THE KID MINCED BACK INTO THE BAR WITH HENRY, LOCKER SLUGGED BACK ANOTHER SHOT OF JAMESONS.

SHOULDN'T BE THIS WAY - NOT AFTER ALL THIS FUCKING TIME.

BACK IN THE DAY, HENRY WOULD'VE BEEN SAT RIGHT THERE WITH HIM: KINGPIN AND RIGHT-HAND MAN. NOT ANYMORE THOUGH. NOT NOW AN INTRUDING GOTH HAD STUCK HIS FAGGOTY CLAWS INTO THE BOSS. *RAYMOND ATTICUS* – EVEN THE NAME SOUNDED QUEER. LOCKER WISHED HE COULD DIG A DITCH AND JUST BURY THE PROBLEM.

LOCKER POURED MORE WHISKY AND SWUNG A BLEARY GAZE ACROSS HIS BOSS'S DRINKING HOLE, WHICH LOCKER HAD PART-OWNED FOR YEARS. IT WAS AN ALRIGHT PLACE, HE SUPPOSED: TABLE SERVICE, LOW LIGHTS, BLOOD REDS AND CHOCOLATE BROWNS. PRIVATE LEATHER BOOTHS LINED THE WALLS BORDERING A SMALL STAGE WHERE SINGERS SOMETIMES CROONED. THE BAR MAY HAVE LOOKED OKAY, BUT IT STILL DREW CROWDS OF ARSEHOLES BOTH LEGIT AND LAWLESS, AS WELL AS LAUGHING, JIGGLING WHORES WHO GOT NOTHING FROM LOCKER BUT DISGUST. HE HATED THE SMUGNESS OF IT ALL, BUT IT MADE HIM CASH AND THE STAFF SERVED HIM WHILE AVOIDING HIS EYES.

ACROSS THE ROOM, CORDONED OFF IN THE VIP AREA, BEARDED AND SUITED FRED CHALMERS SAT GULPING CHAMPAGNE WITH TWO BULIMIC SLAGS. WHEN HENRY LAY A HAND ON FRED'S SHOULDER FRED TURNED HIS HEAD, THEN

STOOD UP TO SHAKE HANDS WITH THAT UNTRUSTWORTHY COCKSUCKER RAY. ALL FRIENDLY, AS IF THE KID BELONGED THERE. AS IF HE WAS PART OF THE FUCKING CREW.

LOOK AT HIM. FUCKING GOTH. FUCKING *NOBODY*, WITH HIS MAKE-UP AND FAGGY DREADLOCKS AND TIGHT TOP AND SKINNY 'COME FUCK ME' JEANS. HENRY WOULDN'T HAVE LET ANY OF THE OTHERS WEAR SUCH A CUNTY GET-UP.

FINALLY, THE KID FLOUNCED OVER TO THE EXIT WITHOUT LOOKING LOCKER'S WAY. LOCKER CAUGHT THE BOSS HENRY'S EYE. FELT A SNAG OF PAIN IN HIS GUTS. HENRY GESTURED FOR HIM TO COME OVER, BUT LOCKER TURNED BACK TO HIS WHISKY BOTTLE.

DIDN'T HENRY REMEMBER HOW THINGS HAD BEEN? DIDN'T IT MATTER TO HENRY THAT WITHOUT LOCKER TO BACK HIM HE WOULD NEVER HAVE BEEN AS FEARED, NEVER AS SAFE, AND NEVER AS RICH?

LOCKER STARED INTO HIS DRINK, IMAGINING A WORLD WITHOUT INTERFERING SCUM.

A HAND SQUEEZING A ROLL OF NOTES THUMPED THE WOOD OF THE BAR, AND FRED CHALMERS CALLED, "EXCUSE ME, DARLIN', WE NEED ANOTHER COUPLE MORE BOTTLES, NICE AN' QUICK."

FRED, TONED AND TANNED. NEAT FACIAL HAIR. BIG JAW, STRONG HANDS, TOUGH REPUTATION.

FUCKING PUSSY.

FRED THUMBED A FIFTY INTO THE AIR TOWARDS THE GINGER SLUT SERVING DRINKS. THE NOTE SPUN ONCE AND THEN SWOOPED ACROSS THE AIR LIKE A PENDULUM. CAME TO REST ON THE RUBBER MATTED FLOOR BEHIND THE BAR. THE REDHEAD FORCED A SMILE AND FRED WATCHED WITH A GRIN AS SHE BENT OVER TO COLLECT THE MONEY. TURNING TO LOCKER, FRED ASKED, "WHY DON'T YOU COME JOIN US, MATE? YOU LOOK LIKE THE WORLD JUST TOOK A DUMP IN YOUR HAT."

THINKS THAT'S FUNNY. BEARDY PRICK THINKS HE SOUNDS

LIKE THE BOSS WHEN HE COMES OUT WITH SHITE LIKE THAT.

LOCKER SHIFTED HIS BULK SIDEWAYS TO REST HIS EYES ON THE MAN. "JUS' THINKING," HE SLURRED.

"BIT RISKY, ISN'T IT?" FRED SAID WITH A SMILE.

FRED LOOKED PRETTY GOOD TONIGHT: SMART AND TRIMMED. MADE LOCKER WANT TO KNOCK THE CUNT'S JAW OUT OF PLACE.

IN A LOW VOICE, FRED ASKED, "WHAT'S THE PROBLEM? ANYTHIN' I SHOULD KNOW?"

"NO," LOCKER GRUNTED, KEEPING HIS EYES SCREWED TO THE PRICK. PICTURING HIM NAKED. PICTURING HIM DEAD.

FRED GLANCED BACK TOWARDS THE TABLE WHERE THE WHORES WERE CACKLING AT ONE OF HENRY'S JOKES. DISTRACTED, FRED SAID, "BUSINESS IS GOOD THOUGH. GOOD EARLY SEASON SO FAR. AND HENRY'S PLEASED WITH THINGS, RIGHT?"

WITHOUT MOVING HIS HEAD, LOCKER PICKED UP HIS GLASS AND TOSSED BACK A SHOT. IMAGINED PUSHING HIS THUMBS INTO THIS SMART PRICK'S EYE HOLES. LOCKER SAW THROUGH HIM. KNEW HE WANTED TO SIT IN HENRY'S CHAIR ONE DAY. KNEW HE COULDN'T BE RELIED ON.

JUST GIVE ME AN HOUR ALONE IN MY WORKROOM WITH YOU, FRED.

" WE AREN'T BEING HASSLED BY THE BOYS IN BLUE," FRED WENT ON, KEEPING HIS TONE CHIRPY. "AND HANCOCK'S KEEPING HIS DISTANCE FOR NOW, LIKE A ... LIKE A SCHOOLKID SCARED O' THE BULLIES."

THERE HE WENT AGAIN: ANOTHER BAD IMPRESSION OF THE BOSS.

"IT'S ALL LOOKING ROSY," FRED BLATHERED. A SMILE SPREAD THROUGH HIS BEARD. "TELL YOU WHAT, THAT LANKY STREAK O' PISS RAY IS A FUNNY FUCKER..."

THE MENTION OF THE INTRUDER MADE LOCKER SNARL, "THAT KID'S A *CUNT.*"

FRED CHECKED BEHIND HIM, AS IF SOMEONE MIGHT HAVE HEARD LOCKER OVER THE MUSIC AND THE PUNTERS' CHATTER. "THAT'S A BIT CONTROVERSIAL, ISN'T IT?" HE ASKED. THE BARTENDER PASSED HIM AN ICE BUCKET. "I MEAN, NONE OF US WERE TOO SURE AT THE START BUT HE'S NOT CAUSIN' A PROBLEM, IS HE? AND HE'S NOT STEPPIN' ON ANY TOES ..."

"HE'S STEPPING ON *EVERYONE'S* FUCKING TOES," LOCKER SPAT. HE KNEW HE SHOULD PROBABLY SHUT UP, BUT COULDN'T STOP. JABBING HIS FINGER ONTO THE COUNTER FOR EMPHASIS, HE GROWLED, "HE'S STEPPING ON *YOUR* TOES, ON *HENRY'S* TOES, AND HE'S SURE AS FUCK STEPPING ON *MINE*."

FRED SPOKE CAREFULLY. "WHAT DO YOU MEAN? HAS THE KID DONE SOMETHING TO OFFEND YOU?"

"HE'S NOT THE RIGHT SORT," LOCKER SAID, SUDDENLY FEELING WASTED. "HE'S JUST A KID AND HE'LL BE TROUBLE. HE'LL DIP HIS TOES INTO THE BUSINESS AND RUN PISSING SCARED AT THE FIRST SIGN OF PROBLEMS."

"IT'S NOT EVEN A DEAD CERT THAT HE'LL BE GETTING INVOLVED, YET." FRED LAID A HAND ONTO LOCKER'S THICK SHOULDER. "DO YOU THINK YOU SHOULD HEAD HOME, PERCY?"

LOCKER LOOKED DOWN AT FRED'S FINGERS AND DRAWLED, "DON'T ... EVER ... CALL ME THAT."

FRED FLINCHED HIS HAND AWAY, HIS EYES STRETCHING WIDE.

FOR A SECOND, LOCKER CONSIDERED HOISTING THE WHISKY BOTTLE UP AND DOING FRED RIGHT THERE: A SMASH AND A STAB AND A TWIST. HE WANTED THE POETRY. WANTED HIS STUPID, STRAIGHT-LINE BRAIN TO OPEN UP AND SEE THINGS MORE CLEARLY, BUT IT WOULDN'T BE WISE. EVEN SO, JUST TO TAKE FRED'S TUFTY THROAT IN HIS HANDS AND *SQUEEZE* ...

"GO BACK TO THEM," LOCKER SAID. HE NEEDED TO REGAIN CONTROL SO HE POURED MORE LIQUOR TO GIVE HIS HANDS SOMETHING TO DO.

FRED WASN'T QUITE FINISHED, THOUGH. "YOU WEREN'T THERE THE FIRST NIGHT, PER... LOCKER. YOU DIDN'T SEE THE KID THEN. NEVER SEEN ANYONE SO QUICK..."

LOCKER'S TEMPER FRAYED. "FORGIVEN HIM FOR THAT NOW, HAVE YOU? TELL ME, DO YOU THINK THAT SHITSTABBER WILL STILL BE WITH US TEN YEARS DOWN THE LINE?"

"I HONESTLY DON'T KNOW. THE BOSS SEEMS TO HAVE TAKEN A REAL SHINE TO HIM."

"YEAH, AND MORE'S THE FUCKING PITY," SNEERED LOCKER. HE POURED OUT THE BOTTLE'S DREGS AND KNOCKED THEM BACK LIKE A FULL STOP.

"WELL, PAL, I'M GONNA HEAD BACK TO THE BOYS BUT, ER, YOU KEEP YOUR HEAD UP, EH?"

UNABLE TO STOP HIMSELF, LOCKER GOT TO HIS FEET. HE TOWERED OVER FRED, LEANED IN TOWARDS HIM. BEARDY FUCKER SMELLED LIKE CINNAMON AFTERSHAVE. LOOKED LIKE HE WAS ABOUT TO TURN AND RUN. TASTING WHISKY FUMES, PERCY LOCKER SPOKE SLOWLY. "I'LL TELL YOU SOMETHING, FRED. IF THAT LITTLE SHIT STEPS AN INCH OUT OF LINE, HE'S *FINISHED.* I'VE GOT FRIENDS, YOU KNOW, AND THEY'D ALL LOVE TO MEET HIM. EVERY FUCKING ONE OF THEM."

FRED STEPPED BACKWARDS. "NO NEED TO BRING YOUR TOOLS INTO THIS, MATE. I'LL JUST... GO BACK TO HENRY AND THE GIRLS NOW..."

LOCKER WATCHED HIM RETREAT. HIS FACE PUMPED HOT BLOOD. HIS SKIN PRICKLED LIKE NETTLE STINGS. HIS BOSS'S LAUGHTER BOOMED OVER THE MUSIC, MADE LOCKER WANT TO PULL OUT HIS OWN EARDRUMS. HE STOOD UP UNSTEADILY AND HEADED FOR THE BAR'S PLUSH, WHITE TOILETS. WENT TO THE FAR URINAL AND PISSED, PLANTING A HAND ON THE SPARKLING WALL TILES FOR BALANCE.

"HEY MAN, FRESHEN UP?" CAME A BLURRED VOICE.

LOCKER TURNED, COCK STILL POKING OUT OF HIS SUIT TROUSERS. SAW HIMSELF IN THE MIRROR BEHIND THE ROW OF

GLITTERING SINKS. SQUINTING, SWAYING, HE STRUGGLED TO FOCUS ON A BLACK MAN WITH A CLEANLY SHAVEN HEAD. A DOZEN OR SO FRAGRANCE BOTTLES STOOD AT THE GUY'S SIDE.

"NO SPLASH, NO GASH," THE BLACK SAID, TEETH BRIGHT AGAINST HIS DARK SKIN. "NO SPRAY, NO LAY."

WHAT WAS THIS? LOCKER NEVER GAVE THE OKAY FOR A BATHROOM ATTENDANT. HE PICTURED THE COON'S BROWN HEAD SPLITTING OPEN ON A TAP, GOUTING BLOOD INTO A PORCELAIN BOWL. A GRITTY CRUNCH OF SKULL. WHITE, ROLLING EYES AGAINST SKIN THE COLOUR OF SHIT.

"YOU THINK I'M PAYING TO TAKE A SLASH, YOU CHEEKY FUCKING CUNT?" LOCKER MUMBLED, ADVANCING. "FUCKING BOG-WOGS EVERYWHERE. COMING TO MY CITY IS BAD ENOUGH, *BUT MY FUCKING BAR?* I DON'T THINK SO."

THE BLACK CUNT SEEMED TO LOOK AROUND FOR SUPPORT, BUT IT WAS JUST THE TWO OF THEM. EVEN IN LOCKER'S TOPSY-TURVY VISION HE COULD SEE THAT THE GUY WAS AFRAID.

"HEY MAN, CHILL A LITTLE, HUH?"

LOCKER LURCHED FORWARDS AND GRABBED HIM BY THE COLLAR. THE CUNT TRIED TO PULL AWAY, BUT WHEN HE SAW LOCKER'S EXPRESSION THE STRENGTH DRAINED FROM HIS BODY. IF LOCKER HAD LET HIM GO, HE WOULD'VE DROPPED LIKE A SACK OF TWIGS.

"PLEASE," THE COON MURMURED.

LOCKER PRESSED HIS FOREHEAD AGAINST THE OTHER MAN'S. DRANK IN THOSE TREMBLING FAT LIPS, THE SOUR SCENT OF SWEAT. LOCKER WANTED THE POETRY TO COME, THE INSIGHT, AND THE INTELLECT HE GAINED WHEN HE WREAKED PAIN AND DAMAGE ONTO SOMEONE HELPLESS.

"I'VE GOT FRIENDS, YOU KNOW," LOCKER TOLD HIM. "LOTS OF FUCKING FRIENDS. YOU WANT TO MEET THEM? I'LL INTRODUCE YOU, IF YOU WANT..."

LOCKER WAS DRUNK, THOUGH. WOULD THE POETRY COME, EVEN IF HE TORE THIS FUCKER TO PIECES? HE PUSHED HIS

HEAD FORWARDS AND BENT THE GUY'S NECK BACK. THOSE BROWN ARMS DANGLED, BONELESS, AND HIS SPINE PRESSED AGAINST THE SINK WITH NOWHERE TO GO.

"I WONDER IF YOU'RE WORTH IT." LOCKER BROUGHT HIS HANDS UP AND WRAPPED THEM AROUND THE ATTENDANT'S HEAD SO THAT THE FINGERTIPS WERE ALMOST TOUCHING. THE BLOKE TRIED TO PUSH LOCKER AWAY AGAIN BUT IT WAS JUST A SCARED HALF-GESTURE. LOCKER URGED THE MAN FARTHER BACKWARDS, VERTEBRAE BENDING EVEN CLOSER TO THE WASH BASIN. BOTTLES OF FRAGRANCE TOPPLED, CLINKING LIKE POPPED LIGHT BULBS.

"I COULD BURST YOUR HEAD LIKE A MELON," LOCKER SAID, TENSING HIS FINGERS AROUND THE GUY'S SKULL. "A FUCKING *WATERMELON*, EH?"

THE DOOR TO THE BATHROOM SWUNG OPEN AND, STILL HOLDING THE ATTENDANT, LOCKER WATCHED A SMALL, BALD BUSINESSMAN SCUTTLE TOWARDS A CUBICLE. GUTLESS LOSER PRETENDED NOT TO SEE.

SHOULD LOCKER GO FOR IT RIGHT THERE AND THEN? HE'D HAVE TO DO THE BUSINESSMAN TOO, AND THEN SHUT THE TOILETS UNTIL CLOSING TIME. IT'D BE RISKY, BUT BY *CHRIST* HE WANTED TO STOMP ON SOMETHING'S FACE.

HE BREATHED DEEPLY, CLOSED HIS EYES, WILLING THE POETRY TO COME, BUT THEN...

NO. GET A GRIP.

HE DROPPED THE PETRIFIED ATTENDANT. THE NIGGER'S KNEES BUCKLED AND HE SLID DOWN THE SINK COUNTER TO THE GROUND.

"LISTEN TO ME," LOCKER TOLD THE SHUDDERING BODY. "*YOU DON'T WORK IN THIS CITY ANYMORE.* NO ONE SHOULD HAVE TO PAY FOR A PISS, SO IF I SEE YOU AGAIN, YOU'D BETTER RUN. YOU CUNTS ARE MEANT TO BE GOOD AT RUNNING, AREN'T YOU?"

THE GUY LAY PROPPED AGAINST THE UNIT, PANTING, HIS

HEAD DROOPED AGAINST HIS CHEST.

PLEASED WITH HIMSELF, LOCKER STAGGERED BACK TO THE BAR AND ORDERED ANOTHER BOTTLE OF WHISKY.

IN THE NEAR-DARKNESS OF HIS WORKROOM, CROSS-LEGGED AND NAKED ON THE STICKY FLOOR, PERCY LOCKER POLISHED HIS FRIENDS.

IVA.

BRUTUS.

O'NEILL

EACH HANDLE, EDGE, POINT, SWITCH, CORNER AND CURVE WAS A TRUE COMPANION. HE IMAGINED WHAT THEY WOULD SAY IF THEY COULD SPEAK, THESE TOOLS HE'D BEFRIENDED.

AN HOUR PASSED. CARING FOR HIS FRIENDS HELPED SOBER HIM, CALM HIM - FELT INTIMATE, STROKING AWAY THEIR BLEMISHES. IT NEVER LASTED LONG, BUT WHILE LOCKER CARED FOR THEM HE NEVER THOUGHT ABOUT THE WHORES, THE PAKIS, HIS PARENTS, OR EVEN THE GOTH CUNT.

DEXTER.

JACKSON.

TAYLOR.

FOR JUST A MOMENT, LOCKER DRUNKENLY WONDERED IF ONE OF THEM – IVA - HAD SHIFTED BETWEEN HIS FINGERS, LIKE A RESTLESS PET. HE FROZE, BUT IT DIDN'T HAPPEN AGAIN.

WHEN EACH OF PERCY'S FRIENDS WAS SPOTLESS, HE SIGHED. THEN, IN THE DARKNESS, HE PICKED UP THE FIRST IMPLEMENT AND BEGAN TO POLISH ONCE AGAIN.

Thomas

In the 6am heat mist, in his Pokemon PJs and slippers, Thomas creeps out through the kitchen door and into the tree-cluttery shade of the Gardden. Honestly, The Flyflyfly Game is the *best* way to start the day!

There's an excited war drum in his chest and the air seems to whizz-crackle as he pads towards the end of the dry pathway, the sun seeping through the branches. As usual there's no birdsong, but insects whirr and zip through the leaves, darting across his vision. He passes the elm tree, gulping respectfully, and then sees his daddy's rickety old tool shed, the only building out here now that all the barns have gone. A little way down, the path narrows and the archway shrinks.

After several minutes of easing himself through the undergrowth, the atmosphere seems to ... wobble. Thomas's eyebrows dampen. Electricity scampers down his spine.

I want to fly...

Slipping out from the trees, a stream splashes and trickles at his feet. Over the water, hills sprawl across the land like a giant's stained bed sheets. Thomas can see a mobile home trundling along a wide grey strip, passing over land that had once belonged to his family, the Bosworths. Long ago, it had been a farm, but Thomas's daddy had sold a load of it to make way for a big ol' road.

A voice like a breeze tells him, *"Don't stop."*

For some reason, at that moment Thomas remembers Simon's warning. "We're not *really* going to play The People Game, are we, Simon? Everything's still okay, right?"

There's no reply, not even a giggle.

He tippy-toes forwards and the water laps over and into his slippers, slurping at his feet. In just a few hours, Thomas will be working at the Green Emporium, chatting with Ratan or standing behind the till serving smoking stuff to holiday makers - but here, in the Gardden, the rules are different.

At almost the same moment that Thomas realises that his foot is stuck beneath the sloppy mudwater, a warm wind strokes his back.

"*If you want to fly, just do it,*" one of the children's voices coaxes.

"I want to," he says. "Just help me a little."

Thomas feels a rush of vertigo, and with a gurgling plop his feet burst from the shallow marsh. He scales the air, feeling lighter than a moth, and the surprised trees rustle and gasp.

Whooping, Thomas soars high above the Gardden. When he looks down he sees that the whole forest has become a grinning face with black shadows for eyes. He doesn't like looking at it so he cranes his neck towards the clouds and rockets towards them.

Ray

With the shower flow warm on his ass, Ray enjoyed his morning's varied and obscure masturbatory fantasies.

First, spreading Helen Mirren's varicose-bedraggled legs and chowing down on her pink-and-grey folds.

Oh yeah.

Then, getting blown by JFK, while at the same time rimmed by a priest.

Then massive, bouncing breasts, right in his face.

Then a flash of steel and a shaft of evening sunlight. A leering face. Blood, and a sense of something vast and deceitful.

yes yes yes that's right

He stopped jerking, trying to shake his mind clear. That was the problem with having a psychedelic imagination: it could be tough to control.

He forced himself to picture Dita Von Teese bending her clean, plump white ass towards him as he teabagged Josef Goebbels.

Oh, that's the one, alright - that's the one!

Oh, Dita, Dita, your ass is amazing.

Oh, Josef, tickle that sack.

Oh Josef.

Josef!

Josef!!!

He came with a tight grunt, sucked the moment in, blew it out, and prepared for a new day.

Aftewards, as he dried himself, he wondered vaguely why Dita's eyes had appeared so black.

Pouting into the mirror, Ray flicked a string of purple dreadlocked hair over his shoulder in a well-practiced gesture that to his satisfaction aroused both girls and guys.

He'd completed the first part of his morning ritual: the indulgence of his rampant libido, which was apparently a trait he'd inherited from his fragile late father. Styling came next, and that day he would grace the world with one of his all-time favourite ensembles: huge, spiked boots that stretched his tall stature even higher, baggy black jeans festooned with silver buckles and chains, and a skin-hugging, Dennis-the-Menace-striped sleeveless that accentuated his androgynous frame. He admired his arrogantly elfin face and then slipped in a pair of devil-red contact lenses.

For a while now his boss and friend Henry had pestered him to alter his style, told him to dress "more like a man", but Ray wasn't about to dilute his appearance simply because his life had changed during the past year. He leaned close to the glass and stroked eyeliner across his lower lids, his face framed by the cluttered, adolescent surroundings. Beside his fiery red bed, a grimacing half-scale Jesus Christ stood nailed to a cross, and a leering demon dragged a spiked crown deep into the Messiah's brow. Subversive books stacked the floor, gruesome film posters splattered the walls, and plastic models of silver screen killers stared menacingly out from each shelf.

The last part of his routine came from his desk drawer, from which he removed and unrolled an A2 world map. He felt the familiar, barely-contained excitement once again; the dream was really going to happen. Lying the map flat against his desk, he drew a black fingernail across the route he had marked in fine-liner: from London to Japan, then a flight to exotic Indonesia, up to Singapore, Malaysia and Thailand, and finally another plane to the vast expanse of Australia.

This time next year...

A sense of uneasy purpose had unfolded within him. What he had never thought possible now seemed within his grasp, and parties, night clubs and promiscuity no longer filled his days. Not now that he knew Henry, his meal ticket out of Seadon.

He replaced the map, winked at his reflection, and pointed two fingers towards the mirror.

"*Ka-blow!*" he hissed, picturing his head bursting into fragments.

Bolstered by his morning ritual, he left the room. A picture of a blonde, buck-toothed younger self smiled gormlessly from the narrow hallway wall.

Downstairs, his mother Rose sat silently at the kitchen table, stirring a mug of weak tea in endless circles. Her blonde hair drooped in wet strings and her unmade face wore a look of wry disappointment. Ray prepared an espresso in a brown-spattered percolator, impatiently gnawing his nails as it brewed. After the mechanism ceased its whirr he poured his coffee, blew on it hard, and swallowed it in two swift gulps. He fought the urge to speak, knowing the direction the conversation would take them.

Still silent, his mother sighed her old sigh; the one that said, *Don't mind me, I'll struggle on alone. I can manage.*

Ray would skip breakfast and grab something on his way to the shop. He needed to stay focused on his upcoming lunch with Henry, because for some reason, Ray had a sense that it was going to be important.

When he turned around, Rose looked gaunt. In a rush, the predictable urge to soothe her took hold. "Look," he said. "It's going to be a terrible film. Anything that Hollondaise is going to direct is doomed to fail."

"Actually, it's going to be very good," Rose countered, her tired eyes drifting over to him. "Frederick Hollondaise is a profoundly talented man. I wish that my achievements were even half that of his ..."

"Oh come on." Ray tried to keep things light. "He changed his surname, *legally*, to 'Hollondaise'. Doesn't that tell you enough? He chose to name himself after an egg-based sauce."

She sipped her tea and laid the back of her hand against her forehead. "He directs films and documentaries that change the world, alter views, confront the important questions ... while I audition for bit parts and earn my crust scanning tinned food and frozen mince."

She glanced at Ray again, probably to make sure he was still watching, and then laid her head against the table with a bump.

What had happened to her since he had grown too old to be mothered? As her acting roles diminished she seemed to spend more of her everyday life in performance.

Ray circled the breakfast table and took a different approach. "What did Lucas say?"

The table muffled her reply. "Lucas said what any agent would - that there other parts out there."

"Well, there you are then," Ray agreed. "We live in a city that must be filled with more creative souls than Broadway, so for once I think of Lucas has a point."

Rose stood with a flourish and swished balletically to the window. Framed by the morning sun, she gazed across their meagre garden. "It's been months since I've had any acting or singing work, and it's taking its toll. I'm finding it hard to feel inspired."

"You're just going through a quiet patch, mum," Ray said, sitting down.

"I just ..." she began, her voice trembling. She returned to her chair and met Ray's eyes. "I just wonder if I should, you know, direct my energy elsewhere for a while."

"Don't feel guilty if you need to take a rest. All artists go through doubtful times." He laid his hand on hers. "Something will come up."

Rose looked at him. "I wonder what your father would have thought. I imagine he would have agreed."

Ray tensed, as though his skin had tightened. He had little idea what his father would have thought, and he felt anger stir at the very mention of him. His chest clenched and heat spread through him but then his mother moved swiftly on, skipping over the subject as if it was irrelevant.

She continued, "Am I ... oh, it doesn't matter."

"What?" he asked.

She seemed to try and swallow, but the question emerged regardless. "Well, sometimes I just need to know ... am I still pretty?"

He squirmed and took his hand away from hers, drinking in her wide eyes, elegant cheeks, thin but shapely lips and still-smooth complexion.

Oh shit, Freud, I hope you aren't listening.

"Yes, mum. Yes, you are. You're still gorgeous."

"Thank you, Raymond."

"No problem. I've got to head to work now."

"Okay. I don't suppose you've had any luck looking for another job yet, have you?"

Ray tutted. *This again.*

"No, I told you, I'm happy being shop manager

for the time being. I'm building up my cash so that..."

"But you deserve better than working in a druggy shop. If you really are serious about leaving Seadon..."

"And I certainly am."

"...then you need to build up a set of skills. You know that you're never going to truly make something of yourself working for *that man*..."

Ray became irritable. "Jesus, what have you got against Henry? He's a great boss! I've never been paid so well."

"Oh, Ray ..."

"What?"

"You're just so strong-willed, and I think you could do something special with your life, something good, if you just make the right choices ..."

"I will, so it's all fine. I'm fine. Everything's fine!" Their eyes met and he softened. "Look, why don't you go and get yourself made up and then grab some lunch at the Red Kite this afternoon? Probably cheer you up."

"I don't have the money, I'm afraid," she said. "Have a good day, Raymond."

He pulled some notes from his back pocket and placed them beside his mother's tea. "Treat yourself."

"Raymond, you can't afford that ..."

"Yes I can. I'm doing well, so don't worry."

She looked at the money, exhaled, and then took

it coyly. "Thank you. I love you, Ray."

"You too, mum. I've got to go to work now, but I'll see you later." He turned to leave.

"Okay." There was a pause. Then he heard, "And Ray?"

"Yes mum?"

"I've asked you before, if you *have* to wank in the shower, please make sure that it all washes down. I'm sick of the plughole being blocked with your purple hair and spunk."

Thomas

Every morning it takes Thomas a whole *booooooooring* hour to plod to work, so he always stocks up on energy before he leaves. Today, he snap-crumbles half a pack of choccy biccies into a breakfast bowl before glopping milk over them. He should clear up soon – it's come to the point where he can't see the kitchen tiles because there are too many soda cans, plastic packets and empty boxes.

He's still excitable after playing Flyflyfly, but by the time he lands in front of the computer in the lounge his heart has stopped ka-booming. He devours his breakfast while watching a couple of clips from his two favourite movies: Toy Story, which he once watched with Simon, and Natural Born Killers, which Ratan recommended to him. Toy Story makes him feel like he's got some pals, while Natural Born Killers is super-batshit-bonkers and makes him feel an ickle bit less of a weirdo.

After watching Woody and Buzz escape from a toilet he watches Mickey and Mallory murder a bunch of people, and then gets up from the PC to grab a shower. His boss

Ratan taught him that it's important to be stink-free at work, so Thomas has started taking extra-special care to stay clean. On that wicked-awesome day eight months ago when he'd first started work at the shop, Ratan had sent him home to shower, telling him that he smelled like an 'overworked bile duct'. Thomas remembered the words because he'd gotten Ratan to write them down so he could look them up when he got home.

Thomas showers, trims his scraggly beard, and dresses in baggy jeans and a blue t-shirt featuring the cast from Rainbow. Before he sets off he goes back to the old fridge and grabs a cold meat pie and a chocolate cake to take for lunch. "Bye!" he calls to the children, because the children are probably watching him.

As he steps onto the door step –

– Thomas considered the difference between the hurry-flurry of the city and the quiet of his home. At home, there was only the grumbling of insects and the background whinge of traffic, while at the shop Thomas faced the everyday people, with their cigarettes and mobile phones and world news and pop songs. He still wasn't used to them, because the children had only let him get a job after he'd ... well, he didn't like to think about the suitcase.

The dual carriageway began at the end of a dirt track leading away from his front pathway. He munched through a bag of onion rings as he walked in the squinty sun, looking forward to seeing Ratan and not thinking too much about the task the children had set him for the day.

After, like, thirty minutes of walking beside the busy road, he reached Seadon's outskirts. A queue of young school kids in blue blazers and shorts were waiting to board a bus driven by a scowling middle-aged dude with a big fat lower lip. Thomas tried not to stare, but it was tough. Children made him feel like he was being watched, even when he wasn't. They confused him. He kind of wanted to take care of them, while at the same time wished they would just go away and die under a bush somewhere.

The high street was quiet but would soon be heaving. Street performers were readying for a day's busking, and Thomas grinned at a dwarf lining up three chainsaws on the street. Farther on, a guy with a shaved, swoopy red haircut was playing an old, bashed-up guitar.

"So, I'll tell you what I want, what I really really want," he sang. "So tell me what you want, what you really really want..."

It still felt exhilarating to be out in public. Holidaymakers were already shuffling down the high street, sunburned and sleepy, or grumpy and whiffing of last night's booze. Thomas had no idea what a hangover felt like, but judging by their blood-veiny eyes and grim-grey skin, it was pretty horrid. Thomas saw guys and gals preparing tills through shop windows, but none of the other stores were as rad as where *he* worked.

When Thomas reached the locked door of the Green Emporium, he peered in through the windows at the shadowy stock: weed smoking kits, pills, weapons, circus toys and a bunch of other weirdy-weird stuff. The only things that Thomas didn't like were the sex gadgets, which made him feel super-lonely whenever he looked at them.

Thomas turned back to the street and saw his boss Ratan coming towards him, looking like a purple-haired vampire mixed with a girly catwalk model.

Yay!

Ray

Ray headed towards Thomas and the Green Emporium, cringing at the sight of the holidaymakers. Parasites. Vultures. Seadon locals shared a contradictory relationship with those who flocked to their postcard beaches, welcoming the end of the city's off-season emptiness but resenting the tourists' intrusion. The early risers plodded past him: families and stag groups, students and hen parties, pensioners and couples. Some would be nursing sore heads in their guesthouses, while others would be dragging their spoilt spawn out of bed, desperate to secure prime spots on the beach. They were the city's red-fleshed medicine, resuscitating the economy after the chill of winter.

Thomas, tubby and grinning, waited patiently at the Green Emporium door. When they had first met, Ray had found himself instantly endeared to him.

Thomas had come to the shop for the first time just over half a year ago: a spotty, bearded and overweight oddball. Thomas had stepped in from the wind and immediately been hypnotised by the movements of Ray's nimble fingers. Ray had been sliding two glass balls across the contours of his hands, like fist-sized water droplets. Thomas, stinking of body odour and sour milk, had wandered wide-eyed into the shop, as if it was a dazzling palace rather than a slightly seedy head shop. Revolted customers had backed away but the childish wonder in Thomas's eyes had appealed to Ray. Henry had given Ray his managerial position much to the annoyance of other, arguably more deserving employees, so to recruit a non-judgemental ally seemed to make sense.

Despite the fact that Thomas had never heard of a "CV", and in spite of his tramp-like smell, his buoyant belly and his food-stained white t-shirt, when Thomas had asked for a job Ray had offered him a trial month - as long as he cleaned himself up. Ray also appreciated that his chubby underling didn't mind having a younger superior and that he called Ray by his old nickname, 'Ratan'.

After a couple of months' resentment from the other two staff members, Ray had blasted the pair of them. Now Thomas and he were the shop's sole employees.

"Morning, Thomas," Ray said.

Thomas

"Morning, Ratan!" Thomas beamed, saluting with all his might and then bending into a low, silly bow.

"How are you today?" Ratan asked. "Coming down, coming up, stoned, or wasted?"

Thomas chuckled, feeling his lips rasp. "You know that I don't do any of that stuff!"

" True," Ratan said, unlocking the door and heading inside. "But the idea always gets a grin out of you, doesn't it?"

"Yep," Thomas agreed with a smirk.

As Ratan swept through the store he said, "One day I'll

get you some Molly, then you'll learn all about it."

"Who's Molly?" Thomas asked, as Ratan switched on the lights.

The Green Emporium seemed pocket-sized to Thomas. The shop floor was split along the middle by a tall shelving cabinet filled with rows of pretty knives, as well as bongs shaped like willies and space aliens. Ratan prepared the tills and switched on some Bob Marley, which he claimed was the only music that 'stoners' wanted to hear. Thomas had come to love the warm shake and sway of the tunes.

Tapping his feet, Thomas picked up a plastic bum on four wheels and began to make a noise like a car engine mixed with a deep, rumbling fart.

Ratan looked up from the till. "Come on, hoover the place up before you start playing with that crap."

Thomas slowed the toy in the air with a squeaking, trumpy skid and put it back on the shelf. "Okay then," he sighed, heading to the till. Scratching his beard, he asked, "So what you been up to since the weekend? Anything rad?"

"Rad? Haven't heard that word for a while," Ratan said. "I went out for drinks with Henry and some of the boys. Just the usual."

"Did you have a good time?" Thomas asked, hoping to hear an outrageous tale. "Did you go to Lashes after?"

"No, I didn't and – meh – just the usual." Ratan vanished into the corridor behind the till.

"Oh. Did anyone get their gun out?" Thomas asked.

Ratan popped his head out from the passageway, looking agitated. "Look, Thomas, just because I tell you something, it doesn't mean you should just ... come out with it like that. I suppose that it's okay right now when it's just the two of us, but remember to pick your timing, alright?" He came back into the shop and plucked a silver contact-juggling ball from a bucket on the wall. After inspecting it for a second, he rolled it along the palm of one hand and then up the back of his forearm. "Anyway, no. No one got any guns out. That was a one-off and everyone keeps their guns hidden, except when we're at Henry's shooting range."

Thomas stood mesmerised by the reflective ball. Ratan made it run smoothly over his upper arm and then, dipping his neck, steered it across the back of his shoulders, down his other arm and into his awaiting fingers.

"Wish I could do that," Thomas said.

"I know you do, Tommy-boy," Ratan smiled, his red eyes twinkling as the ball passed from his knuckles along his wrist and then slotted into the crook of his elbow. With another twitch it sailed up into the air before rushing down Ratan's shoulder at, like, a million miles-an-hour. Ratan caught it and winked. "Takes years of practice, though. Keep trying with the regular juggling, that's what I say. Anyone can do that."

"Okay," Thomas said, hanging his head. He moped to the back room and fetched the vacuum cleaner.

"Hey! Don't give me that look," Ratan scolded, returning the ball to its home on the wall. "What did *you* get up to last night, then?"

Thomas was used to lying, but part of him was desperate to tell Ratan about The Flyflyfly Game. Instead, he replied, "Oh, you know. Just watched a bunch of movies: Minions, Finding Nemo, The Exorcist, Monsters Inc, Human Centipede 2..."

"That's quite a mix right there, buddy," Ratan said, frown-smiling. "Anyway, I'll be upstairs waiting for Henry. You're alright in here by yourself, yeah? I mean, you may as well be manager these days."

"Yep, except for the wages," Thomas said, trying to hide his disappointment. Ratan had barely been there five minutes.

Ratan stopped at the back room door. "You okay for cash?"

"I'm fine. All I buy is movies and food."

"Then you must spend hundreds a week, right?" Ratan laughed.

Thomas dropped his head.

"Ah, don't be like that." Ratan produced £20 from his pocket. "Go on, take that. Call it a bonus."

Thomas shook his head. "You don't have to. But, if you're not too busy, maybe we could ..."

"If you're looking for a fuck, you're shit outta luck," Ratan rhymed, teeth gleaming.

Even though the children would have forbidden it, Thomas asked, "I was just hoping, could we maybe hang out sometime?"

Ratan looked at him strangely. "I don't have time for *myself* at the moment, let alone anyone else. Need to save up my cash and get the hell out of Seadon."

Thomas felt his guts wibble at the thought of his boss leaving. "You aren't *really* going away any time soon, are you?"

Ratan blinked and glanced towards the locked entrance. A spotty guy in a t-shirt that read "Wank-Trombone" had his face pressed against the glass. He rubbed his balls with one hand and started dry-humping the window.

"Tommy-boy – I'll be riding off into the sunset as soon as I can."

LOCKER

SAT IN A GREASY SPOON CAFÉ, PERCY LOCKER SIPPED BLACK TEA AND WATCHED THE GREEN EMPORIUM FROM THE OTHER SIDE OF THE STREET. A TUBBY FUCKER HAD FOLLOWED THE GOTH CUNT INTO THE STORE A COUPLE OF MINUTES AGO, AND LOCKER HAD WATCHED THEM THROUGH THE SHOP WINDOW, TALKING AND LAUGHING.

THAT MORNING, HUNGOVER, LOCKER HAD WANTED TO SEE RAY IN THE SUMMER LIGHT. NOT SO LONG AGO HENRY WOULD HAVE TOLD HIM THAT IT WASN'T HEALTHY TO BROOD. *WASTE O' FACKIN' ENERGY*, HENRY WOULD'VE CALLED IT. LOCKER HAD

HOPED THAT SEEING RAY WOULD STRAIGHTEN HIS HEAD OUT, MAKE HIM REALISE HE WAS MAKING TOO BIG A DEAL OF THE SCRAWNY LITTLE QUEER.

SEEING HIM HAD ONLY INCREASED THE POUNDING IN LOCKER'S BRAIN. HE LOOKED DOWN AT HIS ROUGH HANDS WRAPPED AROUND THE PLAIN WHITE MUG, IMAGINED THEM CLAMPED AROUND THE GOTH CUNT'S THROAT. PICTURED USING HIS TOOLS, *HIS FRIENDS*, TO SLICE OPEN THE LITTLE PRICK'S THROAT AND BALLSACK. LOCKER GLANCED BACK TOWARDS THE GREEN EMPORIUM AND SAW THE GOTH CUNT, NOW IN AN UPSTAIRS WINDOW, GRINNING TO HIMSELF AS HE PULLED DOWN THE BLINDS.

THE MUG BURST APART IN LOCKER'S FINGERS. SCALDING LIQUID AND BONE-WHITE SHARDS BURST ACROSS THE TABLE. AN OLD HAG OF A WAITRESS GASPED WHEN THE TEA SPLASHED HER LEG. LOOKED LIKE SHE WAS GOING TO COMPLAIN, BUT THEN SHE SAW LOCKER'S FACE. HE MET HER GAZE AND SHE CLOSED HER PINCHED ARSEHOLE OF A MOUTH. WITHOUT BREAKING EYE CONTACT, LOCKER ROSE FROM HIS SEAT AND STARED DOWN AT HER, LIKE A KID INSPECTING A BUG. CONSIDERED, JUST FOR A SECOND, RAMMING HIS FIST INTO HER UGLY, WRINKLED CHEEK. THEN, WITHOUT PAYING, HE CALMLY LEFT THE CAFÉ.

CHAPTER 2
"No matter what."

Sandra

Sandra Pickles sat in the armchair of her tiny, freshly cleaned home, her packed suitcase standing obediently at her side, and struggled *not* to remember the good times.

No matter what ...

The press had lost interest. Friends now kept their distance. On the rare occasions that Sandra ventured outside, even the occupants of their neighbouring flats averted their eyes, as if she was a ghost whose presence was an ill omen.

For a time, while her husband Gary had chattered, sweated and chewed his cheeks raw, Sandra had entombed herself in their wardrobe-sized bedroom. Lying foetal, for hours on end she would fix her gaze onto a jagged, v-shaped crack in the skirting board.

Despite having always been careful to observe The Ten Commandments – after all, there was nothing in the Bible that condemned mushies, cocaine or marijuana – Sandra's religion had ceased to grant her light. She had learned that living a sinless life did not keep those dearest to her safe from harm, and with this revelation had come the cold breath of nihilism. If her 'all-loving' God could abandon a loyal subject in their most troubling hour, why should she continue to live according to His word?

Why live at all?

On the far side of the country, Sandra's well-meaning mother had offered her a place to stay. She had never approved of Sandra's relationship with Gary, and no doubt held him solely responsible for all that had happened. Although Sandra's mother had never once discouraged her daughter's younger days of experimentation, squatting and free parties, she had openly objected to Sandra's future husband. *A waster,* she'd called Gary. *A troublemaker.* Even, *An addict.* Of course, such disdain had only convinced Sandra that Gary was the key to escape from her middle class upbringing, so they had married in a registry office just over six years ago.

More recently, while the police investigation had trundled painfully on, Gary had worked in a hotel kitchen to give Sandra time off from work. Poor Gary; Sandra couldn't hate his inadequacies even now. Play-acting the man of the house, ignoring the fact that *Sandra* had always supported *him*, his charade had been brief. When the police had stopped calling and the occasional news crews had left them alone for good, the enormity of what had befallen them had split their single, shared life into two distinct paths.

Gary had never meant to harm anyone. He just struggled with responsibility, and always had done. At heart, he was a good man.

Sat on the couch, with her chest tight and stomach rolling, Sandra looked down at her suitcase, a whole life wrapped in a thin sheet of leather. She had allowed herself just two souvenirs from the room at the end of the hall: a photo album and a yellow hat. She could always come back for more when they sold the flat.

In recent days, when her husband had returned home after a long night out, sunlight would usually be glowing behind the drawn curtains. He would shuffle into the bedroom, demon-eyed and disorientated, and if Sandra was still in bed they would talk in stilted, uneasy tones.

Without inflection, Sandra would say, "Where have you been."

"Here and there, you know." Gary's voice would be distant, drained, his body wafting stale chemicals as he lay behind her. "You alright?"

"Yes."

"Good."

Gary would sometimes place damp, jittery arms around her and Sandra would try to feel something. If they'd just found a way to *talk about it*, perhaps they would have taken the first steps towards closure, but it was never long before Sandra slipped from the bed and made her way to the television in the lounge. There, until Gary left the house again, Sandra had rested her eyes on the screen, its images merely colours, movements and an echoing grey buzz.

Well, no longer. One of them had to put things right.

Gary

Gary had taken rare night off from the clubs, because something was proper wrong with Sandra, wasn't it? Well, things had been wrong for eight shitting months, hadn't they, but this was different. His wife was getting stronger, and it scared him.

That morning, Gary had left the house and taken a stroll across Seadon's main beach. The beige sand was dotted with early season holidaymakers, reminding Gary that summer was just around the corner. The idea of the streets clogging up with visitors made Gary feel sick, so he focused on the sea's navy-blue waves and imagined he was all alone, there on the sand.

The trouble was that, for Gary, it had always been about tablets, trips and long white lines. Some people liked sports, and others liked TV or computers. Gary preferred to drop a few Es, drink some beers, snort some blow if there was any going, and finish the night in a blur of ganja smoke and swirling black K-holes. When all the bad stuff had gone down late last year, it hadn't been a tough choice for Gary to get back into partying. It was ironic that chemicals were partly to blame for all this bollocks, but screw it – he needed a helping hand. No one could go through something like this without a pressure release, could they?

Returning to the old group had felt more like coming home than coming home did, these days. Despite having families now, some of his old mates still gurned and sniffed as energetically as they had back in the day, and they'd welcomed Gary back to the fold.

Beneath the constant blur of coming up and crashing back down, Gary took relief in the fact that what happened late the year before hadn't been his fault – not really, anyway. He'd just been helping out a friend, and there was nothing wrong with that, was there?

Gary stuffed his hands into his pockets and punted a smooth, round pebble towards the shoreline, the yellowish foam lapping close to his scuffed trainers. He could see a ferry way, way out to sea, and towards the end of the beach stood Seadon's crappy pier. The pier arcades would open again once the season was in flow, and the small-time dealers would sure as hell take advantage of them, wouldn't they?

For a few months, getting wasted with the old crew had been total gravy, and much better than rotting at home on the sofa beside the wife. Shit – some folks might have said that he should've stayed there with her, but in the end she had her way of dealing with things and he had his.

Part of Gary wished that Sandra could have enjoyed the class Al's and the tunes. After all, there was no reason to restrain themselves any more, was there? Those days were dead and gone, like decent techno.

Sandra had started to look rough. She didn't seem to sleep much – though he was one to talk – and she was always glued to that shitting armchair, staring at nothing at all. He still loved her - he told himself he did, anyway. He knew that by chasing highs he was dodging the bullet, but at least he'd kept going, kept active. And anyway, shit, it all went down *eight months ago*. At some point they had to start pulling themselves together, didn't they?

Gary stood at the edge of the sea, wondering why it had taken him so long to get around to talking to her. One evening, when the guys had decided to go out to some shitty Goth night for a laugh, Gary had come home early. He'd slept beside his wife and in the morning he'd gotten up and showered himself fresh. Seeing Sandra on the couch, staring dumbly at the screen, he'd decided to try something new.

Sandra

Stroking the suitcase like a sleeping pet, fighting the urge to cry, Sandra thought back to when Gary had broken his routine. A month or two back, clad in his favourite blue tracksuit with his shaggy hair washed and as red as the flesh of a sweet potato, Sandra had been stricken by how spruce he had looked.

"I was home early last night and I'm not in the mood for it today," Gary had explained, perhaps sensing her surprise. "Fancy doing something?"

She had glanced up from whatever talk show, cooking programme or soap opera was on, and asked, "Like what?"

"A walk. It's good out." Something kind had touched his long white face, and he smiled. "The sun's trying to put his hat on."

The thought of what he was asking had petrified her. It had been so long since they spent had any real time together. What if she joined him and found her own husband's company repugnant?

When she had hesitantly agreed, Gary had led her by the hand towards the city. She'd remained apprehensive, because the furthest she had travelled in months had been to the corner shop at the end of their road. The air had been chilly; not cold enough for frost, but enough to make the wind feel crisp at the back of her throat. They had huddled together as they'd walked, and to her surprise her husband's scent had been of fabric softener and Lynx after-shave. In their closeness, with her heart thudding like a frail, battered tambourine, Sandra's fears had loosened. As Gary had led her through the quieter parts of town, Sandra had found herself considering the future.

They had taken a route through back alleys and quaint lanes, barely passing a soul. Like a real, tragedy-free married couple they had spoken in private voices about the cleanliness of the cobbled streets, how lovely the rolling white clouds had been, and how pleasant the temperature was compared to the constant stuffiness of their apartment, which was perpetually heated by the elderly couple below them who left their heating ablaze throughout all twelve months of the year.

As they'd neared a quiet beach, Sandra had been relieved to avoid serious discussion. Instead, they had drifted wordlessly through the whipping winds of the shoreline, sand and water gusting up around them like a prickling mist. The endless ocean had reminded Sandra of the sense of awe that her religion had once given her.

For a brief time the beach had remained desolate, but then a crowd of intrepid and perhaps drunk young adults had sprinted, howling, into the ocean, and Gary had suggested that they head back home. Gary had wrapped her protectively in one arm, and Sandra had once again breathed in the clean, unpolluted body of her sober husband.

No matter what.

Taking a busier route on their way back through the city they had seen a friend of Gary's awkwardly lighting a roll-up outside The Beatum Inn, using his streaked puffer jacket to shield the flame of his fake Zippo. When Sandra had seen this skinhead– Matt Saunders – she had tried to prepare herself.

Matt had been merry and red-faced, eyes not yet bleary but soon to be. From behind the closed pub door she'd heard the burble of friends, partners and relatives enjoying jokes in the comforting boozy haze. Sandra had noticed the change in Gary immediately. The closeness of his supportive arm had dwindled on her shoulders. His eyes had brightened at the sight of his companion. His voice had risen beyond the low, intimate tone he and Sandra shared to a loutish bray.

"Alright, mate?" Gary blared.

"Nice to see you out, guys, nice one," Matt said, his face a storm of broken blood vessels. "Been too long, Sandy! Why don't ya come in? I'll get you both a drink to warm the cock'oles."

To Sandra's initial relief, Gary overshot Matt's question, telling him that he and Sandra were on their way home. She was pleased to see that Gary understood, that he truly wanted to make things work, and realised that their walk had been their first tentative step towards recovery.

"Come on," Matt persisted. "It's Beth's birthday, or had you forgot? She'd love to see you both. Plus, they've got that 'Viking Slayer' back on draught, and it's running down sharpish."

"It's a good beer," Gary admitted. "It's not really up to me, though ..."

When he looked down at Sandra, she saw that he was torn. His face showed that he was genuinely giving her the choice – they could either go inside or head back home - but, despite having just spent their first quality hour together in months, if it were *Gary's* choice he would have been inside the pub like a ginger bullet.

The cold whisked around Sandra. Gary's arm had gone.

"What do you think, honey?" Gary asked, blowing onto his hands to emphasize the chill.

Sandra's skin tightened across her back. Her forehead slickened with sweat and her pulse slammed in her temples. Why had he asked her the question when he'd known exactly what she'd wanted?

Nausea and dizziness claimed her, telling her that nothing in the world was in her control. There was no God looking down from heaven and the skies were empty. Nothing significant would ever change, and the worst thing? In the end, the vast scale of her loss was as insignificant as a leaf falling from a tree.

She looked at her husband and a trembling, shameful hatred gripped her. He would never alter. Even something of this magnitude, this year of pure hell, hadn't shown him a clearer path. A sound like an alarm shot from her throat and, slipping clumsily, Sandra lunged at her husband with a hand outstretched like a claw. Her nails caught his face, scraping four ugly red tracks from ear to jawline.

But no... matter... what...

She saw the horror in his eyes, the gleaming hurt pride. As she leapt back in shock at her own aggression he raised a hand slowly to his cheek, wincing. Matt backed away, seeking refuge in the pub.

With a gasp of shame, Sandra turned and fled, hearing Gary call after her.

Now, sat on the couch, gazing at the suitcase on her lap and waiting to tell Gary that she was finally leaving him, Sandra watched their silent lounge blur behind a veil of tears.

Gary

Gary stopped walking and looked out across the ocean again, rubbing a hand against his face. Sandra's awful slap had been the last thing he'd expected, hadn't it?

That day, his wife's eyes had darted about

nervously as they'd walked, as if she hadn't wanted to look him in the face. She hadn't cut her hair in months so her fringe had been trailing across her eyes in a way that Gary had found sort-of sexy. They'd chit-chatted, avoiding the main issue, and slowly her shoulders had relaxed and her eyes had stopped their crazy little dance. He'd even managed to take in most of what she'd been saying – half his mind on her, the other half on those pills he'd bought a few days before.

But then she'd just flipped, gone mental! Lashed out with her nails, and in front of Matt, too! Shit – it wasn't on, was it? Shouldn't matter how harsh you feel – you just don't do that kind of thing, do you?

Today on the beach, the sun looked brighter than it had during their walk a month or so before. There were a few surfers out, taking advantage of the swell. Out there, catching wave after wave for no reason at all, they looked completely care-free.

Wankers.

Gary would never work Sandra out, would he? Never. And it was getting harder and harder to remember how things had once been, back before the shitting police and the shitting sniping press.

After that day with Sandra outside the pub, Gary had started to hit the chemicals hard. At about the same time, he'd actually started eyeing up the women, which was something he'd rarely done in the past. He'd never been a big shagger – chemicals were better than sex, weren't they? – but he'd found himself wanting to get laid just for a new kind of release. But whenever Gary had gotten the chance for a poke he'd backed off at the last minute, imagining Sandra sat at home, confused and lost and shitting miserable.

She flinched when he touched her these days.

Flinched – his own wife!

But despite the distance between them, he couldn't face the thought of her leaving him. What the hell would he be if she did that, eh? A 33-year-old with a drug habit and bills he couldn't afford.

One day, a couple of weeks ago, the house had become tidy. The plates and cups had been cleaned and the layers of dust wiped away from the furniture. He'd even come back to an empty flat once or twice, and it worried him.

He looked down at his feet, away from the arsehole surfers. Although he hadn't taken anything for over 24 hours, his pulse was quick and his palms were wet. He needed more time to decide if there was anything left of his marriage to save.

One night, eight years ago, he and Sandra had been at a party, sat on an enormous red bean bag. Sandra had been stoned and he'd been coming up on some strong acid. There had been a tall mirror in the corner and whenever the mingling, gyrating bodies had separated, Gary had seen an image of Sandra sat on the lap of a crumbling, fucked-up version of himself. His head had lolled sideways, the eyeballs melting down his grey, sunken cheeks.

For hours, the room had swirled and twisted. He had taken way, way too much, and the LSD had morphed the party guests into circus freaks, then members of his own dysfunctional family, then blurred, flailing shadows or blinding red-and-blue bubbles. The one constant sight throughout trip had been the two shapes in the mirror: his then-girlfriend and his own corpse.

Hours later, when Gary had stopped whimpering like a child and Sandra was leading him back to the council flat they had eventually come to own, he had vowed that he would take things more easily. For the first time ever he had felt overwhelmed by a drug, and if acid could do that to his brain, what the hell could stims do to his body?

Back home, later that night, Gary had rested his head in Sandra's lap, coloured vapour trails snaking across his vision. With the kindest smile, the smile of a princess or a saint or an angel, Sandra had looked down into his swelling and contracting pupils and promised that she would stay beside him, no matter what the future held.

No matter what, she'd said.

No matter what.

With Sandra's soft fingers combing through his hair, Gary's terrors had dissolved, and he had asked Sandra if she would marry him. She had gently kissed his forehead and told him, of course she would.

Picturing those moments, Gary ended his beach walk and turned back towards the flat. When he arrived, Sandra was in her armchair as usual, but her posture was straight and her eyes alert. A dark red suitcase sat across her lap.

Gary's chest tightened. She was *actually* leaving him, wasn't she?

Sandra

Sandra watched her confused husband standing in the lounge doorway. He'd become frail, his arms thin and his face drawn. His red hair, a feature Sandra had once adored, had become dry and unkempt, like that of a stranger.

Sandra was going to tell him that she had bought a train ticket and was leaving that afternoon, and that there was nothing he could say to change her mind. She couldn't let her life slip by like this, so she was going to accept her mother's offer of a place to stay. Maybe her mum had been right all along: maybe Gary was bad news and always had been, and all that had happened the year before had destroyed their chance of happiness together. Then again, maybe if Sandra vanished temporarily from his life he would be spurred into action, and they would pick up the pieces at a later date.

From the couch she stared at her husband, with whom she had shared so much. When she went to speak, though, Gary interrupted her in his crackling voice of a million adolescent spliffs, and nothing was ever the same again.

Gary

Hiding his panic at the sight of the suitcase, Gary said, "No matter what."

Sandra glanced up at him, looking unsure. "What?"

Her brown hair had become wild and her eyes had lost their spark, but somewhere in that small, thin frame was the woman Gary had married. They had shared the same life for so long – perhaps all it would take would be a push of the right buttons.

"That's what you said to me," he said, pulling a chair away from the table to sit in front of her. "You said that we'd stand together, *no matter what* we came up against. You and me, no matter what. I can still hear you now."

Sandra locked her gaze onto the empty television screen, clenching her jaw. "I'm going to stay up north."

Gary felt a jolt of anger. So, her mother was involved, was she? Interfering cow. She and Sandra couldn't do this to him – it wasn't fair.

Sandra continued shakily, "We both need time. I want us to work something out but I don't think that this is helping either of us." The blankness in her face was gone and Gary saw nothing but sadness there. This was how 'opening up' looked. "You're never here any more, Gary."

"If you leave me," he said, "I don't know what I'll do, I really don't. 'No matter what' – they were your words, not mine."

Her eyes shimmered and her lips pressed tightly together.

He took a gamble. "I need you to help us get through this, Sandra, just like you did when I was hitting things a bit too hard."

"Don't throw that in my face, Gary," she said, turning with a scowl. "It's not fair. I don't know how to help you and I don't know how to change. It's not something I can just snap out of. All I can feel is grief, like it's all I've got left."

"But without you I won't have anything left at all." He paused. "Do you blame me?"

Sandra began to cry with ugly, wet moans. Saliva bubbled at her mouth and her timid shoulders rose and fell like levers.

She did blame him, didn't she? She wanted to scream, *Yes! Yes, it's all your fault! If you were a stronger man, if you were less selfish, and if you cared less about your pills and your friends we wouldn't be going through this! You're pathetic!*

But she couldn't, could she? She wasn't spiteful. She was too kind, and that was her weakness. Shit, after all they'd been through she still loved him and wanted their old life back. He could use that.

Gary slid off of the chair, knelt in front of his wife and took her hands into his own. They felt tiny, like a little kid's. "Don't leave me, Sandra. I need you," he told her, and stroked a tear from her cheek. "I think you still want me, too."

Her lips trembled and she stopped sobbing. The pain of the previous months had crushed the faith from her, but he would give her hope again, wouldn't he?

Maybe we can survive this, he could hear her thinking. *Maybe we can salvage something.*

"We could go away, Sandra," Gary pushed, repeating her name because he knew she liked hearing him say it. "We could sell the flat and just go somewhere new. Start afresh, like."

She exhaled, took her hands from his and laid them back into her lap. "What about the drugs?" she asked bitterly.

"I'll ditch them again, Sandra," he assured her. "I did it before, didn't I? And if we move away from Matt and Daz and that lot, there won't be any more temptations, will there?"

It was as if he could hear the barriers falling inside of her, like frail fences in a storm. She wanted it all. She wanted to leave Seadon, she wanted to move somewhere new, and she wanted to recover. But she was still resisting, wasn't she, terrified to let herself believe in something better.

"I just don't know," she said. Then she asked suddenly, "What if the police are wrong? What if..."

Gary took her hands again and massaged them with

his thumbs, just the way she liked. One more push and she'd be convinced. One more shove.

"Just think about this, Sandra," he purred. "One day, we'll look back and we'll talk about it all, and we'll remember the great times and none of the bad." She looked doubtful. "People *do* get through things like this, Sandra, but not without trust. If you can trust me again, we'll fight through it and we'll win. Then, maybe, when we're settled again, we can think about raising a family..."

Sandra's body seemed to implode. Her head fell, her shoulders hunched, her arms lost all strength. She cried a long and agonized cry, and collapsed into Gary's arms.

"Okay, fine, no matter what," she sobbed into his chest. "No matter what."

Victory.

Gary took his wife by the hand and pulled her to her feet. He leaned down, and when they kissed her lips pressed into his so hard that it hurt. Her embrace almost winded him. He ignored a brief tug of regret as he led her in silence towards their bedroom to make love for the first time in what felt like years.

In honesty, Gary had no idea whether he could do any of the things he'd claimed, and didn't even know if he wanted to try. However, the pill he'd dropped an hour ago was starting to kick in, and his remorse was suddenly flushed away in a haze of sex and chemical euphoria.

CHAPTER 3
"For one man to be on top, a population has to suffer"

Rebecca

As Henry Borders sat tight-muscled at his desk, barking demands into his extortionately expensive smartphone, Rebecca Toulson lay curled on the cream chaise longue, drinking in the week's disasters like measures of exquisite cognac.

RAPE, the newspaper screamed, and Rebecca smiled pleasantly. WAR, the broadsheet bellowed, and Rebecca nodded in agreement, licking her lips as she absorbed the image of a fire-scorched refugee camp. MURDER, ADDICTION, POVERTY, DISEASE, ABUSE, ASSAULT ...

There you are again, world.

Rebecca knew that a bystander would likely

have placed her in her early thirties, but she had in fact recently turned 40. She wore a tastefully suggestive, figure-hugging white dress and her hair was a white-blonde bob dyed two shades lighter than her natural tone. She took pride in the fact that her youthful appearance was the result of fine breeding rather than surgery.

Rebecca would have preferred to have been reclining in her private apartment that Henry paid for, or the library of Henry's larger, out-of-town abode – however, her bed-partner usually insisted upon residing where she now sat, in the apartment above his murky little casino. This irked her, but objecting would have cast a shadow across her meticulous impression of subordination.

With the lounge's tall windows, clear glass surfaces and half-circle of supremely white leather furniture, at least the décor in this apartment was less nauseating than that of Henry's mansion. Only its walls betrayed his clueless tastes, scatter-shot as they were with photographs of 1950s gangsters, rat-pack crooners and seductive cheesecake pin-ups.

As Ben E King wailed from the stereo stack, demanding that his wench stood by him, Rebecca suppressed amusement as Henry wrestled with his ever-looming temper. Slightly her senior, Henry was not a large man by any means – a firm yet positively average frame, aside from his pot belly – but his presence belied his physical shape. The fraying hairline, narrow eyes and stone-baked jaw were animated by an arrogance that suffused his every word and action. That day, he wore a faeces-brown fur-lined jacket far too heavy for the early summer heat, a turquoise vest-top that dipped lower than Rebecca's most daring neckline, and a large, personalised medallion that lay partially buried in the thick, black wires of his chest. This gleaming gold circle was engraved with the image of Henry as a younger, more chiselled figure, his bare torso hairless and thick with imagined muscles.

Rebecca watched from the corner of one eye.

"Just fackin' make sure you're done by midday," Henry said, in his near-cartoonish London accent. "O' course you'll recognise him. He looks like Pavarotti, an' smells like a turd what's just run a marathon." He rubbed his damp forehead with the back of a wide, hairy hand. "Yeah. I'm sendin' you first, Fred, coz o' that silver tongue o' yours, but let him know that if there's any more problems, next time it'll be Percy who pops round for a cuppa. That's right. Now fack off an' get it done." He took the mobile away from his ear and gazed calmly at its screen. Then, with a fierce crack, he slammed it onto the glass desk. "Is it just me, or is everyone a mouthy prick these days?"

"What was that about, darling?" Rebecca asked.

"No questions," Henry snapped. Rebecca heard a teeth-grating whirr; Henry had started to grind two black worry balls in one hirsute paw. "I've got a nice day planned for me an' the boy, an' the last thing I need is to be concerned wiv a loada mundane shite."

Ah yes, 'the boy' Raymond, who Henry spoke so fondly of but whom Rebecca had yet to meet. She was used to being kept separate from Henry's business life, but this particular young fellow seemed to have nothing to do with Henry's pursuit of money and power. "So when am I going to have the pleasure of meeting this 'Raymond'?"

Henry looked at her agitatedly. "When I decide the time's right, that's when."

Facing away from him, Rebecca allowed herself a grin. Henry's guardedness only underlined Ray's importance, like a six-year-old hiding a football under his t-shirt. She folded the newspaper and picked up a book of fairy tales from the long glass table.

So why was Rebecca with Henry, one might insightfully ask – her, a glamorous sophisticate with a wit as dry as a Tanqueray 10 Martini, and Henry, a degenerate criminal with the dress sense of a rich village idiot and the verbal artistry of a cow pat? The answer perched somewhere between begrudging attraction and financial necessity – after all, the world is populated solely by users and the used.

Smiling with equal parts nostalgia and mild nausea, Rebecca wondered if she would have behaved differently upon meeting Henry had she known where her choices would lead. Of course she would have; returning to her career as an escort would have been an idyllic vacation from all she now endured.

Rebecca remembered Nicholas, her wealthy ex-partner of ten years, as a simpering, frugal elitist who, even when patronising those he considered beneath him, would speak with an air of loathsome remorse. He had provided richly for her as he had once promised, but boredom, bitten tongues and a barren womb had provoked Rebecca to boff the gardener.

One afternoon, Rebecca had been so immersed in riding, clawing and strangling the dim groundsman that she had failed to notice Nicholas stood in the bedroom doorway, aghast at the sight of his darling viciously fucking the hedge-trimmer. Even when his eyes had met Rebecca's, Nicholas had remained dumbstruck while her loins unleashed an adulterous orgasm.

In spite of Nicholas's generally restrained demeanour, a fight had ensued. Nicholas had thrown Rebecca off the bewildered man and attacked him, but as soon as Rebecca had pulled on her clothes, Nicholas had returned his attention to her. Rebecca had lost her perpetual cool and sped from the house, pursued by her rabid, bellowing partner.

It was a scene the like of which Rebecca had witnessed but until then never experienced. Resisting the indignity of running, Nicholas had bounded awkwardly after her, expelling insults at the top of his voice even as they'd approached a busy Seadon drinking area. Rebecca had ducked into an alleyway leading to the rear of a restaurant, with Nicholas's steps close behind. There, out of sight from all but a pot-washer puffing on a sly joint at the back door, she'd faced Nicholas directly. He'd grasped her by the shoulders and shaken her, demanding to know the reasons for her betrayal. Incensed but once again calm, Rebecca had berated the inadequacy of his genitalia, and explained that his hatred for those lower in status and intellect was merely a symptom of his own emotional shortcomings, reflected by his adoration for a cold-hearted ex-hooker who would never return his love.

Perhaps unsurprisingly, he'd hit her. As a younger woman, Rebecca had been punched by angry Johns who'd failed to 'rise to the occasion' or who'd gotten off on mistreating her, but never by Nicholas. With wounded puppy-dog eyes he had swung for her a second time, his half-closed fist propelling her into a brick wall and firing stars across her vision. Dazed but still standing, she had noticed the pot-smoking kitchen porter slip quietly back into the restaurant, but then on her opposite side she'd seen someone new advancing.

She had recognised Henry Borders from some of the bars she frequented, but had never spoken to him. Henry had tapped Nicholas politely on the arm and Rebecca had watched bafflement cross her lover's face. Then Henry had delivered a kick to the side of his leg, so sharp and precise it had almost certainly snapped a bone. Before Nicholas had even hit the floor Henry had commenced his own, far more brutal beating, informing Nicholas between blows that "only a coward beats his woman in public".

Leaving Nicholas in a groaning, bleeding heap, Henry had driven Rebecca to his mansion on the outskirts of town, and Rebecca had thanked him silently with her lips and tongue. As she'd tasted his skinny, freckled length for the first time, Henry had declared that he'd been delighted to witness her being chased and then assaulted, as it had given him the prime opportunity for an introduction.

Although Rebecca had been unsurprised to find that she had entranced yet another man, she had been quite astonished to hear Henry's offer of renting an apartment for her. If only she had realised sooner what becoming Henry's 'special lady' would involve.

Distracting her from her musings, Bruno, Henry's gunmetal-grey Great Dane, padded into the room to lap noisily at a water bowl at Henry's feet. Henry rubbed the dog's sleek skull affectionately, and his posture visibly loosened. "Yeah, I know I'm gettin' uptight, pal, but it's all gonna be peachy, ain't it?"

Rebecca gazed blankly at the pair before returning to her fairy tales.

"Be a darlin' an' pour me a glass o' that whisky, would ya?" Henry said.

The whisky to which he referred was a rather exceptional Balvenie Thirty. Rebecca would have described it as "silky smooth, with light traces of marzipan, nut and honey, and a deceptive, lingering sweetness." In contrast, Henry simply dubbed it "fackin' well tasteful". She went to the cabinet – just an arm's length away from Henry – and poured him a large measure. When she placed the crystal tumbler down before him, he groped her backside.

"Thanks beautiful. I don't know what I'd do

wiv-out ya," he said, and downed the glass in one. "Phwaor, fackin' well tasteful."

She slid around, placed her rump on his lap, and kissed his sweat-sheened forehead. "Glad to be of service, darling."

God, he reeked; the stench that showers couldn't remove seemed to grow by the day. That Christ-awful, inconsistent, fake cockney brogue was close to the top of her list of complaints, but there was so many more: his small-town ignorance; his clumsy attempts at 'class'; his limitless self-importance; his stress-thinned hair; his nostrils that flared like gaping mouths whenever he spoke.

Not to mention his tastes in the bedroom.

Bruno lapped noisily at his water again and Henry, reminded of the dog's presence, pulled Rebecca's lips to his. He slid his chair back and lifted her from his lap, turning her around to straddle him. Her tight dress rode up from her knees to her hips.

Henry's angular face made Rebecca think of a conscious Easter Island rock. He wasn't an ugly man, and his hard, square jaw and calculating brown eyes appealed to Rebecca. She kissed him again, feeling the sandpaper scrape of his stubble, and tried to remember the last time she had enjoyed his company. She decided to test her luck: "Could we, for once, just you and I..."

She then realised that although one of his hands was massaging her lower back, the other was at the side of the chair, amiably rubbing Bruno's crown.

"Not today, doll," Henry replied, his eyes

twinkling like shards of glass on a blanched beach.

Henry

After the mornin's exertions, Henry woulda thought the dog woulda bin happy to have grabbed forty winks, but nope. In the back yard o' Henry's casino, wiv the midday sun beatin down on him, Bruno raised his massive body up into the beggin position, one paw hoisted into the air to show how desperate he was to join his master.

"It's alright, pal," Henry soothed, strokin one o' Bruno's silky ears between thumb an' forefinger. "I'll be back before ya know it, an' then I'll take ya to the fields and we'll go for a lovely fackin run. Come on pal, don't be like that."

Bruno dropped his head an' front paws to the grass. He'd bin actin moody all day, an' it was beginnin to grind Henry's gears. "Sorry pal, but I'm spendin the day wiv the lad, jus' the two of us. Got some important news to give 'im an' I don't want no distractions, alright?"

Wiv the thick chain on his neck clankin as he moved, Bruno padded across the lawn an' headed into his kennel to stand wiv nothing but his arse pokin out into the air. That extortionate fackin kennel was ten feet tall, an' shaped like a turreted castle, wiv battlements, Union Jack flags an' an entrance made to look like a drawbridge.

"Fine, you grumpy bastard," Henry said, scowlin. "No steak for you tomorrow – just a can o' the old Pedigree instead."

Bruno squatted his back legs in front o' the drawbridge, tensed, an' squeezed out a giant brown log.

"Like that, is it? Well if ya think I'm cleanin that up before I go, you're in for a surprise." He waited a moment an' then crouched to look into the kennel. Bruno was facin defiantly away, refusin to give Henry even a glance. "Oh, sod ya then."

As Henry headed away from the kennel towards the garden's tall gate he heard a bark. Bruno had backed out of his castle an' was starin at him. He alright – just havin a little strop, that was all. Gets more like a fackin woman all the time.

Before Henry left the yard he tipped a wink to his sad-lookin pet. "Be back before ya know it."

It was gonna be a fantastic day. Look at that sun winkin above the skyline. Fackin beautiful, an' the perfect wevver forecast to help wipe away the boy's thoughts about leavin Seadon. Deep down, Raymond didn't really wanna go. People often need a bit o' directin, an' in the end Raymond would thank Henry for makin the right choices for him.

On a separate note, Henry wasn't keen on the boy leavin either. He'd dropped into Henry's life by pure coincidence, an' it'd taken Henry just a few hours to recognise the boy's worth and, more importantly, his heritage.

They'd met a year or so ago, durin an evenin out on the tiles, while Henry had bin pissin a coupla bottles o' Krug up the wall at the back of a nightclub. It'd bin just Henry an' Fred, merrily laughin at fack knows what, but then along had sauntered skinny Raymond, wearin what'd looked like a long, black ballgown an' a loada white facepaint. Soppy sod. Fred had noticed an' yelled out somethin like, "Who's that? The Corpse Bride?"

Raymond had kept his pace. After all, Henry an' Fred were two hard-lookin blokes waitin at a rear entrance, an' Raymond had looked like he was waitin for a hard entrance to some bloke's rear.

Fred had stepped drunkenly in front of him, shorter but stockier than Ray, met the kid's eyes, an' said, "I asked you who you are, mate. Or am I not pretty enough to speak to?"

Raymond, eyes shadowed an' lips painted red, had shown no trace o' nerves. Instead, in this poetic fackin voice, he'd said somethin like, "If I based who I talked to on looks alone I wouldn't have even noticed you."

Fred had frowned. "You a poof?"

Now, Henry weren't always proud o' the behaviour of his acquaintances, but they were his fellas nonetheless, so he'd pulled up his flies and turned to face Raymond. Henry had known where this little chit-chat was probly leadin – a mid-evenin arse-kickin – but at that point Raymond had been a poofy-lookin nobody, so what had Henry cared?

Fred, that beardy, bear-faced cunt, had jeered, "Well? Do you wanna kiss me, Marilyn Manson? Or d'you wanna kiss this?"

An' for a reason Henry would never understand, Fred had pulled out his handgun. In a grease-lightnin flash, though, young Raymond had plucked the piece from Fred's hand. Anuvver second later, Fred had bin whacked by a pistol whip that'd split his lips open, pissin blood across his cheek. Shoulda seen his face as he'd staggered backwards, unarmed an' hurtin! Fackin hilarious.

Pantin, lookin like he was more surprised by his own speed than Fred was, Ray had stood there wiv the gun hangin at his side like a flaccid todger. Then he'd gone, "So what now?"

Henry, smilin casually, had said, "Now you join us for a coupla drinks, son."

"I'm heading to Lashes," Ray had replied, his attention on Henry – no doubt smellin authority.

Henry had replied, "Son, I can guarantee you a better night wiv us. Come on, give Fred back his piece an' we'll buy you the priciest stuff on the menu."

"That's right, give me my fucking gun back, you–"

"Shut up, Fred," Henry had said.

Ray's eyes hadn't left Henry's. "You got any coke?"

Henry had laughed at that one, big an' gut-bustin. "Son, you don't have a fackin clue who I am, do ya?"

Throughout the night, as he'd filled Ray's throat wiv luxury booze an' his nose wiv the city's best white powder, Henry had pieced togevver the facts. Ray's surname, 'Atticus'. Those sky-high cheek bones. His nimble fingers. An' when Henry had casually asked Raymond his muvver's name when she'd come up in conversation, his suspicions had been confirmed.

Rose.

It was a name that Henry remembered well. Their paths had barely crossed in twenty years, an' Henry's feelin's for her were as dry as a desert's fanny. She was just anuvver slag he'd known in anuvver life – but this lad here, even wiv his dreadlocks an' his tranny get-up, was a different kettle o' fish. He was confident an' ballsy, smart an' quick-witted. An' while Henry had felt no desire to raise an ankle-biter a coupla decades ago, things had changed. Henry was no longer a young squirt, an' his long-term squeeze Rebecca could no more have kids than she could fart the national anthem.

So that night, two words had flashed bright neon in Henry's brain.

SON, one had spelled.

SON ... an' maybe HEIR.

So, keepin a lid on his astonishment, Henry had offered the lad a job that very night ˣ a legitimate one an' all. The kid had been lookin for work, the job had bin well-paid, an' the manager's position shoulda bin well outta reach for a young lad wiv-out experience. The rest, as they say, is history.

After biddin farewell to Bruno, Henry eased himself into his red sports car, which was big, powerful, an' had cost as much as a small flat. That bright afternoon he coasted round the back o' the tall white beach apartments to avoid the one-way shite. Seadon seemed to have too many roads for such a small place - could walk for an hour an' get from outskirt to outskirt, but take one wrong turn in the car an' you'd double your journey. After every few corners Henry spied the sea glimmerin between the apartment blocks; one o' the powerful magnets that drew thousands o' visitors away from their northern shit-holes each year. Although the season was just beginnin, clumps o' holidaymakers cackled like seals on each side. They buffed Henry's ego as he reflected that, in the space o' less than two decades, he'd transformed the entire city. When he'd bin a kid, the sea an' the sun had been the *only* draws for the visitors, promptin a population soar in the summertime an' a great plummet in winter. But back then the police had bin a far straighter breed, the streets clear o' lawbreakin except for an occasional scuffle due to one too many shandies. Now, coz o' Henry's single-minded determination, every drinkin hole, every guesthouse, an' every beach was awash wiv high-quality, low-cost Colombian marchin powder.

Fackin *beautiful*, an' when Seadon had gained its rep as a drug haven the tourist season had boomed across most o' the year. No one needs a sunny day to make snortin fun.

Henry pulled up in the grotty alleyway behind the Green Emporium. Shit name that. Shoulda called it somethin more, 'down wiv the kids', but the shop's stock weren't the reason he'd bought the place. Didn't hurt, o' course, but it was more important that the Green Emporium was one o' Henry's several 'front' businesses.

As he got out, a blonde, beachy toe-rag from a little further down the alleyway called out, "Alright, mate?"

One o' Seadon's typical fackin plebs: floppy hair, a t-shirt wiv a picture of a surfer, an' a spliff-shaped rollie hangin from his trap. Fackin clown. Henry stopped an' stared at him. Didn't say a word – cunt wasn't worth it – but he kept his gaze cold an' steady for a few moments.

"S-sorry," the waste o' skin stuttered, wiltin, no doubt sensin the presence of a big fish. He stepped on his ciggy an' facked off back into his own shop.

Henry unlocked the back door an' went inside. A damp-smellin corridor led down to the main shop an' a set o' stairs ran up to his left. Henry could see the side o' some chubby twerp's head at the counter. The bloke looked flustered. Probly embarrassed at havin to sell that double-ended dildo to the redheaded slag standin at the till.

Henry chuckled as he climbed the steps, an' at the top knocked politely on the closed door.

"Henry?" came a voice.

"Nope, Rumpel-fackin-stiltskin," Henry said.

The door opened an' there was his boy, wiv his purple dreadlocks an' red eyes, Henry's young champ, the dog's fackin doodahs. They hugged firmly, clapped backs, an' went back out to the car.

Ray

Henry was the only person Ray had ever met who seemed to have sculpted his life into the precise shape he desired. He was a man from a working class background who had taken the world by the scruff of the neck and demanded better. Ray felt as if he had befriended a fearsome wild animal: an ineloquent Shere Khan, or a grizzly bear moulded by cockney stereotypes.

The sun shone through the open window behind Henry, turning his face craggy and shadowed. He puffed on a large Cuban cigar as he used three fingers to brush the wheel of his Tesla Roadster. Through the pluming smoke, his eyes were agile, sweeping searchlights. He wore a characteristically outlandish outfit: tartan trousers, a shining silver jacket over a white shirt, and a flat green golfer's cap. Ray had formed a theory as to why his boss dressed such an eccentric way: Henry must scour the internet and purchase the most expensive clothes he could find, but pay no attention to their style, colour or source. This way, his wardrobe contained not a single matching theme, save for each item's exclusivity.

"How did you get into the business?" Ray enquired as they cruised through the city.

Henry nose-laughed a blue cloud. "That's not a story I should be tellin' a youngster like you," he teased, glancing out the window towards a cackle of short-skirted women. "You want one o' these cigars? Fackin' delicious."

"Thanks." Ray took one from a compartment loaded with them, each the size of a hot dog. Beneath the cloying stench of smoke, the sports car smelled of deep, rich leather. "I mean it, though. How did you start out?"

Henry shook his head, smirking as he circled a roundabout and moved onto the dual carriageway. "Give you nightmares, I would, tellin' a sensitive soul like yourself."

The jibes were like stones in Ray's shoe. "Look, I know you're a tough businessman," he said. "I know you're seen as a bit of a local legend. And I know you've got access to some tasty products."

"Go on," Henry replied, clearly enjoying Ray's spiel.

"I've gathered that you pay off the police," Ray

said, a little more carefully.

Henry's smile shrank a millimetre. "I jus' give some of our officers a little financial gratitude for protectin' our city."

Ray plunged. "And I'm assuming that no one becomes as rich as you without burying a few bodies ... so to speak."

Henry's lips contracted into a tense pout. A familiar chill climbed the ladder of Ray's back, scaled his neck and dispersed across his scalp. As long as he didn't start to tremble, he knew it wouldn't become another full-blown anxiety attack.

"Alright," Henry said, withdrawing the cigar from his mouth and leaning an arm out of the window. "I'll tell you a fackin' story, shall I?"

Ray swallowed. He clipped his own cigar with a cutter from the dashboard, placed it between his lips, and lit it with Henry's golden zippo.

Keeping his eyes on the road, Henry spat a tobacco crumb. "Mine can be a sticky business. I wouldn't patronise you by sayin' uvverwise. I've seen blood, but I didn't pop out me mum's arse'ole wiv a magnum in my hand. It takes time to toughen up, an' a lot o' sleepless nights."

He glanced at Ray.

"Ysee, when I was fourteen, I began to cotton on to my dad's game. Started to understand who the men in black coats were. Realised why he always had the cash to buy nice clothes, a swish car, an' good stuff for the house. Sometimes jewellery for me mum, too, God rest 'er.

"Dad used to make up stories when I was a nipper, tellin' me about all the great things he did. Solvin' crimes in New York one day, savin' the world from Communism the next. But he wasn't a spy like I'd once thought, or a secret agent. He was just a small-time hood."

Henry steered the car onto a slip road leading to a thin country lane.

"I was already gettin' into trouble: liftin' from shops, an' sellin' a bit o' dope to the older lads. I'd already grown an 'ealthy disrespect for the law, an' I didn't take shite from any Tom, Dick or Harry.

"One night I was crossin' the Elwood estate, knowin' I probly shouldn't be there at that time o' night but, like I said, I was already a ballsy little facker." He cleared his throat and sniffed, his eyes dreaming. The car rumbled softly as it navigated the pockmarked road. "It was pure coincidence, son, jus' like when I met you. Took a trip through an alleyway an' then, *bam*, there I saw my big, bad daddy bein' held down by three blokes. His face was bleedin' an' he was cryin', wailin'."

"Christ," Ray murmured, enraptured. Because Ray had been raised by his mother alone, he found it hard to place himself in such a situation. Ray imagined fierce loyalty and determination in Henry's case, rather than the hollow rage Ray felt when he considered his own father's cowardice.

Henry continued, "It was quiet out that night, so I waited round the corner. Sounded like they were tryin' to drag dad to his feet. I'd seen fights before, been in a couple, but these fellas had weaponry. Two blades, one pistol I could see, an' no doubt more besides. Gutsy cunts, doin' all that outdoors - dad musta pissed off someone big. I remember hearin' one of 'em tell dad he was a dead man, so there was no way I was gonna run. In the end I jus' walked out, bold as you like."

"What did they do?" Ray asked.

"Told me to fack off, o' course. Said they'd cut me if I didn't. Then when my dad started bleatin', they realised who I was. They decided I was hilarious." Henry chuckled dryly. "That put my back *right up*, I can tell ya, but you should never show a tough guy they've got to ya; they're like dogs, an' smell fear. Anyway, dad was yellin' at me to make myself scarce, so one of 'em, this pale guy who looked like an undertaker, slashed dad's arm. Matey wiv the pistol strolled towards me, tellin' me he was gonna kill dad while I watched.

"I still hadn't said a fackin' thing - I was jus' focused on that tall bastard in front o' me. I'd decided what I was gonna do, an' my age was workin' wonders for me. They thought I was a pushover. They thought I was a fackin' *joke*, but they was *wrong*.

"They didn't know that a few months before, I'd found dad's gun in his tool shed. They didn't have a clue that I'd been practicin' in the woods, nickin' from dad's stash o' bullets an' then puttin' the piece back where I'd found it.

"So he was comin' at me, this cocky cunt, an' before he'd realised it I'd whipped out the gun an' popped off two shots – one in 'is cheek, an' anuvver that knocked a lump out his jaw. Wasn't so mouthy when he'd lost half his face an' was whinin', like a kid who'd lost his teddy bear. I put anuvver one in him, an' he shut up at last.

"The uvver two jumped offa dad, dropped their knives an' held up their hands – for me, *a fackin' fourteen-year-old*. If they'd just run, I mighta let 'em be, but I could tell they still thought I was a little kid, a little nobody. So I took out the undertaker's knee, an' as he was fallin' down I blew off the top of his fackin' skull. The uvver one couldn't believe it, but he'd had his chance. I did him in the chest, so then there were just three bodies, one teenager wiv a gun, an' one sobbin' daddy."

Ray was silent as Henry's pad appeared before them. The car's interior had started to gyrate and Ray's back was hot and tingling, his hands threatening to shake. Another attack was coming.

Not now. Not in front of Henry.

"While dad was still lyin' on the floor, he composed himself. Suddenly got all fatherly, an' told me everythin' was gonna be okay, like I needed comfortin'." Henry looked at Ray hard and Ray's chest filled with frost. "He had no right talkin' to me like that, his face all wet wiv snot an' blood. I was fackin' disgusted." Henry snorted and spat a green lump through the window. "What kind o' man needs his son to save his skin, eh? What kind o' man needs his son to do anythin' for him?"

The question hung.

"A failure, that's who. A fackin' failure, who's jus' watched his son do what he couldn't do himself." Henry's nostrils flared. "So you know what I did? I put the barrel against the bridge o' daddy's nose, an' I put a fackin' hole in him, too."

Ray's breath caught. Nausea bloomed like a pungent flower in his throat.

"Best move I ever made. I took the gun an' stashed it, an' by the time the coppers searched our house I'd already moved what I wanted from dad's shed. When the police found the bits I'd left it just confirmed that dad had bin a naughty boy, an' probly deserved it. So *they* had four less crooks to worry about, an' I got a gun an' my dad's money stash. Everyone was happy."

Ray let the words sink in.

"I'm not sayin' it was easy, son; far from it. But wiv that cash, an' that gun, I built the foundations of an empire." The end of Henry's cigar glowed proudly as they drew into the enormous, immaculate gravel driveway.

It was the first time they had openly discussed the violence of Henry's career, and Ray's heart felt as though it had stopped.

They pulled up and Ray stepped out of the car, eager to taste the fresh air. The sun burned at their backs.

Henry said, "Cor. That was a bit intense, weren't it?" He led the way with an ungainly swagger, chest puffed out and chin held high.

Grass carpets edged the drive that led towards Henry's pristine mansion. At either side stood a green figure shaped from tall, preened bushes. Henry had told Ray that they were trimmed in likeness of his idols, London's notorious Kray twins. Henry had said that the pair encapsulated how gents such as he should behave: devious, gutsy and determined. Ronnie's bulk loomed straight-armed on their right, while his slimmer brother Reggie stood with his arms crossed to their left. An identical and ornate silver fountain gushed at the feet of each sibling, and ghostly fish missiled through the waters below.

A grey-haired man in dungarees was balanced on a short platform before Reggie, diligently clipping his elbow with a small pair of shears.

"Mornin', Ralph," Henry called out.

"Good morning, sir," the frail-looking chap replied warmly, doffing an invisible cap before returning to his work. He must have been in his seventies.

When they had passed, Henry murmured, "Whatever you do, don't *ever* fack wiv Ralph. You'll regret it."

Ray grinned politely, but Henry looked serious.

"I mean it. Anyway, come on. The sun may not yet be over the yard arm, but I fancy somethin' strong to see in the day."

Between two stone pillars, a short row of steps led them towards the carved wooden door of the house. At three storeys high its extravagant size, remote location and modest stone-carved nymphs spoke of wealth and, misleadingly, a refined taste.

Henry unlocked the heavy door to a vast, white-and-black marbled reception, above which a gigantic chandelier dangled from a chain that stretched two floors up to the ceiling. A gold-edged staircase climbed in a high spiral, alighting on a first floor balcony before rising to the next.

They stepped inside between two oil paintings of similar style, each depicting Henry. In one, Henry was clad in the outfit of a general and gazed proudly towards the viewer. Behind him, a battalion of loyal infantry stormed the darkness of No-Man's-Land, bayonets and gun barrels raised. In the other, Henry sat on a high throne in a long white shawl and a laurel-leaf crown, eyes closed and face solemn. A maiden stood on either side of him, one offering him a bowl of grapes and the other a flagon of red wine. A crowd of subjects knelt before him, with their right hands pressed to their hearts.

At Ray's feet, a rug lay stretched over the gleaming, gold-dappled floor: two tiger skins neatly stitched side-by-side. One roaring head stared sightlessly towards Henry and Ray, while the other gazed past the staircase to a door on the far wall. Ray had seen behind that portal to the aquarium of tropical fish, swimming in a windowless gloom punctured only by low spotlights and ultra-violet strip lamps.

"Ah, home sweet home," Henry said, and led them towards his well-stocked alcohol reserve.

Henry had told Ray that upon purchasing the house he had paid an architect to design the bar as if it was an upmarket but traditional country pub. Calm greens and forest browns coated the floor and seating, and a grand fireplace lay beneath three severed deer heads: a pretty doe in the centre of two grandly antlered stags. An array of typical pub adornments lined the walls: framed knots and farming tools and photographs of local Seadon scenery. The buffed wooden surfaces of five tables reflected the light that poured through the windows and 1950s pop music jived from hidden speakers.

A glamorous twenty-something brunette with tied-back hair stood at relaxed attention behind the bar wearing a shirt, maroon waistcoat and perfect smile. She had been there other times Ray had visited, too - a bartender for hire by the hour. Ray tried not to stare, determined to keep his sex drive cordoned off and restricted to the mornings.

"Now, whaddya want, son?" Henry said, opening his hands towards four rows of spirit bottles behind the bar.

"What beers have you got?" Ray asked, looking down into the low refrigerators.

"No, no son, you don't want any o' that pissy-knickered shite. Come on, love, get us a coupla Richard Hennessys, and make 'em large, as it's an occasion."

Ray watched the gorgeous tender turn and pour the drinks, and at the sight of those tight trousers gripping her rear felt something stir in his underwear.

"I thought we were shooting after lunch?" Ray said.

Henry grinned wolfishly. "Raymond, I've fired

guns when I've been too pissed to even remember doin' it. A cognac an' a bottle o' wine over lunch won't hurt."

As they sat down, sun rays glinted across Henry's silver jacket, pouring in through sliding glass doors that looked out over the roofs of Seadon's distant horizon. Their host delivered their drinks and when she slipped away, she left a soft scent of pressed flowers. It felt like so long since Ray had had sex that he couldn't stop an image unfurling in his brain: the bartender punishing him with a strap-on as he bent over the bar, handcuffed to the beer pumps and lapping at a trough filled with pink champagne.

"Try that, Raymond-son," Henry told him. "It's *well* old, an' there's about two 'undred different cognacs in it. Or is it a thousand? I dunno, but some of 'em are dead rare. Anyway, it cost a fackin' mint, so enjoy it."

Ray sipped from his glass and, although he would have preferred a cool pale ale, Henry was right; it *was* good. "Thanks."

"Yeah, too right. Stick wi' me, son, an' you'll be perfect. When we've finished this, we'll grab lunch. I've got the chef from Ronaldo's to fix a feast for us, so it's gonna be pukka."

Ray's stomach rumbled at the thought - Ronaldo's was a three-star Michelin grade restaurant. "You really just do as you please, don't you?"

Henry swirled his glass. When he spoke, 'Baby Love' by The Supremes began to play over the speakers. "You wanna know the key to gettin' your own way? It's realisin' that equality is a heap o' shite, same as fackin' charity. Sure, there's a lotta fackers out there who wouldn't agree, but that's why I'm where I am, an' why they're still suckin' on *society's* tits." He spoke the word 'society' as if it was gristle in his mouth.

On some mysterious level, the words rang true. Ray had watched his home city degrade, deform, and stagger drunkenly away from the safe, family realm it had seemed to him as a child. In the country-wide media and in the minds of many who lived there, Seadon had become synonymous with crews of lads and lasses doing drugs and flashing arses; a place to go to fight, fool around, and get fucked up. Oddly, a large part of that was due to this man and his empire of white powder; this braggard who now sat across from him, spouting crooked philosophies and supping ancient cognac. Perhaps Ray should have felt anger and resentment, but Henry's life demonstrated a dangerous truth: for one man to be on top, a population has to suffer. Ray's mother had always tried to teach him otherwise, but what had she ever achieved?

"Now listen, son," Henry said, his scheming eyes narrowing. "I've known something since the moment we met: there's someone special trapped inside o' you, an' I wanna let the poor facker out."

"How are you going to do that?" Ray asked, genuinely curious.

Henry shifted his chair to sit beside Ray and leaned his granite head in close. Ray caught a tang of cigars, sweat, and bitter aftershave. There was something else too; a trace of wet canine. Henry said, "When ya find someone wiv enough good will to help you out, you gotta grab that opportunity hard an' firm. It's you against the world, son, an' while I've got everythin' I could ever need, most fackers have only got their floppy cocks hangin' outta their flies."

A sensation hit Ray: he was being led through an unfamiliar, lightless corridor.

"You wanna be like them?" Henry asked. "The little ants, all workin' togevver for everyone else? Or d'you wanna carve your own path an' lead the fackin' way?"

Ray suddenly knew what Henry's next words were going to be, and felt as if the ground behind him had opened to reveal a yawning pit.

Henry's face was expressionless. "I want you involved."

In that uncertain, flittering moment, Ray saw his mother filling a supermarket shelf with tins of baked beans, choking back tears as she considered another failed audition. Ray fought to clear his mind but the image stayed as clear to him as the unblinking eyes of the multi-millionaire sat across the table.

"Better to be a wolf than a sheep, son," Henry said, as if reading Ray's mind. "You're made for better things than the rest of 'em."

Ray thought hard, feeling his pulse start to pound once more. "What would I have to do?"

"Nothin' hectic, son. Don't worry about it."

"And what would the rest of your... employees think if I did?"

"You're already on good terms wiv Fred an' a couple of uvvers you've met, an' you needn't lose sleep worryin' about anyone else."

Ray looked at the table. "I was thinking about Percy Locker."

Henry screwed his lips into a tight pout and laid a firm hand across Ray's shoulder. "Percy's loyal an' knows what's expected of 'im. The two of us go way back, but in the end I'm the cunt who makes the decisions. So if I say you're on board, he won't make a peep - you got my word on that."

"Did you see him at the bar the other night, looking over at us?" Ray persisted. "He didn't look happy."

"Look," Henry said, slapping Ray's back, hard. "When I say somethin's alright, it's *fackin' alright*. So jus' leave the thinkin' to me, okay?"

"Okay, Henry," Ray replied, disliking his boss's harsh tone.

"Right then," Henry said. "It's important that you trust Percy, coz if ya can't get hold o' me, I want him to be the next cunt ya go to. He's my second-in-command, an' he's a good lad."

Ray pictured Percy's grey eyes, heart-shaped lips, and unreadable face.

"You know that I'll be leaving Seadon soon, though," Ray said. "I just need to save up a good few grand and I'll be off. You know that, don't you?"

"So you say. Ain't no better way to gather funds than by workin' for me."

"Well..." Ray started. "I mean, I'd love to, but I couldn't give any long-term dedication, and ... and I wouldn't want to risk *too* much, and ..."

Henry cut in. "But what you're sayin', after all these conditions an' half-arguments, is 'yes', innit?"

Ray saw Percy again; then his mother looking dumbstruck as another creative endeavour fizzled into nothingness; then the mindless stag-and-hen masses. And then Henry, here in his palace, smoking cigars and drinking champagne, free to do whatever he wanted, whenever he wished.

Fuck it.

"Okay," Ray said, and as he relented, the noisy rush of the sea filled his ears.

Henry remained motionless, the fire of reflected

sunlight burning in his pupils. Then he beamed and his whole body became animated, and his legs and arms juddered like excited dogs. When he enwrapped Ray with a burly arm his body odour became a swarm, and he raised his glass.

"That's fantastic, son! Let's drink to it!"

Henry jangled his glass against Ray's and they emptied their vessels, Henry looking delirious as Ray swallowed his brandy to calm himself. Sweat seeped from Ray's back and the trembling had begun in his hands again, signalling the onset of something unstoppable.

Calm down. Chill out. Everything's fine.

"Here, love!" Henry called to the bar tender. "Bring us anuvver coupla those Richards an' the best bottle o' bubbly you can find! We'll be eatin' next door!"

Ray felt uneasily excited as Henry took them through to the banquet hall, which was an expansive theatre of pompous reds and blues. Their feet clattered against flagstone flooring that lay far beneath a ceiling of swirled ivory. A vast, 30-foot long wooden table stood at the centre, an elaborately carved chair at either end. Ray had eaten there before and knew that the distance between the seats would force them to raise their voices during conversation.

The bar tender opened a bottle of 1990 Louis

Roederer Cristal, and their food arrived on a cloud of succulent aromas that coaxed a deep, rewarding hunger from Ray. Henry had organised for his favourite local chef, Davide Macchione, to prepare a feast of fusion dining. Davide emerged from a door at one end of the echoing hall before each dish to explain precisely what they were about to eat. They swilled champagne alongside a foie gras crème brûlée speckled with Tonga beans, followed by rib-eye steaks of wagyu beef smothered in a white truffle caramel and Sicilian pistachio purée. Henry blustered and boomed with good humour throughout the meal, allowing Ray to enjoy his lunch without speaking, drowning his nerves with delicacies and vintage alcohol. Just as Ray began to doubt whether he could fit any further culinary luxury into his digestive tract, Davide brought them a rich, twelve-fruit compote that may have been more delicious than anything Ray had ever tasted. Finally, they sipped eye-wateringly strong double espressos to clear their palettes and heads, before Henry told Ray that it was time for a spot of shooting.

Out back, they crossed Henry's back field in a warm, dopey haze. Before they reached the soundproofed barn containing Henry's practice range, Henry pointed in an offhand way towards a patch of grass in the distance.

"In case you were wonderin', that's where they end up."

"Who, Henry?" Ray asked, light-headed.

"Anyone who steps in my fackin' way."

Henry drove Ray back to the Green Emporium after a couple of hour's target practice. Even after brandy and bubbly, Ray's aim with a handgun remained dignified. Still tipsy, they laughed as Henry navigated the fast lane and took them back to the city.

Henry parked at the back of the shop and led Ray up to the piping hot office.

"I see you've made yourself more at home, now," Henry said, nodding at the framed pictures and posters that lined the walls. Screen villains filled the room with gun barrels, blades, and cold, hard stares.

"Yup, couldn't bear the blandness any longer," said Ray, smoothing down the rolled-back edge of a Pinhead poster. "Had to get the place feeling a bit more 'me'. Coffee?"

"No thanks, I'm runnin' on full, son," Henry replied. He paced a slow circle, hands clasped behind his back. "Now, you've agreed to come on board, and I've got one last thing to tell you before leavin' you in peace."

Ray grinned. "Firing me already, are you?"

"Got it in one," Henry said, pointing a finger. "Bam."

Ray lifted his hand. "Caught it."

"Thought ya might, son, thought ya might. Quicker than a gunshot, aren't ya? An' that's why I'm givin' ya this place."

Ray hesitated. "The office?"

Henry angled his head and raised his eyebrows. "An' the rest."

Ray's chest tightened. "You're... giving me the Green Emporium?"

"I am."

"Henry, that's very kind, but are you sure you..."

Henry closed his eyes, looking aggravated. "Look, son. One thing you're gonna have to learn is that when I say somethin', I mean it. Anythin' you think you need to point out, I'll have considered several times over. So just be grateful, okay?"

As ever, there was no arguing. "Thank you so much, Henry."

"That's my boy. Now come here."

Ray followed his boss over to the corner of the room where Henry bent over and slid a finger beneath the grey carpet. He pulled it back and revealed varnished floorboards. "Now, you gotta understand that what I'm givin' you here ain't just a shop, son. No. It's a diamond dressed up as a zirconia. A priceless antique stuffed up a whore's arse'ole."

Henry laid the mat back in a triangle and used a key to pry up a board.

"What have you got there?" Ray asked.

Leaning down, Henry turned to Ray with glittering teeth. "A little slice o' the pie."

Under the board, a stack of queen's heads and high numbers lay bathed in shadow. Ray stepped forwards and Henry dislodged another board, pulling it up and propping it against the wall beside the other. Below, there were more faces, more crowns, and more double figures.

Ray looked into Henry's leering face. "What do I do with that?"

Henry straightened and sniffed a laugh. "You fackin' look after it an' watch it grow. Now, I'm not askin' you to be a debt collector, or to give cash out to the fackin' losers I loan to. You'll be a middle man for a select few o' my boys - you'll take over from me. Sometimes they'll need to collect a little extra fundin' for loans, an' uvver times they'll have cash to deposit. Won't happen every day, maybe not even every week, but you'll keep checks on whatever leaves the buildin' an' make sure that the pile just keeps gettin' bigger. An' each time some profit comes in, I'll make sure you get your reward. Alright?"

Ray's mouth was dry. He'd never seen so much money. "How much is in there?"

"Not enough," Henry said, replacing the board. "Never enough. A lot o' my fundin' gets moved through legit businesses, but it's useful to have ready notes that Mr Taxman and Mrs fackin' Banker aren't clued up on. I've got little stashes all across town. They're important, so you do me proud, okay?"

Ray swallowed. He was going to be out of Seadon in no time. "You have no idea how much I appreciate what you're doing for me. I mean, you've taken me in like ... like I don't know what. Like a guardian. I just hope I never disappoint you."

Henry took Ray's face in his hands, clasped it tightly. "Ya wouldn't, son. Ya couldn't – I know ya too well. I know that all you wanna do is make good, an' ya will. You've just gotta believe, trust in me, an' nice things will keep happenin'. Alright?"

Henry's palms felt huge and hot around Ray's face. He seemed to be looking into Ray's mind.

"Thanks again, Henry. I mean it," Ray said, and wrapped an awkward arm around his boss.

Henry's hands remained locked around Ray's face for another moment before he returned the embrace. "You deserve it," he growled into Ray's ear. Again, Henry seemed to hold on to Ray for a few seconds too long, and when he stepped back he was rubbing his eyes. "Anyway. I can't stick around here teachin' you life lessons all day. I've got a to-do list that's longer than a horse's todger."

"Sure, Henry," Ray replied, but suddenly it was as if he was slipping from the room, inch by inch.

Shit, here it comes - run or collapse ... flee or fall...

"I'll see you very soon, son," Henry said.

As Henry left, thin grey tentacles crept across Ray's vision. His legs felt primed to sprint but in the silence of the office the world closed in around him. He saw that flash of steel from his wank fantasy once again, and then Dita's coal-black eyes. His sight contracted, faded. He back-stepped towards the desk. If it hadn't been for the chair he would have dropped like a tree to the wiry carpet.

CHAPTER 4
"Pee in a pod"

Thomas

Up until that strange, belly-squirmy moment, Thomas had been enjoying his morning. Having played Flyflyfly just after he'd woken up, the children had set him his challenge for the day: The Kid Count Game. Thomas, relieved, knew the rules already: he just had to count every young person who came into the shop.

The children set him a task most days, and it was often a real hassle. One time, he'd had to play The Voices Game, which was where he had to talk in a French accent to every third customer, and like a Chinese woman to every fifth. That day, although he'd got some funny looks, he'd succeeded. For his prize, the children had helped Thomas's mummy and daddy to walk around the farmhouse again for a week, which had been a bit weird, but still nice.

Or what about that time when he'd played The Squishy Animal Game? He'd had to look through the shops nearby, trying to find a stuffed animal that was part beaver, part rhino. He'd failed that one, and his forfeit had been having to push cocktail sticks through the webbing next to his thumbs.

Then there was the time he'd played The Limping All Day Game. And then another time, The Mug An Old Man Game. He'd played so many that he couldn't remember them all.

Today, working alone in the shop as usual, he had counted eleven kids so far. Most parents didn't seem happy for their littl'uns to gawp at fake willies and druggy stuff, so Thomas was sure he'd be able to keep track of them and win, no prob.

His morning had been bimbling along nicely, but then this guy with a baseball cap came into the shop with three kids – one girl, two boys. Thomas almost dropped the glass bong he had been examining for a barcode, and the moustached man he was serving became annoyed.

"You alright mate?" Tash-Man asked, all haughty. "You gonna sell that to me, or what?"

Thomas stared at the guy with the kids. They were of different ages to Simon, Hanna and Benny from the Gardden, but that didn't matter. Simon had warned Thomas that he wasn't going to be the Gardden's keeper for much longer, and when Thomas looked at the man in the cap he imagined the guy as his replacement. Nasty pictures filled his brain, and for a few seconds Thomas wanted to thump the man, to kick him and cut him and make him cry.

"I'm not leaving. I'm going to win the stupid People Game, whatever it is," Thomas said, though he hadn't meant to speak out loud. "*You're* leaving, and *you're* going to lose."

The guy with the cap and the kids scowled back, puffing out his chest. "What did you say, pal?"

When Thomas realised what he had done, he said hastily, "Sorry. It was ... a joke."

The guy, his kids and the man with the moustache left soon after. When they were gone, Thomas started to feel like he was going a bit mad. The idea of The People Game was big and scary and horrid, even though he didn't understand it, so he distracted himself with work until the shop cleared out at lunchtime.

"'Ere, mate," a teenager with green doodles on his bald head said. "You got any o' them legal pills what makes yer face feel like it's on fire?"

Thomas shook his head. The teen's expression became so sad that, as he was leaving, it was like his whole face was going to fall off.

A noise made Thomas turn around: a herky-jerky drum roll of boots clonking on stairs. Down the back corridor, Ratan's pale face was even whiter than usual, and his red eyes drooped dopily.

"Thomas..." he said, clutching the bannister and swaying. "Um... will you come for a drink with me?"

Surprised, Thomas struggled for words. "But Ratan... we're still open."

Ratan's red eyeballs focused on him. "Just come for a fucking drink with your superior – *and don't argue.*"

"And just shut the shop?' Thomas asked.

"No, we'll keep the place open with a sign telling people to leave their money on the counter." Ratan's sarcasm seemed to bring back colour to his face. "Of course we'll shut the shop. So get the place locked up while there's still no one in here and meet me out back."

Down an underpass, beside a grotty-looking public loo, The Runway looked to Thomas like a cross between a dungeon and a fairground. Inside, multi-coloured lights twinkled and blinked lazily, while others hung from cords and thin chains, forcing Thomas to duck as they moved through the bar. There was no music, there were no other customers, and the room smelled of damp wood.

Thomas sucked in his surroundings with nervous glee. He was doing something naughty. He wasn't supposed to have *other* friends, but how could he think straight when the room was boggling his eyes with rainbow-lights that danced like fairies?

Two long tables surrounded by chairs stood in the centre of the floor, and benches ran around the room's edges. Behind these long seats, shelves lined the walls, bearing weirdy-weird oddities that goggled through thick metal bars. A dead-eyed Hitler mannequin with a swastika on its chest leaned an arm out from its prison, surrounded by burned stuffed toys. Leading to the corner, a row of dark green candles were rooted to their spots by melted wax, and in between each of these a stuffed rat stood on hind legs, each wearing a funny-looking outfit from a different world culture.

Thomas tried to absorb it all but there was too much. There were pale-faced dolls, a painting of a ship sailing through a sea of leaves, a huge red owl, a bell the size of a basketball, an acoustic guitar with someone's autograph scribbled beneath its strings and a big rusty blunderbuss, like the ones that fired out garbage in old cartoons.

"This place is ... magical ..." Thomas managed.

"Yeah, it's not bad," Ratan agreed, scanning the bottles behind the dusty bar.

A pot-bellied woman of about forty wearing a short denim skirt stood ready to serve them, hands on her hips. "Haven't seen you for a while, Ratan. How have you been?"

"Better than most, thanks, Tara. Get me two straight glasses of the big man."

"What did you order?" Thomas whispered, distracted from the bar's freakish zoo.

"Johnnie Walker."

Thomas's mind was blank.

"Scotch," Ratan clarified.

"Wine?"

"Jesus, Tommy, what planet are you from? You're about to learn a life's lesson in booze."

"Have they got crisps? I'm starving."

"I'll get you some."

"Three packs?"

Ratan smirked. "You're a greedy sod. Go sit down."

Thomas went to the bench closest to the exit.

"Not that one!" Ratan called. "Who's going to notice us all the way over there?"

Thomas came back obediently, but muttered, "It's not like there's anyone else here."

A minute or two later, Ratan came over with two little drinks and three bags of steak-flavoured crisps. Before he sat down he juggled the crisp packets, swirling them in circles before clawing them out of the air. Thomas grinned and gave him a quiet applause.

Sitting down, Ratan nodded back at the bar lady. In a low voice, he said, "She's *crazy*, by the way. A couple of years ago, she wanted a threesome with me and this 70-year-old woman, who might have been her mum. Proper weird." Ratan drank some 'scotch'. "Get that down you."

"I...I don't normally drink," Thomas admitted, tearing open a bag of crisps and tucking in. The truth was, he'd *never* tried alcohol.

"Well, you do today," Ratan said firmly. "I'm feeling strange but I'm still looking fine, and as usual you're looking like shit but apparently feeling okay. So let's see if we can meet somewhere in the middle."

"But what about the shop?"

"You'll get paid, don't worry about that. It's mine now."

"You bought the Green Emporium?" Thomas asked in surprise, squinting at the dark liquid inside his glass.

"No, but it's mine. I earned it."

"Wooooow," Thomas marvelled. He sipped his drink and then coughed explosively. "That tastes...*so yucky...*"

Ratan raised an eyebrow. "Steel yourself, prepare for the burn, and try again."

Thomas was doubtful but he took another gulp and managed to keep the splutters at bay. Apparently 'scotch' burned like acid and tasted like cauliflower farts, but he made an effort to smile because he was meant to be enjoying himself. "Lovely," he wheezed.

His grin must have looked ultra-fake because Ratan laughed. "You look hilarious, buddy. Wait a moment." Ratan went to the bar and bought another drink. When he came back, he poured it into Thomas's glass and turned the 'scotch' a gloopy orange. "Try it now."

Thomas clenched his stomach mega-hard, but the drink was actually scrumptious – sweeter and much less fiery. "Tastes like Battenberg cake," Thomas beamed, and swallowed the rest.

"Better go easy on that stuff, it'll creep up on you," Ratan warned. "I used to have that before I went out to Lashes. I call it a Drag Quim."

"How come you don't go there anymore?" Thomas asked. "When I started at the shop you seemed to love it."

Ratan's red eyes flashed. "I outgrew the place."

Lashes was where Ratan had gained his nickname. Ray...Satan...Ratan. Apparently all the popular people at Lashes had special names, like Sichopath, Ade Blade, and Kat-scan. Ratan had once told Thomas that he could have the nickname "Tommygun" if he wanted. Thomas hadn't.

"You don't miss it, then?" Thomas asked, as a pleasing fuzziness crept through him.

"Not really." Ratan crossed his legs and leaned back, as if he ruled the room. "This city, it tugs you down. Makes you think that all that exists is shagging and dancing and getting wasted." Ratan downed his drink. When he looked at his empty glass he shook his head and rose to his feet. "This ain't gonna do it today."

Thomas was gutted; he'd never been to a pub before. "Are we done?"

"We're far from done, Tommy," Ratan said.

Thomas opened his second bag of crisps. When Ratan came back from the bar he was carrying the rest of the bottle of 'Johnnie Walker' and a wine glass filled with the amber splosh he'd added to Thomas's drink.

"Wow, are you alright?" Thomas asked.

"I will be by the time we get through this," Ratan replied, and tugged off his hair tie. With his red contact lenses and puffy dreadlocks fluffing out over his cheeks, he looked like a cartoon demon.

"What's wrong with you today?" Thomas asked. "I mean,

you came down the stairs looking like a total zombie, and then you told me to shut the shop in the middle of the day. And now we're, like, drinking booze."

Ratan flicked a purple sausage of hair over one shoulder. "I'm fine, Tommy. I've just had better days, that's all."

"I thought you said Henry had given you the Green Emporium? Doesn't that make this an *ace* day?"

Ratan picked up his glass, balanced it on the tip of his middle finger, spun it, then caught it and took a slug. "I'm still ... adjusting to being friends with Henry. I sort-of told him I'd get involved with his main business, and..." He stopped. "And I tell you way too frigging much. Henry would be seriously pissed if he knew how much I told you, and he's not a man you want to antagonise."

"I know that, Ratan," Thomas said, and slurped from his second glass. It tasted great and made Thomas feel all grown up.

"*I'm fucking serious,*" Ratan hissed. "Henry's got power, money, and a lot of influence. And he told me today that he murdered his dad."

"Woah. Really? That's pretty nutty."

"That's right. 'Pretty nutty'," Ratan agreed. "So just use your head, okay? Jesus, why do I tell you this stuff, anyway?"

Ratan was irritable, but he got like that sometimes. Thomas wanted to say something to cheer him up, but he felt fidgety. The children had forbidden him from having other friends, but the drinks were working some kind of hocus-pocus on him, turning his brain into a dizzy dance hall where everything seemed less important. "Maybe they won't be too bothered, anyway," he muttered.

Ratan looked up. "What? Who won't be bothered about what?"

Darn it, he'd said that out loud, hadn't he? He *hated it* when he did that. "Nothing. No one."

Ratan shrugged. "You got plans for this evening?"

"Not really. Just a few things I've got to do," Thomas

lied. He hoped Ratan would either talk about something else or stop talking altogether.

"Like what?"

Thomas was about to lie, but then just shrugged.

"Do you ever go out with friends?" Ratan asked.

"I, um, haven't got too many."

"Didn't you keep any of your mates from school?"

Thomas fumbled for words. "I ... er ..."

Ratan clicked his fingers suddenly. "You were schooled at home, weren't you?"

He was close enough. "Yep. How did you know?"

Ratan grins. "Just a hunch. Explains a lot, really."

Thomas picked up his glass and let his eyes wander around the room, glad that Ratan seemed satisfied.

"So what about finding someone to screw, then?" Ratan said. "You like girls? Boys?"

Thomas was getting hot and uncomfy, as if the rotating bulbs had all focused onto him. He was beginning to understand why the children didn't want him making other friends: too many questions. "Yeah, I like girls, but ... I haven't got the time. I don't want the hassle. I keep myself to myself and I don't need a girlfriend or any friends." Then he snapped, "*Alright?*"

Ratan wasn't put off, though. "Well, if you don't need friends, I suppose you won't want to do this again, will you? You won't want to hang out with little ol' me, drinking and talking shit?"

Thomas scowled, but then grinned. "Okay, fair point. This *is* pretty awesome." Thomas thought for a moment, drained his drink, and then said, "Can I ask you something?"

Ratan looked straight at him. "Sure - shoot."

The booze was making Thomas dwell on stuff he didn't like to think about. "What if Henry told you to hurt someone?"

Ratan's face dropped. He began to tap a rhythm on the table and leaned forward again, looking serious. "Before I answer that, let me ask *you* something. When you look around Seadon, what do you see?"

Thomas thought for a second, wondering how open he should be. Ah, to heck with it. "I see a bunch of other people who I'd rather be than me."

Ratan sneered. "Well I see nothing but fucking vampires. And not the cool kind, either - just unhealthy creatures who come here and suck the city for all it's worth." He chomped his teeth down onto his fist as if he didn't want to say any more, but it seemed like he couldn't stop. "I've watched this city go from a family place to a greasy fuck-pit. A drug-ridden, cultureless shell." The words came faster. "Smackheads on the outskirts, pillheads in the clubs and cokeheads in the bars. Tasteless morons cluttering the streets and beaches. I know that there are good things here – theatre, music, art – but it's all tainted. Seadon's a lost cause, Tommy, and I want out."

Thomas closed his eyes, trying to think clearly. "But if you think that, aren't you just adding to the problem by joining up with Henry? Isn't he some kind of gangster?"

"I just don't care anymore, mate. Sometimes, it's better to be a wolf than a sheep."

Thomas thought of the Gardden and forced himself to speak. "So, like I asked: what if Henry told you to hurt someone? Would you do it?"

Ratan shook his head. "Henry wouldn't force me into anything. He likes me."

Thomas had been hoping Ratan would turn out to be an ally, and fine with doing mean things if they were necessary. He opened his last crisp bag and changed the subject, suddenly feeling a bit sad. "So, you're just going to vanish once you have enough cash, then?"

Almost half the bottle had disappeared and Ratan nodded woozily. "Yup. Gonna go see the world." Suddenly he looked like he was on the verge of blubbering tears. "Sometimes I feel responsible for my mum, and I think I should stick around for her. Then I remind myself that she made her choices and I've got to make mine."

"I guess..." Thomas began, but Ratan blurted, "She's not had it easy, you know! Having her partner hang himself when she had a kid on the way must have been tough. What a fucking coward!"

Ratan raised his fist as if he was going to smack the table, but then thought better of it.

Thomas hadn't known that Ratan's daddy was dead, or that he'd topped himself. Thomas said, "If you ever need anything...you know. Maybe I can help." He sucked on his alcoholic concoction again, feeling relaxed, a little sleepy, and something else... affectionate? Maybe this was what it was like to go drinking with a proper pal. "I don't know why, but I think that you and me are like pee in a pod. No, two peas. You know what I mean."

Ratan smiled blearily. "No I don't. What do you mean?"

Thomas giggled and the room span. "I haven't a clue."

Thomas pushes his front door wide open and stumbles a few steps inside, stops, wibble-totters, and kicks the entrance shut with his heel.

Ratan is such a good guy, a really great dude. This has been the best day that Thomas can remember: first Flyflyfly, and then getting to hang out with his awesome matey.

He flicks a switch and the corridor lights up with a pop. His head is rolling and he doesn't feel too well.

I'm fine.

He staggers down the hallway to the front room. Doesn't bother turning on the lights because a few moon rays are riding through the tall windows. Ratan had told him to get a taxi home but Thomas had wanted fresh air, and the stars had lit his long, stumbling way home.

Thomas plonks down onto the computer chair and feels for the PC's power button in the darkness.

What a day.

He's decided that drinking alcohol is wicked-awesome,

despite the odd, see-sawing feeling in his tum.

He's just about to start watching videos online – maybe some Disney clips, or some Saved By the Bell, or a bit of real death – when he starts to think that he's going to be sick all over the keyboard. The screen seems much too bright in the blackness of the lounge and makes his stomach lurch. This, he supposes, is what being 'pissed' feels like.

Flipping hell.

His mouth waters and he rises too quickly, his legs squirling like candy laces. He falls back down but only half his bum lands on the seat, and he slips off and hits the floor hard. A nasty, sicky taste rises into his mouth. He needs to lie flat so he pushes the chair away and falls backwards, but that just makes his belly flop and his head thump.

"Don't puke, don't puke, don't puke," he chants.

Grunting, he twists himself onto his front. He should have switched on the lights, but there's a shadow in front of the window so he drags himself towards it, hoping to find something to grasp onto to help him get to his feet. When a cloud drifts away from the moon the silhouette above him seems to grow.

At first, Thomas thinks that it's the booze just flip-flunking his mind, but it isn't. With a whoosh and a growl, two blazing red eyebulbs light up the room and glare down at Thomas. The silhouette is a huge towering man-thing with ropes dangling from its skull. In the light of the flaming eyes, Thomas sees chains, boots, arms that are too long and a pouty, scary-grin clownface at the top of a skinny neck.

Thomas tries to shriek but all he can do is whimper. The clowny man-thing teeters, unstable and looming over Thomas with the top of its snakey hair brushing the 12-foot ceiling. When Thomas sees one of its arms swoop down as low as its knees, the fiery glow from its eyes reveals that it's holding a hairy ball.

No, it's not a ball. It's a child's head.

Thomas knows that it's the Gardden, the children, the house that's doing it all, freaking him out and rattling his cage, but it's only when this giant clowny man-thing starts to juggle that he realises what the joke is all about. The man-thing hurls the giggling heads of Simon, Hanna and Benny upwards and catches them, and Thomas recognises what the purple hanging head-ropes and the scorching red eyes and the black clothes and shaky chains are supposed to be.

It's the children's huge, horrid impression of Thomas's friend Ratan.

"Did you have fun with the silly man?" Simon's head asks as it shoots into the air.

Bile slops into Thomas's mouth and he chokes, whining, "I'm sorry, Simon, I went to a dungeon. We had drinks and they made me lose track of everything."

The glaring eyes suddenly puff out and darkness smothers the room again. Lit only by the moon, Thomas sees the man-thing collapse in on itself, nothing but empty clothes, and then all he can see is shadows.

"So, Tommy-Tom-Tom," he hears Simon say, from somewhere close by. "How many children came into the shop today?"

The room swirls. "Simon, I..." Thomas begins, planning to lie, but the sound of Hanna's and Benny's giggles tell him that he mustn't. They'll know.

"You didn't finish counting," Benny's voice gloats from the black. "Tut tut, Fatty-Tom-Tom! That means that we won the Kid Count Game!"

The room tilts like a rocking horse and the shadows around Thomas sway and shudder.

Hanna's voice sneers, "You are just *sooooo* stupid. What a stupid, shitty dummy."

"I'm sorry," Thomas groans, trying to push himself up from his belly. "I'll play properly tomorrow. Just, please, let me go to bed. I'll come see you as soon as I wake up in the morning. Promise."

"No, Thomas. You can't go yet," Simon says, now behind

him.

Benny titters from above, and begins to sing: "Nuh-uh, nuh-uh, nuh-uh!"

"It's all happening, just like I said," Simon says. "Others are going to come to our home, and then you're going to lose The People Game."

"No, I'm going to win it, honest I am..."

Hanna spits into his ear: "You can't. You want *new* friends, don't you?"

"No, of course not..."

"Yes you do!" Benny chuckles. "Stop telling porky pies!"

"I guess that means that we aren't good enough for you, eh?" Simon says. "Well, if that's it, maybe you should go and fetch the suitcase *right now.*"

No.

"Please, I'll count them properly tomorrow if you let me off just this once..."

"Shut up, fatty," Hanna says. "Just shut your stupid, shitty mouth."

"Please," he begs. "Please, just...not that..."

"You'll do it, Thomas," Simon spits. "You'll get that suitcase *right now.*"

"Or the knife, Simon?" Benny suggests. "Maybe he could play the Knife Game?"

Thomas wants to cry, but The Knife Game *is* slightly better than the suitcase. "Okay, I'll do The Knife Game."

Simon sounds disappointed. "Fine. But this time you'll go deep, right? You'll go deep, coz I told you to."

"And coz we're your friends," Benny giggles. "We're your *only* friends."

"Get the knife, Thomas," Hanna says. "Shit, go!"

Thomas doesn't know whether it's the booze, the fact that he'd been out with Ratan, or simply the unfairness of it all, but he suddenly sits up and says, "What happens if I don't?"

The quiet that follows makes Thomas think of the tense seconds in a nature programme before a tiger sprints from a bush and snaps up its prey - then the lounge explodes with blinding light. An ear-crushing drone makes Thomas put his hands to the side of his head, feeling his skull shudder against the noise. The floor shakes, splits, and with a crackling rumble the floorboards plunge into an empty pit. In terror, Thomas scoots away until his back is against the opposite wall, but the ground keeps opening wider, an endless rocky chasm in the middle of the room.

Thomas knows what's down there, but with his hands still pressed to his head he still has to look. It's all part of the Gardden's show, and the only thing worse than disobeying the Gardden is ignoring it.

The two black eyes that fill Thomas's dreams every night, like holes in the universe, stare up at him from the nothingness. They glare accusingly, hateful and nasty but always playful, and Thomas knows he can't disobey. As he realises this, the awful drone stops and the white-hot light and the eyes and the pit suck back and vanish and then there's only silent darkness. Darkness, and the certainty that Thomas has no choice but to play The Knife Game once again.

Later, when his white bed is stained dark in the moonlight, Thomas drops the blade to the floor with a sharp clatter. He falls asleep hearing the children's laughter, thinking that, despite the pain, despite the bleeding that won't stop, and despite the scars that will soon patchwork his fat, horrid belly, at least he'd escaped having to use the suitcase again.

CHAPTER 5
"Yeah, you made this happen"

Gary

"Come on, you raggedy old shitstain!" Gary bellowed at the bookie's screen, gripping a betting slip in one clammy palm and waving his other fist.

There was no need to feel guilty about having a little flutter, was there? Shit, of course not – he'd tried his best to stick around at home, but Sandra wasn't getting any better. He supposed some people would have told him he should stay right next to her, but whatever mate.

It's all your fault and you know it. You're a twat, Gary Pickles. A proper, lowlife twat.

"Don't let that cock-end beat you!" he screeched at the betting shop TV. *"Go on, gal!"*

So, after a silent afternoon he'd spent at the flat struggling to think of something to say, he'd headed out. He couldn't think straight at home, could he? Plus, his nightmares were getting a bit much. Sometimes, when he had nothing to distract him, it was like they were creeping into his daydreams.

"Hit her, she's got plenty of juice left!" Gary yelled to the onscreen jockey. "Fuckin' hit her!"

That's The One was romping home, though, while Gary's horse Bloody Mary was way back in second place. But as they stampeded towards the line, That's The One clipped his front legs on the final jump, rocketing the rider into the air like a crippled superhero before he and the horse collapsed into a single flailing heap.

"*YES!!* Get to the glue factory, you broken-legged bitch!" Gary cheered.

Seconds later, Bloody Mary tore across the line with That's The One and her jockey still struggling on the grass a full stretch behind.

Gary danced on the spot, shouting, "*GET IN!*"

Then he steadied himself and swaggered over to the booth, with the other punters eyeing him jealously.

What a result!

Since he'd told Sandra he was going to knock the powder on the head, he'd been a good lad – hadn't been to Club Straight Lines once, and had only shared a few casual pints with his mates. But what about today, eh? Surely winning on such a cracker was a sign that he deserved a little break. He wouldn't make it a regular thing, but this was a special occasion, right? Who could argue with such a clear sign telling him to party like it was 1999?

So, he'd buy just *one measly gram*, have a good few

hours to himself, and be home in time to join Sandra when she hit the sack. She wouldn't want to join him on a jolly anyway - be far better off watching the TV. Only be concerned, wouldn't she? Probably angry, too, but what she didn't know couldn't hurt her.

Gary made the call. After chatting a little, he decided to go for two grams - didn't have to do it all in one night, did he? And it was good stuff too - no garbage.

After he'd picked up the coke he decided to go for a pint. He'd would wet his whistle, powder his nose, and then head out to wherever the guys were. He strolled into a quiet pub, paid a visit to the bathroom and racked up two long lines on the cistern.

He stopped. If he met with Daz and the others, he wouldn't get back home until the next day, would he? They'd slide him some pills, and then later on when they were coming down they'd head back to Daz's and pop out the ketamine or maybe even burn a couple of dragons. Before Gary knew it, he'd be doing everything he'd promised Sandra that he was going to stop.

twat twat twat twat...

With things as strained as they were at home, getting wasted would be a bad thing. Sometimes he wanted her back, he really did; he just wished she'd give him a sign that she was starting to scrabble her way out of the deep end.

He sighed, opting to compromise. He'd have some ching, he'd drink some drinks, and he'd talk shit at anyone willing to listen – but he wouldn't meet up with the guys. He shouldn't.

Fuck's sake, he thought, and hoovered up the lines.

The bar was a dreary working man's pub. Some people might have called it 'traditional' but Gary, his heart and mind pumping with adrenaline, just wasn't feeling it.

Regardless, he bought a beer and two doubles, downed the doubles, gulped the pint, and looked around for someone to yap at. He resorted to the sag-faced old pisshead sat next to him. Propped wonkily on a bar stool, the wrinkly duffer wore a yellow raincoat and waterproof hat. Weird, considering the dry summer evening's heat.

"How's you, Captain Birdseye?" Gary asked, his synapses thundering. "Caught any whoppers lately? I bet the one that got away was massive. I remember the last time I went angling – didn't catch a thing, not a fucking sausage. Great day though. Couldn't see straight by the end of it."

The old lush glanced up with bloodshot eyes, then pulled his hat over his face and leant back against the wall, apparently planning to take a nap.

"Sleeping with the fishes," Gary muttered, pleased with the comment. He was suave as fuck when he was snorting – the quips came thick and fast. He was about to look for someone else to chat at when his phone rang in his pocket. His mood took a dive.

On the other end of the line, Sandra's voice sounded like rustling paper. "Gary."

"Hey you, what's up?" he asked carefully.

He knew what was up, though: she was checking on him.

"I was just wondering where you were. I'm about to start cooking some food, if you're hungry."

"Food is the *last* thing on my mind right now, darling," he said. "I've got some great news. I've had a bit of luck on the horses and three lovely ones came through – made a grand! I couldn't believe it! I've never won this much! I think someone's smiling on us today, love, seriously I do. You coming out for a couple of celebratory drinks?"

Safe bet to assume you won't.

"No, I don't think so, Gary."

Ha - knew it.

She paused. "Are you with friends?"

Jesus, she didn't trust him at all, did she?

"No, I'm having a grand ol' time by myself." He tred to sound upbeat, but not coked up. "I'm at the greatest pub this side of the Atlantic and I couldn't be having more fun if I tried. It's so good in here that I think we should move in. What more could we want? We'd have drinks, shelter, three different crisp flavours and we'd be surrounded by the salt of the earth. No sir-ree, I couldn't be having more of a ball. So when are you coming down?"

Gary heard her tut.

"What are you on?" she asked.

"Nothing. Just high on life, that's all!"

"You told me you were going to give it a rest," she said. "I really thought that this time, after all we've been through ..."

"Oh for fuck's sake," he snapped. "It's only because I won on the horses. I made more than a grand!"

Sandra sounded even drearier than usual. "I don't care how much you've won, Gary. You promised me that you would leave it alone, but now you've gone and bought some coke or pills or something and I can't believe anything you say."

She was pushing his buttons. "Are you trying to ruin my night, just coz you're still moping around the house? Is that why you're doing this? Coz I think that's a shitty thing to do, Sandra. Real shitty. *You* might not be able to dig yourself out of this rut, but *I* don't have to bury myself right next to you."

People in the pub were staring.

"What?" he barked, glowering at a woman who looked like a thin Pat Butcher. She jerked her white wine in surprise, splashing the table.

"Come home, Gary," Sandra pleaded into his ear.

But he was distracted now, glaring at the scattered drinkers and letting the phone drift from his ear. "Why don't you all just carry on drowning your sorrows? Or d'you want something else?"

Coke was the only drug that sometimes made Gary aggressive, and his temper was fraying. Maybe a little brawl would do him good, chill him out a bit. He'd probably lose though, unless he found someone small. He scanned the room.

"What are you looking at?" he asked a scrawny guy in a patterned shirt sipping an alcopop. "Think it's funny, do you? Think I'm funny?"

The guy focused on his purple drink, shaking his head.

"No? Well how about I make you laugh then?" Gary said as he advanced. "How about I really give you something to chuckle about, you ... you four-eyed poof!"

Gary heard, "Right, that's it," and a thick, hairy arm curled around his throat.

"Fuck off!" Gary squealed. "Fuck off! Who are you? I know people! I -"

The arm yanked on Gary's neck, trapping his breath, and dragged him outside to shove him to the pavement. Gary landed with a light bump, but his phone clattered across the ground. Furious, Gary looked up and saw a burly older man with wire specs and thick eyebrows.

"You broke my phone!" Gary cried through his aching throat. He sprang to his feet but kept his distance.

"Who the *fuck* do you think you are?"

"I'm Bernard," the man replied, in a polite English accent. "I'm the landlord, and you're barred. If you try to come inside again, I'll knock some bloody sense into you."

"Will you?" Gary raged, standing stiffly. "Well how about I come back later and burn your shitty fucking bar to the ground?"

Bernard looked almost sad. "Go home, my friend," he told Gary, softly. "Just go home and calm down. It'll all seem better in the morning."

Gary watched as Bernard turned and stepped back into the pub. "Don't walk away from me, you wanker!" Gary bellowed, as soon as the doors were closed. He peeked through the glass panel in the door. "Knobhead! *I'm* not barred – *you're* the one who's barred, mate!"

He pummelled the window, ready to leg it if Bernard headed back towards him. His phone rang from the pavement. He picked it up, his pulse racing. Sandra again.

"*Just fuck off!*" he snarled at the inanimate, bleeping phone, and drop-kicked it across the street. It scooted towards a shocked-looking Hindu couple. Gary gave them the finger as his phone skittered past them, crashing into a car's alloys with a clunk.

People had started looking at him again. The coke had him on edge and he needed to find a place to gather his thoughts. He'd steer clear of his mates for the moment, but if he was still pissed off later he'd give them a call. He went and retrieved his phone. The screen had become a messed-up patchwork of cracks and dents.

Fuck it. Right. Where should a guy with a thousand squids go to calm down? A pub? Screw that. It should be somewhere special. Somewhere posh. Somewhere he'd never normally drink.

He laughed to himself – somewhere that Sandra would really like, just to spite her.

Most of the pricy drinking spots were close to the pier, so Gary shoved his way through a group of young chanting lads and aimed for the sea. He could feel Sandra dragging his mood down as he walked. Shit, what right did she have, eh? She was pushing him away, blaming him for everything. Even now, sat at home, she'd be wishing for bad things to happen to him, wouldn't she? Probably think it was karma.

She could be a right bitch, sometimes.

The evening buzzed with drugs and booze and tits and music. Throughout Seadon breaks were dropping, banter was blurting, and laughter ploughed the air like gunfire. A gaggle of girls going in the other direction stepped around Gary, but he caught a little brunette's eye and winked. She looked like a sexier version of Sandra, and even though the little minx sneered when she looked at him, Gary knew he could've had her. A couple of drinks, a little dance and a line or two - she'd soon be sopping wet.

Sandra was never going to let him forget the past, was she? He'd keep having nightmares, she'd keep moping, and the whole thing would suck the life out of them both, for good. They were cursed to become one of those miserable couples who'd let resentment kill them.

such a twat. Twat twat twat twat...

The main city streets dropped away and he spotted a tidy-looking bar. Rows of sea-blue flags surfed the wind high above him, and at either side of the grand entranceway a flaming torch burned like a giant match head.

The doorman seemed to measure Gary up, probably considering whether to let him in or not. On the one hand he was wearing a decent tracky, but on the other he was grinding his jaws - a dead giveaway that he'd been snorting. He dipped a hand into his trousers, plucked out a twenty and slid it into the doorman's shirt pocket. He grinned, tried to think of something witty to say, but settled for, "There you are. Get yourself something nice."

The bouncer looked confused, but thanked him with a grunt and swung open the glass doors. Piano music floated into the evening, and Gary stepped inside.

Wow – he'd never seen so many dinner jackets and glittering evening dresses. The lighting was warm, the music low and the conversation polite, punctuated by laughter. Gary would usually feel angry at such a self-important, smug-as-fuck place, but having won so much money that day he should enjoy himself, shouldn't he?

First stop, the bogs. These ones were so much nicer than those in Bernard's shitty pub: twinkling porcelain and no stink of piss or crap. Gary shut the cubicle door behind him and poured out a line onto the toilet seat - a nice hefty one.

"Yeah," he agreed, and sucked it up through a twenty. "Oh *yeah.*"

Back in the main room, Gary puffed out his chest. Right. He had money. He had coke. All he needed now was a drink, and...

And suddenly, the friendly chatter evaporated.

Everything dimmed to a single spotlight.

The clientele's movements slowed and halted, and the beer pumps froze mid-pour.

Gary's tight jaw fell slack.

Who the hell is that?

A figure sat alone in the corner of the room, her eyes stamped coldly onto the busy bar. An image flashed into Gary's mind: this woman in a blood-red wig dressed entirely in dark rubber, with a corset mashing her tits together. A thick bullwhip trailed from one hand and coiled on the floor beside her spiked boots.

In reality, her hair was a blonde bob. A low-cut green dress hugged her slim figure like scales, and beneath the table, a slit showed off her long, crossed legs and strappy high heels. She must have been older than Gary, but those slags outside would have melted beside her. She looked sullen, cruel, and hot-as-fuck. He pictured Sandra, mousey and fragile. Standing there with his mouth twitching, nails dug into his palms, Gary saw this new woman, this vicious-looking queen, straddling him. He imagined coming inside her while Sandra sobbed from somewhere nearby. As the fantasy played in his head, he felt triumphant – *Yeah, you made this happen, Sandra* – and his wife became less solid, her skin and hair and eyes becoming transparent, and then fading away.

You think I'm going to wait around forever, don't you, Sandy? Well, whatever, mate...

Rebecca

Rebecca's pocket book of fairy tales had failed to distract her, so she now sat simmering in the shadows of the wine bar booth. Her philosophy stood true: everyone was either a user or was being used and, at present, her life's imbalances placed her firmly within the 'used' camp.

The establishment in which she sat sold mainly vintage wines and aged spirits, and attracted only the vacuous and wealthy. As they circled each other, these human dregs wore their smug makeup and designer clothes like war paint. Camouflaged in her Percy Bowls green sequinned dress, Rebecca eavesdropped while the men bragged about business deals and recent lays, and the women prattled competitively about the successes of their cheating husbands.

She was terribly sore; the monster had used its teeth again. For a moment that afternoon, in the middle of it all, she had felt hot tears prickle her eyes. With Henry kneeling at the side of her head she had gazed up past his freckled, pencil-like penis and finally objected, but her keeper had simply silenced her with a vulgar jerk of his hips.

Dozing afterwards, she'd had the dream again; the joke her sleeping mind played on her, mocking her inability to procreate. In the vision, her midsection ballooned with the growth of a shockingly deformed mutant. Her body swelled, stretched to translucency, and then finally burst open in a red cloud. It emerged screaming, barking and howling its rage to a horrified world. The black-eyed offspring she had willingly gestated; the product of all she had permitted.

Her decisions may have led her here, but it was no use playing the victim. She had reached this point via her own volition, and she was damned sure she'd remove herself in the same *manner. She had never been a victim. Childhood had delivered no overly affectionate family friends, or uncles with boundary issues or, heaven forbid, a father with wandering digits. Her London upbringing had been tightly structured, perhaps even claustrophobic, but her parents, rich and richly educated, had fed Rebecca and her siblings a wholesome diet of art, culture and warm encouragement. While Rebecca's older brother and younger sister had fallen succinctly in line, Rebecca's thirst for autonomy and, she supposed, her wilful ego, had turned her towards life's less reputable avenues.*

During adolescence Rebecca had decided that all human encounters were transactions: financial, emotional, physical, intellectual, artistic, sexual, and so on. The trick to life, she had concluded, was to offer the world only as much, if not far less, than she received in return. On her twentieth birthday, poised before an audience to blow out the candles of an extravagant cake, Rebecca had declared to three dozen doting relatives her plans for a fruitful career in prostitution. After a moment of awkward silence, the room had erupted into gales of laughter, her family interpreting the line as a daring yet ultimately innocuous quip. But the following spring morning, her head clanging with the bells of a vintage wine hangover, Rebecca had slipped without farewell to Waterloo station, and boarded a train towards Seadon's shores, never to return.

Like a sun-baked, ice-cream-laden Sodom or Gomorrah, anecdotes and frowns of disapproval at Seadon's name had suggested to Rebecca the ideal stalking grounds. Her adolescent years had taught her the power that her smiles and curves commanded, and before leaving home she'd experimented sexually with numerous boys and young men, sharpening her elegant tools upon blunt-minded, prematurely spurting instruments. Thus prepared, in Seadon it had been relatively simple to convince eyes, flies and wallets to open for her. Any initial traces of doubt had dispersed after she'd realised how little she'd felt as these businessmen and professionals had poked parts of their bodies into hers. Like victimhood, degradation is merely a state of mind.

However, even literature, theatre and sprawling stretches of free time grow tiresome and somewhat lonely. After nine years of pimp-less hookerdom, Rebecca had renounced her life as an escort and started a new chapter as the pampered queen of Nicholas: catering company director and yawn-inducer extraordinaire.

Perhaps inevitably, they had pondered parenthood. The idea of raising a child in Nicholas's elegant home had appealed to her on a base, biological level, but in such a selfish world – cold, corrupt and cruel – would it be fair to expel life? Her values were bleak and demanded the upmost mental dedication, so could she truly bear the distracting pitter-patter of verruca-encrusted feet?

The question had eventually revealed itself to be moot. Rebecca was barren, and while Nicholas had been blandly forgiving, Henry had not. When Henry had demanded a son, Rebecca had, as sensitively as possible, explained that she could not give him what he desired. Henry had feigned ambivalence. However, shortly after her confession, Henry had brought a third party to their bed – and after a year or so of such encounters, Rebecca now sat in this dreadful bar, brooding bitterly.

The question was, how could she extract herself from Henry's clammy grasp, and turn her user into the one being used?

From the booth, she signalled to a tuxedo-clad bar tender to bring her another wine. Close to the bar, a bulky man with a thin moustache invaded the space of a gorgeous, petite blonde half his age. The woman was laughing politely and letting him buy her mojito after mojito, her sizable white breasts bulging over the top of a tight flowery blouse. Rebecca smiled at the image of a wheezing, drunken union, and the shame or perhaps cold nonchalance that would follow. She read them like predictable characters in a poorly written book: him married, successful, alcoholic, cripplingly depressed; her naïve, insecure, weak-willed, and ripe for exploitation.

"How's the beer in this place?" a voice rasped.

Rebecca turned and faced a wiry, red-haired man who did not belong in the bar. His face was narrow, his nose pointed, and his skin rough. He wore a striped green tracksuit and his eyebrows were raised moronically.

"You do realise that you took a wrong turn, don't you?" she said. "Wetherspoons is back in town."

His face twitched and he laughed. "Yeah, you're right, I'm not usually into these sorts of places, but I fancied a treat. I was going to meet with some mates, but, um, well ..." He clenched his jaw. "I had a spot of luck on the gee-gees earlier! Tenner on a treble, and one romped home at 17 to 1."

"I have no idea what you are talking about," Rebecca said through glittering teeth. "And in answer to your question, I suspect that the beer in here is much the same as anywhere else: bloating and unpleasant."

The man was clearly a dimwit because he returned her venomous smile with one that seemed genuine. He reached out a hand. "Gary Pickles."

She considered reacting with a show of verbal hostility but idiots could make amusing company, as vulnerable as they were to ridicule. She took his hand gently into hers, softened her rigid posture, and leaned in towards him. "Rebecca Toulson," she purred.

In spite of the room's air conditioning, the man's forehead was slick with sweat.

"I'm rushing a little bit, to be honest."

"Mmm," she muttered. "How many wraps of cheap amphetamines have you enjoyed tonight?"

"No, no, I told you, I won on the horses," he corrected, still not seating himself. "Got a couple of grams of charlie and it's really good stuff. Want some?"

"I'll happily survive without it, thank you all the same. You may want to buy me a drink though; I think that's the customary thing to do when you approach a lady at a bar."

"Oh. Alright then. What do you want?"

"I'll have a large measure of the Remy Martin Napolean. Then you can sit down for a while."

He grinned with the look of a man about to have his seed swallowed, and tottered off to the bar. What she hadn't told him was that her drink would cost more than sixty pounds, so she watched for his reaction when he was told the price. To her mild surprise he pulled a fifty and a twenty from his pocket, and left the change as a tip.

"Lovely," he said when he returned, apparently unfazed. He laid her drink on the table, gulped from a pint of lager, and sat down. He was unshaven but had strong cheekbones, and avoided her eyes when he spoke. "Now, what are you doing here, sat all on your lonesome? A beautiful lady like you should always have company."

"Sometimes ladies need some alone time, Gary." She swirled her brandy, trying to wither the fool with her eyes. "What about you? Are you here tonight to see how the other half lives?"

"Um. Sort of, I suppose. Just thought I'd drop by a new place for a change. It's nice, if you like this sort of thing. I've always preferred a proper pub, but you know what they say about variety being the spice."

Rebecca was enjoying the man's awkwardness, disguised by stimulants but as clear to her as mineral water. "Do you have a wife, Gary?"

"Me?" He shrugged and shook that ridiculous

red mop. "Haven't met the right one just yet."

"I didn't ask if you had met the right one - I asked if you were married."

"No, I told you," he said, gaze flitting to the ceiling.

"Then why are you wearing a wedding band?" she asked.

He looked at the ring, coughed, and then excused himself.

She caught his wrist. "Don't go running off, Gary. I'm not done with you."

He gulped and headed to the bathroom.

Rebecca lifted her glass to her nose and inhaled delicate, aged fire. She took the slightest sip and flames ignited on her tongue, dancing across the roof of her mouth. Aromas of dried and fermented fruits, whispers of pine and deepest plum, a hint of cherries, and an orchid's cremation. As the fluid caressed her throat and drained past the barrier, all it left a trace of smoke behind her lips.

A hot, damp hand came to rest on her bare shoulder and her mind returned to the bar. The idiot was back, redder than before. "Alright?" he asked, dropping heavily onto the seat beside her.

"I'm simply wonderful, Gary," she said. "You decided to come back, I see."

"Yeah, couldn't leave a lady all alone, could I?"

"Unless she's your wife, of course."

"Um...can we not talk about her, please?"

"Pleading already? What would you prefer we talked about?"

"Well, what do you do for work?" he asked,

obviously trying to stay upbeat.

"I don't. I'm provided for. All I have to do is look good and act nice."

"You're married to a businessman?"

"I'm not married but he is a businessman, of sorts. He's a very tough, very cruel, very significant man."

Gary sniffed and said, "Sounds like a cock. I'm no angel, but..."

"What's your wife like?" she asked, sipping more cognac. She was beginning to enjoy herself.

"I asked you to stop talking about her."

"Gary, if you don't like our conversation I'm hardly begging you to stay."

"Alright," he replied, taking a giant mouthful of beer. He seemed to realise that it would be of little use attempting polite conversation, so he said spitefully, "We're not close and we want different things. I'm miserable and fucking bored, and she's clinically depressed."

She coolly deflected his body language, which had become arrogant, like a cornered tomcat. "What a sad story. What's her name?"

He sneered. "Sandra."

"What a lovely name," Rebecca said.

"Mmm," he replied, and his eyes drifted to her cleavage then back up to her face. "Out of interest, what were you thinking before I came over here? You were staring across the bar."

"I don't remember," she said, curtly.

"Sure you do. You were looking over at the blonde and the bigshot over there. What were you thinking?"

Rebecca despised interrogation. "Actually, I

was wondering just how long it would take for that slut to be convinced by that predator to go back to his hotel room."

"Oh," he said, glancing at the pair.

They were still drinking and suddenly both laughed, loud and combative.

"Nah, she won't go for him," Gary said. "Look at her: she's stunning and he's a smarmy old fart. She's gonna drink his money away and then say good night."

"As long as he hasn't slipped something into her drink," Rebecca said.

"He's not the type. With money like that he can buy a woman whenever he wants."

The coke had obviously tipped his ego. His argument put Rebecca in the mood to crush him.

"But Gary, at heart you're all rapists." She smiled, sweet as syrup. "We all live our lives snatching what we can, however and whenever we can. That man is going to take her back to a hotel room, they are going to have shameful, dry sex, and then they are going to totter on home to their respective partners." She raised her glass. "Thank you for the drink, but you've bored me, Gary. I suggest you get back to the gutter where you belong."

For a second his eyebrows flickered in offence, but then a smirk tilted his mouth. "Well, well. Aren't you the harsh one?"

The little bug was teasing her.

"Tell you what - how about a game?" Gary asked, grinding his teeth.

She wasn't looking at him and felt disappointed that he hadn't slunk away.

"*How about this?*" *he proposed.* "*If they leave this bar together, I'll apologize to you, I'll buy you another one of your nice, expensive drinks, and I'll head off into the night by myself.*"

The blazing liquid honey scorched her tongue. Although she was pretending to ignore him, she was in fact intrigued by the idea of a game.

He said, "*But if she turns him down, like I know she's going to...*"

Her eyebrow raised a fraction.

"*Then you can't turn me down.*"

He grinned idiotically.

The blonde at the bar accepted yet another mojito.

Rebecca met Gary's eyes and drained her delicious glass.

Gary

Later on, there was darkness. Gary's lungs were on fire. Rebecca's hands were around his windpipe and his cock was bone-hard inside her.

He opened his eyes and the guesthouse room was a fuzzy red cloud. She was staring down at him, her teeth bared and her body slamming against his. He couldn't breathe. His throat and mouth were dry and clamped shut, he was on the brink of blacking out, but then she released him and he gulped mouthfuls of air.

"This is what you wanted," she spat as she fucked him, digging her nails into his cheeks before returning her hands to his neck.

It was only a game, wasn't it? There was no way she was going to kill him, so he lay still and let her do just as she wanted.

This is what I need.

His eyes rolled back and the room blurred, his body flooding with adrenaline. Just a little longer and he would explode into her and everything would be awesome, wouldn't it? Fucking perfect. And until then, his wife and the past and the little girl with the black eyes from his dreams wouldn't have a chance in hell of touching him.

CHAPTER 6
"Reaping the bounties of a life poorly lived"

Henry

Henry watched as the Great Dane gulped down chunk after chunk o' glistenin brown meat from his golden bowl, which was engraved, "BRUNO".

It was 11am, Rebecca was showerin after another three-way exercise sesh, an' the sun was shinin sluggishly through the lounge window. It warmed Henry's back as he sat at his desk wearin a zebra-printed silk robe an' smokin a cigar. Usually some sex an' a fat Cuban chilled him right out, but not today × not after the way Rebecca had looked at him earlier.

Bruno lifted another morsel o' rump steak outta the bowl with his long, wide tongue. What a prize fackin champ - could out-run, out-eat, out-fight an' certainly out-fack any uvver mangey mutt in the country. An' the size of him!

Breeders called Bruno's colour blue, but he wasn't fackin blue, he was more of a steely grey.

Sometimes, Bruno reminded Henry o' Tonto, the first dog he'd really connected wiv. Henry had never even learned the gallumphin great sod's real name, but Tonto held a special place in his heart.

Henry had met the mutt after he'd bagged this cutey called Charlotte Abbott. That day, many summers ago, he'd bin a 15-year-old virgin wiv-out a single care. While the two o' them had toured the fields just outside o' Seadon, Henry had suggested that they try an' start a fire – just a littl'un, nothin major – so they'd crept into a big old wooden barn near a farmhouse. Gigglin, they'd poured some vodka over a haystack an' tried to light it up. Fackin matches hadn't bin worth a wet fart though, so they'd drunk the rest o' the voddy an' stayed in the barn.

Hadn't bin long before they'd started doin what teenagers often do: kissin an' fiddlin an' laughin. Up until that day, Henry had never gotten more than a cuppla wet fingers, but the two of 'em had bin drunk an' young, an' the barn had felt vaguely romantic.

Trouble was, anatomically, they'd had it the wrong way round. No shame in it, but she'd bin big an' slack, an', despite his length, Henry was quite thin.

"I'll get on top of you instead," she'd gone, after Henry had wriggled around for a minute or two.

They'd struggled into Henry's second ever sex position, an' then Henry had seen Tonto: a Great Dane, jus' like Bruno, standin at the entranceway o' the barn. His massive, foamy tongue had bin lollin out of his mouth, an' as Charlotte had squirmed obliviously on top o' Henry, he'd watched Tonto in terror.

Shit, he'd thought. *Please don't bite me, Mr Dog. And don't bark, because then the farmer will know we're here. Please just leave us alone.*

Tonto had padded a few steps closer and then stopped, his eyes pinned onto Henry.

Shit, shit, shit, Henry had panicked silently, but then Charlotte had started to enjoy herself. Her eyes had closed and her little tits had begun to hop about wiv the effort. She'd gotten excited coz, outta the blue, Henry had become as stiff as a pool cue.

"That feels good," she'd gasped. "That feels good, that feels really good."

Henry had noticed the dog's dignified pose, sat upright, fulla strength an' elegance. Blood'd begun pulsin through Henry's cheeks an' he'd suddenly realised how degradin it was to be stuck beneath this bouncin girl. Henry had thrown her off an' into a pile o' hay. She'd yelped in surprise, but then chuckled when Henry had slipped it in from behind.

"That's nice too," she'd said.

By then Henry was in control an' performin not for her, not even for himself, but for the four-legged fellah a few meters away. His insufficient girth didn't matter anymore, coz he was deep an' she was enjoyin herself an', most importantly, the dog had seemed happy too, pantin an' dribblin gooey strings. Squeezin her arse around him, tryin to create some kinda friction, Henry had held the dog's stare, tryin to impress it while feelin about as tough an' manly as the Lone fackin Ranger. The expressionless mutt had left before Henry had popped his slender cork, but from then on, Henry had often found himself thinkin about the dog he'd christened "Tonto".

None o' them could beat Bruno, though. Four feet tall at the head an' about four feet long – fack, what a beast! But watchin him as he ate reminded Henry of his mornin, an' that made him think about the change he'd noticed in Rebecca.

One o' Henry's gifts was that he could read people like comic books, an' that day Rebecca had given him a trace o' concern. Somethin was different about her, like she was suppressin a smirk or like there was an insult restin jus' behind her lips.

He listened as she opened the bathroom door in the bedroom. Most o' the time he felt lucky to have her – a good, London gal who was full o' class – so what'd brought about this change? Whatever it was, it'd made Henry go hard on her that mornin. Two outta three o' them had loved it, an' anyway, it was better when she wasn't enjoyin herself – sex wasn't for a woman's benefit, was it? After all, it was a trade-off: she got to date the most powerful bloke in the city, an' he got to do whatever the fack he wanted.

"Wanna cuppa, dollface?" Henry called, smoke driftin from his rough lips wiv each word.

"Um... sure," came a shaky voice from the bedroom.

Fackin hell, snap out of it, love. Weren't that bad.

"Nice one," Henry called back. "I'll 'ave a coffee then, when ya get round to it."

The mobile rang on the desk.

"'Ello Percy. Woss the news?"

"I've started talking to people about Robbie," came Percy's monotone.

"Oh yeah?" Henry asked, becomin serious. "Broken any fingers yet?"

"Not so far. Thought you'd want to know that Hancock's already supplying to some people."

"Well we *knew* that," Henry said, feelin impatient. Percy was a good bloke to have on the team, but he wasn't the smartest knife in the book.

Percy elaborated, "I don't think these guys have anything to do with Hancock's crew."

"Okay," Henry said, tappin his cigar. "That means we can do what we like wiv 'em, then. An'–"

"Can we meet up soon?" Percy blurted.

Henry stopped – Percy would never have cut him off like that, back in the day. A good few years back, Percy had taken out the only fellah keepin Henry from bein the top coke supplier in Seadon, so Henry had plenty to thank him for. The cunt's psychopathic tendencies had always bin useful, an' for a good while things'd bin hunky dory between the pair o' them. They'd made a lot o' dough, they'd drunk togevver, and they'd … well, anyway, stuff had turned a little sour for one reason or anuvver, an' nowadays Henry preferred to keep things professional.

Did Percy think that Henry was gonna feel bad, just coz the lug-headed cunt's feelin's had bin stung?

"I'm busy at the moment," Henry said. Couldn't let Percy think that he was at his beck an' fackin call.

Percy said nothin for a few seconds, an' then went, "When will you be free?"

"I don't know, Percy. Soon."

"I've got things to say –"

"Well they'll have to wait, won't they?" Henry snapped.

Silence again.

Wipe your eyes, you fackin pansy.

"Okay," said Percy, an' the phone went dead.

Bruno swivelled his head round from the food bowl, waggin his tail as Rebecca came back in. She was wearin a tight shirt an' grey trousers, an' pullin a suitcase on wheels. Henry liked to see her legs, and she fackin *knew* that ˣ also, what was the case for?

"Leavin me, are ya love?" Henry asked jovially, puttin Percy to the back of his mind an' focusin on Rebecca.

Quietly, she said, "It's just some washing that I'm taking to the launderettes."

Her face was made up beautiful, Henry noticed: her eyes underlined black an' her lips painted a tasty purple. "Get one o' them Polack fackers from downstairs to do it."

She faltered. "There are some items I'd rather do myself. I'm going out."

She was bein short wiv him.

"Oh, I see," he laughed, an' stood up. "Don't matter what I want anymore – is that it?"

"No," she said quickly. "I just want to do it myself, that's all. It's not a big issue ..."

"Oh, ain't it?" he asked. "Right, sorry love. Didn't realise that. I'll jus' mind me own business then, shall I? You go on ya merry way an' I'll just sit 'ere, playin wiv me balls."

She looked at him warily, an' then made to head for the door. Henry weren't havin that though, so he lunged forwards an' grabbed the case. "'Ere, let me take that for you, your majesty. I'll wash these fackers wiv me bare 'ands, then I'll iron 'em nice an' straight."

"No, Henry, I just–"

"*Don't fackin argue wiv me*," he warned, endin the charade. "I've 'ad enough o' your lip today."

But – would you fackin believe it? – the slag pulled the case out of his fingers an' dodged for the door again! Henry was done fackin around, so he clipped her wiv the back of his hand. Her jaw stung his knuckles, but as she gasped he yanked the case back.

"What the fack you got in 'ere, anyway?"

He tore the zip down and a towel flopped out, unfurlin at his feet. There was a dark red patch at one edge, wet an' a bit clumpy.

"Look what you've done to my fackin carpet!"

"Henry, I-"

"Don't say a word unless I tell ya to. Not a fackin word." His temper was risin an' he was strugglin to control it. "Okay, tell me straight. What you up to?"

She looked at him wiv wide eyes, clearly knowin that she'd bin rumbled an' that he was proper narked off.

"I'm sore, that's all," she replied, dodgin whatever the main truth was. "I bled."

Henry's temples felt inflated. "You're sore, eh? Well why d'you think that is?"

"It was just a... bit much today. He bit me. And it went on for longer than usual, and -"

"I know what happened, you cheeky tart. I'm askin you *why* you think it happened."

She seemed confused for a second, an' then that shady look returned to her face. It made Henry realise what the change he'd noticed in her was: defiance. Well, *that* weren't gonna last long - not on Henry's watch.

She said, "Maybe it was because your *pet* can't control himself."

"Are you blamin Bruno for this?" he asked, his cheeks hot an' itchy. "Is that what you're doin?"

She backtracked. "No, I -"

"Coz unless I'm pretty fackin daft, I'd say that's *exactly* what you're doin'."

"Henry -"

He picked up the towel by the wet patch an' stepped towards her. "You wanna know whose fault this is? It's the fault o' the skinny tramp who's started to give her fella the *right fackin hump*."

She eyed him, her chin pushed out like she was tryin to stop it tremblin.

"It's *your* fackin fault," Henry said, drawin his face to hers. "So say it."

She looked dumbstruck – Christ, was he about to see her cry?

"Say it."

She didn't move. Looked fragile, she did, like a china doll.

"FACKIN' SAY IT!"

"It's mine!" she panicked.

"Your fackin what?" he asked, raisin the towel an' feelin how wet the red patch was.

"My fault."

"That's right. That's right, darlin, it's your fackin fault." She was terrified, he could see it. Her body was judderin an' she was breathin in high whistles. He needed to push her farther though, so he grabbed a straggle of her hair an' pulled the towel around her head. Before she could do anythin he'd balled it up, twistin it tight against her nose an' mouth like a balaclava wiv-out holes. She squeeled, the sound muffled behind the towel. Her arms kept dancing spazzily so he batted the side of her skull wiv the flat of his hand, then used the towel to drag her to the floor. The back of her head twatted the carpet wiv a wooden thump.

Bruno barked an' the slag stopped fightin. Her body went limp, pantin an' shudderin through the soaked towel.

"Now I want you to know somethin, darlin," he told her. He batted her masked head playfully, but hard enough to hurt. Pushed his palm flat against her covered face, crushin her nose into her fanny-blood. "If I ever find out you've done somethin' behind my back, there'll be nothin' you can say to patch things up."

She whined under the towel. He'd never seen her like this before – *fackin beautiful.*

"I'm not like uvver blokes," he said. "Some guys forgive an' forget, but not me, you understand?"

She reached up uselessly, tryin to pull the material from her face. Muffled, she bleated, "Henry, I can't breathe..."

"All you have to say is 'yes', love."

"Yes, then! Yes! Yes!"

"That's right. Wasn't tough, was it?"

He pulled the towel away an' her lungs went into overdrive, puffin like she was havin an asthma attack. Silly cow's face was streaked red, an' her hairstyle an' makeup had bin wrecked. Her expression wasn't one o' panic, though – *it was a scowl.*

Crouched over her, Henry said, "Don't you look at me like that, love. You've got your own smart gob to blame for this, not me. You jus' need to know your place, though, don't ya?"

She stared up at him, her eyes lookin extra-white through the smudged gore an' makeup. "Yes, Henry," she said, an' her angry look began to evaporate.

She'd be alright. She was his lady, but

apparently she needed remindin about what that meant.

"Come on then, love," he said, in a soothin voice. "Go an' get yourself cleaned up an' we'll wipe the slate, alright?"

She said nothin as she pulled herself to her feet, but her expression had softened.

"What are you like, eh?" Henry asked affectionately, pattin her arse an' markin the seat of her trousers as she headed to the bedroom. "Oh, an' I'll have two sugars in my cuppa, once ya finally get round to it."

Gary

Gary had managed to coax Sandra out of the house, so now they were walking barefoot across the shoreline. Same beach, same walking pace, and same shitty conversations as usual. Sandra's hand rested flimsily between Gary's fingers, and the cold water kept circling their bare ankles before piddling back to the bathers and boarders.

"Alright?" he asked his wife, watching her reply with a nod and that same blank face.

If it hadn't been for those couple of lines he'd woofed, Gary would've been bored shitless.

He'd expected to feel guilty after his evening with Rebecca, but no - he just wanted more. He'd never known a woman like her. She was spiteful, yeah, but somehow it felt like she'd done him good. There were welts on his face and neck, but Sandra had swallowed his story about a drunken fight. She had even apologised for having nagged him when he'd been out at the pub. It was too late for 'sorries', though – whatever, mate.

They moved in silence from one beach to the next, edging around the grassy cliffs and watching the tourists sun-bathe, swim and lap at their ice creams.

"Thank you for making me come out today, Gary," Sandra said suddenly. "I feel better."

About fucking time.

He bit his lip against a ranting cocaine monologue.

He'd been amazing with Rebecca, hadn't he? He hadn't had sex like it in years, if ever. He had let her do whatever she'd wanted, and it had made her come long and hard.

The size of my cock didn't hurt either.

He grinned. No spooky dreams last night!

"What?" Sandra asked.

"Nothing," he replied. "I'm feeling better too."

She squeezed his hand. "Yes. You seem...different."

"Yeah, maybe I am," he agreed. "Maybe it's the sun, eh? Or the win on the horses, or the fact that I'm taking it more easy with the blow at the moment. It all helps, eh?"

Five buff guys in Bermuda shorts were playing cricket at the edge of the lapping tide.

So what if I'm skinny and you're not – you didn't just get to bang Rebecca, did you?

As they passed, the group's tennis ball soared towards them. Gary dropped Sandra's hand and grabbed it from the air.

"'Owzat!" one of the blokes yelled, laughing. He gestured for Gary to pass it back. "Nice one, mate!"

Gary tossed the ball, and Sandra smiled proudly.

Fucking hell, she was pale. She'd hardly seen daylight in weeks.

They drifted to a stop near the edge of the second beach and turned to face the blue horizon.

"Are we going to sell the flat, then?" Sandra asked, squeezing his hand again.

He looked at her, wondering what the hell she was talking about. Oh yeah. Had he suggested starting somewhere new? The idea no longer fit, though, and looking at his wife reminded him of everything he wanted to forget.

"Yeah, that's a good thought, love, but it might take a while for someone to buy it, eh? And you've got to ask yourself, are we ready for that? I mean, are you?" He tried to control his voice. "This is the first time you've been outside in forever and a day, isn't it? Yeah. And now you just want to sell up and move somewhere new? I'm not so sure it's the right time, love. It's risky, and rash, and..."

"But it might be what we need," she argued. "I thought we could go upcountry and live near Stuart."

Her fucking brother, the banker twerp with the grey personality. Gary shouldn't say anything too hasty, though. Maybe he'd change his mind again, and he didn't want to hurt Sandra unnecessarily – wouldn't be fair, would it? Not after everything she'd been through.

"Well like I said, it's a nice thought, but how long do you think it will take us to get a place up there, eh? I mean, neither of us are working. I know we'd get the cash from the flat, but that won't go far upcountry, will it? It's all more expensive up there. No, I reckon we should stay put for now."

She'd stopped smiling. "But you said you wanted to."

"Yeah, I know love, but I've been thinking..."

About never seeing you again. About doing another line. About Rebecca's tight, tight fanny.

"...that it might be better to wait for a bit."

Sandra

As the five cricketers cheered in unison, Sandra closed her lips and fell silent, as if she was praying. She'd felt queasy all morning – probably the start of a bug - but the fresh air and Gary's company had helped settle her stomach.

It was strange that just a few weeks prior she had been ready to leave Gary, but now the idea of losing him terrified her. Even through her nausea she could read her husband quite plainly, and saw that the subject of moving away had been shifted off conversational limits. Surely this was only temporary. Not so long ago she'd seen how good a man he could be, and how content such dedication had made him.

"Okay Gary, I..." she began, but stopped when Gary let go of her hand and reached into his pocket.

"Hello, there," he said into his smashed-screen phone, sounding at once familiar yet caught off-guard.

The lifeguard's 4x4 droned by and a breeze ruffled Gary's red curls.

"Um... okay," he mumbled. "Sure, of course. Um. Where?"

Sandra heard concern in his voice, so she reached out and stroked his lower back.

"Um. Fine," he said. "Give me twenty minutes and I'll be there."

He hung up, gazing towards the sea.

"Is everything alright?" Sandra asked. "Who was that?"

"Matt," he said into the breeze. "He thinks Kath might actually leave him this time, and he's in a state. Do you mind if I go and be a shoulder for him? You know what a softy he is."

Sandra could not hide her disappointment.

Matt. That dirty, low...

She stopped herself. It wasn't her place to judge, and such bitterness would only lead her to dark places. To forgive is divine, isn't it?

"Of course," she forced herself to reply. He was only trying to help out a friend; it was quite selfless of him, really. "You're a good man, Gary. Do you have time to walk me back, though? Only, I feel a bit shaky..."

"Um. Do you mind if I don't?" Gary said. "I think he *really* needs to see me, like, *right now.*"

"Oh. Okay. You go, then."

"Thanks. He'll appreciate it that." He leant down and pecked her cheek. "I'll send him your love, shall I?"

"Yes. I'll make dinner for later, something nice. Okay?"

"Sounds good."

As he turned to leave, her stomach spasmed. "You're not going to get high, are you?"

He didn't stop but shook his head, saying over his shoulder, "'Course not. Couple of drinks to dilute his sorrows and then I'll be back to the flat. I'll see you in a bit."

As he paced away, Sandra watched the back of his thick red hair with the unnerving sense that he was smiling.

Rebecca

Rebecca careened into the en-suite bathroom. She locked the door and gagged on the smell of her own insides. The cabinet mirror hung like the painting of a rape victim.

That is not you, she told herself.

How had she allowed herself to reach this point? Hadn't she learned anything from her time with Nicholas, from her years playing harlot? In a short time, Henry had shaped her into something she had never foreseen, something she despised. Was she reaping the bounties of a life poorly lived?

Perhaps she had finally found the limits of her acquiescence. A year and a half ago, because Henry had paid for her apartment and kept her from returning to the planet's oldest trade, she had seen no harm in him dictating where they ate and where they spent their time. She had even accepted that he liked her to remain under his influence when they were apart, as well as his overbearing and at times violent sexual behaviour. What she had not anticipated was his need to see resistance in her eyes.

At first she had allowed herself to be crushed by his hairy bulk, and her limbs to be contorted into any awkward shape he saw fit. He had restrained her, choked her, spanked her, and even slapped her once or twice, but, armed by her past life as a hustler, Rebecca had told herself with confidence that she could take whatever Henry could give. It was only kinky sex, even when it hurt. So, by the time he had introduced her to his true carnal obsession, their sex life had become a contest, and one she could only win by total submission.

Her determination to withstand had invited the recurring dream. The snapping beast with the coal-black eyes that gnawed the inner walls of her womb as she slept was her own creation, but as well as being her subconscious's joke at her inability to conceive, it felt like a warning.

You have to stop this.

Perhaps it was time to take a cue from the fairy tales she knew and loved, the cynical stories that disguised their pessimism with pseudo-morals and gleeful bigotry. Hansel and Gretel had slaughtered their cruel captor. Just as the witch had been licking her lips and preparing to gorge on the flesh of her captives, she had found herself burning to death in the very oven she would have used to cook her cannibal feast, and her intended meals had stolen the gold from her bedroom and left her to die.

Yes. Tables can be turned. Users can become the used.

Rebecca stroked her midriff, absent-mindedly imagining the black-eyed creature she dreamed of coiled inside her, like a hideous spring. Her blood-streaked, cactus-haired reflection drew her gaze, its cheeks puffed and stressed, the front of its blonde bob snagged into a peak. She smoothed her hair down, wishing to restore some dignity to her ridiculous appearance.

"Mirror, mirror, on the wall," she muttered. "Who's the most used of us all?"

If she ran away, Henry would pursue her. He would see her flight as the ultimate resistance, and would delight in sending an associate to drag her back. Even if she was wrong about this, did she want to live in fear forever? Did she want Henry to live his life believing she was just another form to twist into a shape of his choosing?

Of course not. This charade had already cost her too much in sleep and self-respect.

For the moment, she would retain her role as Henry's obedient woman - play along, buffer his ego, and regain his trust. Soon though, perhaps just when he believed he was ready to devour her whole, she would pitch him headfirst into the oven.

She showered, dabbing at the aching gashes that riddled her thighs. When she had soaped, scrubbed, shampooed and conditioned, she stood on a towel but left the water running. It battered the glass of the shower cubicle, drowning out her voice to anyone outside of the bathroom.

Her recipient answered his phone almost immediately.

"Hello there," the voice replied.

"I need to see you," she breathed. "I need to see you now."

"Um...okay. Sure, of course. Um. Where?"

"The same place as before. This time, I'm paying."

"Um. Fine. Give me twenty minutes and I'll be there."

She hung up, feeling better. The other night,

Gary, that redheaded little insect, had purchased a room at a low-quality guesthouse. Somehow, it felt appropriate to return.

In the bedroom, Rebecca changed into a gossamer knee-length red dress, dried and styled her hair, re-applied her makeup, and returned to the sitting room looking once again flawless.

"That's better, darlin'," Henry beamed. He was spread across the chaise longue, his canine colossus extended across his lap and the rest of seat. "Lookin' like the heroine o' the movie again."

She sauntered past him to the adjoining kitchen and prepared his coffee. Smiling angelically, she peeked her head around the doorway and gazed into his sly eyes. "You approve, then?" she asked.

"Does a bear shit in a public toilet?" he asked, apparently rhetorically. "'Course I fackin' do. Lookin' stunnin', aren't ya?"

"I'm glad," she said, feigning coyness. When she brought Henry's coffee to him, Bruno swung his mammoth head around, and seemed to look her up and down approvingly. "I'm going out now, but I'll leave the suitcase here, okay?"

"Okay, love," he agreed, scratching behind one of Bruno's giant ears. "Jus' before you go, though, I want ya to apologise to Bruno here – it's only fair. Then ya can do as ya please."

Rebecca looked at the dog, who stared back gormlessly.

I can't do this much longer.

"I'm sorry I complained," she said to the Great Dane, keeping the trembling rage from her voice.

"I know that as long as I behave, you would never hurt me." She rubbed Bruno's head and his enormous tail slapped the arm of the chair.

"That's right, doll. 'Course he wouldn't hurt ya. An' neither would I."

Leaning forward to kiss Henry's rough lips, she caught a waft of his rank body odour.

You're going to regret everything, my darling. Everything.

"I can't stop thinking about you..." the ginger-haired creature squawked, eyes bulging from their sockets. *"I think you're incredible... graaah!"*

Rebecca moved at a leisurely pace as she throttled him. Smiling pleasantly down at the bug inside her, she thought, What a simple, weak little thing you are, with your twitching organ and your silly high voice.

"When I'm with you... glurk... you take me away from everything..." it managed. *"I... craaaark... know it sounds silly... gmph... but I think I love you, Rebecca!"*

She was barely even surprised. Gripping the creature's neck tightly with one hand, she slapped its face hard with the other. "Good."

Users and the used.

The redhead thing's expression told her what mere words could have concealed: it had fallen for her, and it would obey her in any way it could. What traumas had broken this unevolved puppet's spirit? What essential ingredients had its life lacked? In addition, how had it let itself abandon its wife, only to fall for a woman who despised it and wished it nothing but harm?

As she bucked and strangled, slapped and clawed, she pictured the snapping monster of her dreams with its pitiless black eyes. She thought of Henry and how she had come to despise him, of his violence, his love for his pet and his need to maintain control. She absorbed the sight of her insect, struggling for air yet appearing oddly at peace, and behind her, a reedy, excited voice seemed to whisper the same word repeatedly.

yes yes yes yes yes

With a jolt, Rebecca understood that these were the subtle shifts of something much larger than her own sordid tale; something vast and inexorable, whose restless shadow darkened and grew in influence day by day. The revelation was simple and somehow unsurprising, and for one dreadful moment, Rebecca had to suppress a scream.

Thomas

"Time's almost up, Thomas," Simon says.

Thomas is lying on his back in the Gardden a few feet away from the knotty elm tree, stroking the dirt with the palms of his fatty-fat hands. He's gazing up through the criss-crossing branches at the dusty orange evening sky, imagining that he's partying with Ratan. Above him, the tree's scrinched-up arms have arranged themselves into a giant version of Simon's scowling face, but Thomas isn't impressed.

"Things have been happening, and you haven't realised a thing," the giant twig-face says, in a voice that snaps and crunches. "You do *want* to win The People Game, don't you?"

With the back of his skull resting against the earth, Thomas squeezes his eyes shut and lifts the super-sweet bottle of Amaretto to his mouth. The syrupy alcohol burns his throat, slopping over his cheeks. Thomas pictures a thinner, less spotty, less hairy version of himself dancing with the barmaid at The Runway.

"Are you even listening?" the twiggy Simon-face asks.

That'd be super-cool, Thomas thinks, feeling woozy. Maybe the barmaid would let him kiss her, if they were both drunk enough. Ratan would show Thomas how to get a woman, wouldn't he? Ratan understands stuff like that, because Ratan is *awesome*.

"Thomas, this is important."

With his eyes still shut he slurps from the bottle again, loving the way that the booze cuts through his stress.

"*THOMAS!*" Simon's voice booms. "*Thomas - they're coming!*"

CHAPTER 7
"You grab what's yours and you smash what ain't, don't you?"

Rebecca

Once Bruno had finished, he barked once and leaped down from the bed, heading for a pile of blankets in the corner of the room.

"Good boy - ya liked that, didn't ya?" Henry gasped, his chest and round belly heaving. He sagged back down against the headboard and wrapped a wet, hirsute arm around Rebecca, surrounding her with the stink of sex-sweat and rich dog food. The salty taste of him filled her mouth, and something that had no place inside her oozed onto the covers.

Over the previous weeks - since the incident with the towel - there had been moments when Rebecca had almost fled. Her nightmares had become so frequent that at times she avoided lying down and closing her eyes, fearing her dream-progeny's raging howls and the sense of something wrenching itself out of her distended body.

Mummy, it sometimes panted. *Yes yes yes... MUMMY...*

The imagined beast was no longer even confined to the darkness of sleep: occasionally, when she was wide awake, she could almost believe that something real was flexing languidly inside her, biding time and building strength so that one day it could tunnel a ragged exit.

Henry's face was dopey and contented. "That was beautiful, Bex. You have no idea how gorgeous ya look when we're at it, do ya?"

Henry had seemed pleased with her obedient return to form, dictating her behaviour and outfits as well as dismissing and summoning her whenever he saw fit. She rolled onto his reeking bulk, kissing him through the forest of his pectorals. She could sense Henry's tenderness and it made her want to leap from the window. She may have actually done so, had she not been anticipating yet another encounter with her little pet Gary.

"Thank you, darling," Rebecca said. She eyed Bruno, who had curled himself into a cosy ball, and acid gurgled in her belly. Craving distraction, she asked, "What are your plans for the day?"

"Uvver than picturin' what we jus' done, over an' over again? Well, Percy's poppin' over for a chinwag this mornin', an' then I've got a borin' *little errand to run, an' then I'll be joinin' the lad for a spot o' lunch. Busy busy."*

"Am I ever going to meet this Raymond of yours? It would be such a privilege."

Henry grunted. "Too right it would be, my love. He's a gold star - a champion in the makin'."

"What's he like?"

"Young, but quick as a whip. Dresses like a zombified drag-queen sometimes, but he's a good lookin' lad underneath it all. Popular wiv the ladies, I should think."

"How did you meet him?"

Henry looked down at her. "You ain't normally this much of a 'Little-Miss-Curious', Bex. Woss got into you?"

She was genuinely intrigued. Henry seemed to hold his influence and independence above all things, yet this young man had hypnotised him, and Rebecca was interested to learn how. "If I'm being impudent, just tell me..."

"O' course your important, love."

"No, impudent, darling. Impertinent. Overstepping my boundaries. But if it's not too much to ask, I'd love to meet him."

"Oh, I see." Henry sniffed, retrieving a half-smoked cigar from the bedside table. He seemed to think for a moment. The hand he'd wrapped around her strayed down and squeezed a breast, pinching her nipple too hard. "Alright. Tell ya what: as you've been such a good girl lately, I'll let ya come along today. You'll like him." He lit the cigar. "An' if ya don't, act like ya do."

LOCKER

LOCKER THREW A VOLLEY OF BLOWS INTO THE GYM'S HEAVY PUNCHBAG. EACH STRIKE WAS A WOUND TO THE GOTH CUNT'S FACE.

MUSCLING IN ON THINGS AREN'T YOU? I'LL SHOW YOU, THOUGH. I'LL SHOW YOU GOOD.

ALTHOUGH HE WAS ONLY BATTERING A SACK OF SAND, THE TRAINING HELPED LOCKER'S HEAD ALMOST AS MUCH AS IT DID WHEN HE POLISHED HIS METAL FRIENDS. THE POETRY DIDN'T COME - NOT LIKE WHEN HE WAS WORKING ON A REAL PERSON - BUT IT HELPED STRAIGHTEN HIM OUT.

IT WASN'T LIKE HE WAS STUPID, THOUGH. HIS LONG-HAIRED, 60S FALLBACK DAD AND HIS SCRAWNY, HIPPY WHORE OF A MUM HAD SENT HIM TO A GOOD SCHOOL AND DECENT COLLEGE. IT WAS TOUGH TO REMEMBER MUCH OF WHAT HE'D LEARNED WHEN HIS BRAIN WAS FILLED WITH SO MUCH NOISE, THOUGH. TOO FULL OF JABBERING PAKIS, MINCING POOFS AND DISEASED SLUTS.

ONE TIME, WHEN PERCY HAD BEEN BREAKING THE LEGS OF SOME OLD CUNT WHO OWED HENRY MONEY, LOCKER HAD REALISED THAT HIS... ISSUES... WERE PROBABLY HIS MUM AND DAD'S FAULT. AS HE'D SLOWLY TIGHTENED A VICE AROUND THIS PENSIONER'S LEG, HE'D FELT SOMETHING THAT HE'D SINCE COME TO CALL THE POETRY. THE VIOLENCE HAD CREATED THE POETRY, AND THE POETRY HAD MADE HIM REMEMBER THAT HIS PARENTS HAD FED HIM, CLOTHED HIM, WIPED HIS BABY ARSE AND CLEANED HIS TODDLER NOSE - BUT THAT WAS ALL. THEY HADN'T READ TO HIM. HADN'T GIVEN HIM TOYS. HADN'T TAKEN HIM FOR DAYS OUT OR TOLD HIM TO MAKE FRIENDS. AND IF THEY'D SPOKEN WHILE HE WAS NEARBY IT HAD ALWAYS BEEN ABOUT HIM, AROUND HIM, OR OVER HIM; NEVER *TO* HIM.

THE ELDERLY GUY'S RIGHT LEG HAD SNAPPED, AND WITH THAT SOUND LOCKER HAD REMEMBERED THAT HIS BROTHER MOONBEAM AND SISTER ROSEPETAL HAD BEEN HUGGED AND

SQUEEZED AND SHOWERED WITH AFFECTION. TOLD ABOUT PEACE AND LOVE, MAN, AND ALL THAT FUCKING PIG SHIT. ROSEPETAL HAD ONCE TOLD PERCY THAT HE PROBABLY WASN'T HER DAD'S SON. SHE'D SAID THAT WHEN THEIR MUM HAD BEEN PREGNANT WITH PERCY THEY'D HAD ROWS ALL THE TIME, LOUD AND NASTY.

MAYBE FREE LOVE HAD DIED WITH THE VIETNAM WAR, AND IN THE 70S IT WAS JUST CALLED CHEATING.

SHIFTING THE LEFT LEG OF THE OLD CUNT INTO THE VICE, IGNORING HIS FUCKING WHINGING, LOCKER HAD REALISED THAT IT HADN'T JUST BEEN HIS PARENTS WHO'D IGNORED HIM. HE'D ALWAYS BEEN A BIG GUY, BUT FOR MOST OF THE TIME THE KIDS FROM HIS SCHOOL AND COLLEGE HAD TRIED TO PRETEND HE DIDN'T EXIST, TOO. BECAUSE OF THIS, INSTEAD OF PARTYING, SHAGGING AND PLAYING SPORTS LIKE MOST TEENAGERS, LOCKER HAD TAKEN TO DRINKING, FIGHTING AND MUGGING. PEOPLE COULDN'T IGNORE HIM WHEN HE WAS-POUNDING THE SHIT OUT OF THEM. WHEN HE'D TURNED 18 HE'D LEFT HIS CRUDDY LITTLE RURAL TOWN AND, PENNILESS, HEADED FOR SEADON. IN LESS THAN A WEEK, THREE PIGS HAD ARRESTED HIM AND DRAGGED HIM TO A POLICE CELL WHERE, PERCHED ON A BUNK BED AND SMIRKING COCKILY, HE HAD MET A MAN WHO HAD CHANGED HIS LIFE FOREVER.

HENRY BORDERS.

LOCKER ENDED THE PUNCHBAG SESSION WITH A BONE-POWDERING HAYMAKER. IMAGINED THE GOTH CUNT'S SKULL CAVING IN LIKE A DROPPED EGG.

"LOOKING GOOD, CHAMP!" A WHITE-HAIRED TRAINER CALLED BOB YELLED FROM THE RING. TWO FLYWEIGHTS SPARRED BESIDE HIM. "WHEN YOU GONNA LET ME START MANAGING YOU AND MAKE SOME REAL MONEY?"

THAT OLD BASTARD WAS ALWAYS TRYING TO GET FRIENDLY. SOMETHING QUEER ABOUT HIM.

"DON'T NEED ANY MORE CASH," LOCKER SAID.

BOB GRINNED. "I MEANT FOR ME!"

AFTER A QUICK SHOWER, LOCKER DROVE HIS BLACK 4X4 TO HENRY'S PLACE. HE PULLED UP AT THE REAR OF THE CASINO AND SAW HIS BOSS'S AGING SLAG LEAVING THE BACK YARD.

DIE OF AIDS, YOU DIRTY COOZE...

SHE GLANCED UP AND GAVE HIM A LITTLE NERVOUS WAVE. HE IGNORED HER. ALTHOUGH THAT FUCKING CUM-BUCKET HAD BEEN WITH HENRY FOR ABOUT A YEAR, PERCY HAD SO FAR MANAGED TO DODGE ANY REAL CONTACT WITH HER. SHE WAS JUST ANOTHER ONE TRYING TO MUSCLE IN.

RIGHT, HE TOLD HIS BRAIN AS HE CROSSED HENRY'S LAWN. *PLUG IN, ENGAGE.*

HE WISHED HE'D PLANNED BETTER. SHOULD HAVE WRITTEN HIS ARGUMENT DOWN SO HE WOULDN'T FORGET ANYTHING. NOW HE WAS WORRIED THAT HIS TONGUE WAS JUST GOING TO FLAP ABOUT, MAKING GRUNTS INSTEAD OF WORDS. IT HAD BEEN TOUGH ENOUGH GETTING HENRY TO AGREE TO SEE HIM AT ALL, SO HE NEEDED TO MAKE SURE THAT HE GOT THIS MEETING *RIGHT.*

INSIDE, LOCKER WAS HIT BY THE GABBLE OF FOREIGN VOICES. THROUGH A PAIR OF GLASS DOUBLE DOORS, SOME OF THE CASINO WORKERS WERE ON THEIR BREAKS. THE NOISE OF THEIR FUCKING YAMMERING HURT HIS HEAD.

AT A SOUNDPROOFED METAL DOOR, HE PUNCHED A CODE INTO A KEYPAD. UPSTAIRS, HENRY WAS SAT BEHIND THE LAPTOP AT HIS GLASS DESK WEARING A SMART, BRIGHT BLUE SUIT. THE ROOM WAS NEAT EXCEPT FOR A PATCH OF RED ON THE CARPET NEXT TO THE CHAIR. PROBABLY WINE.

HENRY LOOKED AS FINE AS EVER, LOCKER NOTED. NOT IN A QUEER WAY, OF COURSE. JUST... TOUGH. POWERFUL.

THE GREAT DANE CAME BOUNDING PAST HENRY'S DESK TOWARDS LOCKER, LOOKING PLEASED TO SEE HIM. "HELLO, BOY," LOCKER SAID, SCRATCHING BRUNO'S CHIN AND RUBBING HIS EARS. THE DOG'S WET TONGUE FLOPPED FROM

HIS MOUTH AND HIS BROWN EYES MET LOCKER'S. MADE HIM WONDER IF HE SHOULD GET A PET. MAYBE TRAIN IT UP TO HELP HIM IN THE WORKROOM. TEACH IT TO ENJOY A DIFFERENT KIND OF MEAT.

HENRY JUST SAT THERE, RUBBING HIS TEMPLES. "I TRUST YOU'RE ALRIGHT AT THE MOMENT, PERCY," HE MUTTERED, AS IF IT HADN'T BEEN WEEKS SINCE THEY'D SEEN EACH OTHER FACE-TO-FACE. HENRY WAS JUST ABOUT THE ONLY PERSON WHO LOCKER DIDN'T MIND CALLING HIM BY HIS FIRST NAME. INSTEAD OF SOUNDING WEAK AND POOFY, IN HENRY'S GRUFF VOICE THE NAME SOUNDED DIGNIFIED.

"HELLO, HENRY," LOCKER SAID. HE FELT AWKWARD, BUT HE WAS GLAD TO BE THERE, JUST HIM AND HIS BOSS.

"YOU WANT SOMETHIN' TO DRINK?" HENRY ASKED.

"UM, NO THANKS HENRY."

"OH. WELL I DO, SO MAKE US A NICE STRONG COFFEE, WILLYA?"

"SURE, HENRY," LOCKER ANSWERED, AND WENT TO THE KITCHEN BESIDE THE LARGE MAIN ROOM.

"AIN'T SEEIN' YOU MUCH AT THE MOMENT," HENRY CALLED CASUALLY, FROM HIS CHAIR.

THAT'S BECAUSE YOU'RE ALWAYS WITH THAT ANOREXIC GOTH CUNT.

"JUST BUSY, THAT'S ALL," LOCKER REPLIED, FILLING THE COFFEE MACHINE AND LETTING IT BREW. BROWN JUICE DRIPPED INTO THE JUG. LOCKER SUDDENLY FELT ANGRY. "YOU WANT TO GET RID OF THOSE FUCKING WETBACKS YOU'VE GOT DOWN THERE, IN THE CASINO."

"HARDEST WORKERS I'VE EVER KNOWN, PERCY. HARD AN' RELIABLE, AN' THEY KNOW WHEN TO KEEP THEIR MOUTHS SHUT TOO."

LOCKER SNIFFED AND MUMBLED, "THEY DO MY FUCKING HEAD IN."

"WELL THEY'RE STAYIN', PERCY, COZ THEY'RE GOOD

WORKERS." HENRY'S VOICE GAINED AN EDGE. "AN' WHO D'YOU SUGGEST I EMPLOY INSTEAD? TELL ME, WHO'S IN YOUR GOOD BOOKS AT THE MOMENT?"

THE COFFEE SLOWED TO A DRIBBLE. WHY DID THEY HAVE TO ARGUE? IT NEVER USED TO BE LIKE THIS.

"ANYWAY," HENRY SNAPPED IRRITABLY FROM THE FRONT ROOM. "HOW ARE YOU GETTIN' ON WIV HANCOCK'S LACKEYS?"

"SLOW AND STEADY," LOCKER SAID, GLAD TO CHANGE THE SUBJECT. "I'VE SPOKEN TO A FEW NOBODIES. TOLD THEM THEY CAN'T KEEP SELLING COKE. IF THEY AREN'T PUT OFF BY A FRIENDLY CHAT, I'LL TRY SOMETHING ELSE."

"YEAH, AN' YOU'LL FACKIN' LOVE THAT, WON'T YA?" HENRY LEERED. "ALRIGHT. THEN THAT BRINGS US NEATLY ONTO ROBBIE, DOESN'T IT?"

"I'VE BEEN SAYING FOR AGES THAT HE SHOULD GO," LOCKER SAID, TAKING THE COFFEE POURER FROM ITS HOME. "HAVE YOU SPOKEN TO FRED YET?"

"ABOUT GIVIN' ROBBIE A SMACK A LITTLE WHILE BACK? YEAH. CHEEKY LITTLE TURD DESERVED IT, PLUS A WHOLE LOT MORE."

"YOU KNOW THAT IT WASN'T FRED WHO STARTED IT, RIGHT?"

"COURSE HE DIDN'T. KNOWS BETTER THAN TO START SOMETHIN' WITHOUT MY SAY-SO, DOESN'T HE? BUT THAT LITTLE INCIDENT MIGHT JUST BE THE STRAW THAT BREAKS THIS CAMEL'S BACK."

LOCKER FROWNED. METAPHORS CONFUSED HIM, AND HE WAS FOCUSING ON POURING HENRY'S COFFEE. "ROBBIE'S BACK?"

"YEAH, ROBBIE'S BACK. HE'S A BAD APPLE, PERCY. A ROTTEN APPLE WIV A NASTY CORE. I'VE LET HIM GET AWAY WIV TOO MUCH FOR TOO LONG, JUS' COZ HE'S GOT A FAMILY. BEIN' A GOOD A BLOKE HAS ALWAYS BIN A WEAKNESS O' MINE."

A GOOD BLOKE. YES. TOO GOOD, SOMETIMES. LOCKER

WANTED TO TELL HENRY PROPERLY, *TO REALLY SHOW HIM,* BUT PICTURING THE GOTH MADE HIM FEEL EMPTY AND LOST. THERE WAS NO WAY THAT LOCKER COULD COMPLIMENT HIS BOSS AFTER ALL THIS TIME, AT LEAST UNTIL THAT SKINNY FUCKING PRICK WAS OUT OF THE WAY.

LOCKER BROUGHT HENRY HIS DRINK, RICH AND BLACK AS HE LIKED IT, THEN STOOD AT THE OTHER SIDE OF THE DESK WITH HIS HANDS CLASPED IN FRONT OF HIM. KNEW HE LOOKED TOUGH WHEN HE DID THAT. MADE HIS BLACK SUIT STRAIN AND SHOWED OFF HIS BICEPS. "SO YOU WANT ROBBIE GONE, THEN?"

HENRY GUZZLED HIS DRINK. "WOULD THAT BE A PROBLEM? SEE ANYONE OBJECTIN'?"

"NONE OF THE OTHERS LIKE HIM. ROBBIE WAS UNRELIABLE, EVEN BEFORE HE STARTED CUTTING THE SUPPLIES."

"*UNRELIABLE?* HE'S A LUBED FACKIN' EEL. EVEN YOUNG RAYMOND AIN'T KEEN ON HIM, AN' HE'S ONLY MET HIM ONCE."

SOMETHING BURNED INSIDE OF LOCKER'S SKULL. HE GRITTED HIS TEETH.

"WHAT'S THE MATTER?" HENRY ASKED. "WHAT YOU GROWLIN' FOR?"

LOCKER PLUNGED. "IS IT TRUE THAT YOU'VE GIVEN... RAYMOND... THE GREEN EMPORIUM?"

"THAT'S RIGHT," HENRY SAID PROUDLY, LEANING BACK INTO HIS CHAIR. "TO WELCOME HIM TO THE BUSINESS. HE'S BIN DOIN' ME PROUD SO FAR, TOO. I CAN SEE HIM DOIN' GREAT THINGS, DOWN THE LINE."

LOCKER TENSED AND AT LAST SAID WHAT HE FELT. "I DON'T TRUST HIM."

HENRY'S FACE HARDENED. HE DIDN'T SAY ANYTHING AT FIRST, JUST KEPT DRINKING, THOUGHTFULLY. FINALLY, HE ASKED, "AN' WHY WOULD THAT BE?"

LOCKER CONCENTRATED. "BECAUSE... HE'S NOT DONE ANYTHING LIKE THIS BEFORE. HE'S NOT LIKE THE REST OF US, IS

HE? HE'S A KID. I MEAN, I DON'T DISLIKE THE..."

...GOTH CUNT, FUCKING TRANNY, INTERFERING LITTLE FAGGOT...

"...GUY, BUT I DON'T THINK HE'S CUT OUT FOR THIS." LOCKER STOPPED, EXHALING WITH RELIEF.

HENRY'S FACE HAD TURNED A FUNNY SHADE OF RED. "AN' WHY HAVEN'T YOU MENTIONED THIS BEFORE?"

LOCKER HAD HOPED HE WAS DONE THINKING, BUT SAID, "BECAUSE YOU SEEM TO LIKE HIM, AND I DIDN'T KNOW IF..."

"IF WHAT?" HENRY ASKED, DEADPAN. "IF I MIGHT TELL YOU TO GO AN' FACK YOURSELF?"

THERE WAS NO GOING BACK. "WELL, IT'S BEEN A STRANGE WAY TO GET SOMEONE TO WORK FOR YOU, HASN'T IT? HE NICKS FRED'S GUN, BASHES HIM, AND SUDDENLY HE'S PART OF THE CREW. I'M JUST CONFUSED, THAT'S ALL ..."

"NO SURPRISE THERE."

"I MEAN, WHAT'S GOING ON? WHY ARE WE WORKING WITH A SHIRT-LIFTIN' GOTH?"

"TREAD CAREFULLY, PERCY. THINK HARD ABOUT WHAT YOU'RE SAYIN'."

"I THINK THAT SOME OF THE LADS ARE CONFUSED, TOO."

"ARE THEY?" HENRY ASKED. "WELL MAYBE I SHOULD LET 'EM KNOW WHAT'S GOIN' ON, SHOULD I?"

"I DON'T KNOW, MAYBE THAT WOULD BE..."

"AN' MAYBE I SHOULD TELL 'EM WHAT I'M THINKIN' TOO, EH? AS WELL AS WHAT I HAD FOR BREAKFAST, WHAT POSITIONS I LIKE DOIN' MY LADY IN, AN' HOW MANY SHEETS O' TOILET PAPER IT TAKES TO WIPE MY FACKIN' ARSE!" HIS VOICE ROSE. "YOU NEED TO RE-LEARN YOUR FACKIN' PLACE, PERCY! STICK TO WHAT YOU'RE GOOD AT, WHICH IS SCARIN' THE WET SHIT OUTTA PEOPLE!" HE ROSE, SPILLING HIS COFFEE ACROSS THE GLASS DESK. "AS FOR THE REST OF 'EM," HE SAID, SLAMMING A FIST INTO THE TABLE. "IF THEY'VE GOT A PROBLEM WIV THE WAY I RUN THINGS, THEY CAN COME TO ME THEMSELVES,

INSTEAD O' MUTTERIN' UNDER THEIR BREATHS! BUT MAYBE I WON'T TAKE SUCH A CALM FACKIN' STANCE WIV ONE O' THEM!"

"HENRY, I JUST THOUGHT I NEEDED TO SAY SOMETHIN'."

"WELL NEXT TIME YOU CONSIDER THINKIN', *DON'T*, ALRIGHT? I DON'T PAY YOU FOR THAT. I PAY YOU TO KNOCK CUNTS OVER, IS THAT UNDERSTOOD? OR ARE YOU STILL FEELIN' CONFUSED?"

"I UNDERSTAND, HENRY. BUT..."

"BUT WHAT? WHAT ELSE D'YOU WANNA GET OFF THAT BIG BARREL CHEST O' YOURS?"

LOCKER WANTED TO SHUT HIS BRAIN DOWN FOR THE DAY, BUT HE NEEDED TO SAY MORE. THERE HAD TO BE SOMETHING HE COULD SUGGEST THAT WOULD CHANGE THINGS, THAT WOULD GET RID OF THE KID AND BRING HENRY BACK TO HIM. HE THOUGHT OF ALL THE PROBLEMS HE HAD SOLVED FOR HENRY, ALL THE FUCKERS HE'D LEFT POWERLESS OR DEAD IN HIS WAKE. IMAGINED HIS TOOLS, *HIS FRIENDS*, FLEXING IN HIS HANDS.

HE STARED INTO HIS BOSS'S FUMING FACE.

THEN, FROM NOWHERE AT ALL, THE IDEA CAME TO HIM.

Henry

Henry's chat wiv Percy had left a sour fackin taste in his mouth. He wished he coulda rearranged this particular visit for anuvver time, but the nurses could be funny about missed appointments. The fact was, lately he'd bin dreamin about the dodderin old fart who lived here: horrible, stressful fackin nightmares that made him feel like he needed to do somethin, but couldn't remember what. He'd decided that maybe comin to the home an' seein the codger face-to-face would jog his memory.

"I can't stand comin here," Henry told the shrivelled-up body on the bed.

The room was a joke, wiv its peach walls and its countryside paintins and its plain, functional furniture. This place was supposed to be a step above the norm, wiv its hydrotherapy pool and cable TV. Well, if this shit-hole was luxury, Henry supposed that the norm must involve nothin more than a blow-up bed and a rat infestation.

"It's not your stink that's the problem – though ya do smell like a fackin drain," Henry went on. "And it's certainly not how much you've changed since this disease started eatin away at ya. No, I just don't savour bein reminded o' my roots."

Henry cringed as the bag o' bones, propped up by the pillow, sucked its lips with a snappin sound. "Do you have a pen I can borrow, please?" it asked. "Only, my wife likes to do the crossword."

Henry chuckled humourlessly. "Do you put it on? Or do you ask that same fackin' question, even when I'm not around?"

"She doesn't read the stories," the wrinkled thing dithered. "But she loves the crossword."

"Jesus. Your 'wife' has been gone for 20-odd years," Henry pointed out, raisin his voice. "And you know what the joke is? Even when she was still above ground, she couldn't *stand* crosswords."

Henry leaned forwards in his chair, watchin

the idiot's head nod from side-to-side, its hands pattin each uvver in its lap.

"Christ knows why, but Nurse Whatever-'er-name-is says that you calm down when I visit ya. Says you're all uppity the rest o' the time."

Its head lolled sideways and its hands stopped spazzin, as if it'd exhausted itself.

"I've got a hunch that they're gonna put the price up again," Henry said. "That bitch said she wants anuvver chinwag wiv me before I head home, but I'm facked if I'm droppin into her office again. If she wants to talk, she can give me a bell. Anyway, I must be off. I've got lunch with two people that actually matter to me."

As Henry stood, the yellow skeleton shut its eyes. Somethin crept up Henry's back. Nothin frightened him usually – certainly not this useless old duffer – but he suddenly believed that when those wrinkled eyelids opened up, the eyes were gonna be black an' glitterin, jus' like they were in his dreams.

yes yes... black and nice and funny... yes yes YES

He stood there a few moments longer, wonderin what he would do if he was right. Then the old fart's eyes opened again an' they were still brown, jus' like Henry's.

Right, fack this. Lunch time.

Rebecca

Rebecca remained at the table when Henry went to meet Raymond at the door.

The city's handful of auspicious holidaymakers came to the Casual View Restaurant to take refuge from the rabble. The decor was minimal and the drawn curtains tinted the room a meditative, oceanic green. A solitary violin hummed from speakers discreetly hidden, and the scattered couples and dignified families ate in formal quietude. Mouth-teasing scents of fresh seafood haunted the air, drifting like ghosts from the most glorious dishes Rebecca had ever seen.

The pair on the closest table, a small ginger man and a gesticulating Italian woman, each in business suits, ate from typically audacious plates. The man's was a work of art: a whole lobster lay surrounded by a moat of oysters, and between its two pincers a king prawn stood up straight. Caviar lay in a coiled mound at the lobster's maw, and upon its head sat a crown of scallops. Hers was a platter of exquisitely arranged langoustines, Siberian crab claws, Chilean crab legs, plus sections of red snapper, smoked salmon, escolar, rainbow trout and halibut, all underlined by a meticulously crafted paella salad.

As Rebecca's stomach began to rumble, Henry returned, bringing with him a tall, androgynous, black-clad young man.

"Rebecca, my darlin' - meet Raymond."

She stood and offered her hand, which the

young man took into his soft, dry grasp. "It's truly a pleasure to meet you," she said, disarmed by her own piercing sense of curiosity. Having had such an immediate effect upon her, she decided that, for once, Henry was right: there was something special about the lad.

Raymond's smile was a warm glow. "The pleasure's mine."

Henry had told Rebecca that there were times when Raymond wore outlandish makeup, but today his face was bare. His top and skinny trousers clung to his frame, contrasting with the loosely tied ponytail of purple strings that waterfalled from the back of his head. Her first impression of him was of a man in his early 20s eager to shed the baggage of his teen years, yet determined to retain some souvenirs.

"I wasn't expecting anyone else to be joining us," Raymond said, settling himself in the seat across from Rebecca. "It's great to put a face to your name. Henry often talks about you."

Rebecca could not imagine this, but replied, "I could say the same about you. It seems that you're proving yourself to be quite an asset."

"Fackin' 'ell," Henry blared. "Why don't ya just bang each uvver already?"

Rebecca was appalled to feel a blush pass across her cheeks, recognising the sense of protectiveness for the boy that had already stirred inside her. Although she had no doubt that he hid the truth well, she did not believe that Raymond was an experienced criminal - so what on Earth had gained him access to Henry's business?

Pronouncing the wine names atrociously, Henry requested one bottle of Albariño and one of Pouilly-Fissé. They then ordered their lunches.

At first, conversation skipped comfortably between the town's economy and each of their tastes in art. Henry remained on the outskirts of the chatter, allowing Rebecca to relax into Raymond's entertaining company. The boy smiled a great deal, the wine went down easily, and, to her pleasant surprise, Rebecca felt greatly at ease with the young man.

"Do you have your own flat, or do you still live at home?" Rebecca enquired, picking at her entrée.

Looking sheepish, Raymond replied, "I'm still at home with my mum, actually."

Rebecca saw Henry flinch. "Are you alright, darling?"

"Just a bone," he said hoarsely, plucking a mangled chunk of orange fish from his mouth and smearing it on the side of his plate.

"I don't seem to spend much time at home anymore, though," Raymond explained.

"Too much partying?" Rebecca smiled, still trying to isolate the reason for her interest in the boy.

"Well, I used go to Lashes," Raymond said. He grinned tipsily. "A different lay every night."

Rebecca laughed. "I thought you might be a hit with the girls, young man."

"And don't forget the boys!"

Henry spluttered into his wine. "Yeah, but there's none o' that anymore, is there?" he said. "Poofin' about don't suit a man in our line o' work. Nothin' against it, o' course, but it means that a fella ain't trustworthy, dunnit?"

Rebecca stared into Raymond's eyes, sharing his amusement. He raised an eyebrow and quivered it suggestively. She suppressed a chuckle.

"So why did you stop going out to... Lashes, did you say?" she asked.

"I've got more important things to do with my time, and better company to keep!" He motioned towards Henry.

Henry cackled, "Yeah! Too fackin' right you have, son. Got the city at yer feet an' everythin' to play for."

"And my friends at the club just don't seem to get it," Raymond continued.

"Get what?" Rebecca asked.

Raymond sipped his wine, and his fingers performed a dainty dance against the glass. "That if you don't rise above your circumstances by taking what you can, life is just going to 'F' you in the 'A'."

"Too true," Henry agreed. "You grab what's yours an' you smash what ain't, don't ya? An' if someone causes you a problem, you twist their arm until either it pops off or you get yer own way."

"That's not quite what I meant," Raymond said, politely. "For me it's about finding a balance, trying to dodge too much turmoil, and learning to give and take. There isn't much I can do to change the world, so I reckon I'm better to accept things and work around them. We're all just users in the end, aren't we?"

Rebecca raised her glass. "Users and the used," she smiled, and Ray tapped his wine against hers.

Their mains arrived, each a culinary masterpiece, and Henry asked for more wine.

Towards the end of the third bottle, Raymond said, "Henry, did you know that the stash has gone up by almost 50 in just two weeks?

Henry coughed and said, "Let's not upset our stomachs by talkin' business at the table, shall we?"

"No, no, it's interesting," Rebecca assured him. "So what is it that you do for your boss, Raymond?"

Henry looked testily at Rebecca, but allowed Ray to answer.

"I'm like a banker," Raymond said, proudly. "I look after the Green Emporium, and give out any cash that some of Henry's employees need. You see, under the office floorboards in that shop, there's more cash than I've ever..."

"That's enough, son," Henry interrupted firmly. "My lady don't wanna hear about that borin' rubbish, does she?"

"But she said..."

"Don't argue," Henry said, and his eyes bored into Raymond. "Business is business, an' social is social. We don't mix the two."

Rebecca noted the altercation.

How interesting.

Raymond took another gulp of wine. "Sorry. I've been meaning to say though, Henry: I've nearly got enough now."

"Enough what, son?" Henry asked. He chewed

through a mouthful of white fish with a squelch and unleashed a cataclysmic belch.

"Enough money, Henry. I'll be leaving soon. Time to head somewhere new."

Henry stiffened. Rebecca, whose two wines had not affected her vision, thought she saw his hands tremble. His eyes came back to rest on Raymond but he said nothing, and his face remained placid. Rebecca knew the signs, though, and held her breath.

"I'm going to travel, first of all," Raymond continued, smiling innocently at Rebecca. "I've planned a route through Asia that'll eventually take me down into Australia. I never thought I'd manage it, because I'd never had a decent job until I met Henry," he beamed. "It won't be long before I can finally afford it, and then whenever I fancy coming back to good ol' Blighty, I should still have plenty of money to settle somewhere new."

Henry's jaw twitched and a vein pulsed at his temple. His rough cheeks reddened, his eyes narrowed to coin slots. Rebecca wondered for a fleeting instant whether he was going to keel over, the victim of a sudden stroke.

"I'm so grateful for all you've done for me, Henry - you know that, don't you?" Raymond asked. "I said it from the start, though: I've always planned to leave at some point, so, I'm thinking that in a month or two, I'll..."

Henry stood up, focused on the door, and spat, "Well p'raps if you're so fackin' loaded, you'll be good enough to take care o' the bill, won't ya?" He reached out a hand to Rebecca.

Rebecca's mouth opened in shock but she felt incapable of arguing. She rose, embarrassed, and said, "It was wonderful to meet you, Raymond." She extended her hand to him but Henry tugged her other arm and dragged her out of reach. As Henry hauled her towards the door, Raymond looked traumatised. Rebecca could only gaze back helplessly, mouthing an apology, longing to enjoy more of the young man's company. Raymond remained glued to his chair, his eyes glassy and his hands still gripping his knife and fork.

Out on the street, Henry pounded ahead of her, yanking her in his wake.

Despite the meeting's abrupt conclusion, it had offered Rebecca one useful piece of information.

How very, very interesting.

Perhaps Henry had opened the oven door, and was leaning in towards the heat. Perhaps it was finally time for Rebecca to give him the shove he deserved.

CHAPTER 8
"You're going to end up on his plate"

Ray

With his head thudding, Ray sank into his nest of morning bath bubbles.

The day before, sat in the Casual View restaurant following Henry's outburst, the sweating and trembling and vision-blurring had come on so hard he'd nearly blacked out. When he'd recovered he'd ordered another bottle of wine, and that evening he'd returned to his old haunt Lashes. They'd all been there - Sichopath, Venomandy and the rest - but they'd kept their distance, making him an exile surveying a realm he'd once ruled.

Ray knew he should never have told Henry his

plans to leave Seadon in such an offhand manner, so now, hungover and tired, he distracted himself with thoughts of tits. Really huge tits, bouncing like basketballs and poking him in the eyes.

He'd experienced ... *issues* ... with his sexual appetite in the past. During his teen years he had immersed himself in perversion to such an extent that it had practically ruled his life, and it was a wonder he'd never contracted anything considering the amount of care-free fucking, felching and, once, even fisting he'd enjoyed with the locals and tourists. Age, gender, fetish and partner number had never been a concern; Ray's ravenous hunger for warmth and wetness was an equal opportunities employer.

Ray assumed he'd inherited his springboard genitals from his father. In one of his mother Rose's most awkwardly candid moments, she had once hinted that she had never met a man as virile as Ray's late dad. In spite of her distasteful honesty, Ray had found himself smiling, wondering just how similar he was to the mysterious man who'd conceived him. The fond moment had passed swiftly, when he had wondered whether his father's depressive mental health would one day beset Ray, too. How cowardly his father must have been. The word "suicide" graced the act with dignity, and Ray considered it nothing more than a wave of the white flag.

His father had been called Bernard; a banal title that made Ray think of pipe tobacco and holey slippers. On his mother's bedroom mantelpiece, a frameless photograph leaned against the wall showing a neat, prim-looking gent alone on a beach, with the tide far behind him. He stood beneath a stormy sky wearing spectacles, a blue scarf, and a fitted charcoal suit. The camera's gaze appeared to make him uncomfortable. It was the only picture Ray had ever seen of his late father, and aside from his name and eager erection Ray knew little about the man, beyond the fact that he had been a business-to-business stationary salesman - perhaps the least glamorous job Ray could imagine. Bernard had been good enough at his occupation to allow Ray's mother Rose to focus on her creative endeavours, and perhaps it was this generous faith in her abilities that had brought Rose and he together.

Rose had always seemed reluctant to divulge too much about Bernard, and had responded dismissively to Ray's questioning when he had been a child. She had dropped occasional hints and casual references over time, but following several confrontations that had led to a bitter atmosphere, Ray's intrigue had faded. It was hard to remain interested in a man who had abandoned him before birth, particularly when raising the subject evoked such vehemence from his mother.

There was apparently a cemetery up North where Bernard had been interred after his self-induced end, but with such a vague understanding of the man and a rotten resentment for his choices, Ray had never visited.

Ray didn't want to dwell, so he returned his thoughts to tits smothered in whipped cream, stiffened nipples standing pink against a sweet lather.

Erm...

Then, sodomising Locker in a back alleyway.

Yep! That'd show the asshole. Show his asshole, too, the goddamned closet-case.

Then, Marilyn Manson fucking Rebecca while Ray jacked off over her. Soon, Rebecca was easing a banana into Ray's ass while he fucked Mr Manson standing, as Marilyn fucked Rebecca from behind.

While Ray continued to massage his hangover-hard cock, he envisioned a great hall filled with nude human beings.

yes... yes yes yes

Oiled, supple and varied, from barely legal to barely alive, from the palest white to the darkest black, they licked their lips and beckoned to Ray, stroking and squeezing, gyrating, drooling over moistened crevices and rigid muscles, a mass of fragrant entrances, willing flesh and blank, lightless eyes.

From the edge of the bath, Ray's phone let out a strident cry.

Wincing, he answered, "Hey Henry."

"I'll pick you up in an hour, son."

Ray had barely slept, he was hungover and horny, and all he wanted to do was wank the day away. "Um... what's going on?"

"Everythin's fine an' dandy. I jus' need ya to come wiv me to the house. There's somethin' I want ya to see, alright?"

The phone fell silent before Ray could protest.

"Goddamn it," he sighed.

He pondered for an instant and then reached between his legs.

Time for just a little more.

Henry

Its head, crinkled like a giant, white-haired sultana, turned towards Henry. "Can I have a pen, please?"

Henry shifted in the chair beside the bed and replied, "If I had a pen right now, I'd shove it so far up your fackin hooter, that..."

He shook his head.

"Christ. You're like a cunt wiv no hole, you know that? Fackin useless."

"My wife loves doing the crossword."

Henry nibbled a hangnail, trying to swallow his temper. He knew that the only reason he was bein so curt was coz o' the fackin dreams. Horrid, they were: visions of this ghoul scowlin at him wiv a stare that was all wrong, its skin covered in sores and its eyes showin nothin but darkness.

Tense, Henry asked, "Did I ever tell you the story that I give people about you?" He chuckled, checkin his watch. "I tell 'em that I killed ya years ago, an' sometimes I wish I had. I'd do it right now, but I'm too careful these days."

Henry watched the old facker's hands do their tremblin dance again, veiny an' gnarled like tree branches.

"You were always too soft. Always tellin me I needed to make somethin of meself, but never *showin me how*. Jus' left me to me own devices." Henry sat up an' puffed out his chest. "I know jus' where you went wrong, though, an' why I turned out the way *I* wanted instead of how *you* wanted. I ain't makin the same mistakes: *my* lad's gonna take this world by storm. All he needs is some help from yours truly. Unlike you, ya mush-brained twat, *I'm* gonna be a *real* dad."

But his face was doin somethin familiar: his eyes stingin an' his lips startin to wobble. He reached down to the spindly fingers on the bed and gave them a soft squeeze, mutterin, "I don't mean it."

He leaned forwards an' picked up a cup from the floor. Henry's hands shook, just like they always did whenever he was about to leave. He raised the water to his father's mouth so that the elderly man could take a sip.

"You know I don't mean it. I just get stressed, don't I?"

Henry wiped his father's dry lips wiv a tissue. "I'm sure ya did ya best, didn't ya?"

The frail old duffer's eyes drifted shut. Henry wondered if there had bin a time when his pa coulda met Ray and seen past the kid's crazy hair an' clothes, to the the champ the kid would one day be.

"Yeah, I'm sure ya did ya best," Henry repeated, gettin to his feet. "It jus' weren't enough, though."

Ray

Feeling rough, Ray dressed as casually as his wardrobe allowed: skinny jeans, a peaked beanie hat and a tight black vest.

He went to the drawer and took a quick glimpse of the route he'd carefully drawn over his world map.

Just keep reminding yourself: it won't be long now.

Before he left the house he went to see his mother, who was standing in the middle of their small lounge clutching a creased script, with her other hand raised in a fist. She had her blonde hair tied in a bun and her face was bare of makeup.

"How's it going?" Ray asked from the doorway.

Rose clicked her tongue irritably. "Fine. What do you want? You look dreadful."

"Very kind of you to notice. Audition day, is it?"

She sighed dramatically and cast her eyes to the ceiling, so that she resembled a martyr. "Ray, just leave me to my torment, please."

Ray waited at the doorway, trying to work out the precise moment she had managed to regain focus. Then, grinning mischievously, he said, "Nervous, are you?"

"Raymond!" she scolded. "Yes, the audition's today and I need to work!" She softened her tone. "I really think I might have a chance with this one."

"It's not by Frederick Eggs Benedict again, is it? What's this one?"

"A stage play about a woman who discovers a conspiracy in her home town: the authorities are plotting to turn everyone into cats and dogs."

Ray kept his tone expressionless. "Wow."

"Lucas tells me that if I get the part it could be my big break at last."

"Hmm," Ray agreed, vaguely. "So what's your character like, then?"

"I'd be playing Germane Ontario, the sly, conniving head teacher of a struggling primary school."

Ray folded his arms and leaned against the doorframe, studying his mother, wondering how many more failed auditions it would take before she realised that she was not, in all likelihood, ever going to become a successful actress. He genuinely thought of her as a good performer, but show business was a shallow realm and she was past her physical prime. Although she was still undeniably attractive, hints of lines edged her eyelids and mouth, and the skin of her arms had seen firmer days.

"Okay, what's Germane like?" he asked.

"She's a strong, confident, and malicious woman," Rose said. "She's opposed to the authorities, but she's also working her way through the pupils."

"Killing them?"

A pause.

"No."

Ray blinked. "Not *screwing* them?"

"She's a very disturbed lady," Rose said, defensively. "It's all necessary to the play, and it's all done very tastefully."

"But she's screwing the pupils of a primary school?" Ray laughed. "My mother is going to play a kiddy-fiddler?!"

"It's postmodern," she replied.

He frowned. "More to the point, how does 'Germane' even do it? These kids are younger than ten! Does she use a splint?"

"Raymond, for God's sake, it's a serious piece of work. You don't get to see any of it happening..."

"Because that would be illegal."

"...because it isn't about the mechanics of the act; it's about symbolism. And... hang on, don't drag me into a debate. I need to work."

"As you wish, mother," Ray said, straightening up against the doorframe. "As ever, I trust that the grand lord Satan will diabolically assist you on your path, slaying all who wrong you along the way."

"One can only hope," Rose said wryly, turning the script over in her hands. Her expression changed and she muttered, "I'm worried about you, Ray."

Ray hid his surprise. "Why? I'm great. No crippling depression at the moment, I assure you."

She looked at him in accusation. "You're transparent to me, Ray, and you always have been." She bit her lip. "I don't think you realise what kind of a man Henry Borders really is."

Ray eyed her suspiciously. "Did I ever tell you his surname?"

She dropped her script onto the stained coffee table and snapped, "I've lived in this town for over 30 years, Raymond. I know what goes on, and I know when my son is making a serious mistake."

"Don't start this again," Ray snapped, preparing himself for the familiar battle. "He's the owner of a bunch of local businesses, that's all. You just don't like the fact that I'm working in what you call a 'druggy shop'."

Rose's jaw clenched. "Do you think I'm stupid?"

"No, of course not."

"Then don't speak to me as if I am. We both know that there's a lot more to Mr Borders' businesses than a handful of shops. And considering the amount of cash you've been throwing about the place I'm concerned that you've involved yourself in something...underhanded."

"Mother, you've got it all wrong."

The words bounced off her. "He's reeling you in, Raymond, and if you aren't careful you're going to end up on his plate."

Ray laughed, panicking. "You're no poet, mother. Just give it a rest."

Her voice became raw. "Do you think that I raised you alone, just to watch you toss your life away? You're mesmerised by a dangerous man. You think he's your best friend, but you need to snap out of this trance. No good will come of it!"

A car horn buzzed outside. Through the window, Ray saw Henry pulling up at the kerb.

"You don't know what you're talking about, mum. Stop lecturing me like I'm a child."

"But sometimes you act like one! Henry Borders is a control freak. He's ruthless. He's... a monster."

Ray saw violent red. "Well maybe *I'm* a monster, too."

Rose's face tightened in shock. "Don't ever say that," she gasped, her voice hurt and eyes glistening.

Ray snarled, "*I just did.*"

Despite a tug in his chest, he turned, wrenched the front door open and crashed it behind him.

As Henry drove, his receding hair flapped in the warm breeze shooting through the Roadster's open windows.

"About lunch yesterday, son," he said. "I jus' remembered somethin' that needed doin', that's all. Don't go thinkin' that there was anythin' else goin' on, alright? Only fools look to the past."

Ray spoke carefully. "You seemed... agitated."

The engine purred as they turned onto a country road.

Henry shrugged. "Well let me ask you somethin', Raymond-son. D'you think it's easy, bein' me? Havin' people breathin' down me neck all hours o' the day, beggin' for this an' grabbin' at that? Meetin's in the mornin', business deals in the afternoon, an' sortin' out some mouthy cunt in the evenin'? It's a fackin' carnival, an' sometimes the pressure gets to me. I'm only human, despite what some seem to think." He glanced at Ray. "Don't go holdin' it against me, eh?'

Unsure what to think, Ray changed the subject. "So what are we doing today?"

Henry brightened. "Well son, the time's come. As ya know, I want nothin' but good things for ya: jus' rainbows, fairy cakes an' a knob covered in supermodel spit. Remember that, coz you're about to see how things *really* work round here."

They drew into the empty gravel parking area of Henry's mansion and halted with a stony crunch. Ralph was nowhere to be seen, and when they stepped out of the car they were alone.

Henry asked, "Do you remember a scruffy little bastard I employ named Robbie Sport?"

Ray did. "He seemed like a nervous junkie."

"Very perceptive, Raymond-son." Henry headed towards the right side of the building, past the leafy effigy of Ronnie Kray and into a tree-bordered passageway. Henry continued, "Mr Sport looks like a nervous junkie, coz he *is* a nervous fackin' junkie. Cokehead to be precise, which is a bad habit for a drug dealer. Bin on my payroll for several years, an' against my better judgement I trusted him wiv my best stuff: pink coke, an' uvver high-end produce. Started off likeable an' reliable, he did, but the more he earned, the more liberties he started takin'."

The passage led to Henry's back lawn where Ray, Henry and Fred had once enjoyed Henry's giant hot tub, sipping cocktails and wine served to them by the gorgeous barmaid who had served them brandy a few weeks back.

"Robbie could've afforded enough toot to rot the nose off his face, but he got greedy. Started cuttin' it wiv uvver crap, but sellin' it like it was still top drawer product." Henry gave Ray a dark look. "Sellin' it in my fackin' name. To put it mildly, he's caused me some shite. People have bin askin' someone else for their recreational supplies, an' that just ain't on."

"Mr Hancock?" Ray suggested.

Henry nodded. "By helpin' 'em out, Mr Hancock has broken an agreement we made years ago. I'll deal wiv that back-stabbin' arse'ole in good time, but first things first, eh?"

Ray nodded. His stomach felt cold and hollow, though.

In the middle distance, the sun glared over Seadon's grey architecture like a blazing eye.

Henry led Ray across the field. "I gave Robbie a chance, I really did. I'm a reasonable bloke. But even when I asked him about his sticky fingers an' his fackin' Dyson nostrils, he couldn't be straight wiv me. An' I can't stand it when a prick ain't straight."

Ray could see the grass patch Henry had pointed out the last time he'd been there, where those who had dared to cross Henry now apparently lay. A possibility hit Ray - was Henry taking him to an open grave? Had Henry killed Robbie and wanted to show Ray the body before it was buried? A silent grey strand stretched across Ray's vision and an arctic chill traced his spine.

It's okay - Henry's here. He'll show you how to toughen up and get past these fucking panic attacks. He'll show you how to stand your ground, be a man. Not like mum, and not like that fucking coward Bernard...

To his relief, Henry directed them instead towards the shooting range barn.

"As ya know, most o' the time my little operations run smoothly - but every once in a while we get a twig in the spokes."

Henry swung open the barn's thick metal door, invited Ray inside and closed it behind them with a padded clunk. The reception room had a high-planked ceiling that smelled of creosote. A heavy locked chest lay between two doors on the opposite wall, inside which Ray had seen compartments containing bullets, ear protection and several pistols. There was even a handheld submachine gun and an assault rifle, but unlike the handguns, Ray hadn't yet seen those in action.

Ray knew that the left-hand door led through to the shooting range, but Henry stepped smoothly towards the other. He looked back. "You alright, son?"

Ray's throat had closed and his skin felt tight. He nodded. Henry opened the door, and with a sense of surreal inevitability Ray followed him inside.

A bare light bulb lit two men and a room that was no more than thirty feet by thirty. Plastic blue sheeting covered the floor, and the walls were plain white concrete. Something about the sound the door made when Henry closed it signalled to Ray that the chamber was soundproof.

Percy Locker loomed in one corner wearing his usual dark suit and tie. His gently pointed face looked severe.

In the centre, two chairs faced one another. One was an empty leather couch, upon which Henry motioned Ray to sit. The other seat, several stride's away, was an office chair supporting a jittery, rat-like man. Clad in a creased and ill-fitting grey designer suit, he looked up at Ray and Henry, as if he'd been disturbed from important thoughts. A man of constant motion, his hands tapped a beat in his lap and his head jerked in sharp circles. Darting his eyes between Henry and Ray, the man's lips spread wide to reveal small, off-colour teeth.

"Alright, Henry?" the man said in a reedy voice. "Glad you could make it, mate. Pull up a chair. Come here to apologise, have you?"

"An' why would I be doing that, Robbie?" Henry asked, as Ray took his seat.

Robbie's expression fell. He hooked a thumb towards Locker. "*For having this clumsy wanker kidnap me!*"

"Now, now, calm down," Henry said, showing his palms. "Don't want you gettin' all het up over nothin', do we? Ya look a bit peaky already."

"I've felt better." Robbie produced a pack of red Marlboroughs, snorted, and lit one. "Can't get any good gear at the moment, can I?"

"No, I don't suppose ya can," Henry agreed, pacing the room. "Word spreads. I doubt people want much to do wiv you at the moment."

Ray felt his trembling worsen.

Robbie focussed his gaze onto Henry through a veil of acrid smoke. "So what's this deal, then?"

Henry linked his fingers and stopped walking. "Ysee, this is one o' your problems, Robbie. You've no patience." He huffed. "Alright then, cards on the table. It's like this: you could've had all the white powder you could snort, if that's what you'd wanted. Not a great life choice for a family man, but who am I to judge? We all have our vices. However, as reliable as you can be, you like to bite the hand that feeds, don't ya? In fact, you like to use it as a fackin' buttplug."

"You're a waffler, you know that?" Robbie muttered. "Watched 'Lock, Stock ...' one too many times, that's your problem." His face was so pale and thin that when he smiled it looked like a bare skull.

"Jus' tellin' you what I see," Henry replied. "Now, I understand that Locker here has told ya that I've got a deal to offer, so here it is: from time to time, your family will receive a nice, generous package, which should be enough for 'em to live on. Your woman an' your children will be taken care of, an' needn't worry about relyin' on daddy to bring home the cash. I wouldn't want 'em to be affected by your mistakes - wouldn't be fair."

Puffing on his cigarette, Robbie's hands fussed in his lap. "Thanks for the offer, but you're no family counsellor." He plucked the Marlborough from his lips and flicked it across the floor, where it landed at Ray's feet.

Henry stepped closer to Robbie and spoke like a teacher instructing a simple pupil. "The conditions are that you will never take from me again. You will never interfere in my business. You'll never approach me or my associates, an' you'll never be seen in Seadon again."

Robbie's gaze hardened. "And what kind of pay-off do *I* get?"

"Nasty little shits like yerself don't get nothin' outta me, Robbie. I'll help your family out, but not you."

"Cutting me off?" Robbie barked, his expression suddenly feral. "After all the work I've done, all the years of tough graft? Think you can tell us exactly what's what and who's who, don't you? Drinking your champagne, smoking your cigars, and watching the rest of us work the meat from our bones."

Dread rose in Ray like a tingling drug high, draining the muted colours of the room to make his vision swim like a sepia dream.

Stay calm... don't run... be a fucking MAN...

Suddenly, Robbie yelled, "I made you money! A lot of it! And now what?" He thrust a finger at Ray. "I suppose this skinny little dicksucker is gonna take over, is he?!"

The words jerked Ray upright.

Henry lunged towards Robbie and grabbed him by the arms, roaring, "*What's happenin' now hasn't got a thing to do wiv you, ya cheeky little facker!*"

Robbie shook Henry off and went to rise, but Locker dropped a giant hand onto each of his shoulders and shoved him back into the chair.

"You stay where you are," Locker said.

Henry and Robbie eyeballed each other like sparring rams. Hatred twisted Robbie's face and his voice became so shrill that it sounded ludicrous. "What if I say no to your little proposal, eh? What about that?"

Henry smiled humourlessly.

"What if I go and set up my own business, eh?" Robbie continued. "Or if I go an' join Hancock – what happens then?"

Henry caught Locker's eye. "An' how you gonna do that from a hole in the fackin' ground?"

In a single frame of time, Ray watched Robbie's downy eyebrows drop and the cockiness slip from his face. An almost pre-orgasmic blink hid Percy Locker's eyes and Henry took a slow step backwards. Ray heard the low hum of the light bulb and felt acid burn his chest. In despair, he realised the extent of his own immaturity, and knew that he was unprepared for whatever was to follow.

Locker lashed out his right arm. His hand turned a circle above Robbie's head, and Robbie went stiff.

"Get off!" Robbie yelped, but a strip of wire had encircled his stomach and wrists, wickedly thin and strong enough to tear into the sleeves of his suit. Ray heard something unzip as Locker noosed Robbie once across his upper arms and once around his neck, where veins and tendons bulged vulnerably.

Robbie tried to fight the restraints, but Locker looped the wire again and pulled it back against Robbie's cheeks and nose. Robbie's eyes gaped in panic as the wire drew into the meat of his face. Ray saw the rubber handles that allowed Locker to pull the instrument without the wire slicing into his hands.

"More you struggle, more you'll bleed," growled Locker from behind Robbie, tugging open yawning lacerations in the man's cheeks.

"Please," Robbie moaned, as blood began to flow from his jaw. "Please don't..."

Ray's limbs were useless and his mouth had fused shut.

Henry crouched before Robbie so that their eyes were level. His voice was bleak. "Didn't think you was gonna walk out of here in one piece, did ya?"

A droplet of sweat or maybe a tear trickled from Robbie's eye, down into the raw, leaking ditch of his cheek. "Please," he repeated, the cable distorting his expression into that of a Cenobite. "I'll pay you back. I'll do anything."

"*I'll pay you back, I'll do anythin,*" Henry mimicked, laughing. "Silly sod." He paced towards the door. "Don't you go runnin' off now, willya?"

The door closed behind him.

Ray became aware that Locker was staring, his unblinking face for once looking more simian than feminine.

Robbie kept cursing, "Jesus fuck, Jesus fuck, Jesus fuck, Jesus fuck..."

Locker tugged a hand and his prisoner screamed, the lower half of his head now crimson. Locker's eyes never left Ray's.

"Please Henry," Robbie begged, his voice a wet squawk. "Henry I'm sorry!"

"He can't hear you," Locker said, gloating. "You'll have to wait 'til he's back."

At last, Ray found his voice. "Why am I here?"

Locker's lips widened, revealing long white teeth.

The door swung back open.

"Now, son," Henry said, sounding excited. He wasn't looking at Robbie; he was looking at Ray. "Take this."

Ray's mind recoiled.

The gun that Henry held out was beautiful: small, sleek and gleaming.

"This is a Sig Sauer P229," Henry explained. "It'll be good for ya. It's got a nice smooth pull, cushioned recoil, an' it's compact enough for ya to carry about. Feel it. Careful though – the safety's off."

Ray watched his own hand extend and unfurl in slow motion. The heavy stainless steel felt like ice in his grip.

"Now I know that you don't *think* this is what you want," Henry said. "But in time you'll learn. You were born for this. You've got blood in your veins that demands it, you understand?" He reached out and squeezed Ray's slim shoulder. "I'm doing this for *you*."

Robbie's head had lolled downwards, but when Locker pulled at the rubber handles he shrieked, as if awoken from a nightmare.

Henry snapped, "Control that slag, wouldya? Now, Raymond-son. Take a good look at that *thing* behind me. That worthless, ketchup-covered Jack."

Ray did.

"*Please...*" Robbie gasped through his blood, but his tone was no more than a recording in Ray's head.

"What does *that* mean to you?" Henry asked, pointing at the wounded figure.

He's a bastard. A person. A husband. An addict.

"Means nothin' to me," Henry said. "Nothin' to Locker here, either. Ain't no man sittin' there – just an animal that needs puttin' down. No use to anyone, son, so I want you to get to your feet, an' do what needs to be done."

Ray's legs felt unpredictable, but when he stood they became firm. The gun had warmed to the damp heat of his palm.

"Make me proud, son," Henry drawled. "Someone's gotta put this cunt out of his misery, an' I want it to be you."

In his head, Ray tried to rationalise. He wasn't going to hurt this man; he couldn't. He had never harmed anyone outside of a scrappy teenage fistfight or two, so he could not start now.

But this shredded, restrained form was a nobody, wasn't he? Henry had said so. This bastard deserved all he got, and if Ray couldn't accept that, how could he ever call himself a real man?

"Please," Robbie mumbled, his face a torn mask. "I'll leave town...I won't come back...please, just let me go..."

"You shut your fackin' hole," Henry rumbled.

As Ray's legs sleepwalked forwards, he felt Locker's eyes press into him, searching, invasive.

"I know it ain't easy, son. The first time never is," Henry said. "But I wouldn't ask unless I knew you was ready. You were born for this, so I'll ask you again: does *that* mean anythin' to you?"

Ray's mind fell blank and his tongue faltered. The Sig Sauer hung lamely at his side. While Robbie wept protests and pointless negotiation, Locker's stare became predatory. Ray suddenly understood - Locker was willing him to drop the gun.

What would happen if Ray refused, though, after all he had seen? Would *he* be the one in the chair next time, pleading and anticipating death?

"No," Ray murmured.

"Then cock it back, son, jus' like I showed you."

Ray raised the gun, his mind in havoc and his stomach churning like Seadon's yellow-flecked sea. He slid the top section of the weapon back with a threatening clatter. Ray met Percy Locker's cold gaze. He couldn't let Locker know that he was weak - that would truly be dangerous.

Fuck you, Percy.

Ray watched the gun move towards Robbie's forehead, and it was as if someone else was raising it. He knew with total clarity what was happening, knew that he couldn't kill the man. It wasn't in his nature, no matter what Henry said. There was just no way in hell that...

"Pull it," Henry intoned.

The barrel kissed Robbie's temple and he began to struggle once more. Locker dragged one hand backwards and a thin jet of arterial blood hit Ray's chin.

Ray's wrists snapped upwards and, like a grenade, the Sig Sauer's report shook the room.

I didn't mean...

Robbie's left eye collapsed in its socket. The skull whiplashed backwards and Locker's wire stripped twin wings of flesh from Robbie's cheeks, exposing the glistening pink beneath.

Ray's ears howled.

Robbie's ruined head pistoned, seesawed drunkenly, and his lungs expelled a final, stinking gust. In the silence that followed, the dead man's muscles lost their tension and the blood running from his face slowed. Then there was only flesh propped before Ray, meat; a carcass suspended in a butcher's shop window.

"Good man," Henry said proudly.

Ray felt a hand on his shoulder again, but all he could think about were widowed wives and fatherless children.

Still grasping his wire, Locker wrenched the metal cord from its bed of gristle with a defeated huff.

Ray's world lost colour. His chilly, adrenalised body swayed. Feeling Henry's paternal touch, Ray tried to lower his arm but it remained outstretched, his finger tensed over the pulled trigger.

Ray's mind returned to the naked crowd from his fantasies, each tempting form nodding its approval. They reached for him, arms outspread and eyes abyss-black. This time they weren't in a grand hall, though: they were in a lonely, decrepit jungle overshadowed by trees, where something monstrous and mischievous wanted to play games with Ray. At that moment, Ray wanted to do exactly that: to run from all he had done and all that had trapped him, to flee and play games with something hungry, fickle and untameable, to play and stay, forever.

PART TWO
A Summer's Day

CHAPTER 9
"Today really *must be* the start"

Gary

In his bathroom, Gary snorted the morning's first line as quietly as possible. If there was *any day* when he'd need a gram or two of Colombian courage, it was today. The rush hit him like a train, but the gear couldn't have been as good as the stuff he'd been hooting recently, because the buzz seemed to peak immediately. His heart slammed, the adrenaline and endorphins channelling his thoughts, but when his eyes came to rest on the grey backpack sat on the toilet lid, his chest tightened painfully. He fell back against the wall, resting a hand on the edge of the sink.

He couldn't help but picture the girl from his dreams with the black, staring eyes. Although he saw her nodding at him, reassuring him, it wasn't enough today.

Shit, he'd been through it all a thousand and one times though, hadn't he? He was bound to have reservations, but Rebecca was right. This was going to be for the best.

Sandra

Sat at the dining table, Sandra waited for Gary to leave the bathroom. In her lap, she held a tiny, satin-smooth yellow hat, and imagined it warming the fragile head of her unborn child.

At present, it would barely be the length of a finger, but in less than eight months there would be a new person in her and Gary's lives, shaping their future and, she prayed, soothing the scars of their past. What had begun as a queasy walk on the beach four weeks ago had led to a missed period, a pregnancy test, and a sunburst of newly dawned hope. To have conceived via the only intimacy she and Gary had shared in almost a year was improbable, and when combined with their marriage's desperate need for a glint of hope it seemed impossible. She ran a hand across the brim of the bonnet and smiled; they had been blessed with a miracle.

All she had to do now was break the news to Gary.

She relished the sight of the breakfast she had laid out for him: toast with a choice of spreads and jams, orange juice she had squeezed herself, a selection of cereals and, Gary's favourite sugary pleasure: peanut butter Pop Tarts. If Gary wanted eggs, she would cook them for him - probably sunny side up, his usual preference - and as he ate, she would tell him her wonderful news. He would be stunned at first, but with space and time he would come to embrace the new development, and the husband Sandra had known before would slowly return.

Sandra glanced out through the window to the back of

the flats, where morning gulls had crowded around a dump truck, shrilling for leftovers – God's creatures. She had taken to praying again, hesitantly at first, but as the weeks had slipped by without any sign of menstruation Sandra had felt something warm and familiar open inside her. Inch by cautious inch, her religion was returning, and with it came a belief in a possible future.

The past month had not been easy. Although Gary now usually spent his evenings at home with Sandra, she did not believe that he had left the drugs behind. At times, she heard him sniffing in the bathroom, and he regularly vanished for hours on end, claiming to be consoling his friend Matt. Vicious scars had appeared across his body, but rather than explain them, Gary now wore long sleeves and undressed in the dark. He was not the fighting type, but grief can provoke a person to do terrible, unexpected things.

Of course, Sandra's pregnancy would eclipse whatever he was doing in secret, and they would start afresh.

The toilet flushed and Gary emerged from the bathroom at a pace. He carried a backpack and looked preoccupied, deep in thought.

"I've got to shoot off, love, no time for breakfast today," he blurted. "Got a lot on with Matt. We're going to play some pool, right, because he seems to be getting better at last. I want to get him out of the house a bit more."

Sandra rose from her seat. "Gary, haven't you got time for a coffee? It'll set you up for the day..."

"Nah, not right now, darling," he said, pecking her swiftly on the cheek as he passed. "You enjoy it though. Wouldn't want your efforts to go to waste. So you tuck in, and ..."

"Gary. Wait a minute."

He stopped, met her eyes. Guilt flared across his face.

"What's going on?" she demanded. His eyes left hers again, crawling towards the door. "Where are you rushing off to - honestly?"

"Matt's place, I told you, love."

He reached for the handle but she gripped his shoulder. "I don't care if you're using again, Gary. I don't even care if you've taken up smack. I just want you to be honest with me. I've got something important to say."

She released him and picked up the yellow hat from the table, holding it out to him, smiling and willing him to understand.

Gary kept his back to her, fingering the door handle with that small grey bag hanging from his shoulder. "Sandra, love, whatever you want to say, can't it just wait? I'm really doing my best right now, y'know? Helping out a mate, and..."

She waved the hat towards him, wanting to enjoy the moment but feeling something bleak and unchanging pulse from her husband.

He looked back, uncomprehending, and when he saw the hat his brow creased further. "What've you got that for?" He reached past the bonnet and gripped her wrist. "You're just hurting yourself again and you need to stop it, okay? We've been through a lot, but you need to get a grip." He paused. "I can't be here all the time."

"No, Gary, you don't understand."

"Yes I do," he said firmly, his hand still clamped around her. He was trying to be strong, trying not to sound too concerned, but the act was transparent. "'Course I understand. You don't think I still hurt, too? Look. I really *do* need to head out now, but..." His voice wavered. "Whatever happens, you'll be okay."

She lowered the hat, exhausted. It was not the right

time to break her news. It would be better to swallow the announcement and let Gary blow off some steam with his friend. "Fine," she said. "You go off and do your thing and I'll wait here for you, like always."

One of Gary's scuffed trainers pointed downwards, twisting in circles. "Yeah. Thanks, love. Um. I mean it. Thanks for everything, okay?"

The words sounded strange to Sandra. "I'll be here when you get back, Gary. We'll talk then. Don't drink too much, please."

"Yeah," he replied, but didn't look at her. "Goodbye, Sandra."

A few minutes after he had left, as Sandra picked at her dry toast, she realised with a jolt whose grey bag Gary had been carrying.

Thomas

Using a spoon to bulldoze through a breakfast bowl of cookies and cream, Thomas struggle-fights not to turn around. Under his Transformers sweatshirt, the scars from the Knife Game itch. There's something in the air today – something not-quite-right and not-too-nice. He feels as if looking behind him will only confirm his suspicions.

Thomas sits in the lounge in front of his computer, so close to the screen that his breath keeps misting the glass. He wishes that the two YouTube videos – one of them a "best-of" set of Rugrats clips, and the other a snuff film – were enough to distract him from the flicker-flashing at the side of his vision.

From behind, three high-pitched voices speak as one: "Today's the day, Fatty-Tom-Tom. It's time for The People Game."

Thomas sighs, sags, and slips down his chair. He should

get up and grab a shower soon. Thomas will be working alone for most of the morning at the shop, but Ratan will drop by at some point. Ratan has changed so much over the last few weeks. It's not just his new haircut and clothes: he's become quiet, and sort of "on guard" all the time.

"Thomas," Simon hisses into his ear, breath tickling his cheek. "If you don't turn around, I'll reach into your mouth and pull your spine out through your fatty-fat lips."

Thomas gives in and turns. The flicker-flash becomes a blinding glare, a horrid white circle around the burning black gaze of the Gardden. Thomas realises that today really *must* be the start of The People Game, and tears like battery acid flood his eyes.

Henry

Henry's stingin eyes had fack-all to do wiv the phonecall – he hadn't cared about that old facker for years.

He'd woken up wiv Bruno sprawled on top of him, a dead weight, and his first thoughts had bin of the missus, who was comin round later to fix him some grub. For dessert, he and Bruno would grab 'emselves some afternoon delight, then Henry would turf her out and get in touch wiv the lad.

Henry had still bin blinkin the sleep from his eyes when those bloodsuckers from his dad's home had phoned. What really put his teeth on edge was that every nurse sounded the same: like a schoolteacher tryin to control a bad pupil. Henry regretted it now, but he'd started rantin at her straight away.

"Listen, Nurse fackin Ratched," he'd said. "If you're after more money, you can forget it. I already lay out far too much for that mush-brained old sod. What is it now, anyway? Does he need his arse wipin' twice as much these days?"

The nurse-cow had tried interruptin him: "Mr Borders, this is a difficult call to make..."

"Don't tell me what's difficult, love," Henry had scoffed. "What's *difficult* is layin out more than a grand each fackin week for a droolin prat who doesn't know his teeth from his bollocks! Trust me: if your costs rise jus' one more time, the only cash I'll be spendin on him will be for an overdose o' morphine."

Then she'd jus' said, "Your father died last night, Mr Borders."

The gall o' the slag, breakin the news to him like that! It's not as if he was upset, but you'd think that a fackin nurse would have more tact. Well, he'd hung up on her and gone back to bed for a bit, squeezin his eyes shut against a sharp sting.

Now he lay behind Bruno, spoonin the slobberin mutt, smellin the warm crown of his head. At some point, he drifted off to sleep again an' found himself runnin through the fields outside o' Seadon alongside a younger version of his dad. Everythin was cushty, even wiv his dad's eyes all dark an' shadowy.

yes yes... follow me follow me... yes yes yes

They came to a forest, an' although Henry stopped, his dad carried on into the trees. As his pa walked on, he kept turnin back to Henry, beckonin him into the gloom. Henry jus' stood there. For some reason, it felt as though there was a whole lot ridin on whevver Henry followed or not.

LOCKER

LOCKER MURMURED IN HIS SLEEP.

ALL HE COULD SEE WERE WHITE BEDSHEETS AND A WET, MUSCLY BACK. HE WAS LYING ON HIS SIDE AND HE COULD SMELL SWEAT AND A WHIFF OF SHIT BUT IT WASN'T STRONG; IN FACT, IT WAS GOOD. THIS OTHER BODY WAS MAKING LITTLE MOANING NOISES, LIKE THE WHIMPERS HE SOMETIMES HEARD WHEN HE WAS CUTTING PEOPLE UP, BUT QUIETER. LOCKER USUALLY PREFERRED MAKING PEOPLE BLEED, SCREAM. HERE THOUGH, WRAPPED UP IN THOSE SHEETS, HE WAS TRYING HIS BEST *NOT* TO HURT THE OTHER PERSON.

HE WATCHED THAT RIPPLING, TENSING, FLEXING BACK. MUST'VE TAKEN *YEARS* OF WORKOUTS TO GET IT LOOKING THAT GOOD. THE HEAD SHIFTED TO THE RIGHT AND THE HAIRLINE WAS HIGH, BUT PERCY COULDN'T MAKE OUT THE FACE.

"*GAWD YEAH...*" IT WHISPERED, ENCOURAGING, REASSURING HIM THAT IT WASN'T IN PAIN.

YES YES YES

"WHAT ELSE CAN I DO?" LOCKER ASKED.

FINGERS GRASPED HIS HAND. WHILE HE MOVED, EASING HIMSELF FORWARDS AND BACK, HE REALISED THAT HE TRULY MISSED THIS. IT WAS ALL THAT MADE SENSE TO HIM, AND MAYBE THE ONLY THING THAT COULD SAVE HIM FROM REPEATING THE SAME OLD CRAP, AGAIN AND AGAIN FOREVER.

FUCK THE VIOLENCE OF THE POETRY — *THIS* WAS WHAT MATTERED.

BUT WHEN THE FACE TURNED ROUND, IT WASN'T WHO LOCKER HAD THOUGHT IT WAS. THE BUFF, WIDE BACK VANISHED, AND NOW IT WAS A BULIMIC FUCKING BONEBAG COATED IN CHICKEN SKIN, AND A GRINNING FACE WITH A THIN NOSE AND STUPID FUCKING PURPLE HAIR. THE EYES WERE THE WORST PART: NO WHITES, NO COLOUR – JUST A BLACK THAT SEEMED DARKER THAN THE DARKEST COON.

LOCKER YANKED HIMSELF BACKWARDS AND OUT. HE FOUND HIS METAL FRIENDS IN A BAG ON THE PILLOW, SO HE GRABBED ONE AND BROUGHT IT DOWN WITH A FLASH. BLOOD FIREWORKED ACROSS THE SHEETS.

YES YES YES! TAKE HIM KILL HIM EAT HIM YES YES YES!

HE TOOK ANOTHER FRIEND OUT AND RAMMED THAT DOWNWARDS TOO, THEN A THIRD AND A FOURTH, BATTERING AND STABBING AND CHOPPING UNTIL THERE WERE ONLY PIECES, GRISTLE, ORGANS LEFT ON THE BED. SOMEHOW, THOUGH, EVEN AFTER HE HAD SLASHED AWAY THE BODY AND THE SKIN, THE SMILE STAYED THERE, FACELESS AND LEERING BENEATH A PAIR OF COAL-BLACK EYES.

LOCKER AWOKE WITH A JERK.

HOW FUCKING *DARE* THE GOTH CUNT INTERRUPT HIS DREAM? IT WAS AS IF THE KID HAD CLIMBED INTO HIS HEAD, JUST TO LAUGH AT HIM.

IN HIS SINGLE BED, LOCKER CLASPED HIS HANDS BEHIND HIS HEAD. LOCKER'S THIN CURTAINS GLOWED YELLOW – IT WAS GOING TO BE ANOTHER HOT ONE. LYING THERE, ENRAGED YET SOMEHOW CALM, PERCY LOCKER THOUGHT TO HIMSELF, IF THERE WAS *EVER* A DAY TO SLICE APART THAT SKINNY POOF'S SNEER, IT WAS A DAY LIKE TODAY.

Rebecca

With a snarl, Rebecca spread her fingers across Gary's face and pushed him down into the pillow, squeezing his throat with the other hand as she fucked him. With each straddled thrust, air hissed out from between her bared teeth. Veins bulged from her little bug's neck and forehead. As a tickling warmth blossomed inside her, she removed her hand from his red face and let it join the other, tightening her grip on his windpipe, aiming to time her orgasm with the moment he started to black out.

She released him and as he wheezed harshly, she lost herself to the familiar vision: something partly canine bursting from her, in a flurry of gnashing jaws and piercing black eyes. It now persisted in her every nightmare, every daydream, and every unguarded thought, but the time had come: today was about confronting and defeating her many demons.

Rebecca rose to the very end of Gary's length and then ground herself back to the hilt. Her red-haired bug smiled deliriously as she came, sharing her physical joy and emptying himself into her with uncoordinated jerks. Although she wanted to jump from the bed, away from Gary's spurting mess and groping fingers, she resisted. Despite having come to pity and detest the ginger fool in equal measure, she was depending on him.

With parting came their inevitable, one-sided embrace. She rolled off him and onto her back, and Gary twisted sideways to clasp his skinny arms around her. "Thank you," he mumbled, and placed a lingering kiss onto the side of her face.

This guesthouse, with its patches of damp and sachets of instant coffee, had become the sole meeting place for their dozen or so encounters. Its frugal amenities seemed to parallel the limitations of their relationship.

"This will be the most important day of your life," she said. "Aftewards, you can get as high as you please, but for now you need to maintain perfect awareness; crystal clarity."

"I told you, I'll stay straight until I'm done," he said, a little petulantly.

Rebecca looked at the face resting against her upper arm. A patch of thick red hair gathered in an ugly clump against Gary's cheek. "I'm only reminding you, my dear," she said, kittenish, "Because the last thing I want is for you to put yourself at risk."

Her bug's lips spread into a yellow smile. "I know what I've got to do, and it's going to be fine. I'll go to the shop, you go and do whatever you've got to do, and when I see you again we'll be rich and ready to start somewhere new."

"That's right," she crooned, allowing herself to feel excitement, but keeping it firmly from her voice. "So tell me, one last time, what are you going to do?"

"Again?" he whined.

"Yes."

She listened as he explained his duties once more, relieved to hear that he now knew them almost verbatim.

"That's right," she sang. "And then we'll head

off towards the setting sun."

Well, I will.

"Are you sure that I shouldn't hide my face?" he asked. "You know, with a mask or something?"

She shot him a cool look. "Unless you're planning on returning to Seadon after we leave, you've nothing to worry about."

Gary sighed contentedly. "You know that you've saved me, don't you?"

Her mouth twitched in suppressed amusement. "I suppose I have, yes."

"And you know that I love you, don't you?" he asked.

She smiled, turned, and slapped him sharply. "Yes, darling. I know that very well."

With his cheek reddening, Gary settled his ginger hair onto her breast with a contented coo.

"One last thing," she added. "Whatever happens, do not hurt the tall, Gothic boy."

Ray

Shivering naked on his bed, Ray stared down at his flaccid cock and rubbed his palms over the stubble of his freshly cropped head.

Time lay... dormant.

A month had passed since everything had changed, and he hadn't once cracked or cried. He still made jokes in company, still worked hard at the Green Emporium, and still tried to lighten his mother's moods, but in his mind, he still held the Sig Sauer. The trigger remained compressed, the barrel issuing a wisp of smoke, and behind it, just out of focus, a black-eyed legion of naked bodies nodded its assent.

Ray now drank and snorted most nights, not to socialise but to forget. He bought fine drinks, ate fine food, and often rented fine hotel rooms to avoid coming home, whenever things felt like too much to bear. The funds he had saved had withered considerably, but he was too numb to feel concerned.

Back when Ray had been a regular visitor of Lashes nightclub, he had been nicknamed 'Ratan'. This alter ego had been a nihilist, a joyfully debauched libertine. Put in Ray's position, Ratan would no doubt have lain in bed pumping his engorged third leg, picturing extravagant fantasies and scenarios. Ratan would have been invigorated by the thought of murder, and relished working towards a life free of Seadon, of his mother, and of the societal restrictions that he had outgrown.

Ray, however, remained haunted by the gun and his nude audience of approving ghouls. He craved distraction and wished he could provoke a rise from his penis, but whenever he tried, all he saw was a spurting jugular, a jolting neck, a shattered eye socket. Did Robbie's wife know that the man she had married now lay submerged in the wormy soil of Henry's field? If she did, was she glad, or had the thieving addict possessed a caring side?

That morning, the light behind Ray's curtains crept into his dim, adolescent refuge, colouring its freak show of posters and monstrous ornaments. Ray's room was one of the few places that did not drive him to panic. He wished he could remain there forever, but he had responsibilities; he was a man now, after all.

In the week following Robbie's death, Henry had purchased Ray a Valentino charcoal-grey suit, stating that it was a sign of his entry into the team. In the outfitters, as Ray was measured for his new clothes, Henry had told him that a pinstripe commanded respect, and was what *real* men wore. Ray had found no energy for debate, and that afternoon had reserved four more subtly different yet equally overpriced suits. The following day, he had shorn his long, purple dreadlocks and placed them in a transparent zip-lock bag. Those souvenirs of his youth now lay in his desk drawer beside a bottle of Gentleman Jack, Ray's world map, and the pistol that had turned him into a murderer.

Before dressing, he withdrew his map from the drawer. The countries blurred in and out of focus. The idea of a foreign adventure had become daunting, ludicrous, and once again financially out of reach. He considered shredding the map, but doing so felt like too much effort, so he placed it back in the drawer and pushed it firmly closed.

He pulled a black tie around his neck and snapped down the lapels of the same shirt he had worn yesterday and Christ new how many days before that. The mirror reflected a tragic, unshaven Hollywood heartthrob, and not the androgynous alt-model he was used to. A flicker of ego warmed Ray as he made the comparison, but the look in his own eyes extinguished the spark in seconds. He looked brittle, ready to break.

Ray had hoped to sneak from the house without facing his mother, but halfway down the stairs he heard her call: "Raymond?"

He stopped, and in a dry voice replied, "What?"

Rose sat waiting in their modest lounge, still in her dressing gown, her blonde locks running from her head in tangled bed-hair streams. "I'd like to speak with you, please."

"What?" he repeated, wishing he could return to the safety of his bedroom.

His mother Rose looked up at him stood in the doorway, and her lips fell open. "Oh, Raymond."

Despite sharing a home with Ray, she had barely seen him in recent weeks. He must have appeared a stranger. He knew that his cheeks had become gaunt and pinched, and his creased shirt now hung from a matchstick frame that refused to gain weight, despite the rich food and top-shelf alcohol he had taken to consuming. Dark rings encircled his bloodshot eyes and his lips, once boisterously pink, had shrivelled to grey pencil outlines.

His mother rose and reached out to clasp her son's face. Ray considered pulling away, but doing so felt like too much for his emaciated body. Rose's hands slid down to his frail arms, and he allowed his head to fall into the crook of her neck.

"Honestly, my darling," he heard her say, inches from his ear. "You simply *have* to tell me what's been going on. What did that bastard do to you?"

Ray felt himself stiffen: behind her play-acting and her drama queen façade, she always cut to the truth.

"I..." he said, in a voice that was barely there. Nothing more would come, but he was afraid that if he lingered his composure would dissolve and he would break down, drop to the floor of their shared lounge and curl up, weeping for each of the past year's numberless mistakes.

"Oh, my darling," she said into his ribcage, hugging him fiercely. "You've lost yourself, haven't you? You've lost yourself and you don't know how to come back."

"Mum," he gasped, squeezing his eyes shut. "I did something..."

"Whatever you've done, you can make amends," she said. "I've always taught you that I'm here for you."

Anger pricked him. "Feels like *you've* always been the one who's needed *me*."

He opened his eyes, untangled himself from her arms, and saw how his words had stung her.

"I'm sorry," he said, immediately ashamed. He went to the couch and collapsed.

Hesitantly, Rose sat beside him. "Do you want to tell me what's happened?"

He did. He wanted to open his mouth and spill everything, empty himself of all the built-up bile and regret, but the idea of his mother's face twisting into a gnarled mask of disappointment prevented him. She was right. In spite of the support she had always needed from him, she had brought him up to be a better man than the killer he had become.

"Ray," she said. She took his hand, wrapping it warmly in hers. "I know that whatever you've been through, it's because of Henry Borders, isn't it?"

His chest tightened. His skin became cold. Guilty shadows darkened his vision.

"I need to make you see something," she continued. "I need you to wake up. I should have said something before, but you know how it is. You're just the same as me - you let things curdle."

Ray heard the telltale regret in her voice, the warning of something dreadful approaching. He wanted to get up from the couch, because she was going to tell him something he already suspected or perhaps even knew, something that was starting to make the room sway and tremble.

"I don't know how to say this..."

Then don't, mum. Then don't!

"...but, a long time ago, Henry and I had a fling."

A switch was tripped inside him. He breathed out heavily as the world suddenly made sense.

The coke.

The booze.

The Green Emporium.

Robbie...

"It happened many years ago, but after I'd met your father." Her words almost tripped over themselves. "Bernard and I had been together for six years, but we were going through tough times. We had no money and Bernard felt that I should begin looking for a proper job, rather than singing in bars and acting for a pittance. He was trying to control me, so I kept on performing, and after a while we spent some time apart."

Ray had never heard her speak so fast, as if she was afraid that if she paused for even for a moment she would swallow the rest of what she had to say.

"I was stupid," she went on, gazing at the ceiling. "I went with Henry Borders once. *Once*, that's all. I used to sing at his bar and he would leave me flowers before each performance. He was so cocksure. I found his accent oddly charming. I had an idea about what kind of man he was, but when I was at my weakest point, I gave in." She sighed, sucking her lower lip between her teeth. "Your father and I got back together soon afterwards. I told him everything, and Bernard seemed to understand. But Henry harassed me. Pestered me with phone calls, got his men to follow me – then he turned his attentions onto Bernard." She tutted. "Poor Bernard. Henry threatened him in the street, made ugly phone calls. Told him that he wasn't a 'real man', whatever that means. Bernard had always been fragile. He hadn't coped well during our separation, but he wouldn't go to the police." Rose's tone wavered, and for a second Ray thought she was going to cry. "When I found out that I was pregnant with you, the next time Henry called, I told him I was going to have Bernard's baby. After that, the calls stopped, and that seemed to be that." She glanced at Ray. "Bernard told me that having you would be like a new beginning for us. I believed him. I was just so relieved that Henry had left us alone, but as the months passed, and as you grew inside me, Bernard and I drifted again. He stopped sleeping. We argued terribly. He threatened to leave me, and I pleaded with him not to, and..." her voice and head dipped. "And then one night, two months before you were born, I found him in the garage."

Ray felt his mother's body become tense beside him.

"I know why he did it, Ray. I can hear your thoughts, just like I could hear his, but it's not possible, okay? The dates don't add up. The doctors told us when you were conceived but, like I said, Bernard was unstable. I'd betrayed him, and I imagine that added a layer of doubt to everything I told him from then on. To be Henry's child, you would've had to have been born more than a month late. That just cannot be. It *can't*." She seemed to wrestle with her words. "Bernard's genes make you the man you are, not Henry's. I only wish that you could have met him. He wanted the best for everyone and he would have desperately wanted you to get through this, Raymond, whatever it is. Your father would have wanted you to leave Seadon, just as you've always planned, and forget all about Henry bloody Borders."

Ray sat without speaking. How was he supposed to believe her? How could he stop the room from upturning, or the doubt from consuming him when his own mother had lied for so long? He looked at her coldly, absorbing her white face and deflated posture.

Did this revelation make things any worse than they already were? Did it change anything, *really*?

Who was the worst culprit: the lying mother, the conniving drug baron, or Ray himself, the dumb pawn who'd ended another man's life?

The walls were closing in. Ray's sight was blurring once again. He wanted to run.

His mother stared at him expectantly, no doubt needing him to say something, anything.

Ray parted his lips and exhaled air that refused to take shape. No insights came, and the grey, grasping threads returned to suffocate his vision. So instead of replying, he rose, knowing without even looking that his mother's sad, lost gaze never left him once as he turned his back on her and left the house.

CHAPTER 10
"Ain't goin' nowhere"

Gary

In a locked cubicle of the public lavs opposite The Green Emporium, Gary snorted a line off the cistern. Outside on the road he could hear the red-skinned crowds chatting shit in the hot midday sunshine. The coke went down nicely so he chopped up another, then took a minute to think about what he was doing.

He'd scoped out the shop a few times over the past week and each day the same fat geezer had been stood at the till. He didn't seem like anyone to worry about. Judging by his body language, he looked like the sort who'd rather play dead than fight.

From the moment Rebecca had suggested her plan, Gary had begun mentally preparing for the future. He couldn't go on hiding behind Sandra's back. It didn't feel right, and, in the long run, her life would be better if he just fucked off, wouldn't it? Shit - she'd probably thank him, a few years down the line.

Gary had parked the hire car, a metallic blue Ford

Ka, at the rear of the shop, ready to give him a swift escape. They had already loaded Rebecca's clothes into the boot, and the plan was to meet Rebecca at the guesthouse they'd been using as a shag-pad at 3pm. She'd told him that she had her own set of tasks to carry out, and Gary hoped that these "tasks" would involve some kind of payback for her knob-end of a boyfriend. Gary had seen the scars between her legs, and that bastard deserved all he got.

The coke charged through him. Rebecca had said that he wouldn't need to use the shooter - it was just a prop - but it still felt foreign and dangerous against his thigh. Despite the safety catch, he was worried about it blowing off his bollocks. Rebecca had offered to find him a gun, but Gary had wanted to prove himself useful. One of the blokes he sometimes bought coke from dealt more than just drugs, so, with Rebecca's money, Gary had purchased a pistol, just like someone out of a Hollywood film. Well, a Hollywood film where the star had to concentrate on not cacking himself while strolling about with a loaded weapon. Gary supposed that he hadn't really needed to buy bullets, but he would've felt silly buying a gun without anything to fire.

Gary hooted his second line as quietly as he could, and pulled the backpack over his shoulders. Someone came into the bogs and closed the neighbouring cubicle door. The voice of a perky father told a young boy to stop playing with his car for just *one second*, because they both wanted to get back to the beach, didn't they? A glimmer of jealousy ran through Gary.

"Darryl, I told you: stop waving your hands around. You want to get back to the rock pools, don't you?"

"Will the crab still be there?" the child asked. His voice sounded like a cartoon mouse.

Gary ignored both the conversation and the lump in his throat. Back outside, in the brightness of the day, he squinted through the passing figures. It was lunchtime, so surely The Green Emporium would be quiet. He just had to get in, get the shop clear, get upstairs, get the cash and get out.

It will be easy, Rebecca had said, as she'd stroked his scratched chest. *Don't worry, my darling.*

Coked-up and feeling invincible, Gary crossed the street. The shop was almost empty, just as he'd hoped, so he followed a man wearing a shell-suit jacket into the dimness of the store. A customer in a football shirt was paying at the till, and the fat guy with the tufty beard who Gary had seen before was bagging up some goods. Gary feigned interest in a pencil sharpener shaped like an open-legged woman, tapping his thigh to the reggae filling the hot shop.

The football-shirted guy left the store, and the guy in the shell-suit went to the counter. Just the three of them, now – he'd just wait until this last guy left. Gary was going to take control of the situation, because this tubby prick at the till was a little pig, and Gary was a big, badass wolf.

Where was this other guy that Rebecca had told him about - the tall, Gothy one? Upstairs with the money? No time to wonder: the shell-suited bloke strolled past him and outside. Time to move while there was no one else in the store.

Okay.

His skin tingled.

On three.

He licked his dry lips.

One...

He breathed in deeply.

Two...

He drew the gun from his pocket.

Three.

"If I were you," Gary said. "I'd keep my mouth shut and set to locking that door. *Now.*"

The tubby guy looked up from the till, confusion twisting his face. "W-what do you want?"

"I just told you – now move!"

The guy's jowls shook like a bloodhound's and his eyes stretched open. He didn't budge.

"What are you waiting for?" Gary snarled, glancing back through the glass into the street. He edged backwards to bar the doorway, aiming the barrel at the chubber in a way that was out of view from anyone outside.

Through a storm of rushing adrenaline, Gary tried to imagine what a bad guy on the telly might say, and yelled, "Get this locked, or you'll get a bullet in your fat guts."

The shopkeeper fished a handful of keys from his trousers and waddled over to use them, looking petrified.

As he turned the key, Gary warned, "If you do *anything* that I don't like, I'll blow a fucking hole in you. Alright? What's your name?"

The fatty, his sweat-stained pits wafting, stuttered, "T-T-Thomas."

"Well, T-T-Thomas, who else is in here with you? There's supposed to be someone else about, some Goth."

"Ratan's not here," Thomas whimpered. "What's this about? Are you the police?"

Gary opened his mouth to speak but a baffled laugh jumped out. "The police?" he asked, jabbing Thomas's belly with the gun. "Do I look like the fucking police? I'm here for the money. So how about you take me upstairs to the stash, eh?"

Thomas opened his mouth but stayed silent, looking like he was on the verge of a seizure.

Gary poked him with the gun again. "Do you hear me? Lead the way upstairs or I'll *hurt you*."

There was a pattering sound, and liquid puddled on the tiles at Thomas's feet.

"Jesus fucking Christ," Gary complained. "Look, mate: the quicker you get up those stairs, the quicker I'll be out of here."

"Don't hurt me," Thomas mumbled, raising his sausage-and-steak hands in surrender. "Please."

The piss-stained man revolted Gary, with his spots, his unhealthily pale skin, and the rolls of fat overflowing from the arms of his Autobots t-shirt.

"I already told you," Gary said. "I want what's upstairs, so *get up there*."

Wheezing, Thomas led Gary behind the till to a narrow, plywood-boarded passageway. It was stuffy and hot as hell at the back of the shop. The walls were hung with tacky souvenirs, gadgets and dildos. Gary caught his leg on a plastic package that contained a life-sized rubber foot, complete with a bubble-written logo that read, "Sexy-Sexy!"

"When will the Goth be here?" Gary asked.

"I don't know," Thomas answered, shakily.

Gary's stomach rolled. "You'd better not be lying," he said, aiming his gun at Thomas. "If it turns out that anyone else is here, I'm not going to be happy."

Thomas climbed two steps, stopped, then turned back. "Um. I've just remembered. I don't have the keys. That's Ratan's office."

Gary glared at the pudgeball. It hadn't occurred to him that he might be unable to access the stash. Maybe this guy was messing with him, though - could he be acting piss-scared and taking Gary for a fool? Could he already have pressed a silent alarm?

Whatever, mate. This guy's half-retarded.

Gary's pulse juddered in his temples. "Listen to me. I know what's up there, and I'm going to get to it, keys or not. So if you're fucking with me, I'll still take the cash, but I'll leave you lying in a pool of blood."

Thomas shrugged, avoiding Gary's eyes. "I've never been up there."

Gary's body was full of flustered heat and his arse felt loose. This must be why burglars sometimes leave piles of shit in their victim's houses – it wasn't malice, it was *terror*.

For a moment, Gary genuinely considered leaving: just ditching the whole idea and going home. This dumb blob didn't know much, did he? And Gary was pretty sure that he could scare him into keeping quiet. Gary could just go back to Sandra and chomp through his dinner as if nothing had ever happened.

But he wanted a new life, didn't he? He wanted to forget his past, his dole money, his flat, his wife, and, if he was totally honest, every single one of his pals. He wanted to stop dreaming about the little girl with the black eyeballs. He was in love with a new woman and he wanted to please her, and the only way to do that was to see this through.

He dug into his pocket. Keeping the gun pointed at Thomas, he peeled the baggy open, stuck his nose in, and gave it a reckless snort.

Thomas made a sound that was somewhere between a moan and a whistle. His eyes gaped open even wider, as if someone else had just come into the musty stairwell. Rushing, Gary realised that someone was behind him, about to bring something crashing down on his head. He turned quickly, pointing the gun, but there was no one there.

"Out of my way," he said to Thomas irritably, climbing the stairs and shoving past. He twisted the office door handle hard but it just rattled in its frame.

Kick it in?

It seemed pretty sturdy as he shook it, but it couldn't be too hard to boot down, could it? He was wearing sports shoes, but it was only a piece of wood, wasn't it? The problem was that the top step was only a few inches wider than the others, so there was barely any room for Gary to stand. He swung the gun back into Thomas's face and said, "Don't move one *inch* of flab. I'm serious. If I see one ripple, you're dead."

With one hand on the bannister and his gun hand pressed to the wall, Gary pulled a knee up to his chest. He braced himself and then drove his foot forwards, hard. The wood, tougher than expected, stayed firm, and he flew sprawling away from the door.

The world became a tumble dryer and he shot backwards, arms spinning. When he hit Thomas, the guy staggered but stood his ground. Gary continued to fall. He flung a hand out to grab the bannister, and although he managed to steady himself before any painful impact, blood rushed to his head and the edges of the steps dug sharply into his spine. It took Gary half a second to readjust: he was now lying on his back with his feet higher up the stairs than his head, staring at the ceiling and the lower folds of Thomas's belly. The fat man-child could easily crush him beneath churning gallons of weight, so, without thinking, Gary threw a glancing punch into the tubby shopkeeper's calf. Thomas didn't react, so Gary thumped him again and then began to scramble, trying to get to his feet.

"I'll pull you up," Thomas suggested, offering a hand down. "Just stop hitting me, please."

Gary considered punching the fat man again, but couldn't work out what was to be gained. Finally, he waved an arm into the air and Thomas lifted him to his feet. The fat man met Gary eye to eye.

"Are you alright?" Thomas asked. "That looked like it hurt."

"Of course I'm fucking alright," Gary snapped.

"Okay."

As Gary rubbed sweat from his forehead, he noticed the fat man staring past him towards an empty space at the bottom of the stairs. "What is it now?" he asked.

The fat prick looked back at him, lips peeling away from his teeth, like he'd done something wrong. The fruitcake said nothing, though.

Right, Gary told himself. *No more shitting about.*

Ray

Ray found himself at an empty patch of sand between the cliffs of two popular beaches. He sat on the salt-scented rocks without considering his two-thousand-pound suit, as the tranquil sea licked divots into the shoreline.

The wet sand beneath Ray's feet appeared miles away, and the white noise of the ocean stung his ears.

He picked up three pebbles and half-heartedly tried to juggle, but dropped one after just a few seconds and let the others slip from his fingers.

Henry had known who his mother was all along, hadn't he? From that very first night, Henry had decided Ray was his estranged son. That was the only reason he had given Ray the job and later offered him a place in the crew.

Ray imagined Henry's arms around him, clogging his nose with sweat and cigar smoke and that doglike under-scent, squeezing him like a treasured toy. Ray doubted that Henry treated anyone, even Rebecca, with such affection. So why had he turned Ray into a killer? Why do such an awful goddamned thing?

But the answer was simple: control.

If it had not been for Henry, Ray might have known Bernard. The awkward figure in the photograph – the man that his mother Rose had called 'loving' and 'supportive' – might have played a part in Ray's life. Without a husband, Ray's mother had come to rely on her son for strength, and without a father, Ray had become submerged in a world of blurred-lines, drugs and poor role models.

Would he and his mother have struggled financially if Bernard hadn't taken his own life? Would Rose have received an acting break? Would Ray have become a more stable, less bitter

---

Who the hell would Ray be, if not for Henry fucking Borders?

Henry

Henry fackin Borders had woken from his dream to the sound of knockin, an' the smell of Bruno's earthy breath. The Great Dane had turned round an' was lappin at Henry's face. The mutt's saliva smelled rank.

"Dirty bugger," Henry scolded, but didn't mind really. He got up from the bed, stretched, an' wandered into the apartment lounge.

Henry's golden boy musta punched in the doorcode wiv-out waitin for an answer. As he clumped up the stairs, Henry saw that the kid didn't look quite as golden as his usual self.

"Woss 'appened, Raymond-son - didya trade your outfit wiv a tramp again?" He went to hug the kid but the lad stepped away.

Henry examined the boy's face. Although Raymond's eyes were black and drained, they also seemed intense, as if they were measurin Henry up. Cheeky little sod was obviously still mumpty after takin out Robbie.

"Looks like you could do wiv a drink, son," Henry remarked. "Go on, sit yourself down an' I'll fetch you a brandy..."

"Tea," his lad said stiffly. "Milk, no sugar."

Somethin in his tone stopped Henry from arguin, so he went to the kitchen and switched on the kettle. Clearly, the poor sod was still strugglin, but it was only a phase. Henry would straighten him out.

He watched Raymond take a seat on the chaise longue, an' heard Bruno pad into the room, barkin a friendly greetin. While the water boiled, Henry watched the boy give Bruno a coupla strokes but then push him away.

"I know, son," Henry said as he brought Ray's drink in. "It's not easy, is it?"

Bruno had gone to his bed in the corner, lookin dejected.

"Don't take it to heart, pal," Henry said to the dog, an' sat down beside Ray.

The boy was a sorry sight, but he took his drink and sipped it. For once, Henry said nothin an' just waited for the boy to speak.

Raymond got through most of his cup before he went, "I can't stop picturing it. It's like I'm still there, holding the gun."

"Yeah," Henry agreed. "I know, son. Felt like I was sinkin in quicksand after I did me dad in." The lie came so easily, but as soon as Henry said it, he felt sick. He'd tell Ray the truth one day. Half jokin, he said, "Son, you gotta remember that when someone punts the bucket, it's only a life! Plenty more o' them about, ain't there?"

"Why did you make me kill him?"

Henry sighed and sat back. "There are times in every man's life when..."

"I didn't ask for a lesson," Raymond said, his expression hardenin. "Just tell me."

Wasn't like Raymond to be like that. What did the lad want to hear? "I suppose, son," Henry began. "That I wanted to show ya just how strong ya can be."

The lad looked unimpressed. There was also somethin else that Henry couldn't put his finger on.

Henry continued, "Ya said you wanted to leave the city, but that ain't what ya want at all. You'd be makin' a big mistake if you evaporated into thin air. You were made for this, son."

Anger flickered across the lad's face. "And just how do you know what I was 'made for'?"

"Look, Ray, I understand you're upset, but…"

"You don't understand a fucking thing," the boy spat, his face stormy and his body suddenly shakin. "Robbie was right: you think you know what everybody's thinking and what's best for everyone else, don't you?"

Henry sat back. "Go on – have a little rant if it makes ya feel better, son."

"Stop calling me that!" the lad erupted, standin up so fast that his knees bashed the table, sloppin his drink.

"Callin you what, son?" Henry asked, gettin to his feet as well.

"*That!*" Raymond yelled, and *unbe-fackin-lievably*, he stepped forwards and squared up to Henry, crouchin so that his face was just a few inches away. In this gravelly, unfamiliar voice, the boy went, "No matter what you think you know about me, *you don't.*"

In silence, Henry stared back into the kid's tired-lookin eyes. He had wondered how long it would take for that slag of a mum of his to poke her nose in. Actin calm, Henry said, "Is there somethin that you wanna ask me, young Raymond?"

The boy's eyes were icy blue. For just a second, Henry felt sure that his son was gonna say somethin that was goin to *hurt him*. Unnerved, Henry said, "You're angry, an' you've got it into your head that I'm the cunt to blame. Well, that's fine. Get mad wiv me, if you need to. Throw a punch, if ya must. But this has bin for yer own good, an' one day you'll thank me for it."

"You don't own me."

Henry couldn't help but smirk. "So you say."

Raymond kept lookin at him wiv those bright blue, bloodshot peepers. The kid knew that somethin was changin between them – Henry was sure o' that – but it was as if he wanted to test his dad, see how far he could push him.

"Like I said before," Raymond went on, "I *will* be leaving Seadon soon. It'll take me a while to build up my account again, but I'm going, and there's nothing you can do to stop me."

Henry tried to stop himself but he couldn't – the mouthy little shit had pushed his buttons. "You ain't goin *nowhere*, you ungrateful sod. You think that me an' the boys would let that happen, after all you've seen? Do me a fackin favour, son."

"I told you not to call me that–"

"*I'll call you any-fackin-thing I want!*"

Henry bellowed, takin pleasure in the way the kid flushed. "I own this city. When I say 'jump', everyone asks 'how high?' The quicker you come to understand that, the better!" Henry lowered his tone. "Look, son. I've bin expectin this chat, an' we've both probly said things that we shouldn't have. Particularly you, eh? So how about we jus' go on as if none o' this had happened, eh? Ain't that for the best?"

A frown creased the boy's face, like he was holdin back anuvver tirade.

"Go on, Raymond. If you've got somethin important to unload, there's no time like the present. Ask me anythin."

The kid just stared back, half-grimacin, half-questionin.

"Come on," Henry pushed. "Why don't you ask me about your *mum*?"

Henry almost wanted everythin to be out in the open, but then from nowhere the tension left the kid's body. Raymond seemed to shrink back into himself, as if he'd remembered his place in the world.

"I should go," the boy said.

Although Ray's eyes pointed in Henry's direction, Henry had a feelin that they weren't lookin at him. The lad had bin defeated, shoved back into his rightful spot, an' Henry was safe again. He grinned. "Before ya go, Raymond, let's put this behind us. Come over an' give yer old man a hug."

The kid did as he was told.

"That's it, son," Henry muttered into his ear.

"Good lad."

Thomas

What's she doing here?

From the staircase, Thomas had to fight really really hard not to run. In all the years he had been looking after the children, he had never felt so confused and afraid. He understood who the red-haired man was – a 'scally', Ratan might have called him – but he wasn't sure why he was here. Instead of hurting Thomas as he probably deserved, the man was just focused on getting into Ratan's office.

But, even more head-spinning than the ginger guy, was the little girl with the blonde hair standing at the bottom of the stairs. Thomas had noticed her after the red-haired man had tried to bash the office door down, and Thomas was super-confused. How had she gotten there, all the way from the Gardden? The gunman hadn't even glanced her way. Thomas squinted down the steps, half-telling himself she wasn't there.

Gosh. Was this the start of The People Game?

"Just stand stock-still and don't move," the man said, focused on the locked office door.

The girl had moved to the first step, scratching her bright crown and looking perplexed. She began to climb, keeping her large eyes on the red-haired man, as if she had no interest in Thomas at all. Thomas whispered, "What are you doing here?"

Sounding irritated, the redhead guy said, "When I told you not to move, I meant for you to shut up, too." He inspected the crack between the lock and the doorframe. "Get back a bit, in case this bullet goes wrong."

"Are you going to shoot the lock?"

The man's fluffy red hair had started to sag. Sweaty strands plastered his cheeks. "Yes, I'm going to shoot the shitting lock."

To the little girl, Thomas breathed, "Can I get by, please?"

Soil clogged the creases of her blue dress, and smeary streaks trailed through her curly-wurly hair. She furrowed her brow.

The gunman turned back to Thomas and said, "I told you to get back."

"I'm trying," Thomas mewled.

With his eyes all thin and narrow, the man said, "Are you a bit...special?"

Thomas replied, "You can't see her, can you?"

"Who?" the man asked. He shook his head and faced away again, aiming the pistol at the door. "Fuckin' nutjob."

The little girl smiled at Thomas, finally acknowledging him. Her gums and teeth were spattery brown. Thomas backed against the wall with a low whimper and she went by to stand beside the gunman, craning her neck and looking him in the face.

"Right, brace yourself," the guy said.

Thomas had no time to block his ears. There was a thundercrack and splinters flew from the doorframe. The man's hands jerked and he winced, grabbing his right arm. He looked furious and wrenched the door handle. It wouldn't budge. The girl kept staring up at him, so close he could've bent down and kissed her muddy head.

Someone must have heard that.

When the redhead fired three more shots – BOOM BOOM BOOM – Thomas's ears began to ding-dong.

A twist of battered handle dropped to the stairs and fell downwards step-by-step, like a slinky. The guy turned and mouthed something to Thomas before heading inside, and the weeny blonde girl followed.

"Pardon?" Thomas asked.

The room was narrow, the only furniture a paper-sprayed desk with a chair on either side. The walls were coated with posters of movie killers. Everything smelled like coffee.

"I said, sit down and don't move," the man said. He put

down his rucksack, crouched to open it and pulled out a pair of handcuffs. "Got to make this quick."

"Ratan might be back soon. I think someone probably heard you shooting," Thomas said. "If you're going to tie me up, maybe you should wait until Ratan gets here too..."

"Don't tell me what to do, you fuckin' weirdo. Just get on the chair and keep your mouth shut."

Thomas took a seat and watched the little girl pace slow circles around the guy's legs, weaving and darting as if she was playing a game.

"Give me your arms," the man said, slotting his gun into his tracksuit trousers. He pulled Thomas's wrists backwards until they hurt and Thomas felt the cuffs close around them.

The guy scanned the floor. Weirdly, he lifted up the grey carpet near the wall and began to tappety-tap the boards, one by one. "If you know where the right spot is, you might as well tell me now."

The girl sat down cross-legged in the centre of the room, blank-faced but watching the man.

After a few minutes, the gunman squeaked like a guinea pig. A floorboard had shifted and he was trying to dislodge it. "You were right, Rebecca!" he said, beaming a yellow smile as he plucked the floorboard free. He reached inside and pulled out a clump of bank notes, his eyes bugging. "You seen this?" he asked Thomas. "I've never seen so much. Never in my life! *Woo hoo!*"

Thomas watched the man pull stack after stack from the hidden store and shove the money into his bag. He finally understood why it had been so important for the red-haired man to get into the office: he must have been waiting to get the money packed away in his bag first, and *then* he'd kill Thomas.

The blonde girl approached the hole and peered inside, her head once again only a few inches away from the gunman's.

"I'm sorry," Thomas mumbled, but maybe not loud enough for the gunman to hear.

It didn't take long for the man to fill his bag, zip up the rucksack and dangle it over his shoulder. Looking ultra-mega-pleased, he took the gun from his trousers and pointed it at Thomas again.

Thomas cringed and braced himself.

"Well, this has been fun," the ginger man chuckled. "But I'm off now."

"Just...just please please please make it quick," Thomas begged.

The red-haired guy frowned, then a grin spread across his face. "You think I'm going to *kill you?* Christ, fatty – I only want the money. But if you think I'm opening those cuffs before I go, you're wrong."

Surprised, Thomas asked, "How am I going to get out of here, then?"

"That's not my problem, I'm afraid," the guy replied. "But I can't let you call anyone just yet. Because if anyone comes after me, I'll shoot them right in their ugly face. Then, yeah, *then*, I'll hunt *you* down and kill *you*. And then I'll burn your house down and kill your family. And then I'll, like, shag their arses." He paused, as if he was wondering why he'd said that last part. Then he added, "Alright?"

Thomas nodded.

The man stared a second longer. "Okay then." He turned to leave.

As he did, Thomas noticed that the little blonde girl had gone. He leaned sideways and peeked through the doorway. Yep, vanished, just like water down a plughole.

"Must have just been curious," Thomas reasoned.

The man stopped at the door and asked, "What was that?"

Thomas shook his head, feeling dazed and ditzy. "I said that she must have just been curious, that's all."

"*Who* must have been curious? Who the hell have you been talking to?"

Thomas blinked. "Hanna."

The red-haired guy blinked too. Then he made a very strange face indeed.

CHAPTER 11
"The bastard had it coming"

Rebecca

After meeting Gary that morning, Rebecca had visited the hair salon to volumise her blonde hair and raise it into a miniature 50s-style beehive. Back at her apartment, she had used a natural mud facial before applying her makeup with the care and elegance of an artist. She had put on a short, tight silver dress and a pair of strappy black heels that drew her silk-smooth legs to points because she wanted Henry to want her – simply because it would make everything that followed even more sensational.

At the casino apartment, with Henry and Bruno spread together slothfully across the chaise longue, Rebecca had cleared the glass desk of paperwork, placed a tall candle at its centre, and cooked a fillet steak.

"Blimey, what did I do to deserve that

masterpiece, eh?" Henry asked after devouring the meal. He lay his knife and fork down with a clatter and belched, a trickle of beef juice traversing the slope of his chin.

"You deserve everything you get, my darling," Rebecca smiled, reaching across the table to stroke Henry's hands. "And I think that our four-legged friend enjoyed his food too, don't you?"

Bruno had fallen asleep in the corner of the room beside an empty, licked-clean plate.

"That I do, Bex; that I do." Henry appeared relaxed and content, as if Rebecca cooking him steak and herb-coated, pan-fried potatoes confirmed his supremacy over the Earth. He finished his Pinot Noir and smacked his lips, rising to his feet. "An' now I fancy some puddin'."

"Can't we share a little cognac first, darling? Or perhaps some coffee?"

Henry shook his head. "No. I'm done wiv food for the moment."

The question was, how long did Rebecca have?

"Come 'ere," Henry grunted.

Attempting to sound casual, Rebecca planted her chin onto a fist and flashed her eyes seductively. "Why don't you come here?"

She watched him angle his head, presumably wondering whether to grant her this minor submission. She could almost see his thoughts, picturing her spreadeagled on the bed, awaiting the intrusion of his canine counterpart.

Not this time, my sweet.

Shrugging, he approached and stroked her

cheek with a hairy knuckle. "It's been far too long since you've worn a dress like that, darlin'. Even Ronnie Kray couldn't 'ave resisted ya, an' he was a poof. Come 'ere, gimme a kiss."

"Where do you want me to kiss you?" she asked, struggling to think of a way to delay Henry's plans.

Henry's smile did not touch his eyes. "How about we have a few less questions?"

If only she knew how many minutes she needed to kill. She arose and obediently went to kiss Henry, but he simply looked at her, unreadable. Fear uncoiled in her stomach, but then he leaned down and met her lips, hard and hungry. He grabbed a clump of her beehive hair without regard for its craft, tugged her head back and dived down to kiss her again. She loathed him and wanted him ruined, crushed; smeared like a fly on a windshield. He had coerced her in the vilest manner to punish her for her infertility, or simply to revel in her discomfort. It was time to redress the balance – she just needed a little more time.

Henry took her by the wrist and dragged her across the room, suddenly breathing hard. Bruno looked up from his cushions, barked once, and got to his feet to stretch.

Rebecca had promised herself that she would never let the atrocity happen again, and that she would stop her dreams of the part-human, part-animal foetus. As Henry hauled her towards the bedroom, she imagined the black eyes of the beast from her nightmares glittering in the darkness of an unfamiliar corridor.

"Get in there and strip," Henry demanded, pushing her towards the bed before turning to the Great Dane. "Come on, Bruno, let's have some fun."

Rebecca's heart hammered. She did not attempt to undress. Somehow, the idea of one last encounter with the dog and his master was too obscene to bear. She watched through the doorway as Henry spoke excitedly to Bruno, who appeared to be swaying.

"You still half asleep, boy? Come on, wake up for daddy."

But the dog was clearly confused. He took several steps forwards, shaking his head with a snuffled complaint. Lacking coordination, the animal bumped into his master's leg.

"You alright, pal?" Henry asked, crouching down to meet Bruno's eyes. "Woss wrong wiv you, eh?"

Rebecca had realised her error. Research could only go so far, and she had failed to test her armoury. While Bruno may have been experiencing Rebecca's desired effect, Henry was his usual, bullying self. Panicking, she back away, around the bed and into the corner by the window.

Henry was still fussing over Bruno when he glanced up. "I told ya to strip, Bex, so fackin' strip."

Bruno was going to be inside her again soon, barking, slavering and thrusting painfully.

No, no, no...

"Did you hear me?" Henry shouted, with one hand on Bruno's crown and the other pointing angrily towards her. Bruno had straightened, and was looking at Rebecca with increased interest. "That's it, boy - we're goin' to have us a good time, aren't we?"

Bruno padded into the bedroom, butting the door wide and fixing Rebecca with a wet-eyed stare. No malice there; only dumb lust.

She whimpered and heard Henry laugh - actually laugh at her – as he followed his enormous dog inside. "Yeah, you're hungry for it, aren't ya, boy?" Then, to Rebecca, "Get on the bed and strip, Bex, before I knock you fackin' senseless."

Tears burned in her eyes; her carefully laid plan was a failure. Her breath caught and she knew that for the first time in years she was about to weep. She pushed herself against the wall as the dog plodded closer. Gary would be at the guesthouse soon, counting the money while Rebecca repeated the same hideous act she had vowed never to endure again.

"I won't tell you again, Bex," Henry warned, stepping towards her. "I'm just not going to go...to go...to the bed..."

In Rebecca's terror, the oddness of Henry's words did not immediately register – then Henry halted. He shook his head, just as the dog had moments earlier. Frowning, he stepped forwards once and then sideways twice.

Henry looked up, baffled, and then stormed towards her. "You better get on the bed Bex, coz you, shhhr... bare... the bare. Gerron the bare." He stopped, craned his neck upwards inquisitively, and then bellowed,

"Getttonthaaffffackiinbaaaaare!!!"

He clattered into the window frame. Bruno turned in alarm, barking as his master slid backwards down the wall. Rebecca became afraid that Bruno would turn on her, realising that Henry's condition was of her doing, but the Great Dane only shifted his bulk towards Henry to lap at his face. The dog whined in distress, but elation and relief caused Rebecca to laugh ecstatically.

"Are you alright, darling?" she cackled, wiping a tear away with her wrist. "What's wrong, my love? That wine seems to have gone straight to your head!"

Propped against the bedroom wall, Henry's eyes glazed over. Rebecca marvelled at how quickly he had transformed into this useless wreck. How many men had spiked their dates with similar ease, playing concerned boyfriends and helping their victims stagger from the bar, with pink flesh glistening in their minds?

Rebecca circled Henry, who twitched, clearly fighting the GHB now coursing through his blood. He pushed a hand into the floor and drew a leg up in an attempt to stand, looking so disorientated, so un-Henry, that Rebecca laughed once more.

"Oh, my dear Henry, you'll have to try harder than that," she chuckled.

Bruno nuzzled his master's face, but Henry batted the dog away.

"Yurra fucckkn bsshh..." he groaned, writhing spastically and striving to focus on her.

Rebecca took a pace forward, feeling her

sensuous dress slide across her skin, and glanced at Bruno. She couldn't resist, and drove a spiked stiletto heel into the side of Henry's cheek. The blow opened a gash less than an inch away from his eye and he toppled to his right, a dead weight.

My goodness that felt good!

Bruno released a volley of barks, baring his teeth. She leapt backwards and the dog calmed instantly, turning glumly back to his master.

"You can't slip to the land of dreams just yet, my sweet," Rebecca told Henry, brightly. She moved to his side. Bruno remained calm as she shook his master, who now appeared wholly incapacitated. "Wake up, my dear. Come on, there's fun to be had."

Henry's eyes fluttered open again, the wound leaking blood across his nose and forehead. "Whojju gunnadoo?"

She traced a line along the split skin in his cheek, reddening her finger. "I'm going to show you just how much fun your beloved pet can be."

Gary

"Who?" Gary asked, suddenly unable to step through the door.

"No one," Thomas replied from the office chair, like a naughty schoolboy who'd sworn in front of his teacher.

Gary wanted to leave, needed the ocean breeze cooling his red face. Rebecca would be at the guesthouse in less than an hour, but the name that

Thomas had spoken had hooked Gary's mind like a fish.

Thomas couldn't have meant Hanna. Not *Gary's* Hanna — not his little doll.

Gary's legs refused to move. "Who's Hanna?"

Thomas bit his lip.

"Answer me."

The fat man shook his head.

Gary crossed the room. "The sooner you tell me, the sooner I'll be out of here. So who's Hanna?"

"I can't say," Thomas whispered, looking away.

This guy was starting to give Gary the creeps. There was no way that this freak could be the cause of all his problems, but...

But he had to know for sure.

Seeing no other option, he took the gun from his pocket and crouched before Thomas. "Listen. When I came in here, there wasn't a chance in hell that I was going to use this thing on you. I still don't want to." He stroked the barrel, watching Thomas watch the pistol. Gary pressed the weapon against the other man's kneecap. "But seriously, if you don't answer me, I might shoot you. And if I blow a hole through your leg, you won't be able to walk properly, will you? No."

Thomas whimpered again, rattling the handcuffs against the chair.

"So who's Hanna?"

"Please don't shoot me," Thomas begged. Then, "I'm not supposed to say, but she lives in my garden and I look after her."

"Who does?"

When Thomas said nothing, Gary pushed the gun harder into his pudgy knee.

Leave now, you twat. Something isn't right here.

Panicking, Thomas said, "She lives in my garden with

the other two and we all play games together."

"Who is she, and why is she in your garden?"

Thomas's face twisted, and for the first time Gary saw beneath the fat man's 'little boy' mask. "She's with *me* now!" Thomas yelled suddenly. He thrashed against the cuffs. "We play together with Simon and Benny and we're fine just the way we are! So get out of here! *Get out! Get out get out get out-*"

"Are you talking about *my* Hanna?" Gary asked.

"She's not *yours* anymore!"

And for an instant, Gary forgot where he was and what he was doing. Tabloid headlines cut through him, sick phrases like 'sex slave' and 'child molestor'. News stories written about Hanna, his doll - his wonderful little daughter who had once loved to dance to the Chemical Brothers and watch Japanese cartoons and giggle at jokes that didn't make sense.

There had been media reports of every kind: tragic tales supporting Gary and Sandra; opinion pieces about what could have happened to Hanna; police updates; even something written by some bitch of a psychologist discussing how Gary and Sandra had behaved in front of the news cameras, searching for signs of their guilt.

Gary rose unsteadily to his feet.

Thomas, big doughy eyes in a big doughy face, said, "She's happier now..."

The room was scorching. Gary needed time. He wanted to feel the wind but he had to know what the hell this man had done to Hanna.

Picturing his little doll's beaming, precious face, Gary lowered the gun and said, "Let's go for a ride."

Ray

As Ray paced through Seadon's busy high street, past jeering Neanderthals and hot-bodied flakes, the sun roasted his pale skin without mercy.

Something had to happen. He was no longer at ease with his mother, with Henry, with his work. He ripped off his tie and tossed it to the ground as he walked.

It's fine.

He ignored an image of Henry laughing and calling him 'son'. He tried not to see the swamp of pale, empty-headed arseholes that sloshed and burbled on his every side, hungry for coke, booze and brawls. He blanked the tacky stores and stalls bordering the wide street, flogging their beach towels, rock candy and t-shirts that read "Pervert" and "Fancy a Felch?"

It's fine.

Seadon was diseased. The rows of shitty shops were sores, the tourists were lepers, and the buskers sang sick odes to the city's pestilence.

Another image flickered: the unclothed crowd of ghouls, their eyes black, beckoning him... where?

Ray found himself heading towards The Green Emporium. The crowds opened briefly before him and he saw the shop's door closed. The shop became muggy and uncomfortably hot on a day like today, so why the hell would Thomas keep the fresh air from wafting inside?

From a few stores away, the Green Emporium appeared empty to Ray. A guy dressed as a purple fairy was checking out the goods through the window. Reaching the glass doorway, with its sign claiming that the shop was open, Ray saw no one inside. He unlocked the door and entered a sweltering oven, feeling angry that Thomas had shut the store without consulting him. Such banality was a welcome distraction.

"Thomas, you in here?" he called, locking the door behind him. He needed to have words with the tubby little twit before they re-opened. Fuck it; maybe they'd just go the The Runway and drink for the rest of the day.

"Thomas!" he called.

Despite the stereo still playing Bob Marley, a stillness in the air suggested that the building was empty. A sour-scented patch of liquid had spread across the tiles near the till - remnants of some spillage from a careless tourist, no doubt. Behind the counter, Ray pulled the jack out of the MP3 player. Not only had Thomas left the shop without telling him, but he had also left the music playing, a spillage on the floor, the lights on, and the open sign in the doorway.

In the rear corridor, he looked up the stairs towards the office. His guts somersaulted: the door was open.

"No, no, no, no, no..." he chanted, climbing the stairs in leaps.

yes yes yes yes yes

The true horror of the abandoned shop awaited him inside the office. A carpet flap peeled back like a wound, a floorboard leaned against the wall, and the shadows beneath were empty. Ray's first panicked thought was to call Henry's flat, and only when the phone was ringing in his ear did he question what had happened.

Thomas knew nothing about the money. He couldn't have. Thomas was a straight-up oddball who gave off no hint of deception; there was just no way that he had played Ray like a fool.

When Henry didn't pick up, Ray dialled Thomas's house phone for the first time ever, and was promptly informed that the number wasn't recognised.

Fear rising, Ray tried Henry's mobile. It rang and went to answer machine. "Hello, Henry Borders here. If it's business you're ringin' about then don't leave a fackin' message, but if..."

"Fuck," Ray spat.

No matter what Henry had done to him, this was a disastrous development: three hundred and forty two thousand pounds in five grand stacks, *gone*.

Pacing the room, Ray called Henry again.

"Come on, come on."

Both Henry's mobile and the casino rang without reply.

Ray realised his only other option.

LOCKER

THE PAKI WAS THE THIRD TROUBLEMAKER THAT PERCY LOCKER HAD DONE IN A MONTH. THE BASTARD HAD IT COMING.

LOCKER'S WORKROOM WAS ABOUT THE SIZE OF A TYPICAL GARAGE. LOW CEILING. SOUNDPROOFED DOOR. ONCE LOCKER HAD STARTED EARNING DECENT CASH A FEW YEARS BACK, HE'D BOUGHT A HOUSE AND HAD ONE OF HENRY'S BUILDER CONTACTS DIG OUT AN UNDERGROUND SECTION IN HIS GARDEN. WHEN IT WAS FINISHED, LOCKER HAD BOUGHT AND MODIFIED SOME TOOLS UNTIL THEY FELT LIKE GOOD FRIENDS. ALTHOUGH LOCKER SOMETIMES STRUGGLED WITH WORDS, HE'D ALWAYS BEEN GOOD WITH HIS HANDS, AND AFTER HE'D BUILT A COLLECTION OF THESE SPECIAL TOOLS HE'D GIVEN EACH GLEAMING FRIEND ITS OWN NAME.

NOW, WEARING JUST HIS BOXERS, LOCKER CIRCLED THE KNEELING PAKI. SAVOURED THE SHADOWS PLAYING ACROSS THE MAN'S NAKED FORM. HIS NAME WAS EITHER MUMBY OR MOMBY. OBVIOUSLY WORKED OUT, BUT NEEDED MORE PROTEIN. TANNED SKIN WRAPPED AROUND WIRY BICEPS. THE PRICK'S ARMS WERE IN A 'V' SHAPE, TIED BY BELTS AND SPREAD TOWARDS OPPOSITE SIDES OF THE WORKROOM'S DARK, STREAKED TABLE. THE SIDE OF HIS FACE PRESSED AGAINST THE WOOD. HIS THIGHS WERE SPREAD OPEN AND STRAPPED TO OPPOSING TABLE LEGS. BARE ARSE CHEEKS TENSED TIGHT.

MUMBY HADN'T SCREAMED WHEN LOCKER HAD AMBUSHED HIM AT HIS HOME, KNOCKED HIM UNCONSCIOUS AND

BUNDLED HIM INTO THE BOOT OF THE 4X4. EVEN STAYED QUIET WHEN LOCKER UNLOADED HIM IN THE GARAGE, CARRIED HIM DOWNSTAIRS AND SECURED HIM IN THE WORKROOM. THE GUY WAS TOUGH, BUT WHEN LOCKER SWUNG THE MALLET – WHICH HE'D CHRISTENED GEOFF - DOWN ONTO HIS THICK, BROWN HAND, THE CUNT SHRIEKED. SOUNDED LIKE A SKIDDING TYRE.

SATISFIED, LOCKER SAID, "I KNOW YOU WON'T SELL COKE IN SEADON ANYMORE, BUT THIS ISN'T FOR YOUR BENEFIT. YOU KNOW THAT, DON'T YOU?"

THE PAKI'S FACE HAD SCREWED UP LIKE PAPER, SILENT AGAIN. BRAVE LITTLE TURD, EVEN AFTER HIS LEFT HAND HAD BEEN BUG-CRUSHED. THAT BLOW WOULD'VE BEEN NASTY - LOCKER HAD SEEN IT BEFORE. IT'S NOT JUST THE PAIN. IT'S REALISING YOU AREN'T EVER GOING TO HOLD A SPOON OR OPEN A DOOR OR HAVE A WANK IN THE SAME WAY AGAIN.

"I'M DOING THIS FOR THE GUY WHO SUPPLIES YOU: MR HANCOCK," LOCKER CONTINUED. "MY BOSS WANTS HIM WARNED ABOUT WHAT'LL HAPPEN TO HIS *REAL* ASSOCIATES IF HE KEEPS THINGS UP."

MUMBY ROLLED HIS HEAD AGAINST THE WOOD. "I HARDLY KNOW HIM," HE GASPED, HIS MANGLED HAND OOZING A RED POOL ACROSS THE WOOD.

"'COURSE YOU DON'T KNOW HANCOCK. THAT'S WHY IT'S A WARNING, BUT NOT A MOVE AGAINST HIM," LOCKER SAID. "I'VE DONE TWO OTHERS LIKE YOU ALREADY THIS MONTH." HE DIPPED HIS HEAD SO THAT IT WAS JUST ABOVE THE GUY'S BROW. SNIFFED HIS VINEGARY HAIR. "MR HANCOCK CAN WORK ANY BUSINESS HE WANTS, BUT COCAINE BELONGS TO MY BOSS. NO ONE ELSE. I NEED YOU TO PASS ON THE MESSAGE." LOCKER SCRATCHED HIS CHEEK WITH GEOFF THE MALLET'S ROUGH METAL HEAD. "NOTHING PERSONAL."

LOCKER SAW THAT MUMBY UNDERSTOOD. USUALLY, THEY'D BE BEGGING AFTER AN INJURY LIKE THAT, BUT NOT THIS ONE. BRAVE LITTLE SHIT. LOCKER WOULD BREAK HIM, THOUGH.

ALWAYS DID.

"WHAT ELSE DO YOU WANT?" MUMBY ASKED, HIS VOICE WAVERING.

LOCKER ALMOST RESPECTED HIM. "I'LL TELL YOU WHAT I'D LIKE TO DO. I'D LIKE TO INTRODUCE YOU TO SOME MORE OF MY FRIENDS."

THE PAKI STARED AT HIS SHATTERED HAND. THE THIRD KNUCKLE, WHITE AS A BROKEN PLATE, PEAKED OUT FROM THE RAW GASH.

"I'D LIKE YOU TO MEET DEXTER. HAVE HIM TAKE OFF A LAYER OR TWO. THEN I'D LET JACKSON HAVE A GO." LOCKER BEAMED AT THE THOUGHT. "I'D LET HIM BITE INTO YOU FOR A WHILE. THEN O'NEILL COULD SLOW THINGS DOWN. OPEN UP A SLOT HERE AND THERE. SEE WHAT'S INSIDE."

LOCKER WAS GETTING EXCITED. THE POETRY WAS COMING – HE COULD FEEL IT. MEMORIES CROSSED HIS VISION: BLOODSHED AND EXTRACTIONS, SORROW AND PAIN, VICTIMS PAYING HIM THEIR UNDIVIDED ATTENTION.

"THEN I'D LET DENNIS HAVE HIS FUN. LET HIS TEETH CHEW INTO YOU, DOWN INTO THE DARKNESS…"

LOCKER WAS LOSING HIMSELF. WITH VIOLENCE CAME THE RELEASE FROM ALL STRESS AND BULLSHIT, OFFERING HIM INSIGHTS THAT SANDED DOWN THE STUBBLES OF HIS LOW IQ. IT SHARPENED HIS INTELLECT AND WIDENED HIS BLINKERED LOGIC, OPENING THE DOORS THAT THIS AWFUL FUCKING WORLD ALWAYS SOUGHT TO KEEP CLOSED.

LOCKER LIKED THE POETRY.

STANDING STILL, LOCKER SHUT HIS EYES. FELT HIS CHEST FILL AND EMPTY. FOR THAT FLEETING INSTANT, HE WAS THE THINKER AND ARTIST HE ALWAYS COULD HAVE BEEN, AND AS HE MEDITATED, A FACE ROSE BEHIND HIS EYELIDS, BEAUTIFUL, BENIGN AND WISE, YET AS SOLID AS A MOUNTAINSIDE.

"HE UNDERSTANDS ONLY TOO WELL," LOCKER SAID. "HE KNOWS THAT HE WOULDN'T BE WHERE HE IS TODAY, IF NOT

FOR ME. EVERYONE DOES."

BUT THE FACE, NOBLE AND PROUD, THINNED AND PALED. SPROUTED FLUORESCENT HAIR, A NOSE THAT POINTED LIKE A BLADE, AND EYES THAT HAD DARKENED TO HOLES.

PERCY LOCKER RETURNED TO THE STEAMING HOT WORKROOM, AND THE POETRY SCAMPERED AWAY.

THE PAKI WAS MUTTERING TO HIMSELF LIKE A PENSIONER, BUT LOCKER SPOKE OVER HIM. "THE OTHER PAIR I MET THIS WEEK GAVE MR HANCOCK A SPECIAL GIFT, AND I'LL TELL YOU WHAT. BECAUSE YOU HAVEN'T KICKED UP TOO MUCH FUSS, I'LL GIVE YOU A CHOICE."

MUMBY RAISED HIS HEAD.

"WHAT?" THE PAKI ASKED. HOPE IN HIS VOICE.

LOCKER SMILED. "WHICH ONE DO YOU WANT TO LOSE - YOUR LEFT BOLLOCK OR YOUR RIGHT?"

FINALLY, THE PAKI BEGAN TO PLEAD.

LOCKER LOOKED TO THE CEILING AND SLOWLY SHOOK HIS HEAD. THEY ALL SQUEALED LIKE PIGS IN THE END. ALL BEGGED, ALL WEPT, BUT IT DIDN'T HELP A SINGLE ONE OF THEM.

HE STEPPED AROUND THE TABLE AND CROUCHED DOWN BEHIND HIS CAPTIVE. THE PAKI WAS WELL-PACKAGED: HAD A BALL-SACK LIKE TWO FAT PEACHES. WHEN PERCY REACHED AROUND WITH HIS LEFT HAND AND TOOK HOLD OF THE GUY'S THICK COCK AT ITS ROOT, MUMBY WHIMPERED LIKE A KID. WITH HIS FREE HAND, LOCKER KNOCKED GEOFF THE MALLET INTO THE BACK OF HIS HEAD. HARD ENOUGH TO SHUT HIM UP, BUT LIGHT ENOUGH TO KEEP HIM AWAKE.

STILL GRIPPING THE MAN'S COCK, LOCKER DROPPED GEOFF. TURNED TO A WALL-MOUNTED SHELF AND PICKED UP A THIN, CURVED INSTRUMENT.

THE POETRY APPROACHED AGAIN. CALM AWARENESS HOVERED ABOVE LOCKER LIKE A CLOUD. IT WOULD SOON BURST OPEN, AND OUT WOULD CASCADE THE EXQUISITE DEXTROUSNESS OF THOUGHT, EXPANSIVE, TORRENTIAL...

A BLEEPING RANG DULLY FROM LOCKER'S TROUSERS, FOLDED BESIDE THE DOOR. "FUCKING *SHITE*," HE SPAT, STANDING UP AND WIPING HIS HANDS ON A CLOTH.

THE PAKI MOANED SOFTLY.

"*SHUT THE FUCK UP*," LOCKER SNAPPED.

THE PHONE'S SCREEN READ 'GOTH CUNT'.

INTRIGUED, LOCKER ANSWERED WITH AN EXPRESSIONLESS, "HELLO."

"PERCY." THE KID WAS PANTING. "I'VE GOT... QUITE A BIG SITUATION."

"HAVE YOU," LOCKER BREATHED.

LANKY POOF MUST HAVE BROKEN A FINGERNAIL.

"I'M AT THE SHOP. I CAN'T GET HOLD OF HENRY."

LOCKER RUBBED THE BACK OF HIS HAND ACROSS HIS CHIN. "I'M IN THE MIDDLE OF SOMETHING. JUST KEEP CALLING THE BOSS. HE'LL..."

"THE STASH HAS GONE. SOMEONE'S TAKEN IT."

LOCKER HAD TO STOP HIMSELF FROM LAUGHING - THAT *WAS* BIG. HE GLANCED AT THE DAZED FIGURE A FEW FEET AWAY, WITH ITS BLEEDING HAND AND TIGHT ARSE. "ANYONE ELSE WITH YOU?"

"NO ONE. THE PLACE WAS CLOSED AND EMPTY WHEN I GOT BACK."

LOCKER SIGHED.

"WAIT THERE," HE GRUNTED, ANNOYED AT THE KID HAVING INTERRUPTED HIM, YET AGAIN. DROPPED THE MOBILE BACK ONTO THE PILE OF CLOTHES. RETURNED TO MUMBY, WHO GAZED UP AT HIM WITH ROLLING, PAIN-FILLED EYES, RUINED HAND SPAZZING AGAINST THE TABLE.

"PLEASE." THE PAKI SOUNDED DRUNK. "I'LL DO ANYTHING..."

"LOOKS LIKE YOU'VE HAD A LUCKY ESCAPE," LOCKER GRUMBLED.

MUMBY'S PUPILS RE-FOCUSED. RELIEF TOUCHED HIS FACE. *I'LL GET TO KEEP MY KNACKERS*, HE SEEMED TO REALISE. *THIS*

WAS JUST A NARROW ESCAPE, AND EVERYTHING'S GOING TO BE OKAY - PRAISE ALLAH!

LOCKER ALMOST SNICKERED. "NO. THAT WAS A JOKE. I'LL JUST HAVE TO BE QUICK."

HE KNELT BEHIND MUMBY, KNEES ON EACH SIDE OF HIS LOWER LEGS, CROTCH AGAINST HIS ARSE. PICKED UP THE TOOL FROM THE SHELF AGAIN AND HELD IT UP. "THIS IS ONE OF MY VERY BEST FRIENDS. HE'S CALLED ALFIE." LOCKER SQUEEZED THE HANDLE LIGHTLY. A BLADE JUTTED OUT FROM THE END. WHEN HE TIGHTENED HIS GRIP, IT SPLIT INTO TWO AND FLASHED OPEN, LIKE A PAIR OF SCISSORS WITH RUBBER PADS AT THEIR TIPS. HE LOOSENED HIS FINGERS AND THE BLADES CONNECTED AGAIN, CLOSING WITH A CLICK AND RETURNING TO THE HANDLE. "STAB, SPREAD, AND GRAB," LOCKER EXPLAINED.

MUMBY BEGAN TO SQUEAL, STRUGGLING AGAINST THE BELTS. WASN'T GOING ANYWHERE, THOUGH.

THERE WAS WASN'T MUCH OF THE POETRY TO SQUEEZE FROM A RUSHED JOB. WITH HIS CHIN RESTING ON THE PAKI'S SHOULDER, IT TOOK LOCKER JUST SECONDS TO PUSH ALFIE INTO HIS CAPTIVE'S FUZZY SCROTUM, AND FOR HIS TOOL AND FRIEND TO GRASP ITS PRIZE. AMONGST HOPELESS, SHAMEFUL SOBBING, LOCKER HELD A GRISTLY LUMP OUT IN FRONT OF THEM, BETWEEN THUMB AND FOREFINGER.

HE SPOKE INTO THE PAKI'S EAR. "THIS ISN'T YOURS ANYMORE. IT'S MR HANCOCK'S, AND YOU'RE GOING TO GIVE IT TO HIM." HE LEANED IN CLOSE ENOUGH TO KISS THE CUNT'S CHEEK. "AND WHEN WE MEET AGAIN, IF I FIND MORE THAN ONE BOLLOCK IN THAT BALLBAG OF YOURS, I'LL TAKE THE WHOLE FUCKING THING."

Gary

The scenery passed in a blur of cornfields and tall, green hills.

One half of Gary wanted the fat man beside him dead already, shot and killed and sent spinning out of the rent-a-car to burst apart beneath the tyres – but the other half needed to understand.

Thomas sat cuffed in the passenger seat, spouting nonsense: *"Don't do this, please don't do this Simon said I have to play The People Game but I don't want to coz I want everything to stay just as it is but the children can do anything at all anything at all anything at all ..."*

Gary had given up telling him to stop, and had managed to fade the sound out like white noise from a TV. This man had snatched Hanna - Gary knew it, didn't he? He wanted to unleash months of helpless rage onto the paedo cunt, but to stop himself doing just that he drove the hired blue Ford Ka much faster than he should have.

He kept seeing the expression that had broken out across Thomas's face, back at the shop.

She's not yours anymore!

Maybe all this explained the dreams Gary had been having about Hanna, the ones where she'd had cold, black eyes. Maybe the universe had been preparing him for what he was about to learn.

The fatty had said that he lived alone, except for 'the children' who were in his garden. He could've been lying of course, but the shop hadn't been the right place for an interrogation. Years of tabloid reading had painted a picture in Gary's mind: a stinking shed, half-buried by bushes. His starving young daughter shackled by filthy chains. There, each day for the last eight months, Gary's little doll had waited for her fat jailer to come home and talk to her again, to feed her scraps and play games with her.

Games.

Gary's brain boiled. Before he let the violence take control, though, he had to know what had become of his daughter, who had once changed him for the better.

Their drive lasted just a few minutes before the city shrank in the rear view mirror and the woodland surrounding Thomas's house rose ahead of them. Gary knew the building by sight, having ridden the bus past it a few times on his way to parties. It was such a weird-looking place that most people in Seadon probably knew it. Kids probably said it was haunted and dared each other to touch the walls, not knowing that men can be more dangerous than imaginary ghosts.

Gary brought the car back to a reasonable pace, relieved that his speed hadn't attracted any police. He slowed further and cornered the bend. Down a short, sunless dirt track, the farmhouse stood partly hidden by shade and ugly, creeping vines. Three storeys high and ten or so windows long, the dusty glass and peeling paint made the place look derelict.

What a shit-hole.

Gary pulled up. If this guy really lived alone, it made sense that the maintenance of the place had gone to hell. One of the windows up top was cracked like a spiderweb. A bunch of roof tiles had fallen off. The front entrance was crowded with weeds and spiky-looking foliage.

Gary glanced at his passenger, who seemed to be sweating from every pore. The guy was still gabbling, tripping over his words.

"...I've never had this before, I don't know what they will do because you're not supposed to be here, I'm not even supposed to be here but I am, I look after them and play their games and I've always done my best but you shouldn't do this, you-"

Gary gave him a hard, open-handed pelt to the mouth. "You'd better cut that shit out," he warned. "I know what what you've done, and you're gonna suffer. There's worse things than prison, you know that? Worse stuff than getting fucked in the showers." Gary felt his face crease miserably but he got a grip, just in time. "Whatever, mate – I'm Hanna's dad. Do you even know what that means?"

Thomas said, "I didn't have a choice. They made me do it."

Gary wanted to slaughter the fucker. "Just take me to the kids." He got out, gripping the gun. His muscles shivered with adrenaline as he circled the car and yanked open Thomas's door. "Get out."

Thomas shifted his legs sideways but his cuffed hands, still behind him, made getting out of his seat a struggle. Gary grabbed a greasy clump of his hair and pulled him headfirst from the vehicle. With his wrists bound, Thomas couldn't balance. He dropped forwards onto the dirt. His guts weren't large enough to stop his head slamming into the stones. Gary swung a kick into his throat, then another into his kidneys. Thomas squawked, whimpered, and flopped onto his side.

"How do you like it?" Gary yelled. "Nice, is it? Nice feeling everything turn on its fucking head?" He booted Thomas again, relishing the sound of the air shooting from his fat fucking mouth. "Shit – you think I'm gonna stop, don't you? Whatever, mate. Fucking whatever." He punted Thomas in the stomach. "Just get up and get moving."

It was wishful thinking. Even if Thomas hadn't been reduced to a weeping heap of snot and tears, his enormous belly and disabled arms stopped him standing up by himself. Gary took the keys from his pocket and said, "If you do *anything* that I don't like, I'll kill you. I'll do it in a blink. Seriously."

As Gary unlatched the cuffs, Thomas spoke through a mouth smudged with dirt and a couple of spots of blood. "This is what Simon meant when he said that people were coming. This is The People Game."

Gary asked, "Who *is* Simon? Is he in the house?"

Freed, Thomas rolled onto his back, wheezing. To Gary's revulsion, through the smears of grey and red, Thomas grinned. "Simon's in the garden," he said, sounding spiteful. "I don't think he's going to like you."

Gary aimed the gun at Thomas and said, "You might be right. Get to your feet."

As Thomas rose, Gary found himself thinking of Sandra. What had *she* been going through, while Gary had been out bingeing with his mates?

"Take me to Hanna," Gary said.

Thomas wiped the muck from his face and trudged towards the overgrown entrance, rubbing his neck. Thorned bushes grew from the grey borders of the farmhouse, and tufts of long grass and weeds wrestled up between the paving slabs, thickening as they approached the entrance. At the roof - way, way up - Gary could see stray branches reaching down over the splintered guttering.

Branches from the garden out back?

There was also a buzzing, grinding noise from somewhere closeby, but as Thomas fished a key from his pocket and pushed it into the lock, the drone seemed to stop.

Gary watched the scabbed door swing backwards and a stink like sour milk gusted out. "Jesus...what's that smell?"

Thomas turned back dreamily and asked, "What smell?"

Gary covered his nose with his wrist. "Just keep moving and get me to Hanna."

Rebecca

According to her research, Henry was likely to remain unconscious for at least an hour. Rebecca allowed herself a moment to breathe. She had plenty of time to fulfil her plan and intended to leave the apartment long before Henry awoke wondering why he was in such pain.

When she went to her dainty leather handbag in the lounge room, Henry's smartphone rang and vibrated on the glass table. She ignored it and from her pouch removed her own mobile before returning to the bedroom. After selecting the 'videocamera' function, which shot wondrously clear HD footage, Rebecca recorded Bruno solemnly licking his master's face.

"Once upon a time," she said as she filmed. "There was a rich man who owned many castles, controlled scores of servants, cherished his obedient maiden and kept a ferocious dragon. He lived in a kingdom that he had long ago wrongfully laid claim to, and if anyone ever questioned his rule, he crushed them beneath his heel."

She stepped closer, framing Bruno's wet tongue wiping the crimson from Henry's skin.

"This phony king lived a life of luxury. When he stood before his subjects, he stood tall, stood proud, and never let anyone see his weaknesses. But behind the closed doors of his palace, he was confused, because he couldn't decide who he loved more - his maiden or his dragon."

Rebecca zoomed out until the phone's screen contained the whole of Bruno's bulk as well as Henry's slumped form.

"So one day," she continued. "The maiden gave the king a special gift: she cast a spell to make him drift into a deep slumber, and another to make his dragon fall deeply in love with him. After the king married his dragon, the maiden moved far, far away, and left the king and his pet alone to enjoy their love. And they all lived happily ever after."

Rebecca stopped filming and placed the phone onto the bedside cabinet. She turned her attention to the panting dog. "It's okay, boy." She placed a hand onto Bruno's skull. "He's just sleeping."

The animal's chocolate eyes glistened, as if he had been crying, and his ears hung low against his head. The well-groomed canine scent of him filled Rebecca's nose. In spite of the recurring nightmares and the revulsion the dog had caused her, she felt no animosity towards him.

"It's okay, ssshhh." She held the Great Dane's

head with gentle fingers and lifted his ear. In the voice of a wife explaining to her husband why she had to leave, Rebecca whispered, "We've had our ups and downs, haven't we? But I understand. You're just a cock on four legs instead of two, aren't you? And that's just the way you were made."

The dog seemed uncertain of where to look, as if her intimacy made him uncomfortable.

"You didn't know that what you were doing was wrong. You were just being loyal to your master."

She stroked Bruno's silken ears back. He liked that, and his attention appeared to drift from Henry.

"You're just like the rest of them, aren't you? Just want somewhere warm to put that thing between your thighs." She pulled Bruno's face to hers, as if eye contact would prove her sincerity. "And that's fine, because today you can try something new. I promise that it will bring you closer to your master – but you'll have to trust me."

Bruno had become aroused again. His limbs jittered and his sticky penis waggled, but, like a gentleman, he restrained himself. This was surprising because Rebecca had spiked the dog too, but with a rather different drug to Henry's GHB: Viagra.

Keeping her eyes on Bruno, she shuffled towards Henry on all fours. Henry snuffled, his eyes still closed. She shook him, just to make sure that he wasn't about to wake, and then began to move him. He was heavy, but determination *was a powerful catalyst. Bruno watched with curiosity, apparently less hungry for her body without Henry's encouragement.*

In usual circumstances, Rebecca's only exertion occurred when being vaginally plundered by Bruno, so it took her several minutes to heave Henry's body over just once. His face thudded against the carpet. It took great effort to shift his bulk across the floor, and by the time that she pulled the unconscious man's arms up onto the bed, her biceps were on fire. She knelt upon the sheets and looked over at Bruno, who now lay with his head to the ground, apparently bored by the proceedings.

"You'll be interested very soon," she reassured the beast. "You know that this is just a game, don't you? He wants you. He has always wanted you."

Henry muttered and Rebecca stiffened. His eyes remained closed. All was well – she had given him plenty of the GHB that Gary had sourced for her. Thankfully, Henry's unrefined palate had allowed her to pollute his wine with the salty solution without raising suspicion. He would not stir until after Bruno was finished - that was how date rape worked - and by then, Rebecca would have the precious video footage that would keep her safe from harm. In a note she had written the night before, Henry would soon be informed that if he ever had her pursued, his amusing little film would be distributed by an unnamed third party amongst his closest allies, thereby reducing his 'legendary' status to that of a joke.

Digging her knees into the bedsprings, Rebecca dragged Henry's hands towards her so that his arms stretched over the covers and his chin perched on the edge of the mattress. She tutted at the impracticality of forcing a dog to rape someone, but was now in the full swing of the chore. She climbed down and tugged at Henry's legs until, finally, he was propped up into the thoroughly appropriate 'doggy style' position.

"There, Bruno," she said, her chest heaving. "Doesn't he look lovely?"

The dog's ears flapped. He rose from the carpet, as if summoned.

"That's right, boy."

Rebecca opened the small bedside cabinet door and the furniture released a sweet, evocative stench. Inside, a kingsize jam jar stood, filled with the yellowish goo of Henry's preferred lubricant, a vile, Vaseline-and-KY amalgamation. She removed the jar, as well as a tin of luxury dog food bearing the picture of a happy, wet-nosed pooch.

She felt the sensation of being watched and swung her head towards Henry.

He was still motionless.

She turned the phone's videocamera back on and winked cheekily into its lens. Then she balanced it against a lamp perched on the cabinet so that it aimed directly at Bruno and Henry.

"Now, my little lovebirds, how about some foreplay? Are you hungry, boy?"

The Great Dane's tail began to wag, his

ridiculous member bobbing jauntily.

Rebecca snapped the ring pull and inhaled the aroma of the glistening chunks.

"Smells delicious!"

Bruno's pink tongue lolled from his mouth.

When Rebecca crouched and put the tin onto the floor beside Henry, Bruno instinctively moved towards it.

"Not yet!" Rebecca scolded playfully, pushing his head away from the can.

Prevented from eating, Bruno shifted himself mindlessly behind Rebecca. If she had been slower, the beast may have crushed her, but she managed to rest her hindquarters safely against the carpet.

Scowling, she turned back to Bruno and shook her head. "You and I are no longer lovers," she said, sternly. "You belong with your master."

She tugged Henry's belt free and wrestled with his trousers and underpants, then pulled both down to his knees and revealed his hairy backside. Henry drooled onto the bed, his breath coming in soft snorts.

"Lunchtime," Rebecca said, and scooped the cold meat and marrow out over Henry's buttocks. Some stuck to the base of his spine, some caught in his rear beard, and the rest fell between his calves and onto the carpet. Bruno lowered his head to the food on the floor, but Rebecca pushed his huge mouth towards the lumps caught between Henry's cheeks. After a moment's guilty pause, the dog began to eat. Rebecca wanted to applaud as she watched, but instead took her phone from the cabinet and

filmed the proceedings closely.

As the dog licked and swallowed, Rebecca tried to picture her new life. She would go far away, that much was clear, but would she learn the language of a new culture? Buy a property beside the sea, or overlooking a lush green forest? Would her new home have an apple orchard in the garden and a stone fireplace to heat the house in winter? The world seemed a much larger place after twenty years of having lived in the same cursed city.

Once Bruno had slurped all the meat from Henry's hirsute bottom, Henry's cheeks were slick with saliva and gravy. Bruno looked up. Tingling excitedly, Rebecca placed the phone back onto the cabinet so that it continued to hold Henry and the Great Dane in shot.

There was no way that a little soft rimming would open Henry wide enough for Bruno, so Rebecca dipped her hand into the lube. Under Bruno's gaze, she ran her fingers between Henry's furry crack to find the right spot, massaged the entrance and pushed a digit into the tight heat.

"Is that good for you, Henry?" she asked the comatose man.

A bubble formed between his lips and burst, becoming a single thread.

"I'll take that as a 'yes'."

Despite his obvious closeness to the animal, Rebecca liked to think that, in truth, Henry had never viewed Bruno as a lover. Theirs was the macho lust of two straight men spit-roasting a woman, sharing the mutual pleasure of using her body for their own enjoyment but never for hers. Perhaps they would even high-five as they pumped joyously away, but would never extend the act to the other man's body, never kiss stubble-to-stubble; such things were unthinkable. Threesomes with Rebecca and Bruno made Henry a pervert, yes, but still a man; this scenario would reduce him to the status of a 'faggot', a 'whore' - a 'woman'.

She tried inserting a second finger into the tight passage, found resistance, and added more of the yellow sauce. Henry's lungs crackled but Rebecca understood by now that she was safe. His phone rang in the lounge again.

Mimicking an operator, Rebecca said clearly, "Hello. We're sorry; Henry is about to be ravished by a Great Dane, so please leave a message." She met the dog's eyes, opening Henry's back passage with scissoring fingers. "Now, Bruno, I know you must have reservations, but you have to trust me."

Bruno was inches away from her face, and when she took his penis in her free hand the Great Dane yelped but stood firm. Rebecca had learned from bitter experience that Bruno, and presumably all dogs, did not enter his mate erect. A small bone in his length allowed him ingress, but it was only as he thrust that he became engorged. She had been careful not to let Bruno thrust too deeply for too long, fearing that the tennis-ball-sized bulb at the base of his erection would damage her insides. It was as close to "safe sex" as Henry allowed.

Rebecca ran her slick fingers against Bruno's

nostrils. "Smells good doesn't he?"

Bruno hesitated as she tried to drag him into position behind Henry, but the dog soon understood; his owner had taught him well. Rebecca pushed Bruno's front quarters upwards to signal him rise to the bed. In a lolloping bound, Bruno heaved his front legs up onto the mattress, with one on either side of Henry's outstretched arms. When Bruno rested his torso against his master's spine, his lower jaw bumped Henry's skull.

Now that the she had them correctly posed, Rebecca gripped Bruno's shaft and pulled it towards Henry. The dog's legs shuddered as the deformed summit of his phallus nudged Henry's puckered opening. Keeping one hand between the eager dog's legs, Rebecca outstretched the other towards her phone on the cabinet in order to capture a close-up of the initial penetration. She could not quite reach, so she released Bruno for a moment.

A mistake.

The dog lunged forwards and in one forceful stroke, he entered his master all the way to the root. A wretched, inhuman shriek filled the air.

Rebecca fell back, astonished. While the scream rose to a peak she sat uncomprehending, limbs stiff with shock.

Sleeping Beauty awakens.

The dog frantically pumped his hips, and Henry howled, "Wosssssssss goinnnnnnnnn onnnnnnnnnn?"

Henry's arms whirred into life and his face ballooned red, the veins on his neck protruding *like worms. Bruno hammered behind him and Henry tried to claw himself up onto the bed, and the pair seemed like some part-human Cerberus tearing itself in two. Barking, Bruno fell sideways, pulling Henry with him. Henry's scream became a disbelieving gasp, and for a second he was still, clutching the bed for support. His eyes crawled to Rebecca, and he begged, "Help me."*

Rebecca marvelled at what perfect footage the surreal deflowering made. She scrabbled for the phone. Mad laughter rose inside her as she filmed, the sheer joy of her abuser's abuse eclipsing her concerns.

Bruno's movements became frenzied and the pair slipped sideways to the floor, where Henry was spooned by the humping dog. Henry dropped his hands to the carpet and tried to drag himself away from the organ he was impaled upon, digging his nails into the floor for purchase. The dog kept thrusting but with a burst of energy, Henry wrenched himself forwards with a gurgled cry. There was a vicious squelch as anus and grotesque erection came partially dislodged, and Henry's voice climbed horrifically high.

Like a documentarian shooting a dangerous natural disaster, Rebecca kept filming.

Bruno, enslaved by the point of no return, still pistoned his hips even as his master tore free with a sound that made Rebecca's stomach overturn. Suddenly Henry was on his knees, inches of rectum protruding from his violated hole like a deflated pink balloon. Gasping wordlessly, some trace of understanding appeared to run through him. He turned a drunken half-circle, tore open the bedside cabinet drawer and withdrew something small and dark.

Rebecca sprang for the door. Henry's gun exploded as Rebecca reached the relative safety of the lounge. Something yelped and then moaned behind her, but in the wake of the gunfire came sounds that signalled Henry's pursuit.

This is when I'll die, she thought vaguely as she hurried towards the stairs that led to the apartment door, anticipating the white hot impact of a bullet. Without thinking she tore a high heel from her foot to help her run, but balancing on the other ankle caused her second shoe to topple and twist. She almost collapsed in pain, but Henry's staggered footsteps and a second gunshot kept her moving. As she hobbled towards the staircase that would lead to her escape, Rebecca turned back once. Her ex-lover had entered the lounge, pants around his ankles, face a bleeding calamity, and freckled, skinny penis batting from thigh to thigh.

"Come 'ere you facking shllaaag!!" he raged.

A third thunder-crack and a hole appeared in the wall to her side. She reached the top of the stairs, shoeless but alive, and caught a glimpse of Henry's blur-eyed, red-faced apparition overturning the glass desk. In a flare of agony, a fourth shot shredded the flesh of Rebecca's bare arm. She cried out but battered a path down the stairs, determined to survive.

And still he came.

His garbled fury followed her down the staircase as she pressed the button to release the door. A fifth shot but no more pain, and she found herself limping towards the staff area of the casino. A rapid series of thumps came from the stairwell and then Henry was groaning behind her, far closer than he should have been. She turned again – couldn't stop herself - and Henry was at the bottom of the steps, trouserless but pointing his gun.

Rebecca slammed open the double doors to take her to the staff area. A middle-aged man stepped out of a canteen to her right.

"Get her!" Henry bellowed, and there was another shot.

The bullet found the immigrant's stomach and he buckled, wearing a look of disbelief.

Rebecca ran.

CHAPTER 12
"They have entered a belly"

Gary

From the doorstep, the hallway looked to Gary like a little kid had decorated it.

Jesus.

He stepped inside and –

- sees posters of cartoons and movie characters coating the flaked walls, crawling with brown and green mould. Spider webs fill every corner while grime covers the bannisters and skirting boards. Thomas wades though a pile of unopened cardboard packages and Gary follows, holding his breath against the rank air.

A high, carpetless corridor leads thirty feet towards a kitchen. To their left there's a closed door but through a split in the wood Gary can see rows of picturebooks in the next room. Bare wooden stairs climb up to what looks like a huge first floor landing. Gary's pretty sure that whatever is giving off the stomach-turning smell is up there, and he prays that whatever it is has nothing to do with his little doll.

Their footsteps echo as Thomas takes them to the kitchen. Gary cringes when he sees the lightshade hung above him, patterned with characters from a children's TV show called "Action Dan". Hanna had loved that programme, especially when Action Dan was pummelled by the bad guys. Gary had often sat with her, enjoying his little doll's giggles and gasps.

He'd been so proud watching her learn, seeing her grow into a curious, tottering toddler, then a girl of nursery age (already with her daddy's potty-mouth), then a petite, confident schoolgirl, and then ...

An empty bed. A hole in his marriage.

Gary's legs feel as though they're going to give way.

"No," he mutters.

"What?" Thomas asks, entering the dim, neglected kitchen.

"*YOU SHUT YOUR MOUTH AND KEEP WALKING!*" Gary wails, swinging the gun. "*HANNA! WHERE ARE YOU? I'M COMING!*"

"I'm sure they already know you're here," Thomas mumbles.

Gary clubs his shoulder with the butt of the gun, satisfied with the dry thump. "I told you to keep quiet," he says, and Thomas cups his collarbone in silence.

Stacks of filthy plates bury the kitchen's ancient-looking stove; scraps of leftovers smear the tiles and counters; a lake of empty cans and plastic packaging covers the floor; a shallow pile of dead brown-and-black insects clogs the sink.

"Jesus fucking Christ, what's wrong with you?" Gary asks.

Through the window, a thick barrier of leaves and

branches shields the kitchen from sunlight.

"Out there?" Gary points towards the back door, struggling not to throw up. "Yes or no?"

"Yes."

"Then go."

Thomas licks his lips and hesitates, but then shakes his head and opens the door to the garden with a soft creak.

As the damp summer warmth drifts into the kitchen, Gary feels something tug in his chest. It's as if an invisible line attached to his ribs is pulling him through the doorway, and the feeling is almost painful for a moment. Gary could believe that something is drawing him into the garden. He pictures his little girl, but the way she appears in his dreams: pale, smiling angelically, but with eyes that are black and shadowed.

Gary isn't kidding himself – Hanna has to be dead. Standing there, looking through Thomas's doorway into a thick, green clump of leaves and rotten wood, he knows that everything is, and always will be, broken. He can't stop the words. "I was doing better when I had Hanna to care for." His voice trembles. "She was only five."

He imagines her - not the black-eyed girl from his dreams, but his daughter – wearing her cute blue party dress.

He won't cry.

He.

Won't.

Cry.

"I was only gone for a minute, for Christ's sake."

Paused in the doorway, the fat man turns back. "It was longer than that."

Gary sobs, like a hiccup. He wipes his eyes with the

back of his gun hand. Why is he opening up here and now, of all places? "I wasn't even scoring for myself. I'd stopped. I'd stopped because of *her* but I was doing a favour for a mate." He can't move; can't step outside into the heat. "I left Hanna in the park on the swing. I told her to stay there and she told me she would. She waved to me while she was swinging and I told her to hold on properly with both hands, and she said 'okay', and then I went."

The last time he'd seen his daughter she had been smiling in the drizzling rain of the empty Elwood Estate play park, still swinging one-handed, waving goodbye to him. He'd gone to pick up one measly wrap of speed for Daz, who'd said he'd needed it to work his night shift. Daz had begged Gary to help him out, and despite Gary saying that he was looking after Hanna and that he was off drugs for good, in the end he had given in. He'd never been any good at saying no to a mate, had he?

Gary sees her again, his little doll in her favourite blue dress that shimmered, even in dull weather.

Bye bye, daddy, see you in a little while...

Gary snaps, "Where's this Simon guy?"

"Simon's out here too," Thomas says, and passes through the doorway.

Gary crosses the boundary and walks behind Thomas towards the knotted forest. "And who *is* Simon?"

"He's another one of the children. The first. He's my..."

"So there's just kids out here?" Gary asks, trying to make out a path through the trees.

"Just children," Thomas says. Twigs snap drily as he slips beneath an archway of branches that Gary hadn't noticed a second before. "And the garden."

Gary searches the area, jerking the gun in different directions but seeing nothing bar trunks and green shadows. Insects chitter in the shadows, humming from both the air and the ground at their feet. The sound isn't high or intrusive, but for Gary it's somehow intimidating, like a giant struggling to hold its breath.

Wanting to break the quiet, Gary calls, "Hanna?"

The buzzing swells and Gary flinches.

"This way," Thomas says.

Gary is led through the trees and onto a narrow trail, and although the sun still boils above them the route is surprisingly dim. The trunks and branches seem to huddle closer the further they move into the tangle. "Hurry up," Gary says, but his throat is so dry that he can hardly even whisper.

"It's not far," Thomas replies.

Gary hears a sound like a child singing. When he turns towards the noise, the gnarled bark of a collapsed tree seems to grin at him.

I could really do with a fucking good line.

He resists taking the coke from his pocket, though.

Thomas halts at a narrow clearing and bows his head. To Gary, he looks like a condemned man waiting at the gallows.

"What are you doing?" Gary demands. "Take me to Hanna."

"She's here," Thomas breathes, like he's afraid of waking something. He turns from Gary towards a withered elm tree, then crouches his hefty bulk close to the floor. On his knees, he lays his hands against the leafy ground and speaks to the soil.

"I tried to stop him," Thomas says. "You know that I would never have asked anyone to come here. It wasn't supposed to be like this."

With a sickening rush, Gary lifts his hands to his mouth. It's like coming up on the worst trip he's ever known and he sucks in the stale woodland air, feeling unsteady and faint.

Hanna's down there, isn't she? My little doll's buried under my feet.

All the drugs, all the running, all the secret fucks, all the hopes and dreams and prayers for something better have brought Gary to Hanna's burial mound. A moan falls from his mouth. He knows that in a few moments he'll be punching, kicking and ripping at this child-man, this *child killer*, but for now, all Gary feels is self-pity.

He doesn't deserve this, does he? Sure, he's made his fair share of mistakes, but what father deserves to be taken to his child's grave by the piece of scum who'd murdered her?

The whole fucking world had conspired against him.

Thomas is still talking to the ground, begging it to believe him, when Gary leaps forwards and whips the gun barrel down onto the fat bastard's head. Thomas topples flat. The weapon flies from Gary's fingers but he lands on top of the fat man, throwing punches into his spine, kidneys, shoulders and face, drawing red tracks with his nails and screaming out for his little doll, his little girl Hanna.

"*I had gotten better!*" he shrieks. "*You killed her! You killed my baby!*"

Thomas makes no attempt to fight back, and soon Gary's fists and fingers ache with the effort of the attack. His final blow is a heavy, clumping slap to the back of Thomas's neck, and then he stops, his chest heaving, arms tight and drained. Gary collapses sideways and sees that Thomas's eyes have closed.

Spent, Gary drags himself across the ground and leans against the tree – Hanna's tombstone.

Thomas's face is a gore-streaked Hallowe'en mask. He appears to be weeping blood, his lips are torn and his nose looks broken. Gary notices that the garden's drone is rising, as though the insects, trees and bushes are as shocked as he is, and waiting to see what will happen next.

Yeah, keep watching.

It takes Gary a few minutes to compose himself. To his surprise, his first clear thoughts are of Sandra. Although he's partially responsible for what happened to Hanna, his wife can't be blamed at all, can she? The only reason that Sandra had placed their daughter into his care so regularly was because he couldn't hold onto a job. She'd had to work at that shitty café, hadn't she? Some horrible, overly-Christian coffee house that had paid her minimum wage for too many hours a week. While she'd slogged through the days serving drinks and cleaning, Gary had tried to raise their daughter responsibly, avoiding his old friends, drinking moderately, and trying to teach Hanna the lessons that Sandra would want her to learn. Sandra, always supportive, had taught Gary that there was more to life than friends and drugs. Between shifts, plus cooking and housework, she had even assured Gary that he was a good father. And then what had he done? He'd gone and proven her wrong.

Gary takes his mobile out from his pocket.

Sandra

After realising that her husband had taken their daughter's bag from her room, Sandra had enlisted help from the only source that she felt was capable of saving her.

Dear God, she had prayed, sat alone at the breakfast table surrounded by an uneaten breakfast, still stroking her lost child's silk-smooth yellow hat. *I know I've doubted you. In fact, to be honest, I still do, but I don't know where else to turn. Mum's not any good - she just tries to interfere, and blames Gary, and ... well, you know. Anyway, if you really are up there, and you really do care, please help me do what's best for my baby.* Sandra had opened her eyes, trying to discern what she was actually asking for before closing them again. *Give me the strength to face the future. Give me the power to become a mother again. Give Gary the wisdom to turn his back on the things that harm him. That harm us.* She opened her eyes, uncertain of whether to ask for what she truly desired. Screw it - if God sees fit to punish those who have done no wrong, then the least He can do is punish those who do. *And please, although I know that forgiveness is a virtue and all that – could you make the person who took my Hanna pay for their sins? Please. Thanks. Amen.*

Feeling better, Sandra had cleared the food and pottered around the flat, and then after lunch headed into town. Gary's assumption that she had been torturing herself with Hanna's bonnet had been incorrect, but she had reasoned that perhaps she should buy a brand new item for her unborn child; cement its presence in their lives and distinguish it as something way beyond a 'replacement' for Hanna.

No - not "it". Her.

It was when Sandra was standing beneath a

department store's blessedly cool fan, running her fingers across a cutesy bib that read, *"More please, mum!"* that her mobile phone rang in her bag. "Gary? Where are you?"

"Sandra," she heard him say, sounding weak, sucked dry.

"What's wrong?"

"Sandra. Something has happened."

"What? What's happened?"

He sounded hoarse. "I... I want to say that I'm sorry for everything I've ever done."

He's wasted, isn't he? He's been drinking with his stupid friend.

"Are you drunk?" she asked, her tone softening. There was no point in having an argument with him if he'd been drinking, especially when he was trying to apologise.

"Sandra, I've done many, many bad things, but I want to do better. I want to make up for everything." His voice was shaky, as though he had been sobbing. "I know you've heard this lots of times before, but I mean it now, and I'm not drunk, and I'm not too high."

Ah. There it is: chemicals, not booze.

"You're high? Oh, Gary."

"Yes, I've had a little something today," he said, but his voice remained even. "I've realised that I should have been supporting you, properly. That we should have been supporting each other. And now everything's going to change, Sandra."

She couldn't just listen to Gary criticising himself – he was too fragile. "Gary, you *have* been supporting me. In your own way."

"No I haven't," he said, firmly. He was usually so quick to take shelter behind her defences. "Not properly. And I've done so much worse, but I want to make things up to you. I want to get better again. Just like before."

Something in his tone made Sandra leave the shop, out into the crowded street and the sunshine. As they spoke, she followed a narrow alley away from the tourists. She emerged onto a path bordering a bowling green where a group of smartly dressed pensioners were playing. Sandra sat on a bench to watch the bowlers and, beyond them, the sapphire sea.

"Okay. So we still have problems," she admitted. "But how do you plan to 'get better'?"

"First of all, I've got a question," he said. "And I need you to be as honest as you can, okay?"

"Okay, Gary."

"Even after everything that's happened, everything I've done, do you still want to be with me?"

Without a pause, because she wanted nothing else, Sandra said, "Of course I do. Nothing's going to change that."

"Then let's move away."

Her breath snagged in her throat.

This again.

But she was desperate to believe him. She wanted to forget all the times he had let her down and just disappear with him. Surely people can change for good, can't they? Otherwise, what's the point?

Her husband continued, "If you really want things to work out for us, go to the estate agent right after this call and put the flat on sale."

Tears sprang to Sandra's eyes, and she was speechless. *He means it this time. He really does. Thank you, God...*

"We'll move away to anywhere you want, Sandra. Just say the word and we'll go."

"Oh Gary," she gasped. "I love you so much..."

"I love you too," Gary said, and she could tell that he

meant it. He remembered what their lives were once like, and he wanted to rebuild them.

"Okay then," Sandra said shakily, but there was joy in her voice. "If you really are sure, then I'll go and put it on sale right now."

"You do that. I've just got a couple of things I have to do before I come home, okay?"

"Okay." Sandra felt that it was her turn to spill some news. "Gary, I know that I should wait to tell you this, but you've made me so happy calling, and I think that, with God's will, you really mean it this time, so..."

"What is it?"

Sandra let her gaze trip across the wide sea's twinkling horizon. "I'm pregnant. We're going to have another baby."

"That's... that's amazing," he marvelled, and his reply was everything she needed. "What are we going to call it?"

"Oh, I don't know Gary," she told him. "We'll think of something when the time comes. I'm just over two months in, so we'll have her early next year."

"Her? How do you know it's a girl?"

"I can feel her already," Sandra explained, and she could. Inside her, she could already sense the tiny form of Hanna's sister. "I just know."

As if reading her thoughts, Gary said, "So if she was still with us, she would have had a sister. Our Hanna."

Upon hearing him speak the name that had been absent from their home for so long, Sandra finally felt the touch of God again; a warmth against her skin, deeper and more resonant than the sun itself. Gary meant every word. "What's happened, Gary?"

"I'll tell you when we're together again, okay? I'll tell you everything. We're going to leave this shitty place, and when we've had the baby we'll be a family again."

She sighed. "I believe you. I love you. How long will you be?"

"Just a short while. Go to the estate agents and I'll see you at the flat soon. Okay?"

"Okay. I'll see you soon."

When she returned the phone to her handbag, a smile, so foreign to her these days, spread across her face, briefly returning her to the woman she had been before tragedy intruded upon her simple, wonderful life.

Gary

Putting his phone away, Gary focuses on Thomas, on the hands that had snatched and killed his daughter.

An animal growl rises in him. He pictures Sandra in court, watching this sick fuck being led away to prison. No one would convict Gary in light of what had happened, would they? No jury in the world would fail to understand that he had simply lost his way after his young daughter's murder. And this scumbag would have it tough in prison, wouldn't he? Beatings, shanks, and violent rammings in the shower.

The truth is, Gary can't let a bunch of convicts have the joy of punishing this bastard. Shit, Hanna had been Gary's daughter, *his own flesh*, and Thomas had stolen her away. It should be Gary who made Thomas pay, and in the only way that he deserved: a life for a life.

Gary retrieves his weapon from the ground and crouches beside Thomas, who still isn't moving. "Wake up," he says, pushing the guy's bleeding face with the gun barrel. *"Wake the fuck up."*

Thomas's bloody eyes flicker open but he doesn't move, despite his awkward, sideways-twisted position. That feeling is with Gary again – the sense that the trees are watching him, waiting...testing him?

"I would like to torture you," Gary says, ignoring the forest. "I would like you burned, carved up, and cut apart slowly."

yes yes yes... slooooooowwwlllyyyy...

"But I don't have it in me. I can't go thr-... I can't put *Sandra* through a court case, listening to you spout off all the stuff that you did to my little doll. It just wouldn't be fair on her, so you die here. Now."

He shoves the gun between Thomas's lips with a wet clink. Thomas lets the metal pass between his teeth and meets Gary's eyes sadly.

Gary asks, "You got anything left to say?"

Past the gun, Thomas says, "Fi-muh here."

The sense of something watching Gary intensifies, a tingling rush like MDMA shivers but more powerful, looming over him, looming *behind him*.

Gary resists turning around, though. He pulls the gun back an inch from Thomas's lips to let the words escape. "What?"

Thomas's gaze drifts past Gary. "Simon's here."

Gary frowns, tensing his finger against the trigger. "Whatever, mate."

Then there's nothing but pain.

LOCKER

HE PARKED THE 4X4 AT THE BACK OF THE GREEN EMPORIUM. THE GOTH CUNT WAS PACING OUTSIDE, LOOKING GUTTED, AS IF SOMEONE HAD SMASHED HIS FAVOURITE MAKEUP KIT.

YOU'VE REALLY FUCKED THINGS UP, KID - DO YOU REALISE HOW BAD THIS IS?

LOCKER'S DAY HAD BRIGHTENED. SURE, HE'D BEEN DISTRACTED FROM THE POETRY HE WANTED FROM THE PAKI, BUT AT LEAST IT LOOKED LIKE THIS TRANNY FAGGOT'S DAYS AS TOP BOY WERE OVER. BEFORE HE COULD RELISH THAT, THOUGH, LOCKER WANTED TO KNOW WHO HAD THE BALLS TO STEAL SO MUCH FROM HIS BOSS. ONE OF HANCOCK'S LADS? A PIG ON HENRY'S PAYROLL?

LOCKER STEPPED DOWN FROM THE 4X4. "HEARD FROM HENRY YET?"

THE GOTH SHOOK HIS HEAD, LOOKING ABSOLUTELY FUCKING USELESS. DIDN'T MATTER THAT THE LAD HAD GOTTEN RID OF HIS POOFY DREADS AND HIS GIRLY CLOTHES; HE WAS AND ALWAYS WOULD BE A QUEER GOTH CUNT.

"LET'S SEE," LOCKER SAID, TREADING PAST THE GOTH AND INTO THE SHOP. HEAT SWALLOWED HIM, AND HE LOOSENED HIS SHIRT COLLAR.

"I CAME BACK FROM HENRY'S AND THE SHOP WAS EMPTY," THE KID EXPLAINED.

"WHO WAS LEFT IN CHARGE?" LOCKER ASKED, SCALING THE STAIRS TOWARDS THE OFFICE.

"A GUY CALLED THOMAS," RAY SAID AS HE FOLLOWED. "HE DIDN'T KNOW THERE WAS MONEY UP HERE. I THINK HE'S A BIT SIMPLE."

"BUT THE SHOP WAS CLOSED?" LOCKER SAID, STOPPING AT THE DOORWAY. HE INSPECTED THE HOLE WHERE THE HANDLE HAD BEEN.

"YOU MEAN, WAS IT LOCKED UP?" RAY ASKED. "YES."

LOCKER WENT INSIDE AND SAW THE GAP IN THE FLOOR. "YOU CALLED HIM YET?"

"THOMAS?"

"YEAH, THOMAS."

"YES, BUT THE NUMBER DIDN'T WORK."

LOCKER GRUNTED, THEN CLIMBED ONTO HIS KNEES AND USED A TORCH FROM HIS PHONE TO VIEW THE CRACK BETWEEN THE BOARDS.

"WHAT ARE WE GOING TO DO?"

AN IMAGE SLIPPED INTO LOCKER'S MIND: THE BOSS, SMILING AT HIM LIKE HE USED TO, BUT BENEATH THE SHADE OF A HUDDLE OF OLD TREES. "WE'LL GO AND SEE THIS THOMAS GUY," HE SAID, AND STRAIGHT AWAY –

YES YES YES YES YES

– LOCKER KNEW THAT IT WAS THE RIGHT DECISION. "WHERE DOES HE LIVE?"

"ON THE OUTSKIRTS, BUT IT'S NOT HIM; HE HAD NO IDEA WHAT WAS IN HERE."

LOCKER STOOD UP. THE SKINNY FUCK DESCENDED A FEW STEPS TO LET HIM INSPECT THE OFFICE DOOR. "MUST'VE BEEN A LOT OF GUNSHOTS. SMASHED THE HANDLE TO PIECES. MAYBE A STRUGGLE, BUT NO BLOOD AND NO ONE AROUND." LOCKER SNIFFED THE STUFFY AIR. "DOESN'T MAKE SENSE."

"I *KNOW* THAT. THAT'S WHAT I'M TELLING YOU. SO WHAT ARE WE GOING TO DO?"

"ALREADY SAID. GO AND SEE THOMAS."

"WELL HE'S NOT GOING TO BE AT *HOME*, IS HE? NO MATTER WHAT'S HAPPENED, THAT'S THE LAST PLACE HE'D BE, ISN'T IT?"

LOCKER LOOKED COOLLY AT THE PATRONISING LITTLE SHIT. SAW HIM SHRINK. NO MATTER HOW SMART HE SPOKE, THIS LITTLE SPASTIC WOULD SHIT A BRICK IF LOCKER WANTED HIM TO. THEY ALWAYS DID, AND THIS CROSS-DRESSER WASN'T SPECIAL, NO MATTER WHAT HENRY THOUGHT.

STILL PICTURING THE BOSS BECKONING FROM THE TREES, LOCKER SAID SIMPLY, "THERE'S NOTHING ELSE TO GO ON." HE PULLED HIS PHONE OUT. "I'LL CALL HENRY'S MOBILE, YOU CALL THE CASINO."

THE KID PUFFED OUT A BREATH, LIKE A PISSED OFF 5-YEAR-OLD.

LOCKER LISTENED TO HIS BOSS'S PHONE RING. HEARD, "'ELLO, HENRY BORDERS HERE, AN' IF IT'S BUSINESS YOU'RE RINGIN' ABOUT-"

HE HUNG UP AND SAW THAT THE GOTH CUNT WAS STILL LISTENING TO HIS OWN PHONE. "COULD'VE BEEN A BETTER FIRST MONTH FOR YOU, COULDN'T IT?" HE COMMENTED.

LOOK AT THAT PRICK: STANDING THERE, SWEATING HIS GUTS OUT HIS FACE, TRYING NOT TO BLUB. WHAT DID HENRY IMAGINE WAS IN HIM? WHATEVER IT WAS, LOCKER WOULD NEVER SEE IT. BUT AS MUCH AS HE WOULD HAVE LOVED TO HAVE DITCHED THE LITTLE QUEER, HE COULDN'T - IT'S NOT WHAT HENRY WOULD WANT, AND IT DIDN'T FEEL QUITE RIGHT.

"NO ONE'S PICKING UP. TIME TO MOVE," LOCKER TOLD HIM.

AS THEY HEADED OUT INTO THE BRIGHT BACK ALLEYWAY AGAIN, A REASSURING THOUGHT HIT PERCY LOCKER.

YOU'RE GOING TO GET IT TODAY, YOU LITTLE PRICK. I CAN FEEL IT.

Thomas

It's like the worst dream *ever*.

Lying flat and achey, Thomas gags when the gun metal hits the back of his throat. It tastes gross.

Perhaps this is what he deserves, though. For eight months, Thomas has tried to forget all about this red-haired, crazy-eyed man. After Thomas had hugged and hugged Hanna all those months ago, Simon and Benny had given Thomas an ickle bit of leeway. They had pestered him for so long about using the suitcase, but it had only been when they'd offered him a bargain – told him he could go out into the city and find himself a job, like a normal person – that Thomas had reluctantly agreed. Thomas had used the suitcase, Hanna had become the children's new friend, and Thomas had been allowed to start working at the Green Emporium.

Standing over Thomas with the stretchy-tall trees huddled around him, the gunman looks like he's going to keel over. He's soaked in sweat, his bobbly hair is strung together, and he's nibbling on his lower lip really really hard.

The children must be watching from nearby but, trapped under this man's gun, Thomas wants them to stay away.

Thomas is ready to go, because this red-haired man's super-sad sadness has made Thomas realise what he really is.

A slave.

A babysitter.

A horrid, mean man who took two children away from their mummies and daddies and killed them with his own pudgy hands.

Leave me be, Simon. Let Hanna's daddy do whatever he wants with me.

The gunman grips his weapon so tightly that it shakes against Thomas's teeth. For a micro-milisecond, he imagines what it might feel like if the man pulled the gun's tiny lever. Would it hurt? Would he taste the gunpowder when it ka-boomed a bullet straight through his spine?

The red-haired man breathes out purposefully. "You got anything to say?"

Before Thomas can answer, though, there's a movement in the trees. Behind the gunman a short, dark shape rises into the air, thin at first but then blooming and uncurling, slip-sliding from the ground like smoke.

Thomas sighs in disappointment and says simply, "Simon's here."

"What?" the guy asks, and pulls the gun barrel backwards an ickle bit. Behind him, the waist-high darkness is making way for patches of grey skin, a stained blue t-shirt, soil-smeared corduroys and a deepening scowl.

"Simon's here," Thomas repeats, but then the figure behind the gunman changes again. Simon's upper half lengthens, darkens, and black scribbles expand into a row of what looks like shadowy, reared-back tails. One snaps downwards, sticking into the gunman's wrist with the sound of a boot sinking into mud. His eyes roll upwards, and when his fingers spread wide the gun drops from Thomas's lips with a plop.

Simon's upper half has become a jumble of dark tentacles and tails, and the redhead's body jerks as these black threads dive-swoop into his cheeks, chest and arms. Some are as thick as slowworms and some as thin as hairs, and after a series of thuds each one attaches itself to the gunman. The man is still, his face and body trickling red streams from where the shadowed ropes have skewered him.

From the corner of Thomas's eye, a smaller shape appears, wearing a blue dress that wafts like sheets on a washing line. Hanna stands just inches away from her daddy's outstretched hands, but the man doesn't see a thing. Thomas first thinks that Hanna's face is straight because she's looking at her daddy and hiding how teary-sad she is, but that isn't right.

That's not her daddy. That's not his ickle girl.

This is a new and scary thought. If Hanna isn't the man's ickle girl, then maybe Hanna isn't Hanna. And if Hanna isn't Hanna, then maybe Simon isn't Simon, and... that's just something Thomas can't consider.

As quickly as the black serpents had appeared, they dissolve and flicker-fade. The ginger man's knees buckle. The tension in his arms softens like a melting Wham bar and he flumps to the Gardden floor. The smoky, faceless thing shrinks, folds up, gains colour and becomes Simon again.

Simon looks at Thomas accusingly. "You were going to let him kill you," he says. "You're a big fat scaredy-cat."

Benny steps out from behind the elm tree, red-faced, angry, fists bunched at his sides.

Hanna, as gaunt as Simon, turns to Thomas. "*You* did this. You hurt my daddy."

He's not your daddy.

But he must be.

Simon opens his mud-smudged mouth. "What do you think would have happened to us if you'd kicked the bucket?"

Thomas pulls his aching body up to a sitting position. He shakes his dizzy head. "I don't know."

"If you'd popped your clogs," Simon said, "There might never have been a People Game, and we'd have stayed here, all alone, with no one to look after us."

Benny sounds even more spiteful than usual. "You don't care though, do you, fatty? You can't *wait* to get away from us."

For the first time, Thomas considers the thought. If he really *did* leave, wouldn't there be people out there in the big wide world who would help him? Help him become "normal"?

"You would love that, would you?" Simon asks. "You'd hop and dance and spin all day, without us."

"No..."

"Yes you would, you stupid *shit*," Hanna rasps. "You *hate* taking care of us. You don't want to play games anymore. You want to vanish into *fat* air."

"That would be just fine," Simon adds. "We're bored of you anyway."

Simon's words are like stabby knives in Thomas's throat.

"You don't like our games, you always argue with us, and you want to disappear. You're no fun anymore, and that's why we've invited the other people along – to see if we can make some new friends."

Although Thomas wants to argue, to say that he's happy and wants to stay in the Gardden with the children forever, he remembers the misery on the red-haired man's face when he'd spoken about Hanna. Thomas recalls the ripped-up sound of the man's words, like the ghost of a voice that had drowned in its own tears. Thomas had never wanted to hurt anybody. He'd never wanted to use the suitcase. The children, the house, the Gardden had *made him do it.*

Thomas pleads suddenly, "Why couldn't you have just let the man do whatever he wanted with me? I just want to make up for everything. I just want something regular!"

"*I just want something regular*" Benny laughs, a grin spreading across his cruel face. "*I just want something regular.*"

Hanna giggles too, but Simon just says, "Well you can't, Thomas, and that's that. Mummy and daddy are gone. And until someone new comes along, we've only got *you* to take care of us, haven't we?"

"Yes," Thomas says.

"Yes," Simon agrees. "Before you go running off, though, think about this: do you *really* think that there's someone out there who will play with you like we do? Do you think that *anybody* out there will like you – a fatty-fat-fat who talks to the trees and kills ickle kiddies? Yeah right – they'll *burn* you!"

"Yeah!" Benny cheers, starting a little dance and pumping his fists in the air. "Burn him, burn him, burn him!"

Hanna smirks. "Shit, they'll need an awful lot of fuel..."

Thomas imagines a group of police officers tying him to a post and setting light to a pile of wood at his feet. "They...they might help me...you don't know..."

As soon as the words pop out of Thomas's mouth, he feels a tingling in his arms, a sting and a rise in temperature.

"Yes, Thomas," Simon says in a level voice, stepping towards him. "They'll burn you alive."

In sudden pain, Thomas rises to his feet. In the gloomy shade, his bare arms are reddening. "Stop it..."

"When they do it, you'll feel the blubber in your arms simmer and sizzle," Simon gloats. "Your hair will turn to smoke and your blood will bubble in your veins." Simon blinks, and when he opens his eyes again they're black – the black of the Gardden.

Although Thomas can't see any fire, his arm hairs are vanishing in patches, as if something invisible has singed them. "Simon, that hurts!"

Stopping in front of Thomas, Simon says, "It doesn't hurt as much as it will when they pour a bucket of petrol over your head and throw a match at you!"

Thomas scoots away from Simon and his sore spine bumps a tree. Blisters form across his wrists and the back of his hands, swelling like miniature balloons. He knows that if he keeps panicking or yells, Simon will make it worse, so, wincing and clenching his teeth, Thomas tries to sound calm. "Simon. Please make it stop."

Behind Simon, Benny and Hanna take each other by the hands and start twirling in circles, giggling to each other.

"Don't you like it, Thomas?" Simon asks. "This is what they'll do to you if you leave us – isn't it *fun?*"

A hot pustule on Thomas's forearm bursts, splashing his wrist and t-shirt, but not with pus; with warm blood. Others follow suit, throbbing with heat and popping messily. Thomas begs, "*Please!*"

"What's the matter, Thomas?" Simon asks, as Benny and Hanna spin dizzy-wizzily behind him. "I thought you didn't want to play The People Game? I thought you wanted 'something regular'? Well, out there, this is what's 'regular' for fatties who kill ickle kids. You should be *begging us* to let you stay."

With a *WHOOMF,* Thomas's hands burst into flames, and as the heat of his cooking skin hits his face, he shrieks, "*Okay okay okay! I'll play properly! I'll play The People Game!*"

The fire vanishes. The white sacs that had inflated and burst across Thomas's arms heal instantly, and the rusty blood staining his skin and clothes becomes see-through, like it had been nothing more than sweat all along.

"That's a good boy, Thomas," Simon purrs, and reaches

down to pat Thomas's head. His grey hands are cold against Thomas's flesh, a relief after the flames. "You shouldn't leave us, but if you insist, we're going to need someone new to play with."

"Simon, I'm not *going* to leave." But Thomas no longer feels so sure. Not long ago, he couldn't have imagined abandoning the children, the Gardden, but now it's as if he isn't just considering it, he's being *pushed*. Maybe the children *want* him gone.

But would Thomas be safe in the outside world? If he stayed out there for too long, would they use their special computers on him, the ones Thomas had seen in crime movies, which helped the police work out who the bad guys were? Thomas had done some very bad things in his life, so maybe he shouldn't be too hasty. "So," he says, rubbing his arms and leaning back against the tree. "How do I win The People Game?"

A sneaky grin spreads across Simon's face. Hanna and Benny stop spinning roundy-roundy-round and join Simon, one standing on either side. They are each suddenly wearing the same nasty smile, and all six of the dead children's eyes are as black as caves.

In unison, the trio tells Thomas, "You have to use the suitcase, again."

Ray

Locker hid his distaste for Ray like a fire behind the doors of a burning house, but Ray could feel it; its heat surged from him.

They drove in silence, with Locker's only movements being to check the rearview mirror. It was the first time Ray had ever been alone in the man's gruff company and, trying to be subtle, he found himself examining Locker.

Ray thought that such a head did not belong upon such an imposing body. His jawline was arrowlike yet somehow delicate, and muscles flexed constantly beneath his cheeks and bull neck. Softly tanned skin. Large lips, almost feminine. Blank grey eyes that reminded Ray of a statue's, and sideburns that were short and groomed. That morning, Locker must have shaven closely because he had left a tiny red nick upon the point of his chin.

"What?" Locker asked, steering the 4x4 gently around the out-of-city curve.

"What?" Ray asked back, innocently.

"You're staring."

"Sorry." Ray felt mortified that he'd been caught, so he quickly asked, "Has anything like this ever happened before? I mean, has anyone robbed this much from Henry?"

Locker's eyes remained on the road. "No. Anyone who tries stealing gets put under Henry's field. Just like Robbie."

The name jolted Ray.

"Still bothers you, doesn't it?" Locker said, with pleasure in his dull voice.

"I'm fine," Ray said. "Just one less prick in the world."

Locker laughed; a dry hack. "Tough guy."

Ray cringed.

"It's alright," Locker said. "You're still young. Got plenty more years to become a man."

Ray rose to the cajoling, hating himself for it. "I killed Robbie. You saw me do it."

Locker glanced his way. "Yeah, I saw. Amazing what a squirt of blood can do when you aren't used to seeing it. Makes your body jerk, your fingers twitch."

"What are you talking about?" Ray challenged, although of course he understood: Locker knew that Ray hadn't actively decided to fire the gun.

They circled the next roundabout, and a police van took the first exit while Percy went straight across. Henry had taught Ray not to fear the law, saying that most of the city's officers were on their side.

"So how long are you thinking of sticking around for?" Locker asked.

Ray knew that Locker was interrogating him, and felt a stab of anger. "Percy, what's your problem? Because you're about as subtle as a school kid."

Locker's pupils shrank to dots, and Ray realised that he had called Locker by his hated first name. Locker's jaw tightened, but he asked, "Has Henry ever told you about my friends?"

"Who?"

"My friends. The ones I carry in the boot."

Ray ignored his anxiety. "Oh, yes. I know about your 'friends'. They're about the only ones you have, aren't they?"

Locker's knuckles whitened against the wheel. "Maybe you should meet them."

Ray ignored the ice spreading across his skin. "Are you threatening me?"

"No, of course not. Wouldn't want to upset the golden boy. But when a few hundred grand vanishes without a trace, opinions can change."

Rather than submitting to the chills and the panic, Ray felt righteous rage. "You're telling me that this is my fault, and that it's going to alter the way that Henry thinks of me. I think you underestimate the situation though. Henry wants me on board, and I'm sorry if that doesn't sit well with you." A flash of fury caused him to add, "After all, we both know that Henry's never going to fuck you, Percy."

As soon as the words left Ray's throat, he regretted them. Locker's head turned slowly, muscle by muscle, away from the road. He nailed Ray with those cold, dead eyes and his entire face seemed to shift, the cheeks and jawline crawling like a swarm. He maintained the car's speed but ignored the road, drawing close to a motorbike ahead. A white estate car to their side blared its horn, but Locker ran his tongue from one side of his shapely mouth to the other and intoned, "Tread carefully."

Panic hit Ray like a fist. "Locker, you're going to collide with..."

"You don't know as much as you think you do, and in the end, you're going to wish you'd never met my boss." Locker's tone became a croak. "You're going to regret *everything*."

A horn blasted again and the motorcyclist accelerated, narrowly avoiding a collision. Locker kept Ray pinned for a moment longer, squeezing the moment dry. Finally, he returned his vision to the road.

As they drew nearer to the house, Ray became nauseated. Locker's threat, his encounters with his mother and Henry, the theft at the Green Emporium... and Thomas. Maybe someone had held up the shop and Thomas had fled. Maybe he was hurt, in hospital somewhere, shot by whomever had left those bullet holes in the the office door. But if that was true, wouldn't there have been blood? And wouldn't police have been crawling all over the shop?

Ray was certain that Thomas didn't have the brains to have carried out such a robbery - at least not alone. Perhaps that was it: Thomas had a partner in crime, someone who had known about the money and had put him up to it.

"I think that's the place there, up ahead," Ray said, pointing into the distance. Beech and ash trees half-hid the dark, tall form of a farmhouse, which in turn stood against the backdrop of a thick forest. It looked like something out of a fairy tale: a building slowly being devoured by foliage.

Locker decelerated and pulled the 4x4 off the dual carriageway. Trees from either side entwined their limbs above them.

Jesus, Ray thought when the house came into clear view. *Thomas can't live here, surely.*

"Nice place," Locker mumbled, stopping the car. Ray wasn't sure if he was joking.

The structure was at least a couple of centuries old, and appeared utterly abandoned. The walls were rampant with ivy, and each of the farmhouse's ten or so windows revealed drawn, mildewed curtains. Jealous branches reached from behind the building, stretching over the roof to grasp possessively at the tiles. Bushes, weeds and lifeless shrubbery jutted and weaved from the dry earth, making what was once the garden an impassable tangle. Only the protruding entranceway with its rotten-looking door was free of vegetation.

It shouldn't have been there, Ray decided. That anybody should live in a place that appeared so... unclaimed... was wrong. Ray's head throbbed just to look at it.

Welcome, the building seemed to say. *Come say hi, yes yes yes...*

Locker got out of the car. Ray didn't move.

Locker turned back with a scowl and gestured with his head. Ray once again ignored his intuition and stepped into the dust. Up ahead, a blue hatchback was parked at an angle.

"I didn't think that Thomas drove," Ray said.

"Then who does that belong to?" Locker asked, reaching the farmhouse door. He tried the handle and it opened. He backed away a step. "Fucking stinks."

Ray clawed through arguments in his head. "Look, Locker, don't you think we should try and get hold of Henry again? Surely he should know what we're doing."

"Try again if you want, but he's not answering. We're here now. We're gonna look for this Thomas." He crouched down at the doorstep. "Might not be too hard to find, either."

"What do you mean?" Ray asked.

Locker held up a red palm. Blood.

Ray stepped closer and saw a red trail polka-dotting the bare concrete floor, running from a door twenty feet into the farmhouse to gather stickily at the foot of a staircase. From there, it scaled the bare wooden steps.

Ray took another step. A stench hit his nose and his stomach lurched. He withdrew and tottered back from the entrance, waving his hands to dissipate the fumes. "Oh God!" he exclaimed, squeezing his eyes shut as if the smell might burn them in their sockets. "What *is* that?"

Locker's lips had curled upwards. "Something here has been dead for a while."

Ray's food re-settled. "A dog that got in under the floorboards?"

Locker's gaze was empty, the quarter-smile gone. He drew a handgun from his jacket. "Maybe you should stay here. Maybe this isn't for you."

Ray angled his head. He'd show this arrogant bastard. "No, I'm coming."

Locker began to climb the stairs. "Just stay quiet, whatever happens."

Ray cursed himself but followed, surprised to find that when he stepped –

– inside, things feel different.

The hallway walls are damp with long patches of mould, papered erratically with posters from kid's TV shows and comic books. The cartoon animals, superheroes and goggling eyes remind Ray of a room at his primary school in which the pupils had been allowed to decorate with any pictures they had wanted, opting for a mish-mash of pasted magazine photographs as well as their own crayon doodles.

Beneath some of the pictures, Ray can see rectangular bulges. He approaches an A3 poster of a blue-skinned animated girl in a cape, who is flexing her biceps. A wooden frame pokes out from beneath the picture's lop-sided base. Ray can see a triangle of painted grass bearing the illegible scrawl of an artist. The colours of the hidden painting are washed and murky, in total contrast with the primary hues of the posters. It's as if someone has tried to disguise a home that had once been decorated by an adult.

A door with a wide split in its frame stands at the bottom of the stairs. Through the gap, Ray sees several shelves of children's books, as well as what appears to be an old rocking horse.

The smell worsens as they follow the blood trail up the stairs. At the top, the mottled, rotten bannister turns back on itself to border a wide landing. To the left, a corridor runs twenty metres or so beside several closed doors. Up here, walls that were once white have faded to beige. Again, no carpet, no tiles; just splintering, dank wood.

They have entered a belly; Ray can feel it. A hum in the air suggests something nearby, not yet willing to betray its presence. Something curious, something huge. Ray feels as if the walls should be shrinking and expanding like lungs, the doorways blinking like the eyes of a giant.

Locker glances back and once again Ray is aware of the man's disgust for him - but this sense has become dwarfed by an irrational belief that the very farmhouse aches to consume them both. The house? Perhaps the garden.

Expressionless, Locker raises a red finger to his lips. He pokes a thumb towards the door behind him. Ray casts a glance along the unwelcoming entranceway to their side, and his mind fills with gaping mouths, dark soil, and pints of roaring blood. The house is greying, and Ray is sure that he should leave.

no no no... play and stay

The buzzing rises, still low but now indisputably present, like the moan of a short-fused neon strip light.

Run, the grey panic tells him. *Flee.*

Ray almost cries out at the sight of a dead animal, but then realises that it's only a draft excluder shaped like a winged serpent, with bulging eyes and a lolling tongue.

The buzzing comes from the other side of the entranceway, as does the terrible smell.

Ray's legs have locked, one foot on the penultimate step and one on the landing. He meets Locker's hateful but somehow empty eyes, and feels true despair. This is where his life has been leading. This house, this hallway, and this door.

Don't open the door, Ray thinks, watching as Locker raises his gun and reaches for the handle. *Don't open the door, don't open the door, please, just don't open the door...*

Locker opens the door.

CHAPTER 13
"I'm done"

Henry

Henry awoke to a dreadful yammerin.

Jesus Christ on a khazi, woss goin on?

The gabble wasn't English × it sounded Slavic.

When he fluttered his eyes open, he had to squint against the light. He was lyin on his belly on a bed in a bleary red room, an' some ugly, stupid mug wiv a bouffant-beard an' frantic eyes was wafflin at him, goin on an' on an' on. The voice, thick wiv phlegm an' panic, suddenly switched to pigeon English. "I teck Lubos to hospital now? I think he still breathing."

An' it all came firin back: the bitch an' her steak meal, the blast o' the bullets, the pain of his ravaged arsehole, an' Bruno.

The foreign fellah was one o' the Slovaks from downstairs. Henry concentrated, groggily tryin to work his tongue. When he spoke, a nasty, unintended tightenin of his back passage almost made him cry out. "Calm down," he managed.

The stupid face fell an' the bushy eyebrows plunged.

"Find my phone," Henry said. "Call Percy an' tell him to get over 'ere, *now.*"

The fellah vanished an' Henry was left to his thoughts. Grief an' revulsion filled him when he gazed down at the butcher's shop carnage splattered and slopped across his lovely white carpet. He clenched his whole body against the vision, wishin he could turn away, but no. Sights like this needed drinkin in, analysin an' pickin apart.

Bruno lay on his front, at a right angle to the bed. Henry's gun lay muzzle-first against one o' Bruno's spreadeagled legs, an' the poor bastard's skull lay in chunks beside the wall. One brown eye had gone, an' Henry could see a few runnels o' brain pokin out from the smashed egg o' the dog's broken skull. His other eye was intact but glazed, an' an impact spray o' claret had slapped the wall an' run down to the skirtin board.

"Sorry, ol' mate, but what else could I do?" Henry asked. He wanted to say more but his throat had closed, tighter than an amster's chuff. Henry gulped air an' shut his eyes.

That vicious slag will pay.

While Henry had bin kippin - well, out cold - he'd had more dreams. He'd seen his dad in the forest again. Weird what your brain does to you when you're all strung out. Henry an' his dad had come to a clearin, an' Henry had seen his own young son standin there, tall an' tough but facin away so that Henry couldn't see his eyes. The only thing was, it hadn't *looked* like young Raymond – it'd bin stockier, hairier...

The Slovak burst back into the bedroom, holding Henry's phone in one mitt. "He not answer."

Henry remembered now. This fellah had helped him back up the stairs an' dragged the body o' the uvver Slovak up here too – the one who'd taken the shot to the guts. This guy was called Jaroslav, and the dead cunt was Lubo. No, *Lubos.*

"I try but he not answer. I can teck Lubos to hospital now?"

"Not yet," Henry said, as firmly as he could manage. "Call Fred."

The man looked like he was gonna question Henry, but after a few seconds' consideration he vanished again.

In the silence of his bloody room, Henry realised that it was time to accept that, once in a blue moon, he made mistakes. That *bitch* had bin a model ladyfriend after the little spat they'd had about the suitcase – very compliant, just as a slag should be. Things had bin goin well for the three ... for the *two* o' them, so why had she plotted behind his back? Why had she betrayed him like this, corruptin everythin they'd built togevver?

As Henry took in the pitiful sight o' the dog, a deep, achin sorrow shivered through him. Bruno hadn't deserved this. He'd bin Henry's best friend, a bruvver-in-arms, an' Henry had known the big lummox since he was a pup. Bruno couldn't o' known that the friendship between a master an' pet was sacred – however, no one could deny that their bond had bin shattered, at the moment Bruno had pushed his poker where it weren't wanted. It was better to end it with a quick, loud gunshot, rather than let things grow sour over time – you rip a plaster off, don't ya?

Lyin there, dizzy, wiv his rectum raw an' sore, Henry mumbled three words: "*She'll fackin pay.*"

Jaroslav poked his head round the door an' said, "I call. He come."

"Good."

The Slovak crept into the room wiv-out makin eye contact. Henry knew what was comin: the cheeky little wetback was tryin the respectful approach.

"Mr Borders," he went. "I need to teck Lubos to doctor. Can I go, pliz?"

Henry matched the bloke's gentle tone, but amped up his own vulnerability. "Look, pal. As you may be able to tell, I've had a rough day. But you've bin stirlin, I tell ya – a real diamond. Dunno what would've happened if you hadn't bin here to help me, an' you'll be well rewarded, mark my words. But for now, I want ya to stick around til Fred arrives. Would't feel safe wiv-out you here."

"But Mr Borders," Jaroslav went on. "Lubos shot in his stomach. It can teck long time to die. He is my friend. He is good man. Pliz…"

Henry kept the irritation from his voice. "Jus' go an' take a seat in the lounge, an' look after your pal. Fred will be here in no time, an' after we have a quick chinwag ya can take ya mate to hospital, okay? Ten minutes, tops. Trust me – I'll make it worth your while."

Through Henry's bleary vision he saw the Slovak eyein him worriedly. Seconds later, though, there were footsteps from another part o' the flat.

"There you are, what did I tell ya? Let Fred through, an' then wait for him to come an' help you carry your pal down the stairs. Alright?"

A relieved half-smile came to rest on Jaroslav's face as he backed outta the room. "Thank you, Mr Borders."

After the Slovak left, in popped Fred. Normally a calm, stand-up, smart-arse kinda guy, the expression behind that trimmed beard o' his was one o' deep concern. "Boss," he said, soundin disorientated.

As soon as this geezer lost his cool an' let something shock him, he lost his air o' snappy mystique. Henry had bin hopin that Fred's easy-goin nature would take his mind off the seriousness o' the situation, but no, Fred looked shaken.

"Are… um…" Fred began, his voice as soft as a fairy's fart. "Are you okay?"

"I've bin better, Fred," Henry said gravely. "Much better."

"What happened?" Fred asked, surveyin Bruno's hairy remains.

"Ya can't ask me that, Fred. Not yet. Probly not ever." Henry leaned his cheek onto his wrists an' shifted his legs. He went to speak again, but a pain ripped through him, runnin from his arse up into his digestive system.

"Jesus, boss," Fred gasped, steppin forwards. "What can I do?"

It felt like somethin was tryin to burrow out of him. "Get me kecks off!" Henry gurgled, archin his neck an' grippin the mattress.

"What?"

"I'm fackin' serious, Fred! Get me strides around me ankles! An' my pants! Oh Gawd, *get 'em off me!*"

Henry had to rock sideways to give his mortified employee access to his zipper, but as soon as Henry felt the air against his arse, the stabbin started to subside. When Henry fell back onto his front wiv a relieved sigh, Fred gave a whoop an' raised a hand to his mouth. The expression of horror on Fred's face as he tore his eyes away from Henry's backside made Henry cringe.

At last, Fred said, "What else can I do, boss?"

Henry looked up. Shocked at his own embarrassment, he said, "Go an' kill that fackin' Slovak. He's bin doin' my head in."

Ray

As the door swings inwards, flies gush out from the widening gap. The stench and the buzzing multiplies, and a howling blur of red-and-white barrels out onto the landing, ploughing Locker off his feet. His gun clatters across the bare boards and a third figure thrusts Locker's spine into the top stair post, which creaks ominously.

The door slams shut, as if propelled by a spring.

Ray watches Locker crash to the ground with another man flailing on top of him. Locker's deadpan body language falls into turmoil, and when his attacker pins his wrists to the floor he shakes his head almost comically from side to side. In a rush of understanding, Ray sees that the second man, who seems to be smeared in blood, is Thomas.

"Who are you?!" Thomas bellows into Locker's face.

"Get him off me!" Locker calls out, kicking his legs. "You deaf, you Goth cunt? Get him off!"

Ray gapes, backing unconsciously away.

Thomas looks up. "Ratan??"

The moment's distraction allows Locker to grasp Thomas by the hands and roll over, crushing them against the floorboards in an effective reversal of their positions. They look like an oddly-matched pair of lovers. Locker drives his knee between Thomas's thrashing legs and blasts the air out of him.

Thomas stops fighting immediately, wheezing like an asthmatic. In the struggle, Thomas's t-shirt has ridden up to reveal his round belly where thin, cruel-looking scars criss-cross his pale skin.

Locker rises and retrieves his gun from the ground at Ray's feet. He meets Ray's eyes, expressionless, and turns back to Thomas. He points at the closed door, and when he speaks, his tone has returned to its usual monotone. "What have you got in there?"

"Just go away. Please," Thomas pants. "It's nothing to do with you. Why are you here?"

"I'll tell you what's my business, and what isn't."

"Don't go in there," Thomas says, eyes squeezed shut in pain.

Locker steps forwards and, with abrupt speed, drops to all fours so that his head is directly above Thomas's. Looking at Thomas's face upside down, Locker speaks in a low, matter-of-fact voice. "You should know that I wouldn't think twice about cutting your head off." A bead of sweat drops from his nose onto Thomas's lips. "Someone stole from my boss's shop today, and you're the last person who was there. So for now, you're gonna lie still and stay quiet." In what appears to be a single, agile movement, Locker stands and returns to the door.

Ray wants to be assertive, *be a man*, but he still feels as though something else is here with them, something in the air, the floors and the windows. Something outside and below, something that wants, commands, plays and stays, sees everyone, sees everything...

Stop being ridiculous.

Still wincing, Thomas notices Ray staring at his stomach, and pulls his t-shirt back down. Although the scars across his belly have healed, his clothes are a mess of rusty red stains, and his face appears freshly gashed and beaten.

Locker braces himself at the door handle.

"Don't let that man in there," Thomas whispers to Ray, and Ray realises that, no matter what has happened or is about to happen, part of him still feels more loyal to Thomas than to Percy fucking Locker.

"Keep quiet," Ray says, soft but firm.

As Locker pushes the door, Ray imagines it opening to reveal ranks of black-eyed nudes - as if this house is the very birthplace of his nightmares. The door swings back and the unbearable smell hits Ray's nose again; rancid milk and bleach and gut gases. There's a grating whirr of tiny wings and a stream of flies pours haphazardly into the landing. Through the gap in the doorway, Ray sees a thick cloud of droning insects and the edge of an old bed. Its bulging duvet ripples with tiny, scuttling forms, and Ray sees with shock that the grey sole of a human foot juts out from the bottom of the covers.

Hiding his face with a sleeve, Locker steps inside. "What have you done?" Ray asks.

Ray's ever-present chills are growing. The shakes have already started, and the edges of his sight are rippling, but he must not run. He can take this. He killed someone, so now he's a real man.

He murdered Robbie. He blew out Robbie's eye.

yes yes yes you smashed through his dirty skullbrain yes yes yes

Thomas sits up. "You have to leave. They know you're here, and if you aren't careful they might force you to play The People Game."

"Who are 'they'?" Ray asks, batting a fly away from his face.

Thomas understands. Thomas knows that Ray has been lured here, maybe Percy Locker too, because Thomas can feel it...

Thomas shakes his head. "The children."

The door opens again and Locker steps out, tugging the door closed behind him. Ray is shocked to see him wearing a crooked smile. "You've been busy," Locker observes. Insects scale his collar and cheeks. He does not attempt to shake them off.

"What's in there?" Ray hears himself ask.

Locker turns with a sneer, and a fat bluebottle clambers across his forehead. "Five stiffs. Two mummies, two rotten ones, and one fresh." He grunts a laugh. "Not pretty."

"Oh no," Thomas moans.

Locker advances on him, and uses the sole of one polished black boot to shove Thomas back to the floor. Thomas flops and Locker steps a leg over his large midsection, crouches low, puts the gun to Thomas's chest and drops his weight onto Thomas's belly. Air blasts out of Thomas.

"I don't mind what you've been up to," Locker's voice grates. "You could be raping kiddies or shooting snuff films for all I care. All I care about is what you've done with my boss's cash. And when you've told me, I'm going to introduce you to one of my friends."

Thomas is becoming red-faced, struggling to breathe under Locker's weight.

Locker's eyes glint in the gloom. "If you cooperate, I'll let you meet Jackson or Warren. You won't like either of them, of course - but if you don't help me out, I'll have you shake hands with Alfie." He pauses, and a look of what could be pride crosses his face. "You *don't* want to meet Alfie."

Ray senses danger, red and broiling, so he asks Thomas, "What happened? In the shop, with the money? How did you know it was there?"

Locker turns and glares at Ray.

With Locker still sat on his stomach, Thomas manages, "A man called Gary took the money, and then afterwards we came here. He left his bag outside, in his car, so you can just take it and go..."

"Not yet," Locker states, prodding the gun barrel into Thomas's chin. To Ray he says, "Go outside and check the car."

"I want to know what happened first," Ray says. "Who's Gary? Why did you come here? Who are the dead bodies, and where's this Gary guy now?"

Thomas points towards the door. "In there."

"You *killed him?*" Ray asks.

Locker stands up and faces Ray. "Go and get the money."

Ray still refuses to let Locker pull rank. It's foolish and dangerous but he needs something to focus on, something to hold onto beyond the bodies and the house. "*You* get the money, Locker, *I'm* staying here. Then we're going to take Thomas to *Henry* and find out what *he* wants us to do."

Locker narrows his eyes in an expression that would have made most men wilt, but Ray needs to stand strong. The death, the panic, the house's presence; they're conspiring against him, dragging him closer to a decision that's been haunting him for weeks.

yes yes you should play the game yes yes

Locker stares coldly at Ray. "If that's how you want it. But I'll remember this."

"Give me the gun," Ray says. "I'll make sure Thomas doesn't try anything."

Locker swallows with a dry click, watching Ray, calculating. "He's not going anywhere. He's just going to lie there like a good boy."

Locker descends the stairs.

Thomas has propped himself up onto his elbows, his breath heaving. Ray meets Thomas's eyes but neither of them says a word. Thomas watches Locker's head disappear from view, listening for the sound of the front door closing. When it does, Thomas hisses, "You've got to get out of here, Ratan. Please listen to me, you have to leave..."

Ray understands that he does not know a single thing about Thomas, despite once having thought of him as a friend. "We're not going anywhere yet, so just shut up for a moment. Christ, what have you done? Did you kill all those people?"

"No, of course not!" Thomas says, sounding appalled. "They all just died. Except for that man, Gary. Simon stabbed him and I brought him up here. I didn't want to, but I didn't know where else to put him."

"Who's Simon?"

Thomas ignores him. "What's going to happen to me?"

"I don't know," Ray says. "It's out of my hands. If you really didn't take the money, but the man who *did* take it is dead ... well, you're going to have a tough time convincing Locker that it wasn't you." He ponders. "Is Simon here in the house?"

Thomas shakes his head. "He's out back with the others. He gets so angry. He came up out of the ground and stopped the man hurting me, and now he's probably going to come for you too."

Ray's body tenses.

He came up out of the ground.

Something fits into place in Ray's head, and suddenly everything makes a little more sense.

Thomas is completely, irretrievably mad.

There is no Simon.

There is no Gary.

The house does not want to eat Ray.

There is only a pile of rotting corpses and an unstable man who needs years of treatment.

Ray gags at the knowledge and steps backwards, an overwhelming panic closing around his throat.

Run... flee...

"Don't let him hurt me, Ratan," Thomas says from the floor, but the house is drifting smaller and Ray's vision is blurring. Down the stairs, Ray sees Locker, a man who probably wants him dead.

Ray lives in a world where everyone is a murderer, where everyone has blood on their hands, and where everyone is fucking *insane*.

Ray retreats and his sight distorts further. Thomas is saying something but for a solitary second, Ray thinks he can see *through* the boards of both the landing and the ground floor, deep into a dark world of mud and crawling life. He feels a sense of devastating loss and an envious, all-consuming selfishness, dreams of genocide and solitude and two all-seeing globes of obsidian black...

Ray's heel smacks into an uneven floorboard. He trips backwards, down onto a twisting metal rod that pushes the surface behind him into a swinging arc. The world fills with a rancid fug as his spine and skull hit the ground.

The ceiling above him undulates with ten thousand swarming bodies. Ray scrabbles to his feet and sees the filth-smeared bedclothes, a row of four decrepit heads lying face-up against the stiff pillows. Two of them are yellow skeletons with sunken eye sockets and lipless mouths, wrapped in each other's emaciated arms. The other two are marginally less decayed but their grey, leathery flesh shudders with maggots and some foul, seeping residue.

Propped in the corner between the bedside cabinet and wardrobe, through the billowing air and by a window darkened by flies, Ray sees the bloody body of a ginger-haired man wearing a tracksuit. He hears a warbling cry - his own - and turns back to the door.

you like the funny dead people don't you, yes ... you want to kiss fuck play taste them yes yes yes
RUN!

Ray dashes for the hallway, a mad part of him wanting to leap the flight of twenty or so stairs to reach the front door. Locker is two steps from the summit when Ray rams into him. Locker pinwheels backwards and Ray follows with a flurry of pumping limbs. The house upends. Ray sees Locker's hands snatch for the bannister and hears a loud crack. Ray's lanky frame vaults over Locker's body and he somersaults once, crashes against the bare wall and tumbles into a world where up is down and left is right. After a series of dizzying, battering impacts, Ray lands in a pile at the bottom of the stairs.

There is stillness. Darkness.

Ray's arms and head throb with pain and his breath crackles in his chest. When he opens his eyes, he sees the front door standing at an odd angle. Groaning, he pulls himself up to a sitting position.

Thomas stands at the top of the staircase, gazing down at Ray with concern.

Percy Locker lies on his back halfway down the stairs, with his feet ten steps higher than his head. His eyes are closed, and a steady red stream trickles from the dark hair of his crown.

Rebecca

Rebecca was going to ignore the disaster of her plans and the burning, torn-gristle agony of her upper arm.

Stay focused. Get through this.

Alone, barefoot, bleeding, with the scent of dog food and Henry's bowels still fresh in her nose, she sagged against an alleyway wall. Having limped down the high street, she had no idea how she had escaped the gaze of the milling throng. Granted, she was used to acting straight-faced when her mind was askew, and she had kept her hand tightly plugged over the wound in her arm, but surely, one of those holidaymaking drones should have given her a second glance. But no. A hot ball of gas, some rocking water, a patch of sand and a flock of screaming scavenger-birds were apparently just plenty, thank you very much.

Forget the people. Forget the hole in your arm. Forget Henry, for now.

Freedom was less than ten minutes away.

She lifted her hand from the tender, leaking divot in her upper arm. A little to the left and it would have been serious, at best breaking a rib, at worst puncturing a lung.

So where did she want to go?

The hospital... the fairy castle... far, far away...

No – first, the guesthouse.

Gary would be there with her money, and with their takings they would drive somewhere new. They would see to Rebecca's wound, drive to another hotel as far away as they had the energy for, and discuss what to do from there. Then, whatever decision they made, in the morning Rebecca would spike him unconscious, abandon him, and find a new life.

Damn it - no she wouldn't. The GHB was still in her bag at Henry's.

At least she still had her phone, and therefore the video footage of Henry's bestial buggery. However, until Henry searched her belongings and found her carefully composed note he would have no reason to delay having her pursued.

She could barely lift her injured arm, so she spat into one hand and rubbed the other limb until the mess of red was just a hazy smudge. It did little to distract from the ragged lesion, but when she pulled her arm close against her side, she looked unwashed rather than wounded, a crazy lady rather than a victim.

Never a victim.

Seconds later, she began to bleed again though. Glistening droplets welled up from the gash and streaked the silver of her dress. She sighed, lifted her hemline and removed her underwear. She used her teeth and fingers to loop the black knickers around her wounded arm, and the material made a passable makeshift bandage. Stepping out of the alley, she laughed at herself wryly.

My my, how well I'm coping.

The neighbourhood surrounding her was one of the city's less affluent areas. Although the streets were mercifully unpopulated, Rebecca pictured cigarette-sucking mothers shoving prams of mewling infants towards miserable childhoods, erratic adolescences and clones of their own stunted maturities. She imagined women gossiping with their friends and ignoring *their wretched offspring to the point of neglect, the men sitting at home buried in fast food packets or at the pub cheering for eleven strangers kicking a piece of inflated leather.*

Rebecca passed down a street lined with rickety-looking houses, rusting cars and unkempt, thirsty lawns. In the road, a chubby child bounced a tennis ball to his bony, red-faced chum, both glancing up at Rebecca but seeing nothing to catch their interest. Perhaps wild haired, barefooted women with underwear knotted around their appendages were a common sight here.

Having barely attracted a glance, Rebecca turned a corner. Before her stood a row of uninspiring guesthouses with names like 'The Sandy Getaway' and 'Beach Bums'. These businesses overflowed with holidaying families, but a little further on was a clump of downmarket hotels known to charge by the hour. Gary's car was not amongst the parked vehicles, and Rebecca wondered how far away he had decided to pull up. The man did have some sense in his head, after all.

She slipped inside a building entitled 'The Ocean's Outpost' and was greeted by a smiling face that quickly crumbled.

"You alright, Mrs Saunders?" a narrow-jawed Slovakian woman with her black hair in a high bun asked from behind the counter. Rebecca had visited enough times over the past month for the woman to recognise her by sight.

"I have never been better," Rebecca replied stiffly, keeping her hand cupped to her panty-

wrapped arm and fixing the woman with a warning stare. She hurried along the cheaply tiled corridor.

"Don't you want your key?"

Rebecca froze, turned back. "Has Gar... Mr Saunders not checked in yet?"

The woman, whose eyes shone vigilantly, replied, "No, I haven't seen him. I've been here all day."

Rebecca closed her eyes, feeling the world sway.

"Then yes, let me have the key," she heard herself say, and the guesthouse reception grew distant. "I need to lie down."

When she lay back on the bed in the empty guest room, where for weeks she and her little bug Gary had shared secrets and secretions, she told herself that Gary would be with her soon. He would show her the money, she would mount him, she would scrape her claws through his skin, she would climax, and then they would leave Seadon forever.

As she drifted to sleep, a dotted patch of mildew on the ceiling elongated, dispersed, and spread damp tendrils across the white plaster above her. They thickened, sprouted leaves, and Rebecca's midriff cramped in response. Somewhere far away, a pet was yapping. Rebecca felt a tug of maternal protectiveness, and a voice that tittered and purred assured her not to worry, that everything was going to be fine, yes yes yes, because Rebecca was one of the special ones.

Rebecca was going to be the best mummy in

the whole wide world.

Thomas

From the top of the stairs, Thomas tries really really hard to think straight.

Ignoring the throb of his crushed nuts, he heads down the steps and comes to a stop before the big man's body. A sloppy red puddle has gathered under his head. His eyes are closed and his mouth gapes open in a sleepy yawn. One arm is twisted behind his back and his legs are bent open awkwardly, with one leaning against the wall and one poking through the bannister struts.

Is he dead? No, his chest is rising. Still, he's not moving.

Maybe Thomas should hug him, just take him in his arms and squeeze him tighter and tighter, like he had done with the children. Would that be another way for Thomas to win The People Game? Would that save him from having to use the suitcase? Ratan might not like it if he did, but Thomas would love to - after all, the large, nasty man had acted as if Thomas's parents' resting room was *funny.*

The way Thomas lives is probably different to most people, but is it *that* strange? Other people bury their mummies and daddies, and they all know that their loved ones are going to fall apart and get eaten by bugs. All Thomas has done is given his mummy and daddy their own place inside the house instead of under the ground. Even though Thomas's parents weren't very nice to him when they were alive, having them nearby makes him feel an ickle bit less lonely.

At the bottom of the stairs, Ratan starts whining.

"Are you hurt?" Thomas asks lamely, treading over the big man.

Ratan has his knees hugged against his chest and his face buried between them. "What's going on?" he sobs.

"Everything's gone wrong. It's all gone fucking *mental*."

Thomas has never seen this side of his pal, and it makes his throat feel tight. "There, there," Thomas says, reaching the bottom of the stairs. "It's okay."

"What does that mean?" Ratan snaps, bringing his head up. "What the fuck is okay about any of this? I just killed a fucking *gangster!*" He snorts wetly and wipes his nose on a creased shirtsleeve. "All I wanted to do was earn enough money to get out of this horrid little city, and now I've ruined everything."

"Ratan..."

"Stop calling me that! It's a stupid, made-up name, and it doesn't mean anything. That part of my life is over. I don't have my old *friends*. I don't have my *dreadlocks*, or my old *clothes*, and you know what? I'm a fucking *murderer*. So do me a favour and just call me Ray."

Thomas tries again. "*Ray.* He isn't dead."

Ratan sniffs. "He's not? Okay then. That's different, but...Jesus Christ. What am I going to do?"

Thomas feels lost. "What do you want to do?"

Ratan shuts his rainy eyes. "I want to go home and forget all of this. I just want everything to *fuck off*. In fact, I want to go back in time and change every single decision I've made this year." He looks up at Thomas, with his short-shaven head and his eyes that shimmer-shine the brightest of blues.

Thomas sits down beside him. "I've felt like that before. But we've all got responsibilities."

Ratan scoffs and hides his face behind his thighs again. "Oh yeah? What have *you* got to do?"

"I've got to look after the children."

Ratan peeks through his knees. "Who do you mean when you say that? 'The children'?"

Thomas swallows. Part of him wants to talk, to spill the jellybeans right there and then. Maybe if he does that, Ratan will realise that the two of them aren't all that different. But Thomas whispers, "*I can't tell you. They're always listening.*"

Ratan lifts his head, and for a second he looks worried, but not for himself – for Thomas. Some people feel better when they have someone else to look after.

"If they're always listening," Ratan says. "And they don't want you to talk about them – why didn't they stop you telling me to leave the house, earlier?"

Thomas gulps – Ratan is right.

"Maybe..." Ratan starts, his voice suddenly soft and soothing. "Maybe they *want* you to tell me."

"You mean, maybe that's part of the game?"

Ratan pauses, and then says, "Yes."

Thomas feels one of his eyes twitch. "Do you already know about The People Game, then?"

"Of course," Ratan says. "Now what the fuck is going on?"

Thomas realises that the rules of The People Game are becoming less and less clear to him. He knows that the children want him to go out and use the suitcase again – a thought that makes his stomach ache – but apart from that, what is it all about? If more people are going to be coming to the house, maybe this is a new kind of game. Maybe Thomas can make up the rules as he goes along.

"The children live out back," he says finally. "In the Gardden."

"Yes, but who are they?" Ratan persists. "I mean, who do you *think* they are? Earlier, you said that someone called Simon popped out of the ground and killed someone. Do you *really* believe that, deep down?"

Thomas chews his lip. Ratan is only the second person he has ever told about the children, and Gary was the first. He doesn't want to say anything that will make him sound any loopier than he already probably does.

Ratan leans his head sideways against his knees. "You know that when Locker wakes up, he'll probably want to kill us."

Although he's confused, and although he no longer has any idea whether he wants to stay with the children or to run away, Thomas doesn't want to die.

Ratan stands up, looking at the mean man's body on the stairs. "Earlier, it felt a bit like there was someone else here with us. But I can't feel it anymore."

Thomas replies, "It's the children. The Gardden. I don't know why, but I don't think they're going to hurt us right now. I think they're happy just watching. We don't have visitors very often."

"Okay, whatever. Let me think." Ratan rises a few steps. and picks something up from beside the big man's body. It looks like a small knife, but with one wheel attached to its left side and one on its right.

Thomas climbs a couple of stairs to see. "What is it?"

The blade has been buffed as clear as a mirror. Opposite the leather handle, there's a cog, which Ray turns curiously. The two wheels clickety-clack and the sharp edges wibble-wobble in opposite time.

"Percy calls them his friends," Ratan says, sounding as if he's in awe. "I haven't seen one before. I don't know what this thing does, but I think he wanted to use it on *you*." Ratan looks at the bottom of the handle. "He gives them all names. Look - this one's called 'Warren'."

The six letters have been neatly cut into the metal base. Thomas can't imagine what it's for, but the idea of it tunnelling into him makes him feel an ickle bit faint. A thought crosses his mind. "What would you have done if he'd tried?"

Ratan doesn't answer. Just keeps turning the cog, watching the light skip-hopping across the metal.

"Would you have fought him?"

Ratan looks hurt. "Of course I would."

"But you don't think that you'd have been able to stop him, do you? So actually, you might not even have tried."

Ratan seems uncomfortable. "None of this is straightforward, Thomas. You're talking like a kid. There's so much to consider..."

"You're such a dick!" Thomas exclaims. "You'd have let him do that to me!"

"*You're* the one with the corpses in your bedroom!"

"What does that have to do with anything? They died of old age. They're my mummy and daddy, and my grandparents, and –"

"And some other guy who you stabbed to death!"

Thomas tries to be patient, but it's becoming tough. "I *told* you: Simon did that because Gary wanted to kill me."

Ratan looks as though he wants to keep on arguing, but a mumble comes from the man on the stairs. Ratan suddenly looks terrified. The man's eyes stay closed but he moans again, his head flopping sideways to show off the boo-boo on his crown. It's still bleeding, but more slowly.

Thomas panics. The bad man is going to wake up and use his horrible tool on him, and there's only one thing to do. Thomas dashes up the stairs.

"Hey, where are you going?" Ratan yells.

At the top, Thomas turns left and into the bathroom, which is lit by just one dirty window. He scrabbles open the cabinet and grasps a medicine bottle half-filled with cloudy liquid, and snatches a grubby towel from the wall. As he races from the bathroom he rips off the bottle top and soaks the cloth.

"Thomas! Get back here!" Ratan calls.

Thomas rushes back down the stairs to see the big man stirring, one of his hands flexing open and closed, the other still holding the gun. Thomas slams the lid back onto the bottle and dives towards the body.

"What are you doing?" Ratan demands, but Thomas ignores him and covers the big man's face with a handful of towel. He's relieved that Ratan does nothing to stop him. The man sleepily tries to pull the material away but Thomas keeps it in place. When the man raises the gun into the air, Thomas gently plucks it from his fingers.

Ratan panics. "What the hell's that you're using – *Chloroform?*"

Thomas pants, "Not Chloroform. I got the recipe from the internet. It'll just give us time to think."

Ratan takes a step back. "Us? I'm here to do Henry's work, that's all, and..."

The big man's arms flop back onto the stairs.

Ratan crouches down and shakes him. "Locker! Locker, get up!"

"He won't be awake for at least a few minutes. It could be up to an hour."

"Locker!" Ratan tries again. He looks like a little kid who has been separated from his mummy, like Hanna and Benny did when they first came to the Gardden.

"Give me the gun," Ratan says.

Thomas holds it out and Ratan tears it from his hand. For a second he aims it at Thomas, but then seems to scold himself and drops his arm.

Thomas rubs his head and sits down onto the stair below the puddle of blood.

Ratan whines, "What did you suffocate him for?"

"You didn't stop me."

Ratan's face becomes thunderous, but he says nothing. He rises tall, and for a moment looks like he's going to hit Thomas. Then his shoulders relax and he says, "This is going to get me killed."

"No it won't." Thomas wonders what the children think, though. There are times when they seem to know everything, so why aren't they here now, helping him play The People Game? Thomas doesn't even know the rules. "What do *you* want to do?" he asks Ratan again.

Ratan twists the gun in his hands. "I don't know. Whatever Henry wants, I suppose."

"What do you think Henry will say?"

"*I don't know! I don't know!*"

Carefully, Thomas asks, "Would you think about getting rid of him?"

"What?"

Thomas nods at the body.

"You mean, kill Locker? No." But he sounds uncertain. "I don't want to kill *anyone*."

"Maybe we wouldn't have to," Thomas says. "Maybe if we took him outside, into the Gardden, he would just ... stop being a problem..."

"And I suppose that The Rugrats will jump out of the stinging nettles and sort everything out, will they?" Ratan says. He holds his forehead in one hand, rubbing it in circles. "I just need to get hold of Henry. He's got to answer now, surely."

When Ratan pulls the phone from his pocket, Thomas rises from the step and reaches out. The darkness returns to Ratan's face. He lifts the gun. "Don't even think about it, Thomas. I *will* pull this trigger."

"Then Henry will probably kill both of us," Thomas says simply. He's sure as heck that he doesn't want any more people involved in The People Game, whatever the hell it is.

Ratan's brow furrows. "Henry wouldn't do that. It would be my word against yours..."

"And *his* word against *yours*," Thomas says, pointing at the big guy's body.

Anxiety jump-skips over Ratan's face. "This is such a mess. It's all such a mess, such a fucking mess..."

"Then let's take him out to the Gardden and just see what happens," Thomas urges. "What else can we do?"

"What else can we do? What else? I could..."

Ratan stops speaking and his gaze hardens. He looks like something super-huge has just occurred to him. Thomas imagines a light bulb popping on above his head, and when Ratan speaks his voice is steady. "You know what? I'm done."

Thomas doesn't understand. "What do you mean?"

Ratan grimaces and looks at the big man's body, at the gun in his hand, and then up the stairs towards Thomas's parents' room. "You're right," he says. "I actually think you've hit the nail on the head." He breathes out long and slow, and Thomas imagines him puffing out all his worries and every drip-drop of confusion. He looks confident again – *he looks like Ratan.* "I *don't* know what Henry will say or do about any of this. Locker hates my guts, so he'll think that I tried to kill him. Maybe he and Henry will even think that you and I took the money together. Perhaps, perhaps not. But Locker will still want me dead. And you, you sorry bastard – you need help. You need to get away from these 'children' of yours."

"No I don't, sometimes they're nice to me..."

Ratan looks at Thomas as if he is telling porky-pies. "Are they *really?* Then why don't you lift up your t-shirt and say that?"

Thomas covers his stomach protectively.

"That's what I thought," Ratan says, as if he's proven his point. "So there's only one thing for us to do that might make things right."

Thomas's world slows to a crawl as he realises what Ratan is going to say. Ratan isn't a bad guy, really. Deep down, he's still the dude who tells Thomas about his bonkers nights out, his sniffy drugs, and his dirty sex. The Goth who reckons he can do anything, but in the end wants to stick to what he knows.

"We'll go to the police and I'll come clean," Ratan says. "I've got to. I can't do this anymore."

Even though what he's saying is, like, the *total opposite* of rebellion, the words make Thomas picture his friend's old purple dreadlocks and tight black clothes.

He wants us to come clean. He wants me to go to court, go to prison, leave the house, leave the children, leave the Gardden...

"Didn't you once say that Henry pays off the police?" Thomas asks, feeling ill.

The look on Ratan's face falters. "Yes...but not all of them. There's got to be *some* good guys still about. Not everyone can be a monster, can they? I mean, you're not properly bad, are you? You're just *lost.* Like the rest of us."

For mad moments, Thomas wonders if Ray is right. Is there any way – like, a one in a bazillion chance - that Thomas has always been wrong? The children, the house, the Gardden – is just his silly imagination? He thinks back to the first time that Simon had acted funny, when he fell – plop! – out of the tree. *Is* there a chance? And if there is, should Thomas maybe, perhaps, find out for sure?

Should he let Ratan tell the police?

The seconds last ages, and in Thomas's aching brain a tennis ball *boings* from one side of a court to the other.

Henry

Still lyin on the bed, Henry considered that Fred was a true cockney gent, and as reliable as a Duracell battery – however, the prissy cunt didn't like anythin that messed up his outfit.

Henry had wanted time to mull, so he'd told Fred that he wanted the bodies – the two Slovaks and the dog – taken outta the flat and driven down to the field. Risky business, doin it durin the day, but that's what tinted windows and a private back yard were for. Fred had taken his time killin the Slovak, but after a few quiet minutes, Henry had heard the satisfyin pop o' the gun, followed by the sound o' feet bein dragged across carpet. Fred had first cleared out the staff area o' the casino to give him privacy to transport the bodies, an' then he'd left Henry alone in the apartment.

Henry lay on bed wiv his broken arse bared to the room for what felt like hours, an' found that he couldn't stop moanin to himself. Musta bin the effect o' whatever that bint had spiked him wiv, coz there was no way in *hell* that Henry was cryin.

He couldn't stop thinkin about his special boy, an' how he'd forced Ray to make his bones killin that thieving shit Robbie. The *really* odd thing, though, was that whenever Henry considered how he could make things up to his son, thoughts o' Bruno kept gettin in the way, until all he could picture was a mangled hybrid o' Ray an' the Great Dane, as if the pair had bin sat togevver in Doc Brundle's teleporter when the crazy sod had flipped the switch. In Henry's mind, BrunoRay stood in a dark, stinky corridor somewhere, hairy, long-jawed, an' reachin out for a hug.

A sound came from the uvver room: a door closin and footsteps passin over smashed glass. For a second, Henry was afraid. If it was Rebecca – *the bitch, the whore* – he'd be defenceless, unless he grabbed his pistol. He shuffled forwards on the bed, wincin at the sticky feelin o' the air on his tortured ringpiece. He reached down and picked his gun from the floor, pointed it at the closed entranceway. His hands juddered like a frightened kid's.

Then Fred came in, his normally spotless suit drenched red. There was even a bloody smear across his lips that made him look like a bewildered, bearded tranny.

"It's done," Fred mumbled, his eyes like plastic. Then he went, almost casually, "That was my first, Henry."

Fred's calm tone showed how upset he was.

"I... um... stuck a shopkeeper when I was younger, but I heard that he was okay after a few months," His eyes pointed Henry's way, but they were unfocused.

This'll stay wiv 'im, Henry thought irritably, lowerin the gun. *It's broken somethin inside 'im.*

Then the moment passed and Fred was back in the room, askin, "Can I have a shower now?"

Henry dropped the shooter an' deflected the question. "Everythin go alright?"

"I left them with your gardener, wotsisname?"

"Ralph," Henry said, layin his head down onto his crossed arms, which felt numb. "Good. Now go an' get my laptop, an' a chair from the lounge."

Fred sighed and retreated into the flat.

Henry's head felt echoey. He didn't feel hungover, but there was definitely somethin weird still travellin through his system.

"Now," Henry said, when Fred was back in the bedroom and perched on a chair, wiv the computer on his lap. "What do you know about spikin drinks?"

Fred looked up, that gory lipstick still plastered all over his gob.

Henry tutted. "Wipe your mouth, Fred. You look like you've been tonguin a bird who's got the painters in."

Fred looked quizzical, but then it clicked. He rubbed his suit sleeve across his lips.

"Now, one more time," Henry said. "What do you know about spikin people?"

"What, like raping?"

"Yeah. What drugs do they use, an' what do they do?"

"GHB or Rohypnol, I think," Fred replied. "The clubbers use it too. We do a pretty good line in it, actually..."

"Not anymore we fackin don't! We ain't sellin that stuff no more!" Henry lowered his tone, mainly because such exertion hurt his mudflaps. "Anyway, what I wanna know is, when's this shite gonna be outta my body?"

"Depends on your constitution, I suppose," Fred said, starin at the blank screen o' the laptop.

Henry breathed in. "Well it's lucky that I'm as tough as an ox, then. Okay, onto uvver things." He paused. "Over the next few minutes, I don't want you makin eye contact wiv me, you understand?"

"Er... yes, Henry."

"Right then." Henry braced himself. "Then tell me - what does my arse look like?"

Fred's eyes floated up from the screen. He seemed to struggle, as if he was scribblin mental crosses next to certain words and phrases. At last, Fred said, "It looks... painful."

Henry puffed. "That's not what I meant, is it? I can feel how much it hurts myself. What I'm askin is, woss the damage? How big is the wound?"

Fred stammered, "Well, it's not a...not a wound, as such. I mean, there's blood, and a bit of, um... but it's more like something has *fallen out.*"

Henry felt his face lose blood. "Jesus fackin

Christ. You mean on the floor somewhere?"

"No," Fred corrected. "It's still attached, but it's hanging out. Like it needs to be...pushed back in, or something."

"Alright, alright," Henry said, holdin up a hand. "Then I need you to get on the internet an' search for somethin."

"Okay," Fred said, soundin glum. "What am I looking for?"

Henry had never felt so much shame. "Type 'prolapse'."

Fred battered the keys.

"Eurgh..." Fred muttered after a moment, peekin at the screen through one eye. "This bird is squirtin hers out her arse." He looked digusted, but then sniggered. "Here, Henry, you might want to see this. She's got her fingers in the..."

When he glanced up at Henry, he straightened his face an' closed his stupid fackin mouth. Then he began searchin again. "This is more like it."

Amongst a load of awful snapshots of anal injuries, they soon learned that what was pokin out from Henry's bumcheeks was part of his rectal wall. Wiv-out expression or comment, Fred read out the details o' the surgery that could put Henry right. After the phrase "an incision is made into the perineum", Henry told his employee to stop.

"Well, now we know that the treatment is fackin horrible, but what *I* wanna know is, what would happen if I jus' left it? Rested up, ate lots o' soup an' that. Would it get better?"

Fred scoured more pages. "Okay, listen to this. It says here that if the lining has only fallen out by 7cm or less, it should slip back within 96 hours. So you'll be alright! No need for the hospital!"

"So it's hangin out less than 7cm, is it?"

"Well, yeah, I reckon it must be."

Henry cocked his head. "Fred - when we're talkin about my ability to shit right, I need to know *for sure*."

"But you said that you didn't want to call a doctor."

Henry shook his head a fraction each way. "Look, I don't care how much cash you want afterwards - it'll be no object, trust me." He closed his eyes. "Go an' wash your hands. There's a ruler in me desk drawer..."

Followin the second most degradin moment o' Henry's life, Fred looked traumatised. Couldn't keep his hands still, and kept shruggin his shoulders.

"Come back round here so I can see ya properly, Fred," Henry said, still on his front on the bed. He attempted wry humour. "You weren't expectin to do somethin like *that* when you were makin your mornin cuppa, were ya? Don't worry, you'll get your reward. But for now

I need you to listen, coz this is very fackin important."

Fred nodded, starin above Henry's eyeline. "What do you want?"

Henry sneered. "I want blood. Nine rosy red pints, poured out o' the twat o' the sadistic tart who did this to me. I want her here, I want her *now*, an' I wanna watch her *die*."

Fred nodded. "Rebecca."

"Round up your contacts: partners, employees, friends, families, pets, an' any uvver cunts you can think of. Tell 'em I'm lookin for her. Get someone to stake out her flat. Check the 'ospitals. Tell the rest of 'em that she shouldn't be hard to find, coz she's wearin a glitzy silver dress an' she's got a bloody great hole in her arm. Tell 'em I'm offerin a lotta cash to the first person who tells me where she is."

A ringin came from the lounge.

"Get that for me, wouldya, Fred? Then start makin some calls."

Fred zombied outta the room and came back wiv Henry's mobile. Henry looked at the name on the screen.

"About fackin time," he muttered.

But when he answered he fell speechless, an' the weight o' the day started to crush him.

Ray

It's not as if a weight has been lifted from Ray; it's as if the glue of a loathsome Hallowe'en costume has come unstuck, and the suit is peeling away from his skin in satisfying chunks. He is in a house that smells of rotten meat, assisting his deeply unstable companion in the manual transport of an unconscious gang member, but Raymond Atticus feels like smiling.

The façade is over. He's made a swathe of irreversible mistakes that have taken him far away from where he would like to be, but for the first time in weeks he feels an ember of resolve. It's so simple: he'll confess. Regardless of the truth of Henry's intentions, or of Ray's mother's affair, or of his father Bernard's suicide, Ray is ready to start the long journey home - even if it means imprisonment.

It's so blindingly obvious, now. Henry has spent the past year luring Ray, coercing him, and finally forcing him to commit murder, all with the aim of cementing him to the spot. Well, forget that. He may have a lot of maturing to do, but no one is in control of Raymond Atticus, except for Raymond Atticus.

He's far from singing with joy, of course. What he is planning is enormous, preposterous - to take down a mid-level crime syndicate by approaching a bribed police force. It's like the plot of a stupid movie, or an even stupider book, but, you know what?

Crazier stuff happens.

The most important thing is that this feels *right*.

It's the best course of action for Thomas, too. In comparison to Locker and Henry, Thomas's mental state seems oddly innocuous. Okay, *innocuous* isn't the right word for the behaviour of a man who stores five corpses in his bedroom, but Ray senses that there's naivety in everything Thomas does. What the poor bastard needs is treatment rather than condemnation.

On the stairway, Ray allows Thomas to soak the towel again and wrap it around Locker's neck. It's probably a dangerous thing to do – people die breathing such fumes – but necessary.

Ray switches the gun back to safety and tucks it into his trousers, and then takes Locker's legs. He feels a sense of odd disappointment at having to leave Thomas's dank home so quickly, as if that squadron of naked bodies from his dreams is somewhere close by, waiting longingly for him behind one of the farmhouse's many closed doors – or perhaps out back, in the garden.

it's okay, yes yes yes... you'll stay for a while longer... you'll see...

Thomas heaves the dead weight of Locker's head and shoulders, and together they carry his heavy-set body down the stairs towards the front door. Before passing the boundary, Ray suddenly feels conflicted, as if what they're doing truly is deranged and what he should actually do is stay there, in the farmhouse. He has a bristling urge to drop Locker's legs, whip out his gun and fire it again and again into Thomas's face.

yes yes yes yes yes!

Feeling a snarl contort his face, Ray is just about to let go and snatch the gun when they step -

- out into the tree-shaded warmth. The sun had dipped in the sky. Ray shook his muzzy head, hoping to clear the odd, creeping sense that the farmhouse was sorry to see him leave.

don't go, no no no... not yet... we can be friends, pleeeeeease...

"Down," Ray said, when they reached Locker's dark four-wheeled monster. His cheeks felt inflamed from heaving Locker along, so it was a relief when they had lowered the body to the dust. Ray crouched and fished in the man's pockets. He withdrew the keychain and balanced it on the back of his hand. Attempting to entertain Thomas, he held his hand up and rippled his knuckles dextrously. The three keys paraded across Ray's fingers like metal soldiers. He squinted up into the sunlight, hoping that Thomas was grinning, but when he got back to his feet, Thomas looked feverish.

"Look," Ray said. "I don't understand what's gone on today, at the shop or in your house, but...

everything is going to be okay. It might not feel as if you want this, but, trust me; things are better this way. You'll get the help you need. We'll *both* get help."

Thomas shrugged.

Ray wanted to say something significant. "I...I killed a man. I, um, I shot him. It hit his head, um, his eye, and he died right there. I don't think I meant to do it. I think he was a scumbag, but..." He was floundering. "There might be people out there who were terribly affected by what I did. This guy had a wife and family and friends, you know?" He looked at Thomas, who said nothing; he barely looked as if he was listening. "Are you going to be alright?" Ray asked.

"I'm fine," Thomas replied, his gaze on the house. "It's probably for the best, yeah."

Ray opened the boot, wanting to get moving before he lost his nerve. "Come on, help me get him inside."

They lifted Locker again, Ray grunting with the strain. He folded Locker's legs at the knee and fitted him awkwardly into the boot. Locker was so large that he had to be laid sideways and curled into a ball, with his wrists lying flat against his shins. A large sports bag in the far corner of the boot space clanked against Locker's spine. With his eyes closed and his spear-shaped jaw relaxed, he appeared strangely at peace.

"Should we tie him up, do you think?" Ray asked.

"I haven't got a rope or anything," Thomas said. "I guess we could try and use towels? He'll stay asleep for a while, though, breathing in that stuff."

Ray chewed his lip, and then slammed the trunk over Locker's crumpled form. "No, let's not waste any more time."

He circled the vehicle, opened the driver's door, and climbed up into the seat. The vehicle smelled clean and well cared-for. Thomas remained staring at the house. If he'd tried to run, Ray probably wouldn't have given chase.

It felt strange to sit in Locker's seat. Ray had only ever piloted his driving instructor's little hatchback and his mother's old crate, and even in these extreme circumstances he felt a twinge of excitement to be hijacking such a beast. Thomas clambered into the 4x4 beside him, wearing a pained expression as he gazed through the windscreen.

Ray asked, "You okay, mate? It's going to be fine, don't wor-"

Thomas lunged and clamped a handful of cloth over Ray's mouth and nose. A sulphurous sting hit his brain. He tried to pull away, writhing sidewards, but only managed to butt his cheek into the window. Thomas's grip was merciless and Ray felt his skull slam back into the headrest. A second later, Thomas straddled him like an ungainly, obese lover, thrusting the cloth harder into Ray's face, filling his throat with noxious chemicals.

Beneath Thomas's lumbering strength, panic and adrenaline swept through Ray. His gear-change arm was pinned against his seat by a heavy thigh, and Thomas had secured his other wrist against the door. Ray tried to thrash his legs but Thomas leaned in closer, disabling Ray with his bulk.

Ray's ears filled with muffled wheezing and the cloth's poisonous vapours devoured the day. With his head tightly restrained, Ray stared into the blurring face of a man he had once called a friend. There was no malice in Thomas's expression, only vacant sorrow.

The car morphed into a dream and Ray's assailant distorted, softened. Life was filling with grey mist, but this was a hungrier, more opaque fog than that of Ray's usual panic - rather than wishing to run, Ray's body craved darkness. Even as the dulling influence of the fumes weakened Ray's limbs he couldn't submit to defeat, and struggled uselessly.

"I'm so sorry, Ratan," Thomas's voice crackled, like distant static. "But I can't let you tell people about me. No one will want to help me, out there. They'll burn me..."

Ray's consciousness drifted beneath a black

curtain.

"I'm sorry," Thomas wept. His roiling face looked out through the passenger window, up towards the tree-scraped, swirling sky. "I just can't go against them. I can't."

When Thomas turned back, his features atomised.

"It might be alright if we do things *this* way, too," said a voice to Ray, from the bottom of a deep well. Then nothing.

CHAPTER 14
"The Gardden"

Thomas

When there were no more panicky, jerky jolts left in Ratan's body and he was dozing soundly, Thomas slipped the rag back into his pocket and wiped his own tears from Ratan's cheeks. After a minute or two, Thomas left the car, opened the driver's side and lifted Ratan out, cradling his head and carrying his legs with care. He could barely take his eyes off his friend's face as he walked.

Friend.

"I'm sorry," Thomas repeated, as he took Ratan back –

- into the house. He paces through to the kitchen. The children seem to sigh musically, like a choir. Still holding Ratan up, he takes his friend's gun and drops it into the bin. It clinks against Gary's weapon, which Thomas had chucked away just an hour or so earlier.

In the Gardden, the leaves rustle, the branches sway.

"I couldn't hurt him," Thomas says when he reaches the rotten elm tree, hugging Ratan to his chest. "I didn't know what I should do, so I'm leaving it up to you guys. I know this probably means that I lost The People Game, and I'm sorry." He bends his knees and lays Ratan down onto the soil, sits down next to him and strokes his forehead. "Simon, do you hear me? Ratan doesn't believe in you, and he wants to tattle-tell on me, so I'm going to leave him here for *you* to decide."

Ratan's silly idea pops back into his brain – the one about the children and the Gardden being imaginary.

"*I* know you're real, but if I come back here and Ratan's okay, then I'm going to go to the police with him." Thomas rubs his pal's shoulder, hoping real hard that he'll get to see him again.

The children do nothing, say nothing, but Thomas knows... thinks?... that they're paying attention.

"Don't hurt him. Please. He doesn't deserve it. He's nice to me. Maybe even *you* guys would like him." He takes Ratan's hand and gives it a farewell squidge. "So, if you *have* to do something bad, make it quick, okay? *Okay?*"

The dead trees mutter and creak, like old joints.

"I hope you're listening," Thomas says, letting go of Ratan's hand. "If you're there."

After another sad glance at his buddy's skinny body, with its creased shirt and tie all askew, Thomas goes to the house to fetch the suitcase.

Gary

Fuck me, what is that?

Sharp pain and a dehydrated comedown rattle through Gary, and a fucking *terrible* stench makes him retch. Static fills his head. Little waves keep splashing against his skin. Gary can see nothing bar a red blur, and it feels as if his eyelids have been superglued shut.

He can't remember anything after standing in the

garden, holding the gun inside the fat prick's mouth. He'd meant to kill the paedo scumbag, but then... then he'd woken up *here*, wherever *here* is.

He can feel cold walls meeting behind him, which tell him that he's sat up in a corner somewhere. He digs his fingers into his crusted eye sockets. The fluttering waves vanish and return, tickling him as he scrapes away something that feels like scabs.

Gary opens his sticky eyes to a dense cloud of buzzing, swirling insects. He opens his mouth in shock and the tiny creatures dart inside, crawling across his tongue, scuttling across the roof of his mouth. He chokes and spits, horrified, flailing to shake off the flies, palming them away, but it's no use. Too many of the bastards!

Flitting bluebottles and dried blood coat Gary's tracksuit. When he attempts to stand, he quickly slumps back into the corner, his legs giving way like a pisshead at the end of a night's drinking. Trying again, he pushes himself up using the walls to steady himself. The humming swarm seems to clear a space before closing in again.

He's in a double bedroom without carpet, the floorboards uneven stretches of damp, splintered wood. There are a couple of old wooden chests and a tall wardrobe in one corner, but the only prominent furniture is the bed. Bugs pattern the sheets, crowd the ceiling and scuttle across the mildewed walls.

Gary freezes when he sees the four bodies. Their eyeless heads poke from the bedcovers, in a row across the stained pillows. Gary has never seen a corpse before, and can't help but whimper. Two of them look like slimy, brown-and-yellow mannequins, while the other pair are more like dusty, unwrapped mummies. Gary covers his mouth. The stink, like bad meat, is almost too much. His heart slams in his throat and he sways, trying not to tumble to the floor again.

Should never have come here. Should never have gone to the shop. Should never have promised Rebecca a single shitty thing.

He shuffles forwards, cutting an unsteady path through the bugs. When he reaches the huge corridor outside he pulls the door closed behind him, chest heaving as he breathes the fresher air. Aside from some droning flies that managed to escape the bedroom, the hallway feels still.

Where the hell is the fat man?

More importantly, is Gary *dying*? Now that he's come to a stop, he notices that he's lightheaded and wracked with pain. He rolls up his sleeves and sees green-rimmed holes speckling his flesh. They leak blood every time he moves, and the pain and the dark patches across his tracky tell him there are more to see.

What did that fucker do to me?

A corridor stretches off to his right and a set of stairs before him lead to what must be the ground floor. Gary begins to shake at the thought of encountering Thomas again. The fat shit had seemed so harmless in the shop, pissing his pants and acting dumb. Now, knowing who the man really is and what he's done, Gary can't bear the thought of meeting him again in this wretched, shitty farmhouse.

He taps his grubby hands over his pockets but finds no gun, no wallet, and, *fuck*, no car keys either. He touches his seat pocket and finds the shape of his phone. That's something, at least.

His legs are unreliable as he heads down the stairs.

Even if he has to walk all the way, he has to get back home. Halfway down the steps, there's a dried, rusty patch. Shit, had the fat guy dragged him out of the garden, through the house and up this staircase? At the bottom, Gary turns to walk the short distance to the front door, but instead meets the familiar, sparkling eyes of his lost daughter.

He stops.

Gapes.

Dry mud streaks Hanna from hair to feet. She has her hands clasped politely behind her, and her smirking face is pale but smudged brown. She's no taller than Gary's waistband and she wears the same pretty blue dress and black sandals she had worn on that awful day eight months ago, when she was snatched.

Snatched and killed.

Dark with smudged soil, she leans her head to the side curiously, grinning as if Gary has fallen for a prank. When she moves her head, curls of her dirty blonde hair drop from one shoulder and down over her thin, six-year-old chest.

"Hi daddy," she says, beaming at him, as if no time has passed since that rainy day in the park.

Gary's throat hardly opens. "Hanna..."

"Did you miss me?" she asks, framed by poster-coated walls and the light from the kitchen behind her.

Gary finds his voice. "My little doll. I thought you were gone." He drops to his knees and pulls her to him. She smells of soil and doesn't hug him back, but Gary is just glad to have her in his arms again. When he speaks, his voice wavers and the words come out in a haphazard rush. "I'm so sorry this has all happened. It's all my fault but I'll never let another bad thing happen to you, honestly love, you're the most precious thing in my life and I thought you'd gone forever and I'm so sorry that I let it happen. I'll do better this time, I promise, honest I will."

She giggles into his ear and her breath smells like a grave. "That's okay daddy, don't be silly," she says, chirpily. "The stupid fat man has been taking care of me. He's going to bring us another friend to play with."

Gary pulls back and looks into her eyes, which are edged with grey but glow warmly, playfully.

"Now listen," Gary says. "I'm going to take you away from here and you're going to tell me everything that's happened. Everything will be alright again. It'll just be you, me and your mummy living far, far away. We'll be really happy again, just you wait."

She laughs and her eyes pinch shut, as they always had whenever she'd found something funny. "No, daddy. I'm going to stay here with Simon and Benny, and maybe the fat man."

Gary's temper frays. "Now you listen to me, Hanna: you're coming home and I don't want any arguments. That man is very bad. He took you away from your mummy and me, and...and..."

Gary feels his face crease.

Hanna's here, Hanna's back, your little doll's here in front of you but she's dead and she doesn't want to leave...

"Just come with me and see mummy, okay?" Gary says. He goes to grab Hanna's shoulder, but somehow she dodges him without appearing to move.

"Daddy," she says, mock-scolding. Her teeth gleam in the dimness of the corridor, clean and white against the soil that crusts her skin. "I'm staying here, I told you. But you know what? We're all playing a game – even you. If you win, maybe you'll get to stay here, too.

You could be my daddy again, and help look after Simon and Benny."

Hanna's voice sounds strangely unfamiliar. It's deeper and more confident than Gary remembers, like a bad impersonation of his daughter. Gary blinks and the sunlight from the kitchen brightens, seeming to cut a beam right through her.

"I don't want any nonsense from you, young lady," Gary says, testing a phrase that he remembers Sandra using. He reaches out but still doesn't touch her. "You're coming with me."

"What's wrong, daddy? Shit, everything's fine, just like you said."

"Hanna, don't speak like that. That's not how nice girls talk."

Hanna's grin widens, and it's like Gary is seeing her through a fish-eye camera lens.

"Are you okay?" she asks, and for a moment Gary thinks that her eyes have rolled back into her head. "Do you want to play with us? Because if you do, first you have to win The People Game."

He shakes his head, trying to take Hanna by the arm again. This time his fingers wrap around her skin and it feels like tree bark, rough and cold. When he looks back at her face, her cheeks seems to ripple like muddy water. Her jaw twitches and her tongue lolls from her mouth, coated in mucus.

"Hanna, are you alri..." he begins to ask, but his words trail away.

Hanna's pupils swallow the whites of her eyes, and something red slithers out from beneath each eyeball, a millimetre at first but growing, widening the gap.

"You never loved me, daddy," the little girl with the coal-black eyes says, in the voice of a grown man. Her lips stretch open and her lower eyelids peel downwards in two finger-wide strips, like red tears. "You let the fat guy take me away because that's what you always wanted, isn't it? Someone to snatch me so that you could sniff up your special powders again."

Gary lets go of her arm but now *she* grabs *him*, with fingers that are like five black, worm-eaten twigs. Gary tries to pull away but sheholds him tight and a dark, splintery digit finds one of the green holes in Gary's arm.

"Mummy never wanted me to leave, but you did," she groans, through a mouth grown several times too large. Her rotten finger slips into Gary's forearm. "You nasty fucking addict. Did you even cry for me?" The pink beneath her peeling eyelids flexes, as if something is trying to break through, and her lips flop down and away from her gums, her jawbone clicking as it opens wider, wider. "*If you really loved me, you'd stay and play with me,*" the thing before him snarls. "*Yes yes yes, you'd play and stay, play and stay, PLAY AND STAY!*"

Gary rips himself free and retreats from the mutating figure, burbling everything that comes into his mind. "I loved you, Hanna, and I was better when you were here, and I did it all for you! Maybe I will come and play with you but maybe not, because I know you aren't here, I know you aren't here, I know you aren't here..."

The waist-high figure advances, still in its pretty blue dress, still shrieking for Gary to play and stay, but now its upper half is a writhing mass of pinks, whites and stringy reds. Gary staggers to the doorway and grabs for the handle. He turns back one final time, to face the figure that is no longer his daughter, and then wrenches the door handle down. Light floods the hall and he runs.

LOCKER

TOTAL DARKNESS.

WHEN LOCKER AWOKE, HE WAS ON HIS SIDE, ARMS PRESSED BETWEEN HIS FOLDED LEGS. HE TRIED TO SIT UP BUT HIS FACE SLAMMED INTO A HARD, WIRY SURFACE. RAW AGONY THROBBED IN HIS SKULL, AND ONE HATEFUL THOUGHT RAN THROUGH HIS MIND.

THE GOTH CUNT.

HE'D KNOWN FROM THE BEGINNING THAT THE KID COULDN'T BE TRUSTED. FELT IT IMMEDIATELY. SOMETHING WOMANLY ABOUT HIM, SOMETHING *SNAKE-LIKE* THAT HAD MADE LOCKER WANT TO CRUSH THE FUCKER'S THROAT. HAVING SHOVED LOCKER DOWN THE STAIRS, THE SLIPPERY BASTARD HAD FINALLY SHOWN HIS TRUE SELF. EVEN HENRY COULDN'T ARGUE ANYMORE.

FIRST OFF THOUGH, LOCKER HAD TO WORK OUT WHERE THE HELL HE WAS. HE LAY IN A CONFINED SPACE AND COULDN'T SEE A THING. HIS ARMS ACHED AND HIS HEAD WAS PRESSED AGAINST WHAT FELT LIKE ROUGH CARPET. HE FLEXED HIS HANDS: NUMB. BLOOD RETURNED TO HIS RIGHT ARM WHEN HE MOVED IT, BUT THE ONE CRUSHED BENEATH HIM STAYED DEAD. HE EDGED HIS FEET FORWARDS UNTIL THEY TOUCHED SOMETHING SOLID. WHEREVER HE WAS, IT WAS HOT, CRAMPED, AND SMELLED OF OIL. SOMETHING DUG INTO LOCKER'S BACK, SO WITH HIS WORKING ARM HE REACHED BEHIND HIM, JUST ABOVE THE BASE OF HIS SPINE.

A HOLDALL, MADE BULKY BY ITS CONTENTS. SOMETHING INSIDE JANGLED.

LOCKER ALMOST LAUGHED. HE'D'VE KNOWN THE SOUND OF HIS FRIENDS ANYWHERE.

THE DIRTY, SNEAKY, GOTH BASTARD HAS PUT ME IN THE

BOOT OF MY OWN 4X4.

HIS TEMPLES PULSED DULLY, BUT THE PRESENCE OF HIS FRIENDS WAS REASSURING. RETURNING HIS ARM TO HIS SIDE, HE FELT A BULGE IN ONE TROUSER POCKET. FUCKING AMATEUR HADN'T EVEN TAKEN AWAY HIS PHONE. WITH EFFORT, LOCKER EASED OUT THE MOBILE AND LOOKED AT ITS SCREEN. FIVE MISSED CALLS FROM HENRY, AND MORE THAN AN HOUR HAD PASSED SINCE THE GOTH HAD PUSHED HIM DOWN THE STAIRS.

ANGER REARED BUT HE STORED IT AWAY. SAVED IT.

HE CALLED HENRY.

"ABOUT FACKIN' TIME," HIS BOSS ANSWERED.

EVERYTHING IMPROVED AT THE SOUND OF HENRY'S VOICE.

LOCKER WHISPERED RAPIDLY, "HENRY. I WAS RIGHT ABOUT THE KID. HE'S LOCKED ME IN MY BOOT. HE KNOCKED ME DOWN THE STAIRS AT..." HE STOPPED. "YOU KNOW ABOUT THE ROBBERY, RIGHT?"

"PERCY, WHAT THE FACK ARE YOU..."

"SOMEONE STOLE THE STASH FROM THE GREEN EMPORIUM OFFICE. MIGHT HAVE BEEN THE FAT GUY WHO WORKS THERE, MIGHT HAVE BEEN SOMEONE ELSE. ANYWAY, WE WENT TO THE FAT GUY'S HOUSE AND IT TURNS OUT THAT HE'S A FUCKING PSYCHO. HE'S GOT FIVE STIFFS UP IN HIS BEDROOM AND THE MONEY, LOOKS LIKE ALL OF IT, IS IN A CAR OUTSIDE."

"PERCY, SLOW DOWN."

"SORRY. SO ANYWAY, I WENT BACK INTO THE HOUSE AND I WAS HEADING UP THE STEPS WHEN SUDDENLY, THE GOTH C... RAYMOND... SPRINTS TOWARDS ME, SCREAMING. KNOCKED ME DOWN THE STAIRS! AND NOW I'VE WOKEN UP IN THE BOOT OF THE 4X4 AND I DON'T KNOW WHAT TO DO."

THERE WAS A LONG SILENCE. THEN, IN A STRAINED VOICE, HENRY SAID, "SOUNDS LIKE YOU'RE ALMOST HAVIN' AS BAD A DAY AS I AM."

"WHAT DO YOU MEAN? TELL ME WHO IT IS AND I'LL SORT IT, YOU KNOW I WILL..."

"NEVER MIND FOR NOW. I S'POSE YOU THINK RAY'S INVOLVED IN THIS ROBBERY, THEN, EH?"

"MAYBE," LOCKER REPLIED, CAREFULLY. "I DON'T SEE ANY OTHER REASON HE'D ATTACK ME. SO ... DO YOU BELIEVE ME ABOUT HIM NOW?"

LOCKER HEARD A SAD BREATH. "PERCY, CONSIDERIN' THE DAY I'M HAVIN', I'D BELIEVE JUST ABOUT ANYTHIN'."

"WHAT'S WRONG AT YOUR END, BOSS?"

HENRY CHUCKLED. "MY *END* IS HALF THE BLEEDIN' PROBLEM. MY EX-LADYFRIEND HAS TURNED ON ME, IN THE WORST POSSIBLE WAY." HENRY'S VOICE BECAME DEEP AND SERIOUS. "I WANT THAT SLAG HERE, IN FRONT O' ME, AN' I WANNA WATCH 'ER DIE. THIS IS THE ONE TIME THAT I'D LIKE TO SEE YOU USE EACH ONE O' YOUR LITTLE FRIENDS TO THEIR FULL FACKIN' POTENTIAL."

"AS SOON AS I'M OUT OF HERE, HENRY," LOCKER SAID. "I'LL DO ANYTHING YOU WANT."

"THAT'S GOOD TO HEAR, PERCY, COZ I'M NOT SURE I COULD TAKE ANY MORE BETRAYAL TODAY. YOU GOT ANY IDEA HOW YOU'LL GET YOURSELF OUTTA THERE? ANY WAY TO OPEN IT FROM THE INSIDE?"

"NO."

"NO, I S'POSE NOT. YOU'RE USED TO SHUTTIN' *UVVER* CUNTS IN THERE, EH? SO WHERE'S THIS FAT BLOKE STAYIN'?"

"BIG FARMHOUSE ON THE ROAD LEAVING TOWN," PERCY SAID. "LOOKS RUN-DOWN AS HELL, NEXT TO THE FOREST."

THERE WAS A SOUND FROM OUTSIDE: A SCUFFLE OF FEET AND A MUMBLE.

"HENRY," LOCKER HISSED. "SOMEONE'S NEARBY. HOLD ON, I'LL CALL YOU BACK. IT MIGHT BE THE KID."

"PERCY, DON'T HURT -"

LOCKER HUNG UP.

FROM THE BOOT, ALL OUTSIDE NOISES WERE MUFFLED. A MALE VOICE WAS SPEAKING, BUT THE WORDS WEREN'T CLEAR.

ACTUALLY, WAS IT TWO PEOPLE? THE FATTY AND THE GOTH? HE STRAINED TO LISTEN.

"...ORT OF. WELL, I...SHOP, NOW I'M...TO IT, BUT...HAVE THE MONEY, ALL OF IT...PARKED UP OUTSIDE A FARMHOUSE...ROAD OUT OF TOWN...BACKED BY...MISS IT."

WAS THE GOTH TALKING ABOUT THE CASH?

LOCKER BEGAN TO FUME.

TAKEN HENRY'S FUCKING MONEY... LOCKED ME IN MY OWN FUCKING BOOT... YOU'RE GONNA FUCKING PAY...

THE 4X4'S DOOR CLICKED AND A RUMBLE PASSED THROUGH THE BOOT. THE GOTH HAD STARTED THE ENGINE.

WHAT THE HELL DOES THAT POOF THINK HE'S DOING? HOW FUCKING DARE HE...

LOCKER'S STOMACH ROLLED AS THE VEHICLE BEGAN TO MOVE. STARS LIKE GUNFIRE SPRANG ACROSS THE DARKNESS AND LOCKER SNAPPED. BECAME RAMPANT. STARTED HAMMERING THE ROOF.

NO ONE FUCKING DOES THIS TO ME!

LOCKER HAD TAKEN BEATINGS IN THE PAST, EVEN BEEN STABBED ONCE, BUT NEVER ANYTHING LIKE THIS. NEVER TRAPPED IN HIS OWN FUCKING VEHICLE.

FUCKING GOTH, FUCKING FAGGOT, FUCKING USELESS SPINELESS CUNT...

THE 4X4 ROCKED FORWARDS. THEN THE ENGINE DIED.

LOCKER STOPPED.

WAS THE GOTH COMING TO GET HIM?

THREATEN HIM?

ATTACK HIM?

IT SHOULD HAVE BEEN FUNNY BUT, THERE IN THE BOOT, FOLDED WITH THREE OUT OF FOUR LIMBS USELESS, LOCKER WAS VULNERABLE. FRANTIC, HE REACHED BACK AND FUMBLED FOR THE BAG. TUGGED AT THE ZIP.

THE CLICK OF THE DRIVER'S DOOR.

FOOTSTEPS IN THE GRAVEL.

BREATHING STEEPLY, LOCKER REACHED INTO THE ZIPPER AND FOUND A METAL HANDLE.
A VOICE OUTSIDE.
A KEY'S CLATTER IN THE BOOT'S LATCH.
LOCKER WOULD FEEL THE LANKY FUCKER'S FLESH TEAR IN HIS HANDS.

Ray

Ray dreams that he is lying on his back in a dark, overgrown

GARDDEN

garden.

When he stands up, his head feels sore and unbalanced. The moonlight paints the sky beyond the trees a silvery grey, and shadowy, scabrous figures reach out to him with withered limbs.

They are the house. They are the children.

They are the Garrden.

we like you little man yes yes yes

Ray freezes, hit by an unfamiliar unease. It isn't just the trees; it is an overwhelming sense of authority, of something watching over him yet craving supervision.

Daddy?

This paternal but needy presence waits within every strip of bark, every stone, every parched blade of grass. It's inside the memories of the *ancient*

young things below him, whose lives were snatched away when they were only beginning. It's behind a wall of undergrowth and inside the huge farmhouse, clogged with its harsh smells and traumatic memories. Ray knows that it's even inside Thomas.

In his dream, Ray understands that

the Gardden

his Daddy is a hungry, jealous thing. Daddy is fickle and playful. Daddy has always been here, and cannot empathise; Daddy can only *overwhelm*.

Beyond these impressions, there lies something perhaps even more disconcerting: Daddy... the Gardden... wants to make friends with Ray.

we'll kill the others, yes yes, eat them, snatch them, son ... we'll imagine everything we want

Ray's dreaming self surveys the green shadows. He mustn't enrage

it

us

them

this fatherly thing, the Gardden, despite the fact that he can feel that it means him no harm - for now.

Ray's breath catches. Although he can see nothing but wizened silhouettes, he *senses* something open a pair of vast, formless eyes. They

it

we

she

see him, *see into him.* Ray feels that he should cower, like a worshipper at the feet of a malevolent god. With a wink of one vast orb, the Gardden could pound every bone in his body to viscous marrow.

I could, I would, I might

no no no we mustn't because we looooooove you Ray Ratan Raymond-son yes yes yes

While Ray trembles beneath the wooden shades, the Gardden reveals a sprawling showreel of images to him.

I will tell you a story yes yes

The revelations are an extended hand, a request for companionship: glimpses of

honest truth

fantasy that are scattered amongst the ragged wood and leaves, flickering purposefully on and off, one at a time, like frameless television screens.

Displayed upon one portal, directly above Ray's head, he sees an image of a lush forest of many acres, engulfed by fire. The Gardden, which, back then, was a nameless, ageless presence haunting the spaces beneath the land, had ignited the blaze itself. Afterwards, the incinerated trees left the soil enriched, perfect for agriculture.

Ray watches the "screen" display a solitary,

buck-toothed man shaping the area into a farm, tending the fertile ground with an enthusiasm that verged on love. When the land unleashed vegetables and could sustain cattle and sheep, this farmer took a wife and raised a family.

The first shimmering screen blinks off and another, at Ray's feet, flashes on, showing him the moment that the Gardden learned the joy of intervention. One day, quite capriciously, the Gardden concentrated - Ray felt it as he watched - and plucked all four limbs from the farmer's youngest son, leaving the toddling boy a wailing, helpless torso.

The sight should have mortified Ray, but Daddy swiftly changed the image on the screen, and showed him many years later

a blink

when the farmer was an old man, the Gardden enticed trees to shoot from the ground overnight. Another screen, another flash forward in time, a later generation, and the Gardden forced a deer to dance like a puppet, before spilling its innards across the grass with a pop and a spurt. On another screen and at another time still, the Gardden caused foot-long horns to erupt bloodily from the skull of an old woman.

Light spills from behind Ray, and he turns. A few feet away, yet another of the forest's shimmering screens has clicked on, bathing him in its glow. He watches as

watch it, son, yes yes yes... have fun... you can win the game if you watch and play and stay stay stayyyyy

a different mother howled in dismay. The Gardden had found a new game: speaking through a newborn. It squeezed noises from the mewling creature, manipulating meat and muscle to form sounds that its parents recognised. In response to the mother's rage, as she knelt and wept on the grass in shock, the Gardden forced her tongue to leap from her throat, extended the thick pink tissue a full three metres above her head, and hanged her from a tree.

Over further generations, Ray saw the family learn that contesting the Gardden's games never reaped benefits. The Gardden

allows

will allow

allowed them to continue their lives, but interrupted ever more frequently with pranks, games and absurdities.

Over time

yes yes funny fun playtime, son, yes yes you like this don't you

SLAUGHTER FUCKING HATRED LONELY CANT BEAR THIS SHITSTABBING MISERY ALONE ALONE ALONE FOREVER AND

EVER

it grew restless.

The families plodded on, squirted out new people, and eventually learned to accept the Gardden's meddling as an unalterable fact of life. They were wary, often on guard, but no longer so fazed when the Gardden animated an oak tree, or rearranged the heads of their livestock, or swelled a family member's body several times its original size. In response to their suffering, the adults warned the youngsters to pay the Gardden respect, to try not to react, and in effect to pretend it wasn't there.

Absorbed by the screen, Ray sensed that their attitudes soon bored the Gardden

no fun, sad face sad face, no no no

and it withdrew, closed its intangible eyes, and slept.

In the dimness, a new, more vibrant screen appears directly before Ray, like a glowing home cinema he's sat too close to. It shows a suited man shaking hands with an old farmer with a lined face and pendulous jowls. Ray's next view reveals men wearing fluorescent, protective clothing laying a road where the farmland used to be.

In his dream - which is, of course, the only thing that this strange vision can be - Ray is suddenly back inside the house; an unseen, silent observer of an extended family of six. In contrast to the way it is now, the house is blandly decorated, neat, carpeted, and lacking any creeping mould, clouds of spiderwebs or layers of grey dust.

watch, son, watch the story so you will want to play and stay and be our happy child and daddy

ALONE AND HATEFUL,

happy happy happy yes yes yes

The family's two eldest are a senile, doddery pair. Until now, Ray knows that the slumbering Gardden had never influenced their lives, but appear to Ray to carry some genetic remnant of unease, perhaps passed down through generations of troubled ancestors. Their son is a tall, careful man who wears a perpetually vacant smile. His grotesquely obese wife is a bedbound matriarch whose sole movements are to swallow the sweet delicacies her husband pushes into her moist lips.

dirty filthy foul sick blubber

funny fatty woman yes yes silly fatty

DEAD AND ROTTING CUNT

One of their sons is a slim, wilful eight-year-old who appears to have inherited his father's body and his mother's authoritarianism; the other is a round twelve-year-old, cursed with his father's servile nature and his mother's large frame. In the echoing currents of his sleep, as the family live their daily routines, Ray watches the two sons learning from and imitating their parents.

The father seems to love the mother while simultaneously despising every repulsive inch of her, and by feeding her unquenchable appetite he neglects his children. Sometimes he pummels his prostrate wife in a bout of frustrated, raging violence, but afterwards always apologises politely, allows the meaningless smile to return to his face, and shuffles back out of the bedroom.

Ray watches them age, and when the man's mother is no longer able to care for herself, her gigantic daughter-in-law offers to share her bed. Gnarled by arthritis, the ancient grandfather soon joins them too, and in that sweat-stained chamber he, his wife and their obscene daughter-in-law are fed, cleaned and beaten by the vacantly smiling man for the rest of their days.

When the grandparents die in that very same bed, the man refuses to move them, partly out of spite for his wife, partly out of shocked grief.

Ray finds himself back outside, in the

GARDDEN

garden again, which is now flooded with foggy daylight. He sees that the elder sibling is by now a teenager, growing fatter and progressively obedient to his younger, bossier brother.

Ray sees for the first time that this overweight adolescent is, in fact, his friend and betrayer Thomas Bosworth.

it is okay Ray Ratan Raymond-son, it is fine fine fine ... you are young, yes yes yes, so we will take you to Disneyland Africa Mars Hell Heaven where we can all play and play and play and play and

The garden... Gardden... is lush and green as the two siblings play together, sharing a cake that young Thomas had taken from the kitchen. Their skin is blotched, unhealthy, but as they enjoy games and chase each other through the trees they appear content. They chuckle and skip, and Ray feels the same sensation he had at the start of his dream: like a deep, internal plug tearing free. The insubstantial eyes of the thing that should never have been

but I am yes yes yes and I will always be

snap wide open and the Gardden is suddenly awake. Its only desire is to play, so it speaks to young Thomas using his sibling's lips. Through the younger child, it tells Thomas to climb to the top of a great elm tree. The tubby young teen complies, clambering up into the branches. When he stops, mid-ascent, the wood creaking unsteadily under his weight, the Gardden uses his brother's smaller body to climb beyond Thomas, up, up and into the highest canopy.

"*Simon!*" Thomas calls.

The younger boy falls like a rock, clattering through the branches and landing on the ground beside Ray, broken, twisted and motionless.

Back on the ground, Thomas shakes his brother's splintered arm, like that of a stuffed toy. He stands up straight and curls his bottom lip, cocking his head as if hearing a distant whisper, and then dashes away before returning with a spade. He pauses after each thrust of the shovel, listens hard, then returns to burying his brother beneath the cold soil.

Thomas will never forget Simon, Ray understands. The Gardden

used

uses

will use Thomas's memories of his stern brother to turn Thomas into a

daddy

slave

friend to play with.

Ray wants to wake up now. He doesn't want to be dreaming about the Gardden or anything above or around or beneath him, telling him its tale and showing him the roots of its past.

It isn't possible, anyway. There can't be any great or godlike presence, coercing Ray to

play and stay and play and stay and play and
stay.

In the misty daylight, every screen that Ray had witnessed before appears and switches on simultaneously. In and amongst the leaves

watch watch watch yes yes yes stay stay stay

they reveal dark glimpses from the house: Thomas's grandparents stiffening and corroding in their stagnant bed, propped beside their son and his colossal wife; Thomas scrawling a crayon picture of two black eyes above a crowd of trees, titled in handwriting far too messy for his age: "THE GARDDEN"; Thomas growing older, visiting the flyblown bedroom to feed his parents cakes and pies that crawl with beetles; Thomas playing alone amongst the trees, pumping his limbs lightning-swift as the lush jungle greens wilt, the leaves drop like corpses, the healthy bark peels and the branches warp; Thomas's weakening parents, their lungs wracked with bacterium that teems from the rancid cadavers beside them; Thomas's mother and father dying, wretched with disease and hunger, clutching each other even in death and decay.

Then, with his family gone, the screens show the Gardden

became

will become

becoming the focus of Thomas's life. On one screen, a lost young boy wanders between the trees, his mousey hair in disarray and a forgotten twig tucked behind one ear. Thomas, encouraged by the Gardden, lurches towards the tiny, trusting five-year-old, crouching awkwardly and taking the child into his broad arms. The startled boy stiffens in alarm but Thomas hugs him tighter, squeezing the child against his own blubbery frame, choking and crushing his delicate body. When the child falls limp, Thomas

disappeared

will disappear

had disappeared

disappears from Ray's sight to fetch the spade again, to bury the little boy in the dirt beside Simon.

Although Ray knows that it's only a nightmare, he reels when on another screen he sees Thomas drag a suitcase into the Gardden and remove the slumped body of a second child: thin, pretty young girl in a blue dress. The images do not react to Ray's protests, and Thomas lays the girl flat against the ground. He reaches down and embraces her, heaving the air from her lungs and smothering her with his elephantine bulk.

Ray panics, pinching his arms in a famous gesture that fails to awaken him.

The screens switch off all at once, and Ray falls to his knees when

no no no don't fall it is good you can do this too yes yes yes you can play the Crying Game and Explore and the Knife Game and Slit The Cat and you can cry and dance and die and laugh and

two vast black eyes open above him, the

Gardden's eyes, the seething eyes of Ray's daddy, their gaze somehow calm and soothing yet utterly final. On every side, circling him, the nude forms of men and women, teens and geriatrics, nod their heads in unison, their oily eye sockets drinking him in, pleading silently for him to remain there with them forever.

Dumb with terror, down on his knees, Ray closes his eyes, telling himself that the all-seeing yet infinitely ignorant Gardden *simply cannot exist.* Absolutely nothing can be tittering into his ears, telling him to stay forever, playful and lonely, happy and hateful. And there's *certainly* no part of Ray that wants to do exactly as it wishes, care-free, snatching children and others for a

daddy

mummy

god

strange, hideously powerful companion, and...

Ray opens his eyes.

Although the world is bright and blurry, Ray knows that the dream is over.

He is lying on his back on the desiccated forest floor, squinting up through the cluttered branches towards the vibrant day beyond them. As his pounding blood slows, the nightmare ebbs away and he smiles with dopey relief.

It's only when Ray's vision clears that he sees the

face glowering down at him, like a mask of cold, leering malice.

Gary

Having sprinted down the front path and pressed his hands against the hot metal of the rented car, Gary turned back to face the farmhouse entrance and the empty passageway where his daughter had just been. He tried to swallow but his throat only clicked, tight and dry. He panicked – *I can't breathe* - but then heard the oxygen rushing in and out of him.

Hyperventilating, aren't you? Like that time you snorted coke, then smack, then special K, one after the other.

It felt different outside, with the rumble of the dual carriageway carrying on the breeze and the skeletal trees stood against the evening sun. Shit, that cool air felt good against his wounds, even though they still hurt like fuck.

The image of the *thing* in the corridor was still fresh in his brain.

His baby, Hanna.

His little doll.

Dead and buried in the fat man's garden but standing right there in the hall.

Fucking hallucination.

He'd seen all sorts of shit before, but never anything like that. Maybe the fat fuck had poisoned him – maybe *that* was what the green shit clogged around his wounds was. That or the bashes to the skull, comedown, shock, loss of blood... they were all working their nasty magic, weren't they? Gary shook his head doggedly, but felt like crying.

Pull yourself together.

Nothing that Hanna had said had been true. Not one thing. He'd loved her so much, hadn't he? Drugs were great and all that, but he would've done anything for his little doll, so that made him a good daddy, didn't it? *Didn't it?*

The farmhouse windows stared at him blankly.

"Fuck you," Gary muttered, under his breath.

It was a stupid, shitty thought, but Gary felt as if the house had lost interest in him.

You're just a twat, Gary. You were never going to win, you twat, twat, twatty twat...

A large black vehicle with tinted windows was parked against the verge. That hadn't been there when he'd got here, had it?

Maybe. Hadn't exactly been thinking straight.

He pulled at the handle of the rental. Locked. Shit, and he had no keys, did he? He went round to the other side.

He tried the other door, and muttered, "Fuck's sake."

He pressed his face against the glass. He wanted to flee, but if he had all the money he'd stuffed into Hanna's bag, Sandra and he would have a real helping hand to start their new life together, wouldn't they? Hanna's grey rucksack still lay across the back seat. He scanned the ground for a rock but saw nothing but gravel and weeds. Taking a deep breath, Gary wound back his fist and delivered the hardest punch he could to the centre of the rear window. There was a dry thud and a shock of new pain that jarred his arm. He cried out, clutching his pathetic, bloody limb.

Hadn't even marked the glass.

Twat...

He really wasn't cut out for all this, was he?

Gary's stomach suddenly dropped further – what about Rebecca? If Sandra ever found out about Gary's affair, there would be *no chance* of them patching things up. He remembered Rebecca's nails against his throat, but today's horrid fuss and bother made shagging Rebecca seem unimportant. How could she matter when Gary had lost so much, or when he compared her to Sandra, the mother of his dead child, and everything they'd been through?

Rebecca wasn't a goddess, was she? She pissed, shat and farted just like everyone else; he'd heard her in the guesthouse bathroom, even over the sound of the running water tap. She was just a bitter woman with a choking fetish. What had she gotten out of their relationship, anyway - a meeting of minds? Not really. A partner? Ha, *whatever, mate*. Great sex? Maybe, but only because he'd let her knock him about while she'd bounced around on top of him. So what else?

The truth slipped into Gary's brain so easily that it must have been there all along: it was because he'd done as he was told.

He took the mobile from his back pocket in a shaking, blood-stained hand – *shit, even reaching behind him hurt* - and leaned back against the car, resting his head beneath a slash of sunlight that glared through the trees. Squinting up at the sky through the branches, Gary called Rebecca's mobile.

"Gary, my sweet!" she cried. "Where are you? What's going on?"

He kept his tone flat. "Listen, just calm down for a moment. I've got things I need to say."

"Have you been arrested? Are you making your one phone call?" He never could tell if she was joking.

"No, nothing like that."

She became harsh. "Then why aren't you here? Why aren't you here with the money?"

"Look," Gary said, a headache brewing in his temples. "A lot has happened. I think I need the hospital."

"Did Henry find you?"

"What? Your boyfy? No, not at all. But the robbery didn't go as planned."

"Tell me *exactly* what's going on, Gary. First of all, do you have my money?"

Gary knew he should have been running to safety, but he needed this shit sorted first. "Yes, I've got the cash. Well, sort of. I'm right beside it." He peeked in through the car window again. "Anyway, you can have it, all of it, if you want. It's parked up in the rental outside a farmhouse. You can get here if you take the main road out of town. It's a massive building, falling apart, backed by a forest – you must know the one. You can't miss it."

Rebecca's voice was cold. "Have you gone back on our plan, Gary?"

"Yes," he replied, relieved. "I'm sorry, Rebecca. I... I just can't do this to Sandra. I never told you this before, but we had a kid. A little girl called Hanna. Hanna was taken away from us, and it was sort-of my fault, so we've been through a lot. I owe everything to Sandra. I can't leave her."

"How *touching*," Rebecca spat. Gary pictured her face, the patronising smile that he had once thought made her look sexy-as-fuck. "And, I suppose, as you're turning over your delightful new leaf, you'll be confessing *everything* to little Sandy, won't you? You'll tell her about the times that you pushed your little worm into me, and how you squirted like a fire hose when I clawed you? That's what she deserves, Gary - the poor bitch should have the truth."

Trying to sound firm, Gary said, "I don't want you speaking about Sandra like that, Rebecca. If you do it again I'll...shit, I'll burn the money, and then neither of us will have it."

That caught her off-guard, didn't it?

She spluttered, "Are you honestly and truly *threatening* me, Gary?"

"If that's what you want to call it, yes," he said, satisfied. "I'm sorry if this hurts –"

She cackled into his ear. "Hurts? *You* hurt *me? How* charming, Gary. How sweet to think that I have ever felt anything but contempt for you."

"It's over," he stated. "I enjoyed our time together, but I'm not sure I'll ever understand why."

"Perhaps I should enlighten you," she told him, in a sweet voice that Gary didn't trust for a second. "You loved me because I *hate* you, and that's just what you need."

Here we go – pop psychology time.

"It's in everything you do. The drugs, the dishonesty, the desire for punishment. I wouldn't be surprised if it was even apparent in the loss of your little girl."

The smile hung loosely from his face, but something stopped him from hanging up.

"What happened to poor little Hanna, Gary?" she went on, her voice mock-sad and piss-takey. "Did your hopeless genes deliver something faulty - some disease, some disability? Or maybe you caused an accident. Is that it?" She paused. "Or, when you say 'taken away', perhaps you mean that *literally?*" She seemed to interpret his silence as a 'yes'. "How did you let *that* happen? Were you lost in some kind of drug trip, or was it due to some other negligence? Maybe you wanted it to happen, deep down..."

"Stop it," he managed, his throat constricted.

A low growl came from the phone and rose into a vicious laugh. "You're a masochist, Gary. You bring misery to every person you meet, and you always will. Everyone, especially little Sandy, would be better off without you."

Gary became angry. "Jesus, Rebecca. What makes you so *bitter?* You act as if being a spiteful bitch will stop you getting hurt. But you're not as tough as you make out. I've heard you in your sleep. You *cry* sometimes, Rebecca, and when I hug you, while you're sleeping, *you hug me back.*"

The silence lasted for so long that Gary thought she had ended the call. Then, maybe for the first time ever, he heard something different in her voice. "So that's it, then? You're done with me?"

Her about-turn made Gary wary. "Look, I don't hate you. I just think that you should find someone else. Find someone who you *actually like.*" She stayed silent. "I mean, there's got to be *someone* out there for you, hasn't there? Aren't you a bit past all this fucking about? Doesn't it get a bit tiring?" He pictured her face, sadly. "You look so gorgeous when you actually smile, Rebecca. Sometimes it's like you've forgotten to hate everyone, just for a second."

There was no reply.

"Rebecca?"

Shit. The line was dead. She must have hung up before his little speech.

Ah well.

After pocketing the phone, he shut his eyes, rubbed them, and then squeezed two fingers into his ears. He stayed like that for a while, blanking the world. When he finally dropped his hands, the house seemed to be watching him again.

"Oh, piss off," he mumbled.

He wished he still had the coke. Maybe when he got to the hospital, they'd slip him some codeine, eh? Perhaps even a dab or two of morphine, if he acted up enough.

Just drift away...

He trudged over to the large black vehicle and, to his disbelief, when he looked into the driver's window he saw keys dangling from the ignition. He tried the door doubtfully but it opened with a satisfying click. Astounded, he climbed inside and into a hot fug of air that smelled of clean leather upholstery.

Fuck me.

The fat bastard had only gone and left his swanky off-roader unlocked, hadn't he?

The seat felt like a soft glove for his exhausted, aching arse. His limbs felt almost useless. Red spots fell lazily from his arms and landed on the plush brown leather. After a few seconds, Gary felt his eyelids droop. He shook himself and raised one suffering hand to the keys. The engine came to life, sounding as powerful as a tank. When he pressed the clutch to the floor and felt for the bite of the accelerator, a violent crash came from behind him.

Gary howled in shock.

Thomas!

The single noise became a series of loud slams, but when Gary swung his head back, he could see nobody through the windows. He scanned the vehicle's controls until he saw four separate buttons, each bearing the picture of a padlock. When he pressed them in turn, the door locks whirred into place.

The furious thumping rose in pitch, sounding like someone was ramming a baseball bat repeatedly into the rear bumper.

Is he beneath the shitting car?

All Gary had to do was drive away and leave the fat guy behind, so he edged the 4x4 a few feet forwards to turn her around. The ferocity of the thumping increased yet again and at last, Gary understood: someone was shut in the boot.

Jesus.

It was a kid, just like Hanna, wasn't it?

But it's so loud ...

Gary killed the engine and the crashing immediately stopped. He listened and heard panicked scrabbling, like an injured rat in a trap.

It has to be a kid. Must be terrified.

He unlocked the door and trod back onto the gravel, taking the keys with him.

"It's alright, I'm going to let you out, okay?" he called to the kidnapped child. "My name's Gary. Don't worry, I won't hurt you."

Surely, saving an innocent life would make up for all the bad things he'd done, wouldn't it? No one could judge Gary if he became a hero, right? *Right?*

With a jittering hand, Gary pushed the key into the boot's lock and twisted it. The trunk arose. He had barely a second to register the sight of the huge man with grey, lightless eyes and thick girly lips stuffed into the compartment.

Something flashed. Gary felt an impact. Startled, he

looked down and saw a clenched fist pressed hard against his stomach. The hand, which seemed to be turning red, clenched tighter and Gary's belly gave a jerk. The man, bleeding from the head, stared coldly as he wrenched his hand away.

Gary's legs lost their strength. He fell back from the 4x4 in agony, feeling as though something inside him was unraveling. His arse and spine hit the ground, hard. Something splashed Gary's face and a collapsing, tearing pain stole his breath. A glistening red trail crossed the metre of air between his navel and up to the man's hand, which he could see poking just over the edge of the boot now above him.

Through the trees, the purples and oranges of the early evening darkened.

I'm going to die now, aren't I? That's just not fair.

Gary Pickles strained his eyes up and behind him, and let them come to rest on a fading, bottom-up image of the farmhouse. Somehow, he knew she was going to be there.

Framed by a window on the second floor, pale and upside-down, Gary saw the unmistakable shape of his little doll. Hanna Pickles seemed to shrug, smiling sadly, almost as if to say: *You had your chance.*

LOCKER

WHEN WHITE LIGHT FILLED LOCKER'S VISION, HE'D RAMMED HIS ARM FORWARDS. SQUINTED UP AT A GRIMACING FACE HE DIDN'T RECOGNISE. HE'D SQUEEZED THE HANDLES AND ALFIE, BURIED IN THE STRANGER'S CLOTHES, HAD GRIPPED SOMETHING. THE FACE, SURROUNDED BY SHAGGY RED HAIR,

WENT BLANK. WHEN THE BODY HAD TOPPLED, ALFIE HAD DRAGGED OUT A LOOP OF INTESTINE, MAKING LOCKER IMAGINE A LONG, GREY EEL.

AS THE MAN HAD COLLAPSED, HIS LIPS GOLDFISHING AND ERUPTING A RED, A BRIEF FLASH OF THE POETRY SWEPT THROUGH LOCKER. THE EXULTANT JOY OF ENDING A LIFE HAD SHUDDERED THROUGH HIM AND FOR ONE RAPTUROUS MOMENT, LOCKER FELT SOMETHING THAT MATTERED; SOME DEEP, ALMOST PRIMIEVAL PURPOSE. THAT PURPOSE HAD A NAME. THAT NAME WAS...

BUT THE REVELATION HAD PASSED QUICKLY, LEFT NAMELESS AND FACELESS BY THE BREVITY OF THE REDHEADED MAN'S DEATH.

PANTING, STILL STRUGGLING TO SEE THROUGH THE SUDDEN GLARE OF SUNLIGHT, LOCKER DROPPED ALFIE. HAULED HIMSELF UP TO SIT UPRIGHT AND HELP THE CIRCULATION IN HIS LIMBS. HE LOOKED DOWN AT THE GINGER MAN. DEAD. STRINGS OF ENTRAILS SPRAWLED BETWEEN HIS LEGS. EMPTY EYES LOCKED ON THE HOUSE.

AFTER A MINUTE OR SO, LOCKER'S BLOOD RESUMED ITS USUAL MOVEMENTS AND HE PULLED HIMSELF OUT OF THE TRUNK. THE SIGHT OF THE UNNAMED CORPSE MADE HIM FEEL BETTER. HE MARVELLED AT THE OFFAL SPILLING FROM ITS TRACKSUIT, FEELING THE REMNANTS OF THE POETRY CLEARING AND FOCUSING HIS BRAIN. THE BODY LOOKED AT PEACE: EMPTY OF LIFE, WITH SUNLIGHT PLAYING ACROSS PARTS USUALLY HIDDEN.

LOCKER STRETCHED HIS SPINE, ACHING ALL OVER.

COULD DO WITH A BOTTLE OF WHISKY AND A GOOD, LONG SLEEP.

HE TOUCHED THE STICKY CROWN OF HIS SKULL. HIS HAND CAME BACK A RUSTY RED.

HAD THE GOTH REALLY HAD THE BALLS TO ATTACK HIM? LOCKER PICTURED THE LANKY CUNT RUNNING AT HIM FROM

THE TOP OF THE STAIRS, LOOKING MORE PETRIFIED THAN THREATENING. HE COULD CALL HENRY AGAIN, BUT THE LAST THING HE NEEDED WAS HIS BOSS TELLING HIM NOT TO HURT THAT SCRAWNY STREAK OF PISS. THAT WAS ALL LOCKER WANTED: TO HAVE THE KID LYING THERE, HELPLESS.

FROM THE CORNER OF LOCKER'S EYE, THE HOUSE SEEMED TO FROWN. SOMETHING IN A SECOND FLOOR WINDOW DREW HIS GAZE, BUT WHEN HE LOOKED, THE SHAPE WAS GONE. THERE WAS NO WAY THAT THE KID WAS STILL IN THE HOUSE, WAS THERE?

A CHANGE IN THE LIGHT SEEMED TO MAKE THE HOUSE WINK. HE REALISED THAT HE HAD TO CHECK, BUT SHOULD MOVE THE REDHEAD'S BODY FIRST.

DIDN'T MATTER HOW MESSY LOCKER GOT WHEN HE WAS AT HOME IN HIS WORKROOM, BECAUSE HE ALWAYS UNDRESSED WHENEVER HE WAS DOWN THERE. HERE, THOUGH, THERE WAS NO WAY HE COULD MOVE THE REDHEAD WITHOUT SOAKING HIS SUIT IN BLOOD. HE CROUCHED AND UNCLIPPED ALFIE FROM THE MAN'S WARM GUTS. TOOK THE KEYS FROM THE BOOT'S LOCK AND WENT ROUND TO THE DRIVER'S SIDE.

FOR FUCK'S SAKE - GINGER CUNT STAINED MY SEATS.

THE 4X4 HUMMED POWERFULLY WHEN LOCKER PULLED IT BACKWARDS TO COVER THE CORPSE.

BETTER THAN NOTHING.

HE GOT OUT AND WENT TO THE BOOT. PLACED ALFIE INSIDE THE NAVY BLUE HOLDALL. ZIPPED IT UP AND HEAVED IT OUT. HIS FRIENDS JANGLED WITH EVERY STRIDE AS HE HEADED BACK TOWARDS THE HOUSE.

CHAPTER 15
"Handfuls and bellyfuls and brainfuls of regret"

Thomas

Thomas tugged the scuff-battered suitcase on its wheels through Gary's neighbourhood, feeling bubbles of excitement popping in his veins. What he was about to do was pretty horrid, but it was also kind of like being on an adventure. He was a private eye, a burglar, a spy sneaking about on a secret mission.

The high rises loomed above him like the tallest trees in the Gardden, and when Thomas craned his neck they seemed to sway in the breeze. Down on the street, kids hung about on bikes and skateboards, poking each other, bragging and chuckling. Thomas thought back to his own childhood: climbing trees with Simon in the Gardden, and being laughed at for his jelly belly in the playground before he stopped attending, when the other kids went to Big

Boys' School.

Across the street, a young teenager with spiked black hair and fingerless gloves looked away from a pretty girl who was sharing his bottle of coke. "Oi, chubs! What you got in the suitcase? Pies?"

The girl guffawed, smacking the boy's arm.

Thomas weighed him up. Stupid little boys must be dead easy to replace – their parents can just squirt out new ones whenever they want. Would Simon, Hanna and Benny like to have *two* new friends, instead of just one?

The nasty boy held out a hand and cupped his imaginary belly, puffing out his cheeks and pointing at Thomas. The girl looked delighted. Sadly, Thomas would never fit two people in his suitcase, so he just faked a smile and strolled into an alleyway, trundling the old suitcase beside him. It had belonged to his daddy once, though Thomas had never known his father to go on holiday - he'd always been too busy looking after Thomas's poor, fatty-fat mummy.

The alley smelled of pee and wild garlic. Beer cans lay flattened on the tarmac like dead metal squeak-mice. A filthy, blackened teddy bear lay face down in a patch of nettles. The sound of an argument leapt over a wall.

"She better looking than me, then?" a woman's voice squawked. "Let you stick it in her mouth did she, eh?"

"Steph, love, I don't know what you're talking about, we're just friends."

"Oh yeah, friends who keep each others' stinkin' pants in their pockets!"

"I honestly have no idea where they came from. I swear, love, they could be anyone's..."

"Anyone's? *Anyone's??* How many slappers have you been pokin' with?"

"Oh, Steph..."

People with their complicated lives. Thomas was lucky in some ways, he supposed. All he had to do was obey everything the children told him.

Unless Ratan's right. Unless they're not really real.

Out the other side of the alleyway, the street was

choc-a-block with dented parked cars and behind them, towering into the sky, was the block of flats. Thomas was sure that this was the address printed on Gary's driving licence.

Thomas's best hope would be that no one else noticed him before he got into the flat, and that the woman - Sandra, Gary had called her - was teeny-tiny and, like, totally fragile. He fingered the bottle in his pocket. What if there were *other* people with her, though? If she had friends, or relatives, or other kids around? As Thomas crossed the street towards the glass entranceway, his guttyworks squirmed. No time to change the plan now, though.

He took out Gary's keys from his pocket and headed up a concrete slope towards the entrance. Thank flipping *goodness* that there was no one in the dim porchway. Which key was it, though? More importantly, where was the keyhole? There was only a funny-looking keypad next to a small black box stuck to the brickwork.

Thomas began to fret when he heard muffled, echoey footsteps. Through the glass, a pair of legs appeared in the concrete stairwell.

Oh dear.

A mummy-type lady walked down the stairs and then came towards the doorway. Thomas forced a smile and the lady smiled back. She looked friendly.

Turn and run?

Pushing a thick pair of specs up onto her plump nose, the lady flicked a switch and the glass door slid-skidded open.

"Ooh, going somewhere nice, are you, or just coming back?" she asked, nodding down at the suitcase. She held the door open for Thomas and ushered him inside.

"Just coming back," he replied automatically, stepping past her.

"Lovely. Nice holiday was it? Where'd you go?"

He racked his mind and said the first place that came into his head. "Town."

"Oh," she replied, sounding puzzled. "Lovely."

The door drifted closed, and after a second she walked away towards the road, leaving Thomas alone in the lobby.

The long ceiling lights painted everything earwax-yellow. The doors to the elevator had a sheet of paper attached to them, which read, 'Awaiting repair'. The children had told him that Gary's home was on the third floor. That would be a mega-whopper-relief when Thomas was pulling along a jam-packed suitcase instead of an empty one.

A baby wailed somewhere closeby and a soft man's voice tried to calm it down. Farther away, what must have been a huge dog barked and barked. Thomas climbed the stairs, his footsteps pinging and ponging as if he was in a cave.

The third floor corridor was empty. Pushchairs cluttered the long hall. Doors banged. Squealy kids' voices floated through thin walls, and conversations that Thomas couldn't make out burbled and blathered like broken radios.

Thomas slipped past two doors and arrived at number 12. Trying to look casual, he pressed an ear to the door.

Nothing.

This was it. She might be in there, sat on the couch reading, or perched on the toilet, or baking a yummy-scrumptious cake. As soon as he went in, she might start howling and bawling. The neighbours might hear and a bunch of big men with arms like tree trunks might pounce out of the flats and pound Thomas's face. He braced himself, looked both ways, checked the bottle, stroked the handkerchief, and then eased Gary's key into the lock.

The door swung back into an empty lounge. Thomas tiptoed forwards, pulled the suitcase inside and gently clicked the door closed behind him.

A coffee table stood in the centre of the tidy room, stacked with magazines and a mug decorated with a cartoon man and woman arguing. The couch and armchair were threadbare. A television was stuck to wall and a vase of yellow flowers stood on a small dining table at the window. Two framed pictures of forests were on another wall, as well as a poster saying 'The Prodigy' with a list of dates and cities. It felt to Thomas like it was missing something.

Photographs - that was it!

Don't regular people keep pictures of their happy lives on their walls, on the tables, and on the shelves? He had seen it in films that he'd watched online.

He wondered, what if there was no one about? How long would he have to wait before Sandra came back? He pulled the bottle from his jeans and drenched the snotrag with the tranq-stuff. Leaving the suitcase in the lounge, he pocketed the bottle and began to move through the flat, holding the handkerchief out, ready to press over the woman's face. In the kitchen, a stack of washed plates was still damp with bubbles. He strained his ears for movement. There were only three other doors in the flat, and the first of these was an unoccupied, plain white bathroom.

Thomas approached the second and took hold of the handle. Sandra might be asleep inside - that would be perfect! Handkerchief held high, Thomas twisted the handle and eased it open.

Behind the door was a cramped bedroom with barely enough space around the unmade bed for him to walk. There was a wardrobe, a chest of drawers, thin green carpet, peach-dotted wallpaper, and cabinets on either side of the pillows. One of them held a lamp, the other a half-drunk glass of water. It all looked really really dull.

Thomas sealed the door again and crept down the hallway towards the final room. He soaked the handkerchief again, because some of it had probably already floated away.

The final door felt mega-stiff, as if it was hardly ever touched. Thomas strained and it opened. He stepped into a child's bedroom that was much larger than the double room and coloured with bright oranges and yellows. The perfectly made bed had covers patterned with the picture of a teen popstar with pigtails, singing into a microphone.

A mega-bright pink table stood at the end of the bed, rowed from edge-to-edge with dolls, ponies, miniature houses, bouncy balls, cuddly toys and a collection of robots holding laser guns. Three sides of the room were wallpapered with a pattern of dancing elves and bug-eyed trolls, while, behind the bed, a huge and gorgeous painting covered the fourth.

Thomas stared in awe. It must have taken a super-long time to draw and colour in, and showed a jungle exploding with wildlife. Creatures hid in lush green trees and hung from the branches, while others prowled the forest floor. Teeny-tiny insects crawled across the leaves and a thin, bright red snake had wound itself about a tree in the foreground. In the distance, past the foliage and a bunch of dangling vines, a family of tigers feasted on a meaty carcass, while fish leapt from a stream running along the woodland's green horizon. Right at the top of the painting, just below the bedroom ceiling, a whole bunch of orangutans jabbered and fussed.

It had to be the most beautiful thing that Thomas had ever, ever seen. At the bottom, near the skirting board, was some painted handwriting: "For Hanna, with all our love and more besides. By mummy and daddy".

Thomas went to the tall window, which looked out over the neighbourhood. A group of ten-year-olds were playing football on the street three floors down, each wearing the same red team strip. Before Thomas had snatched Hanna, this road had been her view at the beginning and at the end of every day.

There were photographs, too, lining a unit of shelves by the window. With a weirdy-weird sleepwalking feeling, Thomas saw that every picture showed Hanna's familiar face. He had never seen her as she looked here – he'd seen her smile, seen her giggle, but he'd never seen her *happy*.

There she was, running a race with her classmates, dressed in a glittery gold leotard. In the next frame, she was younger and playing in a rock pool with Gary, who looked pale and pasty wearing just a pair of black shorts.

He was grinning, as if it was the happiest day of his life. In another, Hanna snoozed on a couch in front of the television; another, she was a toddler in a baby chair, with brown slop proudly spread across her chin; another one still she was an ickle naked baby, lying on white sheets inside of a large plastic container with tubes running from it. In some of the photos, Thomas saw a short woman with mousey, messy hair. She looked fretful even when she was smiling. That had to be Sandra. In one lively photo, Sandra wore a party hat and held a floating balloon-dragon. Hanna sat next to her, blowing out four candles on a cake decorated with jelly sweets.

Here were this family's memories. Here was this home's love, closed off and shut away for no one to see. Here, there was none of Hanna's sniggering, or her meanness; there was only a happy, healthy little girl with a mummy and daddy who must have loved her loads and loads and loads.

Apparently, Hanna's parents had attempted to give her a safe start to her life – so what had Thomas done to them when he'd grabbed and nabbed their little girl? Thomas could have imagined his own parents barely noticing if he'd vanished, but Hanna's mummy and daddy seemed to be a very different kettle of jellyfish.

This is how it should have been for me.

He backed away, trying to keep things together. He left the room and shut the door behind him.

I shouldn't be here.

Something hurt terribly in his chest. Amongst a massive bundle of feelings - anger, frustration, loneliness, misery, fear, wonder - what he felt most of all was regret. Handfuls and bellyfuls and brainfuls of regret.

He couldn't do this.

No way.

Let the children torture him. Let them *kill* him, because he had to leave this flat. He had to run away and escape from both this home and the Gardden while he still felt clear-headed and before that awful, nasty sense of duty came back again.

Ratan had been right.

Thomas rushed to the lounge and lifted the empty suitcase. It was time to get back to his pal Ratan, and time to either save him, or admit to himself that actually, yep, he *was* crackers and the Gardden didn't exist.

As he aimed for the door, he heard a rattle. His heart clenched. Time didn't slow; it sped up, mega-quick.

The sound was a key in the lock and a moment later the woman from the photographs was in the room with him too, her face a Polaroid of dumb-looking surprise and her lips shaped in a pink "O".

Sandra.

And, inside her, a teensy weensy baby.

Henry

Henry had lain in silence after Percy's call, starin at the gun, the phone at the foot o' the bed, and the massive dark stain on the carpet where his canine bruvver had died. He was restless and his front was gettin sore from havin been in the same fackin position for so long. He kept remindin himself that he weren't afraid o' nothin, and that whatever was crampin his guts was just a bellyache, and that was all.

How'd all this happened? What'd he done wrong? He'd given that slag everythin: nice clothes, meals out, an' jewellery. He'd given his lad responsibility, guidance, an' money. But now it seemed that the very two people he'd taken under his wing had turned on him, spat right in his face an' swanned off outta the picture.

He didn't feel hurt, o' course, an' he didn't feel sad. Henry Borders rolled wiv the punches, whevver they were sneaky little jabs or fackin great haymakers. He only hoped that what was happenin didn't reach the wrong ears.

There goes Henry, people'd say. *The silly sod who got bummed by his dog and lost a truckload of cash to a backstabbing little kid.*

Well, Henry would fight wiv every breath left in his body to stop that from happenin. It was true that he couldn't move far, what with his anal what-nots poppin out into the light, but he had connections, loyal an' true. He had his willpower, oh yeah, plus tough guys, big money, an' firepower.

He called for Fred.

"Any news?" he asked, when the beardy cunt was back in the bedroom.

"Nothing yet, Henry. There's a lot of people out there looking for her, though. She can't be far, eh? I tried the hospital and they haven't had anyone who's been shot."

"There's a new problem now, though, Fred," Henry told him. "Percy's bin on the blower. Seems he's landed himself in a spot o' trouble, an' that some cheeky cunt has stolen from one o' my stashes. Percy even said that when he an' young Ray went to the thievin toerag's house, Ray promptly went nuts an' punted Percy down a flight o' stairs. Now poor ol' Percy's locked up in the boot of his own car."

Fred looked unnerved. "Wait a minute – the

Goth tried his luck with Percy and came out on top? And now he's... what? Kidnapped Percy? What's goin on?"

"I want you to go to this cunt's house an' bring the 'ole lot of 'em to me, okay?"

Fred looked surprised. "Um... I thought you wanted your... problem... to stay private?"

Henry looked up, ruefully. "They say that desperate times call for desperate measures, an' times don't come much more desperate than this. Percy reckons that young Ray's involved wiv takin' my money, an' that makes sense, dunnit?"

"Right," Fred agreed.

"Wrong," Henry corrected. "It doesn't make a single ounce o' fackin sense, so I need to look 'em all right in the eyes an' find out what the bleedin hell's goin on."

"Possible Hancock's involved?"

"How'd ya mean?" Henry demanded. Trust Fred to come up wiv some fancy idea about Henry's rival – always had thoughts above his station.

Fred explained, "Hancock's always sniffing around our patches, trying to move into spots we haven't touched. And didn't Percy start a little campaign recently, shaking up a few of Hancock's punters?"

"Don't start complicatin things, Fred. What you're talkin about there is a fackin *war*, an' that ain't in anyone's interest. I don't know what the score is yet, but I haven't seen any reason to assume that Hancock's involved."

"Unless he's offered Ray more funds than you,

of course," Fred persisted.

Fred's argument reminded Henry why Percy was his best employee: wiv Percy there were hardly ever any questions - just "Yes boss" an' "No boss".

"Come down 'ere, Fred. I need to speak wiv you, eye-to-eye."

Fred crouched down.

Despite lyin on his front wiv his broken bum-crack spread to the world, Henry was determined to keep his respect. "Listen to me. If I tell you that somethin ain't the case, it ain't the case, alright?"

Fred swallowed, noddin.

"Right, an' if I tell you that somethin *is* the fackin case, then you can rely on the fact that I've thought it through five or six times already, okay?"

Fred nodded again, an' a bead o' sweat appeared on his brow.

"Good. An' lastly, if I tell ya to whip your pants down, pull your cock between your legs an' run around the room performin Madonna's greatest hits, all I want you to ask is, 'Which songs, boss?' That understood?"

After a breath, Fred smiled uncomfortably. "I get it, Henry."

"I'm glad. Now fack off an' make some more calls."

As Fred paced from the room, Henry's mobile rang again.

When Henry answered, the world collapsed around his ears. He listened and tried to argue, but inside his sore head, buildins were shatterin, bullets were shreddin brains to pulp, an' vaults of his precious money were bein incinerated. The call seemed to last forever, but when it was finally over, Henry dropped the phone an' tried yellin for Fred. Only breath hissed out from his lips, though.

This was it: make or fackin break. Judgement day had come, an' if Henry didn't get back into the driver's seat pretty sharpish, all he'd have left in the world would be a prolapsed poop chute.

"Fred!" he managed, his voice perilously weak. "The plan's changed again."

"How do you mean?" Fred called from the lounge.

"Stay in there, Fred. I'll explain in a minute. There's somethin I've gotta do first."

Fred couldn't be around when Henry did this ⁼ Henry had bin degraded in front o' the guy too many times already. Fack it, this is all that the docs an' nurses would do, if he went to the hospital. Anyway, the discomfort would distract him from how the voice had sounded on the other end o' the line.

Henry reached back an' touched the tender area. There was no way he could use his fingers, even if it *would* make the job easier. Maybe if he clenched the right muscles, it would all pop right back into where it was supposed to be, but he didn't feel quite up to that; it'd be like takin a shite, only backwards. So he grabbed the only usable item within reach: his gun. He

made sure that the safety catch was on –
suicide by a bullet up the arse was one
humiliation too far. Then he closed his eyes,
concentrated, an' put the barrel against his
exposed rectum.

An' thrusted.

Rebecca

Naked and showered clean, Rebecca sat, stunned,
on the edge of the guesthouse bed.

Her arm throbbed ruthlessly. If only she had
a change of clothes and a bandage. The flesh
around the bullet wound had swelled, purple
and shining, and seeped fresh blood no matter
how often she dabbed it. She crossed the room to
the bathroom and viewed the injury in the
mirror. It was small but would need stitches,
and it winked like a gouged eye socket whenever
she uncrooked her elbow. Her eyes passed wanly
across the rest of her body: her large-nippled C-
cup breasts, which were firm for 40, her trim
stomach, which was almost as taut as a decade
ago, and her gently hour glass-shaped thighs and
waist, which hadn't yet succumbed to middle
age.

She heard Gary again: Aren't you a bit past
all this fucking about?

She returned to the bedroom. Using her teeth,
she tore a yellowed strip of pillowcase from the
bed and wrapped it around her arm. Not an

ideal dressing, but it would have to do for the moment.

Although she was struggling to focus on practicality, she couldn't help but admit to herself that she had underestimated Gary. For his words to have affected her was preposterous - she was a grown woman, for God's sake - but the little louse had, somehow, caused her to reflect. Glancing at the bed, she realised with dismay that she almost missed her little bug. From the start, Rebecca had framed him as a lost cause: drug addicted, obsessed by her, and blind to everything else. She had unwittingly reduced him to a stereotype, but now that he had returned to his simpleton of a wife, Rebecca felt a stab of envy. She could never have predicted that her time with such an apparent waste of human skin would end with Gary taking the moral high ground and then turning his pockmarked back on her.

You look so gorgeous when you smile. The words had been ice in her chest. Sometimes it's like you've forgotten to hate everyone, just for a second.

She dried her hair and slipped her pungent silver dress back on, cursing the fact that her clothes were already in the rental car. As she did, her insides cramped.

you will be fine, mummy, yes yes yes, just come and see us

She started, almost scanning the room for the source of a voice that she had obviously imagined.

She called a cab. It was likely that Henry had

told his many local contacts to look out for her, but remaining inside the guesthouse until her transport arrived would surely minimise the chances of her being spied.

Down in the guesthouse's musty porchway, she stood out of sight from the large, haughty-looking woman behind the front desk. A pair of spindle-legged spiders seemed to watch Rebecca from a high corner and she, in turn, watched the road outside. The glass walls had a greenhouse effect and the sun outside, though lower now, drew perspiration from her.

Forget this city. Forget users and the used, abusers and the abused. Just get the money and find something new. Something better.

A cab pulled up and blasted its coarse horn. Rebecca pictured a secluded cottage somewhere thousands of miles away. Despite being loath to admit a change in her views – life wasn't a simple timeline of triumphs, failures and character developments – perhaps there was some truth in Gary's ramblings.

Perhaps, at some point in the far-flung future, Rebecca would remember to forget to hate.

LOCKER

HALFWAY DOWN THE FARMHOUSE'S WEIRD, KIDDY-POSTER HALL, THE ACHE IN LOCKER'S SKULL CHANGES. MUST BE A BAD CONCUSSION BECAUSE HIS BRAIN SUDDENLY FEELS LIKE IT'S INFLATING.

THERE'S SOMETHING ELSE, TOO: VOICES HAVE STARTED

SHOUTING IN HIS HEAD, TELLING LOCKER TO FIND THE KID. TELLING LOCKER TO HURT HIM. TELLING LOCKER TO BATHE IN HIS FILTHY FUCKING BLOOD.

DRINK HIS SKIN AND GUTS AND SPIT, YES YES YES, EAT HIM EAT HIM EAT HIM, CUT HIS HER THEIR FACE TO SHREDS

LOCKER STOPS AND LEANS AGAINST THE CORRIDOR'S DAMP WALL. HE'S ALREADY PLANNING TO KILL THE FUCKER, BUT THIS FEELS ... DIFFERENT.

BASH HOLES IN ITS SKULL AND FUCK THE BRAINS, YES YES YES, PUT YOUR THING INTO HIS SQUISHY TASTY HEAD

CAN'T LET A LITTLE HEADACHE RUIN HIS MOMENT WITH THE GOTH, THOUGH – HE'S WAITED TOO LONG. FEELS WEIRD THOUGH. ALMOST LIKE HE'S THINKING SOMEONE ELSE'S THOUGHTS.

SLICE HIM INTO STRIPS AND WEAR HIM, YES YES YES, WEAR HIM

LOCKER WANTS TO FIND THE INTERFERING LITTLE QUEER, BUT THERE ARE OTHER VOICES AMONGST THE COMMOTION, TOO, SCREAMING OUT CONFLICTING ORDERS.

DON'T HURT THE BOY BECAUSE HE SHOULD STAY AND PLAY, YES YES, PRETTY BOY GIRL CREATURE KIDDIE MAN

THIS ONE SHOULD WIN

NO NO NO THE BOY THE BOY

IT'S HOW LOCKER IMAGINES GOING CRAZY MIGHT FEEL.

HE SHUFFLES TOWARDS THE KITCHEN, THINKING THAT MAYBE OTHER PEOPLE PUT UP WITH VOICES BATTLING OVER THEIR DECISIONS ALL THE TIME. WHAT'S THAT CALLED AGAIN? A CONSCIENCE?

HE'S IN THE GARDEN SO CUT HIM KILL HER STAB IT EAT THEM

SODOMISE

NO, HE'S A CHILD

"JUST SHUT UP," HE SAYS, THROUGH GRITTED TEETH.

WAS SOMETHING PROPER WEIRD HAPPENING? NO. HE'S

JUST WORRIED ABOUT GOING BEHIND HENRY'S BACK.

GET OUT THERE AND SKIN HIM ALIVE AND PULL OUT HIS EYES AND CHEW THROUGH HIS LUNGS

NO, HE CAN BE OUR DADDY FRIEND BROTHER SISTER SERVANT

THROUGH A SMEARED KITCHEN WINDOW AND ALONG A PATH BORDERED BY TREES, LOCKER SEES WHAT MIGHT BE THE GOTH'S HEAD. HIS CHEST TIGHTENS, BUT THE WEIGHT OF HIS BAG OF FRIENDS IS HEAVY AND REASSURING. WHEN LOCKER EASES OPEN THE KITCHEN DOOR, THE GABBLING IN HIS HEAD ABRUPTLY STOPS. THERE'S SILENCE.

IT'S LIKE A DEAD FOREST OUTSIDE. THE DAY'S WARMTH IS DRAINING AND ABOVE HIM, THROUGH THE TREES, THE SUN HAS LOST ITS EDGE. FROM THE OUTSKIRTS OF THE WOODED AREA, THE GOTH LOOKS UNCONSCIOUS. LOCKER SLIPS BETWEEN THE TREES.

THERE HE IS: THE POOF WHO'D COME BETWEEN LOCKER AND HENRY.

THE KID.

THE IMPOSTER.

THE USELESS GOTH CUNT, WHO'D LOST HENRY'S CASH AND SHOVED LOCKER DOWN A FUCKING STAIRCASE.

CHRIST, HE REALLY IS OUT COLD.

LOCKER SNEERS AT THE SUIT THAT THE KID'S WEARING, NOW SMUDGED WITH SOIL. JUST A COSTUME. JUST A SICK FUCKING JOKE.

BE MUCH MORE COMFORTABLE IN A SKIRT, WOULDN'T YOU?

HE CIRCLES THE BODY.

WHAT'S HE DOING OUT HERE? AND WHAT WERE THOSE FUCKING VOICES ALL ABOUT?

HE CAN'T THINK, BECAUSE HE'S BEEN SERVED THE KID ON A FUCKING PLATE. HE DROPS THE HOLDALL AND IN A RUSH TAKES OUT PETEY, HIS PAIR OF POLICE-ISSUE HANDCUFFS.

HE PICTURES THE KID BUMBLING TOWARDS HIM AT THE

TOP OF THE STAIRS AGAIN AND ANGER FILLS HIM LIKE FIRE, LIKE ACID.

THE KID IS LIGHT AND ROLLS OVER EASILY. LOCKER HAD IMAGINED WHAT IT MIGHT FEEL LIKE TO DO JUST AS HE PLEASED WITH THE COCKSUCKER. IT'S NOTHING LIKE THE PAKI, THE BOG WOG, OR ANY OF THE OTHER WORTHLESS SCRAPS OF MEAT. THIS *MATTERS,* AND CLIPPING PETEY AROUND THE GOTH'S WRISTS WEAKENS LOCKER'S KNEES.

THE GOTH SNUFFLES AND HIS BLUE EYES, DOTTED WITH GRIT, FLUTTER OPEN.

LOCKER'S POETRY IS ALREADY ON ITS WAY.

KNEELING, LOCKER WATCHES THE KID STRUGGLING TO SEE. *THAT'S IT, COME ON, WAKE UP.*

HE RUNS THE BACK OF HIS LEFT HAND ACROSS THE KID'S VELVETY SKIN, WHICH LOOKS EVEN PALER UNDER THE TREES. THE KID'S EYES ARE AT FIRST CURIOUS, THEN ALMOST RELIEVED. THEY WIDEN FOR A SECOND AND FOCUS ON LOCKER, AND THE LITTLE FAGGOT GOES TO MOVE BUT THE HANDCUFFS JANGLE BEHIND HIM. CONFUSION CROSSES HIS FACE.

"HELLO," LOCKER SAYS.

THE KID'S MOUTH FORMS A ZIG-ZAG. "LOCKER?"

"YEAH."

LOCKER KNOWS THAT THE KID WILL PROBABLY WRESTLE WITH WHAT'S GOING ON FOR A WHILE LONGER. THEN HE'LL TRY AND JUSTIFY HIMSELF. THEN HE'LL BEG PERCY NOT TO HURT HIM, AND THEN TO STOP HURTING HIM, AND THEN TO LET HIM LIVE, AND THEN, FINALLY, TO LET HIM DIE.

THE KID TRIES TO MOVE HIS WRISTS. LOCKER PRESSES A HAND OVER HIS LIPS. TAKES HIS MOBILE OUT.

LOCKER WILL TEACH HENRY FOR HAVING INVOLVED THIS SKINNY FAGGOT IN REAL MEN'S BUSINESS. THEN EVERYTHING WILL BE BACK TO NORMAL, JUST LIKE IT SHOULD BE.

PERCY AND HENRY.

HENRY AND PERCY.

"'ELLO, PERCY, WOSS THE NEWS?" HENRY ASKS AS HE PICKS UP.

"I'M OUT OF THE BOOT, BUT I THINK YOU SHOULD BRACE YOURSELF," LOCKER SAYS, TRYING TO SOUND CONCERNED.

"WHY? WOSS HAPPENED?"

"IT'S RAY." HE LEAVES A PAUSE. "THE FAT FUCK FROM THE SHOP HAS LEFT HIM IN THE BACK GARDEN. HE'S...IN A BAD WAY."

LOCKER WATCHES THE GOTH AS THE WORDS HIT HIS EARS. LITTLE BITCH IS STILL TRYING TO SEE STRAIGHT, STRAINING HIS NECK BACK IN AN ATTEMPT TO GET HIS LIPS AWAY FROM LOCKER'S PALM.

THAT'S IT, SQUIRM.

HENRY'S VOICE DROPS. "WHAT D'YOU MEAN, 'BAD WAY'?"

"HE MIGHT BE... *DEAD,* BOSS."

THE KID STILL SEEMS TO HAVE LITTLE IDEA OF WHAT'S HAPPENING. THERE'S NO FEAR ON HIS FACE YET – JUST AGITATION. THAT'LL CHANGE SOON. HE'LL UNDERSTAND WHAT'S GOING ON WHEN THE POETRY ARRIVES, OH YEAH.

"I FOUND HIM IN THE GARDEN," LOCKER SAID. "HE'S BEEN CUT UP REAL NASTY AND HE'S NOT MOVING. THE FAT FUCK'S NOWHERE AROUND -"

"WHO'S THIS FAT GUY YOU KEEP BANGIN' ON ABOUT?" HENRY BLASTS. "*WHO THE FACK DID THIS TO MY RAY?*"

"I... I DON'T KNOW, HENRY."

"IS HE DEAD?" HENRY DEMANDS.

"I..."

"*I SAID IS HE FACKIN' DEAD?*"

"I'M NOT SURE, BOSS."

GAZING INTO THE KID'S GLASSY EYES, LOCKER FEELS A MOMENT OF DOUBT. REALISATION SINKS IN – HE'S TRYING TO HEAL THINGS WITH HENRY BY BETRAYING HIM. THIS WILL CHANGE *EVERYTHING.*

"HE LOOKS PRETTY ROUGH, BOSS."

"NOW YOU LISTEN TO ME, PERCY," HENRY GROWLS. "SOMETHIN' ABOUT THIS STINKS LIKE A WHORE'S SNATCH."

"WHAT SHOULD I DO?" LOCKER ASKS.

HENRY'S HAVING NONE OF IT. "I'M GONNA TRACK DOWN WHOEVER'S DONE THIS AN' SLAUGHTER THEIR WHOLE FACKIN' FAMILY!" HENRY FUMES. "RIGHT NOW, PERCY, I WANT YOU TO FIND OUT IF MY RAY'S STILL ALIVE. AN' IF THERE'S *ANY* CHANCE THAT HE IS, I WANT YOU TO TAKE HIM TO THE HOSPITAL, NO QUESTIONS ASKED."

"SURE, OKAY HENRY," LOCKER SAYS.

THE KID HAS FALLEN STILL AGAIN, EYELIDS SLACK AND HALF-CLOSED.

HENRY CONTINUES, "I'M COMIN', AN' I WANT YOU TO TELL ME EVERYTHIN', AS AN' WHEN IT HAPPENS. I'M HEADIN' FOR THAT SHITTY FACKIN' FARMHOUSE *RIGHT NOW.*" HENRY'S LAST WORDS BEFORE ENDING THE CALL ARE A HISS. "AN' PERCY - IF I FIND OUT THAT WHAT YOU'VE GIVEN ME AIN'T THE TRUTH, THE WHOLE TRUTH, AN' NOTHIN' FACKIN' BUT, I'LL MAKE SURE THAT YOU DIE DEEPTHROATIN' YOUR OWN COCK."

HENRY HANGS UP.

LOCKER ALMOST PANICS. WHAT DOES HE DO NOW, WITH HENRY ON HIS WAY? HE'D ASSUMED THERE'D BE PLENTY OF TIME TO INTRODUCE THE GOTH TO HIS WONDERFUL FRIENDS, AND THAT HE'D BE ABLE TO CHOP THE FUCKER UP AND BURY HIM AT HENRY'S MANSION WITHOUT INTERFERENCE. HE'S FURIOUS WITH HIMSELF. USELESS FUCKING BRAIN. SHOULD HAVE CALLED HENRY *AFTERWARDS.*

NOW, IN THE MINUTES BEFORE HENRY ARRIVES, LOCKER WILL HAVE TO CUT UP THE GOTH, CLEAN UP HIS FRIENDS, AND THEN STASH THEM IN THE BOOT.

LOCKER TAKES A DEEP BREATH.

IT'S OKAY.

NOTHING TO WORRY ABOUT.

HE'S A PROFESSIONAL.

Thomas

The woman had enough time to squeak "Gary!" before Thomas leapt forwards and slammed her against the door. It clicked shut just as Thomas stuffed the handkerchief over her mouth.

"Ssshhh, it's okay," he gasped into her frantic face. "I'm going to leave. I'm not going to take your baby any more."

but you are you are yes yes yes you are

Her teeth chomped into his palm and he yelped, snatching back his hand. She turned, shrieking, to the door and scrabbled for the handle. Thomas grasped a handful of her short hair and yanked her backwards really really hard, and then wrapped his other wrist around her throat.

"Ssshhh," he said into her ear. She smelt clean and sweet. "I'm going to leave now, okay? I don't want to hurt you. I just want to go."

As he squeezed her throat, she thrashed like an eel in his arms, burying her elbows into his guts, stamping on his toes and scraping her flat heels down his shins. Huffing with frustration, Thomas dragged her by the neck to the sofa. They dropped into the seat and she landed heavily on his lap, her movements slowing as he squidged her windpipe even harder. He let go of her hair but kept his wrist tightly against her throat until her head sagged against him, her arms limp and her cheeks the colour of beetroots.

Oops-a-daisy - had he killed her? He hadn't meant to, but he didn't want her telling tales. If the police were going to find out about him, Thomas wanted to be standing right next to Ratan while it happened. And it wouldn't be fair if the coppers found out about Thomas breaking in to Sandra's home, seeing as he'd already decided to leave when she got back home.

Thomas let go and the air hiccupped back into her lungs. He lifted the handkerchief to her lips. She didn't struggle this time, and a minute or so later she went totally limp against his chest.

Surely this had been the closest Thomas had ever come to being caught? Phew!

With Sandra's head slumped back against Thomas's shoulder and cheek, he wondered, what now? Leave her in the flat and just hope that the police couldn't track him down? Thomas had seen TV shows where detectives dusted for DNA, which meant tiny body bits, to match with criminals. He'd taken Hanna from a public place where he couldn't have left much hair or fingerprints or skin, but what about here, in Hanna's mummy's home? And even if Thomas cleaned every single spot he'd touched, Sandra would still be able to describe him to the coppers.

Yes, officer, he was a fatty-fat, super-spotty, greasy, disgusting man...

Thomas's belly gurgled sadly.

Maybe the lady he had passed at the entrance would remember him, too. If that happened, he'd *definitely* go to jail, where he'd be locked up with bad men who don't like guys who nab little kiddies.

Thomas felt queasy and hungry and had no idea what to do.

It was also strange to have a woman so close to him. His only other contact with ladies was in the Green Emporium when he was selling sexy toys, and that always made him feel a bit squirly inside. He always thought that those ladies were laughing at him, but this time, the lady he was with was fast asleep.

Thomas lowered Sandra onto the sofa and examined her. She had a nice face. With her short, boyish hair, she looked just like a pixie. Small mouth, button nose, soft skin. Loads of freckles on one cheek but hardly any on the other. She was wearing a saggy blue sweatshirt and faded jeans, and Thomas found himself wishing that he could see what was underneath them. He ran his thick fingers over her wrist, across the back of her hand and along her bitten-short nails, one by one.

Hmm.

If he did as the children had asked, he would get to see *everything*, and, he would win The People Game. Wouldn't that be nice? And maybe afterwards, the children would leave him alone, or at least never ask him to use the suitcase again.

Sandra didn't *seem* pregnant. Thomas had thought she would look gross, all bulging stomach and dangly boobs. Sandra's belly was trim, though, with just the tiniest swelled spot above her jeans. He put his hand against the rough material covering her tummy and felt a thrill, imagining the ickle person trapped inside. Did the children really want the baby *right now*? It couldn't be much bigger than a fist – there wouldn't be room for anything larger. So what kind of friend would it make for them? Simon hadn't aged in the years he had been in the Gardden, so why would whoever was inside Sandra change? Thomas was confused but didn't want to leave just yet.

What he wanted to do was lift Sandra's top, so he took the bottom of the wiry jumper in his fingers and pulled it upwards to catch a glimpse of her pale, warm skin. There were weirdy-weird bruise marks on either side of her tummy, but aside from those, she looked lovely.

Thomas decided that there was no way that he could leave her where she was. He'd already killed her young daughter, and Simon had stabbed her husband about a bajillion times, so wouldn't she be better off dead, too? Without her family, she would be alone, and Thomas knew how horrid loneliness was. It ate you up, so maybe Sandra would be glad if Thomas kept her company for a while.

He wondered what tool he could use to get to the baby. He had hardly any kitchen stuff, because he only ever cooked microwave dinners or ate takeaways. There were no proper knives or anything. Then he remembered the hacksaw that his father had used back when Thomas was young, to keep the trees in the garden neat. It would probably have rusted by now, but its brown teeth would surely be up to the job. It was only a belly, after all.

The thought made Thomas feel a bit sick and a bit sad. It would be such a waste to ruin Sandra's yummy body, and it would be nice to play with her like a *real* adult, not like the silly games Thomas played in the Gardden. Maybe she would even *let* him play with her – maybe she would like him and the children would let her live with them while the baby grew nice and big inside her. And if not, Thomas would get to have some fun at least *once* before he had to cut her open and pull out the children's new friend.

Things always worked out for the best, didn't they?

No one had knocked on the door since Thomas had gotten into the flat and no one had tried to get in, so maybe the other residents were used to shouts and crashes coming from the rooms nearby.

With his heart thud-thud-thudding, Thomas pushed the suitcase over to the sofa and unzipped it. She would fit inside, no problem, and then all he would have to do would be to get her back to the Gardden. He knelt in front of the open case and gently rolled Sandra towards him, then laid her softly into the container on her side. Her legs spilled over so he carefully folded her into a ball, just like he and Ratan had done to the big, nasty man when they'd put him into the boot of the ginormous black car. Sandra's shoulders were a bit wide, but he had no problem flapping the lid over her and zipping the case shut. The brown leather looked a bit lumpy, but not suspicious or anything.

He thought one last time about Hanna's bedroom down the corridor, and then wiped the thought from his mind. He didn't like dwelling on teary-sad things.

The case was heavier with Sandra in it than when it had held Hanna. Thomas tugged it across the floor on its wheels, took one last glance at the plain-coloured flat, and pulled the door open.

A man was standing across the corridor, leaning on the wall beside his open door. A young boy and a girl were playfighting in the flat behind him, tussling and grunting, but the man seemed to be chilling out and gathering his thoughts. He was tall, had a bristly moustache, and had a tattoo of a green lion along one of his skinny arms.

"Hello," he said to Thomas. "How's it going?"

Thomas froze and said, "Great thanks."

Eager to get away, he began to haul the suitcase through the doorway.

"Er... who are you?" the man asked.

Thomas thought fast. "I'm Gary's brother, Steve. Pleased to meet you." He looked up at the man, whose face had softened.

"Oh, nice one. Didn't know Gaz had a brother. I'm Sam." The moustached man reached out a hand and Thomas shook it with one damp, hot palm. "You staying long? Oh, obviously not. Guess you're just leaving, eh?"

"That's right," Thomas said, trying to sound casual. "Heading home now."

Sam nodded, crossing his arms and leaning back against the slate wall. "I hope you straightened him out a bit while you were here. He's been... well, I'm sure you know how he gets. Understandable, o' course, after everything they've been through. But Sandra's a good gal, isn't she?"

Thomas nodded lamely.

"To be honest, she could probably do with some extra support every now and again, without him swanning off whenever he fancies. If you'll forgive me saying so."

"Yeah," Thomas agreed, desperate to end the conversation, to close the door behind him and get the heck outside. "Well, I've got a train to catch, so I have to go."

"Oh, of course. You be on your way, mate," Sam said. But he went on regardless: "It hit *all of us* bloody hard when it happened, you know. Wasn't just Gaz and Sandra. Lovely little girl, she was, little Hanna. So bright and confident. Don't know what I'd do if anything like that happened my little brats." He looked back at them. "Doesn't bear thinkin' about, so I can't imagine what it did to your family."

Thomas went to leave again, but the guy was on a roll.

"We all came together after things had blown over a bit. Tried to throw 'em a little gathering, like a wake I s'pose, but it was no use." Sam pinched his lips together for a second. "You can't heal all that with smiles and a few drinks, can you? Only closure can do that. Only finding out what really happened to their little darlin'." Sam coughed, looking lost in his thoughts, then said, "Steve, was it? I'll remember that. Safe journey."

"Thank you," Thomas said, relieved.

He was about to pull the door closed when the suitcase groaned.

Oh dear.

Sam frowned and asked, "What you got in there?"

Oh dear oh dear oh dear!

He hadn't put Sandra to sleepytime properly, had he? He'd wanted to get her back to the house so badly that he hadn't remembered how quickly the stuff on the handkerchief evaporated.

Thomas released the suitcase and went to run, but Sam grabbed his arm.

"Let me go!" Thomas yelled, as the suitcase howled and fell onto its side.

"I asked you a question, pal. What's in there?" Sam turned to the other doors. "Dave! Joe! Someone get out here!"

"Let me go!" Thomas bellowed again, trying to barge past this unexpectedly strong man. He remembered the bottle in his pocket and reached inside to toss the contents into the guy's face. He took hold of the glass neck but as it slipped from his jeans it also slipped from his fingers, shattering against the wall with a tinkling splosh.

Down the corridor, blocking Thomas's escape, another door swung open and a second guy poked his head out. "What's up, Sam? Who you got there?"

Still grasping Thomas's wrist, Sam called, "I think he was burgling Gaz and Sandra's place, an' somethin' in his suitcase is makin' noises! Get down here, Joe!"

"Get off me *now!*"

Thomas's voice attracted yet another tenant, this one a sour-faced woman in her late middle age with a long cigarette hanging from her mouth.

"Woss gahn on?" she demanded, smoke circling her head.

"Get this fucker!" Sam shouted. "Don't let him out of here!"

With an enormous wrench, Thomas freed himself. More doors were opening though, and a number of concerned-looking tenants now barred his exit.

Seeing nothing else to do, Thomas dodged past the suitcase and back into Gary and Sandra's home. Sam tried to get inside too but Thomas threw his body against the door. The suitcase shot out into the corridor and the latch clicked shut.

"Jesus Christ, there's someone in there!" came a voice from the other side. "Get them out!"

Thomas wondered was this it? Was this what 'getting caught' felt like?

No. Not yet!

He raced to the lounge windows. A long, long way down, there was a row of skips bordering a patch of grass and a few empty parking spaces. One of the open skips was full of soft-looking rubbish. Maybe if he jumped, he'd escape with just a few broken bones. He'd seen it in a film once, but from three storeys up it looked *so high.*

He flinched as someone battered the door.

"Get out of my home!" screeched a woman's voice. It reminded him of an older Hanna – was that Sandra?

This was just another game, Thomas told himself. Like all the others that he'd played before: *The Escape Game.*

Someone kept pummelling the door. Thomas ran to the kitchen and pushed open the window behind the sink. He scrambled up onto the counter, poked his head through the open window, looked down and saw concrete slabs. The frosted glass in the bathroom was too small for him to climb through, so he tried the double bedroom instead.

The residents banged and bellowed from the corridor

as Thomas stepped around the bed, hoping hoping *hoping* that through the window there would be a fire escape ladder or at least a balcony or something.

There was only a vertical drop towards tarmac.

The bashing at the door became less frantic but louder, as if someone was pounding firm, steady blows against the wood.

Help me, Simon, he prayed. *Help me Benny, help me Hanna – just get me away from here. I'll play The People Game properly, I'll get you another friend, I'll do anything you say if you help me out now...*

For a moment, he just stood at the window, staring out over a narrow street and a scruffy grass park.

The noises coming from the front room changed - the door was splintering. Would it be better to give in? They weren't going to kill him, after all. That's not what normal people do - they'd just call the police.

A booming crash came from the other room and Thomas knew that they had broken through. A chaos of voices filled the flat as Thomas leapt back into the corridor. A group of four furious men marched inside. Sam held a cricket bat. Behind the rabble, the sour-faced woman was supporting Sandra, who looked dizzy but really really mad.

Thomas rushed into Hanna's room and shoved the door shut behind him. There was no lock but he couldn't give in yet. He dragged the pink table away from the bed and blocked the entrance. Hanna's fluorescent toys spilled across the floor. Lodged between the unit of photographs and the door, Thomas knew that the thin wooden table wouldn't hold them back for long.

Outside the window and three floors down, the young friends were still playing soccer in the street. There would be nothing soft for Thomas to land on if he leapt – he'd just squish-splatter across the pavement and the road.

The mob began to smash at the bedroom door.

Thomas wasn't going to let them have him. The children wouldn't want him to be caught or die, would they? They needed looking after. They loved him.

The door jolted open a couple of inches and a hand reached into the room, prying open the entrance. The raging voices grew super-loud.

"Out, you fucker!"

"You ain't going nowhere!"

"Give it up, mate! Just give it up!"

Thomas tugged at the the window but it wouldn't budge. It needed a key. Ignoring the screams and the violent crashing, Thomas heaved the bedside cabinet into the air and threw it headlong into Hanna's single-glazed window. The glass exploded but the cabinet bounced and toppled sideways onto the carpet.

"Save me, Simon!" Thomas bawled, panic and terror blowing fuses in his brain. "Save me Hanna! Save me Benny! I'll look after you forever!"

The shelving unit blocking the door lumbered forwards.

Thomas stepped one foot onto the overturned cabinet and, as the mob surged into the bedroom, launched himself at the smashed window. His hands, head and chest hit the air but his midsection hit the jagged edge of the window frame. Glass teeth sank into his scarred belly. Barely feeling the pain, Thomas stared at the pavement far below, wishing he could swoop and soar just as he did above the Gardden when he played Flyflyfly.

Hands seized his ankles.

"Don't let them take me!" Thomas howled, as spikes raked his skin. "Hanna! Simon! Benny! Help me!"

Three storeys down, the young footballers gaped up at Thomas hanging halfway out of the broken window. He desperately wanted to soar or plummet to the ground - whichever came first – but shards snapped and rip-slashed his sides when the furious crew dragged him back towards the bedroom.

"No!" he barked. "They won't let you do this! You can't stop me! Hanna, get them off me! *Hanna!*"

"What was that?" Sandra demanded. "What did he say?"

A man bellowed, "Get him in here!"

Thomas felt glass knives shred his chest and face. Then he was back inside Hanna's bedroom, seeing wallpaper elves close up and streaked dark red. He slid face-first down the wall, his vision a mishmash of blood. Hands turned him onto his back. When he heard sounds of shock, he opened his eyes. There, surrounded by an audience of dumbfounded faces, was Hanna's mummy Sandra.

"What did you say, just now?" she asked, her voice trembling. She dropped to her knees at his side. "How do you know her name?"

Thomas tried to speak, but his torn-up mouth wouldn't work.

"Please," she begged. Everyone behind her had stopped talking. Some were looking away. "Please tell me. How do you know her name? Did you read about her? Is that it?"

Thomas's sight swam like glitches in a computer game, but then he saw Hanna's beautiful mural again, with its creepy-crawlies, big cats and cackling apes. It reminded him that an ickle girl had once lived in this room – a real girl, not the horrid thing who ordered Thomas about and laughed at his pain – so he wheezed, "She likes it in the Gardden."

Sandra's hands flew to her mouth.

As the bedroom's colours faded to grey, Thomas whispered, "She likes it under the ground. I've taken good care of her."

Through her fingers, Sandra asked, "Did you take my baby?"

Thomas could feel that speaking had split his mouth open further, but he wanted her to know. He hadn't wanted to hurt anyone. He was just confused and a scaredy-cat who couldn't fight back, so he nodded weakly.

Sandra's eyes began to stream. "He took her," she said. Then, louder, to the others, "He took her! He took my baby!"

"We need to call an ambulance," Sam said from her side.

Through a darkening blur, Thomas saw something change in Sandra's eyes. "No we don't."

Sandra glanced around the room, at the photographs, the toys, and the mega-gorgeous mural. As she took something from Sam's hands, Thomas realised that the children weren't going to help him. He hadn't noticed before, but now he saw the three of them stood in the corner of the room, watching him blankly: his dead brother Simon, naughty, blonde Hanna, and mean, ickle Benny. Thomas had no idea if they were really with him or not, because in some dim corner of his mind he finally understood that he was loopy, totally crackers and absolutely cuckoo. The children had never been his friends. The children weren't even really children – they were just what the Gardden had used to keep Thomas under its thumb. And whether it was the Gardden or Thomas's broken brain that had caused them to appear in Hanna's bedroom, while he poured blood and was surrounded by a bug-swarm of stranger's faces, he knew that he was alone, just as he'd always been.

"It *was* you, wasn't it?" Sandra said.

Tasting blood, Thomas tried and failed to speak. He settled for another nod.

"You can all see that this man is about to attack me, can't you?" Sandra said, not asking, but telling the others. No one argued, and she raised something long and narrow towards the ceiling. "That's right. So this is self-defence."

Thomas watched Hanna's mummy close her eyes, puff out calmly, and open them again. A second later, she brought the cricket bat down.

CHAPTER 16
"Creation through destruction"

Henry

It was lucky that he'd bought the cane a year or so back, coz he woulda struggled gettin around wiv-out it. It'd bin the silver eagle at the top o' the walkin stick that'd interested Henry, and it was the only thing he'd ever bought that he could describe as 'elegant', wiv-out feelin like a ragin poof.

Henry shuffled out onto the casino's back lawn. He was now clad in an all-white suit and black tie that he hoped would distract the world from his 'just-shat-my-pants' hobble. He supported himself wiv the cane, keen to avoid disturbin the bits and bobs that he'd rammed back up his arse. His breath hitched when he passed Bruno's empty kennel, its drawbridge lowered, the Union Jacks droopin morosely in the breezeless late afternoon.

Fred was leanin against his grey-black BMW, chattin on his phone. Even though Henry couldn't make out what the beardy cunt was sayin, a shiver o' paranoia ran down his spine.

He's talkin about me. Probly laughin about me arse'ole.

Henry suspected that this would be the way of his future: forever frettin about what people were sayin, behind his backside. Although he was maintainin well considerin the certain stressful events, he already understood that, whatever the outcome o' this long, long day, everythin would've changed forever. He'd seen his reflection in the bathroom mirror as he'd grappled to put on the white suit. The usual glint in his eyes had bin snuffed out, an' his complexion was drained. Now, concentratin on every pathetic step, he musta looked like a stroke victim.

"How are you doing, boss?" Fred dared, after endin his call.

"I'm on top o' the fackin world," Henry growled. "Jus' get in the car."

Fred closed his mouth an' climbed behind the wheel. Henry pulled open the passenger door, ignorin the jogglin of his arse-articles, and eased himself down onto the seat. Fred pulled out onto the road. Despite the car's smooth movements, Henry couldn't help makin pained little peeps every few seconds.

"Er...where are we going, boss?"

"We're goin to get my boy," Henry said, and wiv

those words he managed to harden his voice. "He's a good lad, no matter what you bastards might think."

"I like him," Fred said, quickly.

"Save it," Henry barked. "You tell that to my Ray when we get there. I don't need any o' your fackin lies, alright? The boy's at a farm'ouse ten minutes outta town, backed by the woods. Big place, sold off some fields to make way for the connection road. Know where I mean, or do I have to call Percy?"

"I know it," Fred said.

An' the car fell into silence.

LOCKER

HE'D WANTED TO PLAY WITH THE GOTH. WANTED TO KEEP THE PRICK AWAKE WHILE HE'D CLIPPED EACH KNUCKLE FROM EACH FINGER, ONE BY ONE. SLICED OFF HIS EYELIDS AND SMASHED HIS RIBS TO SPLINTERS.

NO TIME FOR DEXTER NOW, THOUGH, OR O'NEILL, OR EVEN JACKO - JUST BRUTUS THE BUTCHER KNIFE, ONE OF LOCKER'S SIMPLEST, MOST BELOVED FRIENDS. HE MAY BE RUSHED, BUT BY *CHRIST* HE CAN FEEL THAT THE POETRY IS ON ITS WAY, THUNDERING TOWARDS HIM LIKE A TRAIN IN A TUNNEL.

THE GOTH IS ON HIS FRONT WITH ONE CHEEK PRESSED INTO THE DUST. PETEY THE HANDCUFFS HOLD HIS ARMS BEHIND HIM. LOCKER CROUCHES, AMUSED AT THE GOTH'S FINGERS FLEXING AT THE BASE OF HIS SPINE, PULLING AT THEIR CONFINES. THE KID HASN'T SAID ANYTHING SINCE LOCKER HAD CALLED HENRY. IT'S LIKE THE KID IS DOPED UP. HIS HEAD LOLLS

AGAINST THE DIRT AND HIS EYES CRAWL UP TOWARDS LOCKER'S. MEETING LOCKER'S GAZE SEEMS TO TRIGGER SOMETHING AND THE KID LOOKS ALARMED, AND TUGS HARDER AGAINST HANDCUFFS.

"YOU AREN'T GOING ANYWHERE," LOCKER SAYS.

"PERCY...WHAT'S HAPPENING?" THE GOTH ASKS. "WHAT ARE YOU DOING?"

"IT'S 'LOCKER'. AND THIS IS BRUTUS."

LOCKER HOLDS BRUTUS THE BUTCHER KNIFE OUT FOR THE GOTH TO SEE. THE METAL IS GREY BENEATH THE FOREST SHADOWS. UNDERSTANDING BEGINS AT THE BOY'S LIPS, PURSING THEM. THEN IT SPREADS OUT ACROSS THE LITTLE PANSY'S CHEEKS AND UP TO HIS PANICKED EYEBALLS. LITTLE POOF SHRINKS FROM THE BLADE.

"DON'T WORRY, KID. IT'LL BE OVER SOON."

THIS IS LIKE NOTHING LOCKER HAS FELT BEFORE – THIS IS LIKE DEFEATING A TRUE ENEMY. EACH OF THE SEVEN MURDERS LOCKER HAD ALREADY COMMITTED HAD BEEN NOTHING MORE THAN A FOCUS FOR HIS RAGE – A FLESH-AND-BLOOD PUNCHING BAG. BUT THIS, *OH THIS...*

THE GOTH'S EYES START TO WATER.

"JUST LIKE I THOUGHT - NO BALLS," LOCKER LAUGHS. HE SWIPES BRUTUS THROUGH THE AIR, THINKING ABOUT PAST SESSIONS IN THE WORKROOM. "THERE'S USUALLY A FEW STAGES BEFORE THEY CRY. THEY SHOUT, THEY ARGUE, THEY SCREAM, THEY ACT TOUGH, THEY FIGHT, THEY BEG, THEY BLACK OUT. BUT HARDLY ANY OF THEM *START OFF* BAWLING."

"PLEASE..." THE GOTH WHISPERS, AND A TEAR ROLLS DOWN HIS FACE. "PLEASE DON'T."

"THAT'S MORE LIKE IT," LOCKER SAYS. HE PRESSES BRUTUS AGAINST THE KID'S FOREHEAD; COLD, SHARP METAL THAT LOCKER HAD NURTURED AND CHERISHED. "BACK ON FAMILIAR GROUND NOW." HE TRACKS THE KNIFE A COUPLE OF INCHES, LEAVING A SHALLOW, HAIR-THIN SLIT ACROSS THE KID'S

BROW, COAXING THE POETRY TO DROWN HIM IN ITS ELOQUENCE. "YOU KNOW, I ONCE HAD A GUY DIE IN MY BASEMENT, SCREAMING OUT FOR HIS MUMMY. I WONDER IF YOU'LL DO THAT, TOO."

THE POETRY TAKES HOLD: THE RARE ARTISTRY BIRTHED BY APPROACHING VIOLENCE. LOCKER'S MIND BROADENS, BLOOMS, THE THOUGHTS AND WORDS STARTING TO CLARIFY, THE JIGSAW PIECES RECONNECTING.

"I DIDN'T MEAN TO KNOCK YOU DOWN THE STAIRS," THE KID SAYS, UNABLE TO MEET LOCKER'S EYES.

ANY DOUBTS THAT LOCKER HAD FELT SEEP AWAY, AS THE POETRY RECLAIMS ITS THRONE. HE SWINGS BRUTUS DOWN LIKE A PENDULUM, INCHES FROM THE GOTH'S FACE. "TODAY, I'M AN ARTIST," LOCKER DRAWLS. "AND YOU? YOU'RE MY CANVAS."

THE KID SOBS, HIS EYELIDS PINCHED SHUT, SQUEEZING OUT A FAGGOT'S WET SORROW. HIS SCULPTED FACE REFLECTS ACROSS BRUTUS'S BLADE.

"THIS IS WHAT I'M HERE FOR: TO RID THE WORLD OF QUEERS LIKE YOU. I DON'T DO IT FOR MYSELF, THOUGH. IT'S ALL FOR THE MAN WHO GAVE MY LIFE MEANING, A LONG TIME AGO."

LOCKER TAKES THE GOTH'S SKULL IN ONE HAND AND HOLDS IT FIRMLY AGAINST THE GROUND. "OH, AND ONE LAST THING: DID YOU KNOW THAT HAVING YOU KILL ROBBIE WAS MY IDEA? NOT HENRY'S - *MINE.*"

THE FOREST FALLS INTO SOFT FOCUS, AND LOCKER ADMIRES HIS FRIEND BRUTUS'S SIMPLICITY. THERE ARE NO SWITCHES, NO BUTTONS, NO TRIGGERS: JUST A LONG, RAZOR-EDGED KNIFE MADE FOR SHEARING MEAT FROM BONES. IN THE MISTY MOMENTS BEFORE LOCKER BEGINS, HE SEES A LOOK OF PERFECT DESPAIR CONTORT THE GOTH'S FACE: THE EXPRESSION OF A LOST CHILD.

SO FUCKING PRETTY, LOCKER THINKS, HOLDING THE GOTH'S HEAD STILL. THE VOICES HAVE STARTED IN LOCKER'S

HEAD AGAIN, BUT HE'S TOO FAR GONE NOW, TOO DEEPLY IMMERSED IN THE POETRY TO HEAR THEIR WORDS. IN ZEN-LIKE MENTAL SILENCE, LOCKER PUSHES BRUTUS'S SHARP TIP INTO THE GOTH'S CHEEK, AT THE CENTRE-POINT BETWEEN EAR AND MOUTH. DIRECTING THE UNWIELDY BLADE WITH THE PRECISION OF A SCALPEL, LOCKER SAVOURS THE EASE WITH WHICH IT DISAPPEARS INTO THE KID'S FACE, EXPERTLY COAXING THE METAL BACKWARDS BETWEEN RAY'S CLENCHED TEETH. ALTHOUGH THE GOTH'S LIPS REMAIN SEALED, BRACING THEMSELVES AGAINST THE PAIN, A NOISE LIKE A SOPRANO'S BROKEN HIGH NOTE SHOOTS OUT FROM THE NEWLY-OPENED WOUND. JUST BEFORE BRUTUS REACHES THE GOTH'S LIPS, LOCKER SPIES A WET GLIMPSE OF TOOTH AND GUM.

THE POETRY GUSHES THROUGH HIM, A CEREBRAL HIGH. LOCKER IS BECOMING A DEITY; THE GOD OF SLAUGHTER.

THE CLEAVER EMERGES BETWEEN THE CHILD'S LIPS. LOCKER SMILES: THE GOTH'S CHEEK HAS BEEN DIVIDED INTO SEPARATE UPPER AND LOWER PORTIONS.

CREATION THROUGH DESTRUCTION, LOCKER THINKS.

THE VOICES SHRIEK BUT THEIR WORDS ARE A BLUR; LOCKER IS LOST WITHIN HIS ARTISTRY, CRAFTING AN INSTALLATION OF PAIN AND RAW HUMAN MATTER. THE CHILD'S IDENTITY WILL SOON DEGRADE INTO GLISTENING RED FOLDS AND INANIMATE SCRAPS, MERE IMPRESSIONS OF THE INTRUDER WHO HAD ONCE STOLEN LOCKER'S PLACE AT HIS BOSS'S SIDE.

AS THE GOTH'S BODY FLAILS HOPELESSLY, HIS BLOOD AND TEARS MERGE WITH THE POWDERY SOIL. LOCKER THE SCULPTOR, LOCKER THE POET, LOCKER THE PHILOSOPHER RELISHES EVERY RAPTUROUS SECOND.

Ray

Ray almost passes out as the steel's cutting edge eases a path through the fat of his cheek. Percy Locker looms above him with a look of near-orgasmic pleasure, his eyes euphoric and his teeth gnawing his lower lip.

A buzzing swarm of voices crowds Ray's head.

don't let him win

we want you that's why we showed you our story, yes yes yes

FUCK KILL HATE THE SCUM

play little man play because then we can touch and kiss and fuck and die and

YOU KNOW WHAT TO DO, CHILD

Despite the sickening slew of voices, Ray's attention is swallowed by the pull of the knife. He wants blackness. He wants relief. He wants his mother, her flighty nature, her silly answers and her constant need for support.

Mummy...

"I've heard this called a Glasgow smile," Locker drools, almost lecherously. "A Chelsea grin. A joker-mask. In America, they call it a buck-fifty, because they say it takes 150 stitches to seal."

A hand drags Ray sideways and he feels his carved face flatten against the dirt. He yelps as

Locker turns him over onto his back, grit sticking to his tongue.

Behind Locker, the trees seem to have changed.

Locker pants excitedly, but the sound is muffled by the hissing, chittering voices.

we need you, child

be our mummy and be our daddy and be our kiddy

win win win

OBEY

he loves him so show him love, yes yes yes, he loves him so show him love

When Locker's hand presses against Ray's mouth, a finger scratches against his gums. Locker's face lingers close, like a grotesque lover. "I'll do this one *slowly*," he purrs. Through the taste of blood and the pain, Ray smells Locker's hot breath and sweet aftershave.

he loves him so show him love, yes yes yes

OBEYUS

it will be funny funny funny

As Ray's injured face bleeds into the sun-baked mud, Locker presses the knife against the unblemished side of his other cheek. Locker's lips open again, just an inch or two from Ray's. "You're going to die, but I want you to know *exactly* what I'm doing. I want you to scream. I want you to scream so hard that you open up your whole fucking face."

Ray clenches his teeth as Locker presses the blade harder against his skin, but even through the terror and raw pain Ray knows that the surrounding trees have become more than dead wood: the gnarled angles have curved and the twigs and branches now suggest unclothed bodies, anatomically incorrect yet unmistakably human. Peach, beige and black skin undulates from the shadows, tree-shaped but now glistening, *carnal.* Where there had only been bark moments before, hips appear to gyrate while fingers and tongues delve into moist, fleshy runnels. Scattered throughout the erotic confusion, Ray sees eyes - eyes without whites or irises, just staring marbles of depthless black.

win win win, little child...fuck us touch us kill us...he loves him so show him love

"Come on, you little queer. Scream for me."

Obey US, child!

A sudden determination electrifies Ray. As the metal of Locker's knife grinds against his molars, Ray stops cringing and cowering, and thrusts his face *towards* the agony. Locker's eyes widen in shock but Ray's abrupt movement is too fast to dodge. It feels like victory, and laughter and excited cheers erupt throughout the garden

YES YES YES

as Ray's ragged lips meet Locker's, painting the

stocky man's chin red. For a second, Locker's eyes flicker shut, and Ray almost believes that the man is going to return his blood-drenched kiss. Then Locker recoils in revulsion.

"The fuck you doing?" he demands, smearing a hand against his face, streaking gore across his cheek in what must be a mirror reversal of Ray's own crimson features.

Ray's mangled words, spoken past the knife and through a lisping, half-torn mouth, come unbidden: "Henry loves you. So just stop."

The forest falls silent. Locker looks perplexed, as if he too had been hearing the unearthly voices. His confusion makes him appear almost innocent, but then a lunatic grin twists his face.

"I always knew that you were a fucking faggot."

Behind Locker, two enormous, featureless shadows emerge from the air, like circular doors to oblivion. They narrow, and Ray realises that something colossal and unearthly has just blinked.

Locker sneers, "I'm going to split you down the middle, from neck to cock. That's how you'll die, you little poof. That's when-"

Before Locker can continue, a third black shape opens like a void below the two enormous eyes behind him. Ray's ears are pulverised by a noise, like the sum total of all the storms that have ever raged breaking at once.

Henry

As they drove, Henry watched the parasites who usually made his life so fackin easy. For the first time he could remember, he wished he was one o' them: sunburned, half-pissed, suckin in the views an' skirtin for minge.

Speakin o' minge, where was the bitch, eh? If she knew what was best for her, she'd be miles away by now, but Henry would find her. Didn't matter how long it took, or how far she went: Henry had contacts all over the shop.

As for Raymond – well, Henry was in two minds. The lad needed to see his errors so, in a way, Henry had wanted him punished. Just enough to make him buck his ideas up an' realise what a saint Henry had bin for givin him such grand opportunities. Back at the start, when Henry had realised who the lad was, he'd looked at the situation casually. The fact that the kid was family was just a technicality, really. One o' Henry's tough little bollock-soldiers had busted open the egg o' some club singer, an' that was just dandy. He'd bin pissed off at first, an' had rubbed the slag's infidelity into the face of her man, but that's jus' what blokes do when they're young – they banter. Henry had no *real* interest in Ray's slapper of a ma, so what was the big deal?

The big deal, he'd since decided, was that

despite Henry's absence, the lad had inherited his old man's potential for greatness. When it came down to brass tacks, what was an emperor worth, wiv-out an heir to inherit his empire?

As Fred drove, in spite of everythin that'd happened, Henry was beginnin to feel as if things were slottin into place. He was coastin along, creepin ever closer to his lad, *his real lad*, an' everythin was gonna be cushty. The boy couldn't be dead – no fackin way. Those dreams Henry had bin havin, the ones of his black-eyed dad, an' the forest, an' seein his son turnin away from him – they'd bin warnins. Some part of Henry had *known* that this day was comin, an' it'd prepared him for the worst. Well, broken arse or not, Henry was ready.

The house wasn't far. It was a buildin that most locals were probly familiar wiv, but one that Henry didn't know much about, despite it bein his responsibility to know the ins an' outs o' Seadon's landmarks. Fred almost missed the approachin lane, but wiv a screech o' tyres he caught it, just in time.

"Jesus," Fred said, as he pulled the BMW into a narrow, overcast dirt track. "No one lives here, surely."

"There's Locker's 4x4," Henry observed. That tank o' Percy's was parked jus' behind a much smaller car, some tiny blue hatchback.

"Out ya get," Henry said. "I don't know woss bin goin' on here, so have your shooter at the ready an' your eyes peeled like oranges."

Henry opened the door an' edged across the

seat, liftin his arse-cheeks off the surface wiv relief. His backside felt all swelled up, as if some of his junk wanted to pop out again, so he used the ornate cane to keep him steady.

It was cool outside, an' the sound o' traffic seemed muffled even though the four-lane road was closeby.

Fred didn't hesitate, an' made his way up the overgrown path towards the front door. He turned back, his gun at his side. "What do I do, knock?"

"No you don't fackin knock, you fackin pillock. You wait for me an' then you find a way to slip inside quietly, ready for anythin. Jus' wait there ˣ I'm not on top form."

"Probably shouldn't be up and about, really," Fred mumbled, turnin back from the door to face Henry.

Henry was about to tell his employee just where to get off, when Fred's eyes widened. The beardy cunt retreated away from the door an' back down the path, passin Henry as he went. "Oh, shit. Boss, look at this."

To the rear o' Locker's vehicle, jus' visible between the wheels, a bloke's head was lookin up at the registration number. A flurry o' ginger hair lay spread across the dirt.

Fred was pale.

"Not goin squeamish on me, are ya?" Henry asked, steppin towards the body. The face was sprayed red, the mouth gapin open. "Who the fack is that?"

"I'm not sure, Henry," Fred said, swayin. He

lay a hand against the back o' Percy's 4x4 an' crouched down. "Oh, *shit.* I think he's been... um... *eviscerated.*"

When Henry leaned over to see, his arse gave off a loose burp. Ignorin the intrusion, Henry said, "Oh yeah. So he has." He managed a chuckle. "No guts, no glory, eh?"

Fred took a glance and shook his head. "I don't recognise him. Did Percy do that, d'you reckon? Looks like his style. Probably used one of his little friends."

Henry scratched his head. "Well, this certainly ain't the fatty that Percy was goin on about. This one's built like a fackin fishin rod." He sighed, heaved himself back up usin the cane, an' starEd at the house. "I dunno woss goin on. Percy ain't called back, so all we can do is get inside to find..."

He stopped. Surely the ground hadn't just quivered, had it? Henry began to ask, "Did you feel..."

A long, baritone rumble mashed his words flat, feelin as though it was shakin Henry's body as it rose, huge an' threatenin. Fred looked confused an' seemed to speak, but Henry couldn't hear anything except the cacophony.

What in fack's name is that? Henry tried to shout, but the deep, burblin racket stole his voice from the air. He covered his ears but the sound was reverberatin his very bones. He staggered backwards, bracin himself against the noise which seemed to be comin from behind the house.

The din kept escalatin.

I'm goin deaf - I'm never goin' to hear again!

Fred clung onto the boot handle, strugglin to stay standin, then thought better an' slapped his hands over his ears an' fell onto his arse.

Earthquakes weren't like this, were they? An' you didn't get anythin more than little gnat's fart tremors in England. Still clutchin his ears, Henry shut his eyes to try an' stop 'em vibratin. The roar kept boomin, impossibly low an' jus' fackin *massive*. He looked up an' saw that the trees reachin over the dilapidated roof were movin.

This is fackin mental, he thought, for a moment believin that the hurricane o' sound was gonna keep getting louder an' louder, until both of 'em lay dead.

Then it was over. One moment there was total fackin chaos, an' then, nothin at all. Almost like somethin had gotten a hold of itself an' calmed the fack down.

Fred stayed flat against the ground, hands over his ears, eyes gogglin.

Henry didn't believe in any o' that *weird stuff*, so the sound musta come from some great machine - maybe a few hundred amps blowin their loads all at once. Had to be an explanation, an' it weren't gonna slow Henry down - nothin would. Henry would kick God himself in the balls if the cunt tried to stop him gettin to his son.

"Oi," Henry said, barely hearin the word,

even in his own head. He kicked Fred's side an' the soppy sod seemed to find himself again. Henry motioned towards the house, an' after a second Fred nodded begrudgingly.

Wiv Fred at his side, Henry stepped onto the weed-strewn path leadin to the front door. Deaf or not, he was gonna get to his lad.

LOCKER

ONCE ITS TEETH ARE EXPOSED, A HUMAN FACE REVEALS THE TRUTH: THAT IT IS JUST A MASK OF FLESH CONCEALING A SKULL. LOCKER MUSES UPON THIS AS HE SLICES THROUGH RAY'S SECOND CHEEK, HIS NOSE CLOSE ENOUGH TO SMELL THE COPPERY BLOOD.

OVERCOME BY THE POETRY, LOCKER IS KILLING HIS PARENTS, THE QUEERS, THE COONS, THE PAKIS AND THE WHORES. HE'S SWIMMING IN THE GOTH'S SPILLING REDS, RELISHING THE UNRESISTANT TISSUE AND THE LOYALTY OF HIS SHIMMERING FRIEND BRUTUS. HE EMBRACES THE KNOWLEDGE THAT EVERY WORTHLESS PIECE OF MEAT ENDS UP HERE, RESTRAINED AND WEEPING ON SOMEONE ELSE'S CHOPPING BOARD.

THAT'S LIFE.

AFTER THE GOTH HAS GONE, LOCKER WILL ONCE AGAIN STAND UNACCOMPANIED AT HIS BOSS'S SIDE, AND ALL WRONGS WILL BE RIGHTED. LOCKER WANTS THE KID TO KNOW THAT HE'S BEEN BESTED, SO AS HE DRAGS BRUTUS'S POINT CLOSER TO THE EDGE OF THE CHILD'S RUINED MOUTH, HE SAYS, "COME ON, YOU LITTLE QUEER. SCREAM FOR ME."

AT HIS WORDS, SOMETHING IMPOSSIBLE HAPPENS: THE KID'S UNFOCUSED EYES, INTIMATELY NEAR, MEET LOCKER'S.

THE PRESSURE AGAINST BRUTUS THE BUTCHER KNIFE INCREASES, AND LOCKER REALISES THAT HE'S ABOUT TO EXPERIENCE SOMETHING HE NEVER HAS BEFORE.

THE KID RAISES HIS HEAD. THE KNIFE SLIPS FURTHER INTO HIS FACE, CLINKS AGAINST TEETH, AND THE KID'S LIPS, BLOOD-CAKED AND FOUL, MEET LOCKER'S. CAUGHT OUT AND SHOCKED, LOCKER CAN'T HELP BUT SHUT HIS EYES. HE OPENS THEM AGAIN AND SEES THE GOTH UP CLOSE, *KISSING HIM*, AND PULLS AWAY FROM THE DIRTY FUCKING QUEER.

THE POETRY DIES. LOCKER THE LUGHEAD RETURNS.

SIMPLE.

VIOLENT.

STILL HOLDING BRUTUS IN ONE HAND, LOCKER WIPES HIS MOUTH. "THE FUCK YOU DOING?"

WITH THE KNIFE STILL BURIED IN HIS CHEEK, THE GOTH MANAGES: "HENRY LOVES YOU. SO STOP."

LOCKER WANTS THE HATRED. NEEDS TO FEEL SURE AGAIN, BUT HE CAN FEEL THAT HE'S BEEN TRICKED.

"I ALWAYS KNEW YOU WERE A FUCKING FAGGOT," HE TELLS THE GOTH, BUT HE'S PUZZLED. THE GOTH HAD ONLY KISSED HIM – DIDN'T MEAN ANYTHING – BUT IT FEELS LIKE SOMETHING MUCH WORSE HAS HAPPENED.

LOCKER FEELS *DEFEATED.*

HE FORCES A SMILE. "I'M GOING TO SPLIT YOU FROM YOUR NECK DOWN TO YOUR COCK." HE DISLODGES THE KNIFE FROM THE KID'S CHEEK. "THAT'S HOW YOU'LL DIE, YOU LITTLE POOF. THAT'S WHEN-"

LOCKER'S EARS CAVE IN. THE GARDEN FILLS WITH A CLAMOUR SO TERRIBLE THAT BRUTUS'S HANDLE LEAVES HIS FINGERS AND DROPS TO THE SOIL. ANY NOISE THE KNIFE MIGHT HAVE MADE IS BLOTTED OUT BY A POUNDING, ONGOING EXPLOSION.

CONJURED BY THE AUDITORY VIOLENCE, THE POETRY AWAKENS IN LOCKER ONCE MORE. LOCKER THE ARTIST LEAPS

TO HIS FEET, FEELING THE GROUND TREMBLE. THE PANDEMONIUM COMES IN WAVES, AND ALTHOUGH HE COVERS HIS EARS, HIS HANDS ARE AS INSUFFICIENT AS SHEETS OF PAPER. HE SPINS AROUND TO TRACE THE SOUND'S SOURCE BUT IT'S EVERYWHERE: BELOW HIM, ABOVE HIM, CIRCLING HIM LIKE A TORNADO.

THE TREES THRASH, THEIR FRAYED LIMBS FLEXING LIKE SNAKES. THE COLOSSAL ROAR SCALES NEW HEIGHTS, AND IN THE SHADOWS OF THE FRENZIED FOREST SOMETHING VAST BEGINS TO UNCOIL. THE GARDEN

GARDDEN

IS ALIVE, AND WHEN LOCKER TURNS, TWO IMMENSE BLACK SPHERES BEAR DOWN UPON HIM, LIKE THE PITILESS GAZE OF AN AWAKENED GOD. BENEATH THESE, A MAN-SIZED, TAR-BLACK ELLIPSIS YAWNS HUNGRILY, *BELLOWING.*

THE DEATHS LOCKER HAS CAUSED, THE PAIN HE HAS AWOKEN, THE TORMENTS HE HAS RELISHED; ALL ARE DUST BEFORE THIS ATROCITY. LOCKER IS PLANKTON CAUGHT IN THE JAWS OF A WHALE.

YOU LOST SO YOU SHOULD NOT BE HERE AND YOU SHOULD NOT BE PLAYING NO NO NO YOU SHOULD NOT HAVE FRIENDS YOU SHOULD BE ALONE ALONE ALONE

PARALYSED, LOCKER STARES BEYOND THE BLACK EYES AND THE MOUTH. BETWEEN THE WRITHING BOUGH AND BARK, A TIDE OF FAMILIAR FORMS IS SWELLING: AMPUTATED LIMBS, EXTRACTED ORGANS, SMASHED BONES, AND A CHURNING RESERVOIR OF BLOOD. LOCKER TURNS TO FLEE, BUT SOMETHING CONSTRICTS HIS STOMACH. THE GOTH SEEMS TO DROP AWAY FROM HIS FEET BUT THEN LOCKER'S MIND READJUSTS. AS THE SKULL-SHATTERING DRONE MAINTAINS ITS ASSAULT, LOCKER REALISES THAT HE IS BEING PULLED AWAY FROM THE GROUND. THE BLACK EYES AND MOUTH MATCH HIS ASCENT, REMAINING LEVEL WITH HIM AS HE RISES METRES ABOVE THE FOREST FLOOR.

YES YES YES NOW IT'S TIME FOR US TO PLAAAAAAAAAAAAAAAAAY

AN ARM HAS ENWRAPPED LOCKER'S WAIST – NO, NOT AN ARM: A MONSTROUS TREE BRANCH. LEGS DANGLING, LOCKER IS LIFTED INTO THE CANOPY, AWAY FROM THE KID AND THE DISMEMBERED TERRORS THAT FLOW AND SHUDDER AND ADVANCE BENEATH HIM.

NO, PERCY TRIES TO ARGUE. *NO NO NO NO NO...*

YES YES YES YES YES

HE GRIPS THE BROWN LIMB IN PANICKED FINGERS AND PULLS, BUT IT'S AS HOPELESS AS TRYING TO SNAP THICK ROPE. THE GOTH STARES UP, HIS FEATURES CARVED INTO A MOCKING LEER – A LEER THAT LOCKER ONCE SAW IN A DREAM.

AMIDST THE CHAOS, THE AIR BECOMES THICK WITH GLITTERING, FLASHING FORMS. THEY CIRCLE THE BLACK EYES AND MOUTH SUSPENDED BEFORE HIM LIKE DISTORTED NUMBERS ON A CLOCK FACE. LOCKER FEELS A SURGE OF UNHINGED RELIEF; HIS DUTIFUL FRIENDS HAVE COME TO ASSIST HIM. FAITHFUL, EVER-RELIABLE, THEY'RE HERE TO SEVER THE BRANCH THAT HAS ENSNARED HIM.

JACKSON, LOCKER'S ROTATING SAW, DETACHES FROM THE ORBIT AND APPROACHES THE TREE LIMB WRAPPED AROUND LOCKER'S MIDSECTION. JACKSON'S TEETH SPIN WILDLY. THE FOREST'S NOISE SEEMS TO RISE IN CLIMAX AS LOCKER WATCHES JACKSON THE BUZZSAW DODGE BENEATH THE BRANCH AND WITH A SHARP DOWNWARD SWERVE, BURY HIS EDGE DEEP INTO LOCKER'S FLAILING ANKLE. LOCKER FEELS THE AGONY OF HIS FRIEND'S SERRATIONS FOR THE FIRST TIME AND SCREAMS OUT, BUT THE WALL OF MOCKING NOISE SWALLOWS HIS PROTESTS. UNDER JACKSON'S UNFORGIVING JAWS, LOCKER'S TROUSER LEG SPLITS APART IN A SPRAY OF CHEWED FLESH.

PERCY LOCKER'S TOOLS ARE NO LONGER HIS COMPANIONS. *THEY ARE MINE*

O'NEILL, A SURGICAL SCALPEL, EMERGES FROM THE RING OF MURDEROUS WEAPONS AND SKEWERS LOCKER'S LEFT PALM, NAILING IT TO THE BRANCH THAT HAS HIM TRAPPED. HE TUGS AT THE SCALPEL WITH HIS FREE HAND AS DEXTER, A BLOWTORCH, SPONTANEOUSLY IGNITES AND DARTS BENEATH HIS CHIN. DEXTER SCORCHES LOCKER'S FLESH UNDER A ROASTING BLUE FLAME, AND THROUGH HIS AGONY LOCKER KNOWS FROM EXPERIENCE THAT HIS LIPS WILL SOON MELT AND ENTWINE.

ONE BY ONE HIS LOYAL FRIENDS TURN AGAINST HIM, AND EACH WAIL THAT PASSES THROUGH THE BUBBLING SORE OF HIS MOUTH IS DESTROYED BY THE GARDDEN'S CATACLYSMIC FURY.

YOU LOST YOU LOST YES YES YES SO THIS IS HOW WE PLAYYYYYYYYYYYY

AS LOCKER WRESTLES WITH THE BRANCH STILL HOLDING HIM CAPTIVE, IVA, AN INSTRUMENT SHAPED LIKE A LONG, SNAPPING PAIR OF SCISSORS, FLAYS HIS FREE ARM. STRIPS OF PINK PEEL AWAY AND THE WORKINGS OF HIS WRIST ARE REVEALED IN A THROBBING DELUGE OF BLOOD. IVA CLIMBS HIGHER. THROUGH INCONCEIVABLE PAIN, LOCKER FEELS THE TOOL AT HIS NECK, UNDRESSING LAYERS OF SKIN BEFORE SCALING HIS JAW AND ATTEMPTING TO UNMASK HIM ENTIRELY.

LOCKER THE SCHOLAR SCREAMS THROUGH HIS ROUGHLY-FUSED MOUTH, BUT STOPS WHEN ALFIE ARCS UPWARDS AND IMPALES HIS THROAT. ALFIE, WHO HAD STOLEN PARTS FROM HALF A DOZEN OF LOCKER'S VICTIMS, TAKES HOLD OF LOCKER'S TONGUE AND WRENCHES IT OUT THROUGH THE RAGGED NEW TUNNEL IN HIS NECK.

LOCKER'S TOOLS DRAG HIS EARDRUMS FROM THEIR HOMES, CASTRATE HIM IN A RED WATERFALL AND TEAR GOUGES ACROSS HIS BODY BUT PERCY LOCKER, A GARGLING, CRIMSON FIGURE UNDONE AT EVERY SEAM, LIVES ON. THE BLACK EYES

AND MOUTH OF THE GARDDEN, INCENSED WITH MINDLESS, PLAYFUL LOATHING, WILL NOT PERMIT HIM TO REST.

ISN'T THIS FUUUUUUUUUUUUUUUUN

AT LAST THE ASSAULT ENDS. THE GARDDEN'S SHADOWED EYES AND MOUTH VANISH. LOCKER'S ATTACKERS SHOWER THE GROUND FAR BELOW. THE GOTH SEES THEM COMING BUT REMAINS STILL AS THEY LAND HARMLESSLY AROUND HIM. WITH LOCKER'S CONSCIOUSNESS IN PIECES, HIS EARS BRUTALLY DEAFENED AND HIS TATTERED NERVES ABLAZE, HE IS LOWERED TO THE GROUND.

THOUGH HE IS LITTLE MORE THAN A SHAMBLING TOWER OF WOUNDS, LOCKER REMAINS STANDING, ALIVE AND IMPOSSIBLY AWARE. THE GOTH GAPES AT HIM, A DEFORMED LITTLE BOY AWOKEN FROM A NIGHTMARE. LOCKER GLANCES DOWN AT HIS OWN TRAUMATISED BODY, BUT THEN FOCUSES ON THE HOUSE BEYOND THE EDGE OF THE FOREST.

ONE SOLITARY THOUGHT IS A BEACON – *HENRY* – BUT IT IS NO LONGER A PERSON THAT REACHES OUT WITH FINGERLESS STUMPS AND PLODS FORWARDS, AS UNSTEADY AS A TODDLER; IT IS BLEEDING, FEATURELESS WRECKAGE. THE HOUSE LOOMS BEFORE IT AND THE ONCE-ANIMATE FOLIAGE MAKES NO ATTEMPT TO HALT ITS PROGRESS. ALTHOUGH ITS WORLD HAS FALLEN SILENT, LOCKER FEELS CRACKLING MOANS DRIFTING FROM THE MUTANT LUMP OF ITS HEAD.

LOCKER STUMBLES THROUGH A SOUNDLESS WORLD. AFTER A LIFETIME OF AWKWARD STRIDES, IT EMERGES FROM THE GARDDEN. THERE, ADVANCING BEFORE ITS LIDLESS EYES, AWAITS A FAMILIAR FIGURE: THE MAN WHO HAD ONCE GIVEN ITS LIFE A CALLING.

IN A FINAL BURST OF THE POETRY, A LAST BREATH OF ARTISTIC GRACE, IT ISSUES A SLEW OF WORDS. GAZING INTO ITS MASTER'S PERFECT FEATURES IT CONFESSES THAT IT HAD ONLY HATED HIS DECISIONS BECAUSE IT HAD LOVED HIM. IT REMINDS ITS KEEPER THAT IT HAD ONCE BEEN THE

INSTRUMENT HE HAD WIELDED TO BUILD AN EMPIRE. IT STATES THAT, BEFORE OFFERING ALLEGIANCE TO ITS BOSS, IT HAD BEEN PATHLESS AND HOPELESS, AND THAT IN DIFFERENT CIRCUMSTANCES IT WOULD HAVE REMAINED AT ITS MASTER'S SIDE FOREVER.

AS LOCKER SPEAKS, IT REMEMBERS THE DAYS WHEN IT HAD MASSAGED ITS BOSS'S ACHING SHOULDERS. WHEN IT HAD TOLD HIM THAT ALL WAS WELL, THAT THE CITY BELONGED TO HIM, AND THAT THE WORLD WAS HIS PERFECT OYSTER. WHEN IT HAD USED ITS ONCE-SOFT LIPS TO PLEASURE ITS MASTER'S MOST SENSITIVE ORGAN, TO HELP HIM FORGET HIS TROUBLES.

THE DECREPIT APPARITION SHUFFLES CLOSER, FEELING SAFE IN THE SILENCE ONE LAST TIME. ITS NAKED FACIAL MUSCLES SQUIRM, AS IF TO SMILE.

CHAPTER 17
"Welcome home"

Henry

Henry shuddered as cold, pungent air spilled from the doorway. His gun loosened in his damp palm. When nothin emerged from the dark hallway, Henry turned back and saw Fred lookin goggle-eyed an' nervous.

Fackin woofter, Henry thought, but he was on edge, willin the sirens in his ears to stop. It didn't matter what that blastin noise had meant; he'd ask questions later.

Henry braced against the smell, an' –

– steps into the damp property. Somethin he can't pinpoint twists the day.

A foot or so inside, Fred speaks from behind him. "Thf... s... na... s... ths?"

"You what?!" Henry booms, still partially deaf. He concentrates on Fred's lips.

"I said, who the fuck lives in a place like this?!"

"Jus' some fat bastard headin for an early grave."

"What?!" Fred asks.

"It doesn't matter!"

A nauseatin smell descends the bare-wood staircase. Henry can see at the end of a hallway decorated wiv stupid pictures, in a rubbish tip of a kitchen, a door is standin wide open. Could Percy and Raymond be outside? He motions for Fred to stay quiet an' points forwards. They edge along the corridor, an' when Fred reaches a doorway on the right he swings his gun inside, checkin to make sure it's clear.

Henry's ears have calmed a little now, an' he thinks he can hear a low hum from somewhere nearby, like exposed wires or a nest o' wasps.

Nothin about this place feels right.

"D'you hear that?" Henry asks, as he follows Fred towards the kitchen.

"What?" Fred asks.

"That buzzin."

"I can't hear much at all, Henry," Fred says. "But I keep thinking there's somebody...sounds silly...somebody behind me."

"Don't talk cock," Henry snaps.

Feelin irrational but refusin to admit it, Henry marches into the cookin room. He gags when he sees the state o' the place: smeared packagin, crunched-up soda cans, brown an' red muck over every surface, bugs swarmin in complicated regiments around a heap o' dead mates in the sink. "Jesus fackin Christ."

His son. Henry has to reach his son.

oh you will yes yes yes you will meet your pretty funny perfect sonny

Above the hot an' cold taps, the window looks out into a mass of shadowy green an' brown. A movement from the wooden trunks catches his attention, a little too far into the dimness to make out. As it draws closer, though, Henry sees that it's a man strugglin to remain upright. "Fred. Look."

They peer through the window as the figure comes closer, its arms outstretched. It glistens all over.

"Er, Henry, that looks like it could be Percy, but..."

"No, can't be," Henry asserts. "Never seen Percy take an uncertain step in his life."

A stream o' light from above the trees reveals the body clearly. It shouldn't be walkin. It stumbles once an' its head lolls forwards, showin off a bare section o' skull. Rags o' black suit an' probly muscle hang from its arms. Christ – it's bin flayed. After a few more tottered strides, the thing readjusts its head, an' Henry sees two mad white globes gazin out from a map o' shredded gristle.

"Fuck me," Fred panics, his voice high-pitched. "It *is* Percy. Fuck me, fuck me..."

"It's not Percy!" Henry yells.

He knows that it isn't Percy, because there's only one person in his world that looks half as facked up as that: a shrivelled, demented man in his 80s who spends his days alone in bed, waiting for someone to lend his late wife a pen.

Henry shakes his head an' goes to the door. There's somethin very wrong in this place, an' if it wasn't for the fact that his son was somewhere nearby he'd have bin runnin for the car. He yanks the door open and steps onto the shaded grass.

"Who are ya? Where's the kid?" he demands.

It ain't Dad. It can't be.

He ploughs into the trees, tryin to blank the details o' the figure even as the mangled mess beneath its eyes spreads out in recognition.

Henry stops.

Fred was right: it *is* fackin Percy.

The man's skinned jaw shifts, an' out comes this wheezin slobber, like the sound Bruno used to make lickin up the scraps of a good meal. There's no time to consider Locker's loyalty, or their difficult past, or their even tougher present. Henry just puts his gun to the doomed cunt's forehead an' pumps out a round, movin past wiv-out stoppin. The body drops behind him. Henry doesn't look back.

A second shape lies on its side further into the glade, surrounded by glintin metal.

"Raymond!" Henry shouts, speedin up into a jog. His lad doesn't respond but Henry can hear him breathin.

When Henry gets close enough, he sees that his golden boy's face is drenched red an' his arms are handcuffed behind his back. Henry recognises Percy's torture tools ˣ his 'friends' – strewn across the clearin. "Woss 'appened, son?"

Understandin dawns on Henry. Fred calls out but Henry ignores him, tryin to compose himself in the face of his worst nightmare.

Even Percy, his old "companion", an' longest servin employee, had betrayed Henry before he'd died.

Henry drops his cane, gets down to the floor an' lays a hand onto the boy's shoulder. "Can you hear me, Raymond-son?"

The kid's eyes roll. He moans a coupla minor-keys. Stricken wiv grief, Henry sees the wounds that now divide the kid's filmstar cheeks. Havin ignored his feelins for so long, Henry can't express himself in a single gesture. He knows that he should be racin to free the lad, helpin him to his feet an' rushin him to the hospital, but he can't process the sight of his special lad's torn-up face. Henry feels the boy tremblin.

"Ray, my poor boy..." he mumbles. He needs somethin to focus his mind on or he's gonna blubber or collapse beside the kid, curlin up into a ball that ain't no use to anyone.

"Boss, what's happened?" Fred calls. "Is he dead?"

Like a strikin snake, Henry rises an' spins around. "*No he's not fackin' dead, you useless cocksucker!*"

Henry lunges at Fred. "Did you know about this?" he demands, grabbin Fred's hairy throat an' crushin the gun against his lips. "Are you in on it?

Fred looks anxious but doesn't fight back. "Of course I didn't, Henry," he says into the barrel, raisin his hands. "I've been with you the whole afternoon, haven't I?"

Henry tenses his finger against the trigger. "You're all against me, aren't ya? Not a loyal bone in yer bodies – not one. Well you know what happens to backstabbin scum like you, don't ya?"

"Boss," Fred says, warily. "We need to get the kid to a doctor."

Henry gives the gun a shove an' Fred's lower lip splits against his teeth. "What else d'you know, eh? What else are you pricks keepin from me?"

"Nothing at all...I swear!" Fred splutters.

Henry's mood has become a combo o' wrath, confusion, an' a touch o' lunacy – but it's better than cryin. "Come on, what else?" he yells, eyebrows dancin, sweat pourin from him. "What've you done, eh? Nicked my cash? Banged my missus? Buggered me while I'm sleepin?"

"Henry," Fred says. "What are we going to do about Ray? He's badly hurt."

"Is that a fackin fact?" Henry spits, but when he looks back down, the sight of his lad brings him back to Earth. He lowers his weapon an' releases Fred, an' then turns back to Ray. Henry's face starts to crumble an' his eyes start to sting, but he composes himself. "Come on, help me get him outta here. I don't like this place."

"What are we going to do about the cuffs?"

Fred asks.

"We've bin standin round chin-waggin for long enough. My lad needs the hospital."

"But boss, what about the police..."

Henry gives Fred a look. Fred shuts his mouth.

Rebecca

The driver, a large, unimpressed-looking Irishman, was the type of cabbie that Rebecca favoured: one who kept his raving views to himself.

As they drove, immersed in the working class scent of old rolling tobacco, Rebecca decided that she was going to leave the drab island of 'Great' Britain for good. Bored with glamour's empty promises, she would travel either to the quaint state of New England or to the icy calms of Canada.

Users and the used, she lamented. Abusers and the abused.

Turning back to watch Seadon's suburbs dropping from view for perhaps the last time, Rebecca considered her life's mottos. Was such simplicity a coherent worldview, or merely the conclusions of a woman who has lived a radical yet ultimately narrow life?

"That's the house," she said briskly as a tattered, branch-draped roof rose into view.

He nodded into the rear mirror, looking

irritated.

Under a blushing red sky, they slowed and left the dual carriageway. The cab slipped beneath a darkened archway of trees and Rebecca's eyes widened; a group of three vehicles were gathered some way down the lane. "Stop here!" she ordered.

"Alright, keep yer hair on." The cabbie pulled up. "That'll be fifteen, please."

"Just give me a moment," she said, leaning between the two front seats to scan the dusty track ahead. Farthest away, she saw Gary's metallic blue rent-a-car. A little behind that a long, dark grey BMW and finally, closest to the cab, a huge black off-road vehicle resembling a cross between a tank and a hearse.

That looks like Percy Locker's 4x4.

Had she been set up? No - not a chance. Gary had no connection to Henry and his crew.

"Listen, love, it's going to cost you a pretty penny if you want me to sit here all day."

"You'll get your money," she said. "In fact, if you stay here until I get back, you can have three hundred pounds for your troubles."

The driver closed his lips.

Rebecca tried to imagine the worst possible outcome of stepping out of the taxi. Then she pictured the money, the wads of paper that could unlock a new future for her.

"Just wait here," she told him, opening the door and swinging out her legs and laying her bare feet against the gravel.

A thick growth of shrubs and trees climbed the cool, shaded air on either side, and the tall trunks to her right obscured her view of the farmhouse. She began a cautious path towards the 4x4, keeping close to the trees, and after ten feet or so caught her first clear sight of the farmhouse.

She was immediately hit by two conflicting impressions. One was a thoroughly irrational sense of menace. Her second (yet by no means more logical) sense was an oddly comforting belief that, standing there, she was in precisely the right place at the right time.

Home.

She craned her neck to take in a full view of the building. The grimy windows revealed nothing of their contents, but its decrepit three storeys and forest-backed roof gave the structure an arresting presence. Rebecca had to concentrate hard to keep her legs from taking her to the doorway. She felt drawn, not to the mysteries of the house itself, but rather to those she felt were at the rear of the property: the trees, the earth, and the garden.

Don't be a fool.

When Rebecca turned around to ensure that the taxi was still waiting, she noticed something beneath the 4x4.

Not something; someone.

Despite his face appearing upside down from her position, Rebecca knew immediately that she was looking at Gary, and that he was dead. As she absorbed his shocked expression and the dried blood daubed across his chin, she was taken back to a moment in their past: gripping his throat in the moist warmth of the guesthouse, drinking in his fear and discomfort just as Henry had no doubt imbibed hers. Rebecca's plan had always been to abandon Gary but now, staring at his pathetic remains, she felt a terrible sorrow.

Gary Pickles had been a man deserving guidance at best, and pity at worst. She did not believe him to have been especially malicious – just self-destructive, supremely lost, spineless, and in desperate need of a saviour.

Anger flared inside her.

How had Gary come to be here, and why in hell's name was he now lying dead under Percy Locker's vehicle? Moreover, were those his innards half-hidden by the transport's underbelly?

Feeling her gullet constrict, Rebecca looked away from her dead lover's body and back to the trail that led to the dual carriageway. Through the taxi's windscreen, she saw an outline of the driver, comfortably oblivious to the carnage no more than 20 metres away. The temptation to bolt rose in her again, but the money was all she had left. Surely her little bug's murderer had taken it from the rental car?

A deep, throbbing ache climbed the buckled ridges of her spine.

welcome home

She gasped, turning back to the house. Its empty windows resembled expectant eyes. She approached the blue Ka, her head feeling muzzy, and saw a small, grey rucksack lying on the back seat.

Rebecca felt no surprise to find all four doors

and the boot locked. Perhaps Gary had died clutching the keys, but she despised the thought of rifling through his pockets with his organs on display. All she had to do was break the window, snatch the bag and return to the cab – but her driver was unlikely to linger while she performed an impromptu B-and-E, or while she emptied the pockets of a corpse.

It was all so terribly inconvenient, but she either had to tell her driver that she could not pay, or somehow claim her money from the car.

no no no, come inside...he she it won't stay long

The cough of an engine drew her attention. The taxi was reversing, creeping away towards the dual carriageway like a wary cat. Although Rebecca was too far away and the windscreen too shadowed for her to define the driver, she envisioned him clutching the wheel with his eyes closed - sleepdriving. When the car reached the slip road, it turned a slow circle and re-joined the dual carriageway, and then promptly trundled out of sight.

bye byeeeeeeeee

Rebecca was now wholly alone, and while she wondered why her driver had abandoned her, she was too aware of the danger of her situation. Gary was dead, murdered, and his killer might still be nearby. She braced herself and crouched at the rear of the huge black 4x4. The faecal stench of her late lover's bowels assaulted her, but she gripped Gary's body beneath its armpits and, in stages, dragged it out from beneath the vehicle.

In death, Gary's eyes gazed up towards his forehead. His mouth stretched open, like a yawn. His fingers were clenched claws. Despite the vision of his tangled innards, Rebecca had an urge to stroke his bloodied cheek, like a mother soothing a sick and sleepless child. She touched his blood-slickened lips, wishing he could feel her finger's comforting trail. She remembered that she was there to find the car keys so she leaned forwards, stretching for Gary's pockets, but felt unable to resist laying her hands against the purple-grey folds of his intestines, kneading them and

yes yes yesssssssssssss

running her fingers through the glutinous threads, just as she might a young child's hair.

She snatched back her hands, stomach rolling, and tightened her lips against a surge of vomit. She wiped the gummy blood from her hands onto the shoulders of Gary's blue tracksuit, fearing that the day's events had loosened something vital in her brain. Ignoring Gary's viscera this time, Rebecca searched his two side pockets, finding only his phone. Then she rolled him over, hearing his entrails slither, to ensure that there was nowhere else he could have secured the keys.

Despairing, she checked her surroundings for something with which to smash the car window. She glanced at the farmhouse and heard or thought those words again.

welcome home

Her belly gurgled.

"I'll be back in a moment, son," she told Gary, noticing but accepting the incongruity of her *words. She rose, picturing a comfortable bed and a family of loving sons and daughters, and reminded herself that all she had to do was find the keys or a heavy blunt object to gain access to the car. Halfway down the weed-ridden path she decided that she would stop, that she had to admit defeat because it was too risky*

no no no no no

but the next thing she knew was that she had eased open the splintery portal and stepped –

- inside, and as she moves forwards, vertigo clutches her throat. Her centre of balance teeters and she bowls forwards, landing onto her hands and knees. Her head fills with a white hiss and, on all-fours, she sees the hallway blur like a dream. Her mind feels swamped, distorted, but oddly at ease. She pulls herself to her feet and her torso spasms sickeningly, but it's okay, it's alright: something has begun, something that she has always feared yet at the same time always secretly craved.

"I'm in shock," she says aloud, but her voice sounds uncertain. Her lower parts lurch like a magnified period cramp.

She does not think it this time, but hears a sharp whisper: "Mummy."

She wants to reply but she is too light-headed. The walls are a garish nightmare of gurning faces and lunatic characters. She needs to find the source of that voice, because it is calling to her; it has always called to her.

After another few steps, she discovers a barren room containing nothing more than a desktop computer and a leather office chair. The walls run with damp, the ceiling crawls with dull green fungus, and the floor seems to shift below her naked feet.

Is there someone else nearby? Something beneath her? Something that pulses through the house, inhabiting every room as well as the garden behind it?

She struggles to remember why she had entered the house, and hears a low, brooding growl. She's confused, fighting to process each strange development as well as ignoring her shock at the death of Gary, her insectile son... no... lover. The cramp in her lower torso comes again and she cries out.

Immediately after she presses her hand against her midriff, she pulls it away. Something impossible had moved.

"Mummy!" someone from the corridor cries. "MUMMY!"

Disorientated and in pain, she leaves the empty room and follows the voice. Her concerns are becoming less substantial, billowing and trickling nearby but no longer immediate, and the phrase repeats like a mantra within her: welcome home, welcome home, welcome home...

The corridor has darkened. Its patch-worked walls pulse in gentle, smoky waves. Dazed, struggling to make sense of the series of disconnected sensations, Rebecca sees two forms in the kitchen: a childlike silhouette without features and a tall, four-legged beast.

The shadow's voice is an ethereal buzz: "Please take care of us, mummy."

The paltry light from the kitchen window

should have been sufficient to uncover the small figure, but its details are as indeterminable as oil. The kitchen window behind it frames a black, yawning passageway, throbbing wetly, like the gullet of a giant. Rebecca back-paces, fighting to rationalise what she is seeing.

Why is she here? What is she looking for?

The creature at the dark figure's side snarls, revealing a set of spear-like teeth. Although the shadow's identity is indefinable, the beast is unmistakeable. Bruno stares Rebecca down, his eyes no longer dumbly passive but rabid, lupine.

"Please, mummy. Please look after us," the inky child begs.

Bruno pads towards Rebecca, his warning growl deep and primal. When his foam-flecked jaws open, something white juts out: in place of a tongue, a long, narrow penis has thrust head-first out of the hound's throat, dotted with brown freckles. It is an organ that Rebecca knows far too well.

Even as the pain in her abdomen rears up and something uninvited flexes there, Rebecca remains calm. She is here, inside this strange house, but the panic she should have felt is entirely absent, and there is something tranquillising about the way those words drift through her head – welcome home, welcome home – as well as an almost-beautiful sense of something alive inside her womb, sustained by her core. Hasn't she always known that her dream would one day come true and she would become home to a curled, unborn trespasser with a wet snout, hairless paws and a stump of bone-white tail? It is hers to nurture, as is this house, this child, and this dog; each to love, embrace and cherish.

yes yes yes... only three left... mummy, you can beat the others

Something inside her jerks. She clutches her lower section and sees with disturbed admiration that under the figure-hugging, glittering dress, her trim belly has flourished to twice its usual size. Something's undulating weight heaves against her bladder.

"Mummy, are you alright?" the shadow in the kitchen enquires as she buckles, bending over.

"Yes, darling."

The pain overwhelms her and she staggers backwards, clutching the underside of her swelled midriff. She lowers herself slowly to the filthy floorboards. Her internal muscles tighten and she grits her teeth against an agonizing expulsive motion, easing whatever passenger she now carries towards its exit. An unstoppable pressure rises, and she lifts her dress up and over her half-sphere belly.

Bruno, no longer growling, comes closer. Rebecca braces herself against another lurch of pain, and the dog lowers his broad skull onto his paws and lies still against the ground, panting as if in anticipation. Between his lance-like teeth, the pores of his cock-tongue ooze saliva, and the Great Dane gazes at the spot between Rebecca's legs that now throbs with purposeful, primal tension.

Rebecca throws back her head and squeals gracelessy, another contraction clenching her inner muscles, more devastating those previous. Pain charges through her, and as the contraction intensifies she feels her pelvis strain, widening impossibly.

yes yes yes... be our mummy

Rebecca hears a gristly crackle as her body attempts to clear a passage, and a burning, insuppressable shift occurs behind her pubic arch.

It's coming.

The black, featureless child stands motionless at the kitchen's entrance as a previously unimaginable agony tears through her. Her pelvis cracks and she senses that something has breached the tight space between her legs. A wet slap fills her ears and she squeezes her eyes shut, wishing she could blank her body's torment. The convulsions climax, dragging a horse-like bray from her, and with a slithering crunch, her womb expels an object that feels the size of a watermelon.

Bruno barks triumphantly.

"Mummy," she hears the shadow-child say. "Mummy, mummy, mummy, mummy..."

She opens her eyes to see a small, slime-coated shape shuddering stickily between her open legs, part pink, part white, and dotted with erratic tufts of dark hair. Bruno dips his vast skull, takes something into his jaws, and with a yank drags a final, gelatinous mass out of her body.

Rebecca is once again filled with the impossible certainty that, despite her circumstances, all is well; she is in the right place at exactly the right time, she is at home, she is a mother, and she has just given birth to the beast that she has always dreamed about, yes yes yes, and then -

Snap! - she became hideously aware.

A lifetime of accepting the unacceptable ended with one foul realisation: she had been fooled.

With a cry, Rebecca fell back against the ground and slid her legs closed, fully expecting to find that her pelvis had been shattered. Despite her exhaustion and the soreness beyond measure, she knew that she had to escape before the docile fuzziness returned. Ignoring the still-powerful urge to take her spawn - was it still growing? - into her arms, she twisted herself onto her front and heaved herself to her feet. The front door was still open, and she staggered on raw, aching legs towards the light.

She could not help but turn back.

The monstrosity she had expelled lay with its fur-dotted spine facing her. Bruno lapped paternally at its neck. It was growing at a shocking rate, already the size of a primary school infant. It yapped, just like a wolf pup, and Rebecca felt a vile maternal tug.

Just as she had always dreamed, the base of its naked spine bore a nub of white tail, and though the shape of its head was humanlike when it turned to face the ceiling she saw its elongated jawline. It snapped its teeth, and grunted. Bruno looked in pleading at Rebecca, but she held onto the fact that none of this could be true, none of it real.

She forced herself to turn away, sensing

something constrict with rage in the corridor behind her.

NO NO NO NO NO MUMMY

Rebecca hobbled towards the door, fleeing the barking, mewling fruit of her loins, the shadowy child that had begged her to stay, and the voice that echoed through her head and bones

OBEY US MUMMY OBEY ME OBEYYYYYYYYYY

and demanded that she stayed.

When she reached for the door handle, a terrible urge held her back.

A dreadful, dazed pain.

A desire to reject desolation and to nurture something other than bitterness.

And a fearful, preposterous certainty that this place was, is, always had been, and always will be the only thing she would ever desire.

CHAPTER 18
"Grasping green darkness"

Henry

Henry supports the boy's waist while Fred struggles to hold his shoulders up, an' the pair half-drag, half-support him an' walk towards the house. Henry had gotten Fred to hunt through Locker's ripped-up trousers until he'd found the handcuff keys, so at least Raymond's arms are free now. Even so, the lad doesn't seem to have a clue what's goin on, an' keeps whinin like an injured cat.

In spite of all the shite that's popped outta this arse'ole of a day, Henry can't stop thinkin about his pesky dreams. Picturin his old dad, a face like a deflated balloon but wiv pitch-black eyes, standin on a forest path, beckonin. Beckonin him to this very fackin garden.

Then there are the voices that he keeps

hearin, or thinkin he's heard.

are you going to stay with us? yes yes yes you could play games with your ickle boy if you did because someone has to win yes yes yes

Henry has almost replied aloud, but that'd make him sound like a schizo – one o' them split-up personalities. He sure as hell doesn't wanna give Fred any more ammo.

It seems to take much longer gettin back outta the garden than it had gettin in. Every time Henry thinks that they're at the edge, he notices that the house is still a bit of a distance away, like it's movin at the same rate as they're walkin. They finally reach a small clearin, an' the house is just a few metres away.

"It's alright, son," Henry says, as much to distract himself as to reassure the boy. "We'll get you fixed up, good an' proper. You've lost blood but you're a trooper, aren't ya? My special lad."

you think that he is but he isn't, no no no, you funny funny man

Henry ignores it. "If ya need a transfusion, you can probly have a few glugs o' mine, can't ya? An' don't worry about yer face – I'll get the best surgeons in the country to sort you out. They'll have you lookin' even better than you did before!"

"Mum..." Ray says, his head hangin, his gob streamin blood. "Mum..."

"Don't worry about her, Raymond-son – I'll make sure she's waitin for you at the hospital, alright? Just stay wiv me, stay awake for ya ol' dad."

silly, soppy man... you could be OUR *daddy, though, yes yes yes*

NO NOT HIM

In the kitchen, Ray shifts one foot in front o' the other. He can't quite support himself, an' gluey strings o' blood still hang from his chin an' onto the collar of his muddy shirt. He's not bleedin enough to make Henry think that he's bust an artery, though.

While they're helpin him down the empty, stinkin hall, Fred goes, "I know we're taking him to a doctor, and I'm on board with that. But shouldn't we decide what we're going to say? Bribes can only go so far, so what are we going to tell them? And what will Ray say, once he can speak?"

Henry stops. He sighs, lookin at Ray's bleary eyes an' ruined face. "Fred - to be honest I couldn't give a badger's toss what he tells 'em. Right now, I'd give this kid anythin. I'd kill anyone who hurt him more than he already is. I'd even get banged up for him. So shut up, keep movin, an' we'll talk about it when we're on our way, okay?"

"Okay," Fred replies, lookin troubled.

They reach the closed front door.

"Hold him a moment, willya?" Henry says. "It's gonna be alright, son, jus' gimme a sec."

He tugs the handle.

Rebecca, the slag who'd ripped up his heart an' his arse'ole, is lyin on the front step. She's face up an' pantin, eyeballs glassier than

Raymond's, soaked in sweat, hair pricked up like a thorn bush. There's grey slime all over her legs, too, the filthy cow.

Henry is too surprised to question why she's there. "Put him down," he tells Fred.

The tart doesn't react – jus' keeps starin at the sky.

Fred's murmurin somethin, but Henry says, "I dunno why she's here. Maybe she's a gift, makin' up for what's happened to Raymond here. Whatever it is, we're takin' her wiv us. Slam 'er in the boot an' deal wiv 'er once Ray's seein a doctor."

bring her back inside, yes yes yes, then we'll have a mummy, a daddy, and a baby

no just one winner just one winner

Henry flinches – the voices sound closer now. Oblivious, Fred lays Raymond down onto the floorboards, ready to help Henry wiv the slag.

"You nasty cunt," Henry rumbles to Rebecca. "If you thought it was bad wiv Bruno, jus' you wait."

KILL THE WHORE KILL THE CHILD KILL THEM ALL

no no no, we just want the child or the mummy

"I'll teach you what happens to people who mess wiv Henry fackin Borders," Henry says, determined to ignore the voices, even though they seem to be swellin.

we need a winner, yes yes yes

SLAUGHTER THEM ALL

"I'll buy three Rottweilers, an' have 'em take turns on ya: one up your clunge, one up your

arse, an' one in your gob. An' you'll *love it*.
You'll..."

bring back his funny hairy son

his REAL son

yes

yes yes yes

YES!!!

Henry is about to step outside when he hears
a rush o' footsteps, like the heavy patter that
Bruno's paws used to make when he was excited.
Henry must be goin bonkers, coz when he hears a
familiar phlegmy grizzle he's almost convinced
that it *is* Bruno, back from the dead.

Behind him, Fred yelps.

Henry turns.

Until today, there's never bin a situation
that Henry hasn't felt capable o' dealin wiv.
Havin lived a life o' such self-certainty, the
moment that he absorbs the sight in the
corridor, his grip on the world takes a tumble.

Somethin's stood in the shadows behind Fred.
Above Fred's shoulder, two calculatin, brown-
yellow eyes are focused on Henry. The owner o'
those peepers is enormous, but it's dippin its
skull an' hunchin its back to reach Fred's
throat. Fred's gone stiff, as if he doesn't dare
move, coz the thing behind him has locked its
long, wolfish jaws underneath his neatly
trimmed beard. Above the teeth buried in Fred's
neck, the black nostrils look wet enough to be a
snout, but flare in a way that makes 'em seem
like a fella's.

When the door behind Henry slams shut, a

fart like a mournin child slips from his bowels. For the first time ever, he's rooted to the spot. He's seen it in uvver cunts – always sneered at such weakness – but here he is, locked to the floor. What's worse, he hasn't frozen simply coz o' there's a great ugly dog-thing chewin on his pal's windpipe, but coz o' somethin much worse: Henry feels *recognition.* He's noticed that, despite the thing's cheeks bein knotted wiv fur, its brow has got a high, maybe even *recedin,* hairline. Henry's also spotted that the pawlike hands diggin into Fred's sides are pudgy an' stubby, like Henry's.

Somethin in Fred's gullet gives way wiv a gravelly crunch. The great towerin thing releases him wiv a smack o' lips. Fred's head rolls back, neck-hole squirtin a red bouquet over a poster o' some tart in a pink cape. Henry still can't move, even when Fred hits the floorboards at his feet, throat spurtin an' arms twitchin.

Henry sees the full form o' the huge, hairy bastard, an' his brain retreats. Its overall shape is curved an' womanly, but its arms an' long legs bulge wiv muscles. The skull is wide an' its face is patched wiv random black fur. A heavy set o' tits hangs above its paunched belly, an' the nipples, large an' pinky-brown, remind Henry o' the bitch lyin outside on the doorstep. However, a lanky, straw-thin dick hangs between its legs, pale an' scatter-shot wiv freckles.

Henry meets its yellow-brown eyes an' hears

two terrible words.

"'*Ello, daddy.*"

Henry feels a weird, acceptin calmness. He turns slowly to his left, like a merry-go-round windin down, an' looks at young Raymond lyin on his back, wiv his ripped face leanin Henry's way. Henry absorbs the boy's long, slim frame an' once-beautiful looks. Wiv-out thinkin, Henry crouches next to him, picturin the blue eyes beneath those closed lids an' observin the narrow, sharp nose an' angelic cheekbones. When all's said an' done, Henry an' Raymond don't look one bit alike. It's amazin what wishful thinkin can do.

Feelin feeble, Henry plants his ruined arse onto the floor, gazin at the boy he'd wished was his son an' heir, while tryin to ignore the freakish figure loomin above him. There's a padded thud as the dog-thing drops its bulk to all fours. It'd truly be a mark o' weakness if Henry didn't face the beast, an' he can't die like that, so he stares into its face just a foot or so away. He can smell its rank breath, an' as he watches, its expression alters, lips slippin back from the knives of its teeth. The sad, connivin eyes narrow to cracks, an' Henry's reminded of a meaner, larger Bruno.

Henry lowers his head wiv what he hopes is composed, purposeful dignity. "I'm sorry, son," he murmurs, either to the boy or the dog-thing. "I'm sorry."

At the first touch o' the thing's taloned paws, though, Henry realises the stupidity o' just sittin there.

"*Jesus fackin' Christ!*" he bellows, forgettin dignity an' poise. "*Fack! Get offa me, you great bastard!*"

He springs to his feet, swingin a fist. The dog-thing pounces, an' its furry weight hits him like a fackin freight train. Henry pratfalls onto his back, crushed beneath it, an' two rows o' sharp enamel dig into his neck. He can't cry out, an' his eyes water like taps. Through the pain, all he can see is the high, mildewed ceilin an' the top o' the thing's pink head, covered in hairy clumps. It drags him sideways, an' Henry finds himself starin once more into Raymond's face, the kid's eyes blissfully closed an' oblivious. Henry coughs an' claret jets across the floorboards, gushin from his lips like it can't get out of him quick enough.

"*Daddy,*" Henry hears. "*Daddy.*"

The thing inspects him wiv its yellow-brown eyes. It looks almost sorrowful, like a child sat at its parent's deathbed, but underneath all that there's nothing but dumb, feral hunger.

"*Daddy,*" it repeats, before snappin its jaws around Henry's neck for a second time. Helpless an' surrounded by the damp, wild smell of its fur, Henry's vision becomes a mush o' brown, grey an' pink.

As he feels the blood pissin out of him, Henry hears one o' the other voices a final time.

two left now, yes yes yes...just two left

The infamous Henry Borders lies on the damp floor o' someone else's home, as somethin awful gobbles on his larynx. He realises he's shat himself. Even worse: he's usin his last few breaths to sob, like he was some sorta poof.

Rebecca

After a time of empty thoughtlessness, Rebecca stirred to the smell of something rank and coppery. She sat up, wrinkling her nose. She was on the cool ground, facing the house's mossy front path that led to the cars. Although the atmosphere was serene, the silence only punctuated by the sighs of vehicles roaming the road beyond the trees, there was a hint of settling in the air, like the aftermath of a great flurry of motion.

Something had happened after she had watched the taxi depart; something she refused to consider.

Beneath the early evening sun, she stretched her arms above her head, easing her stiffened neck to the left and then to the right. She stopped, mid-turn. A chill wave passed over her: from beneath the door's mouldering threshold, something thick and red had oozed into the day, pooling upon the stoop just inches from the back of her ridden-up dress.

Rebecca knew quite certainly that, even though recent memories were fuzzy, the sight of

Jonathan Butcher

the crimson puddle threatened to send her spiralling back into catatonia. At this understanding, she hardened, vowing to distance herself and focus on the one thing that would matter if she survived: the money. Ignoring

the dog the shadow-child THE BIRTH

the pain of her insides and strained pelvis, she hauled herself to her feet and faced the farmhouse door. She should have fled. She should have prioritised life and sanity over the contents of Gary's grey backpack, but, standing one pace back from the gruesome front stoop, Rebecca braced herself, laid a hand against the door, and pushed.

Inside, the floorboards were awash with blood. She stepped back when she saw the suited man lying facedown in a red pond in the hallway. The sight and shape of its hairy cheek told Rebecca that it was one of Henry's associates: Fred Chalmers. His throat had been rent open, exposing the tongue-like tubing of his oesophagus.

Closeby, beside the poster-clad wall, a second body lay on its back, this one far thinner than Fred. Its face was a mask of gore, and Rebecca's breath snagged when she recognised Raymond.

Her greatest surprise was sprawled at the end of the hall, where the obliterated features of a third figure gazed sightlessly towards her. Its blood-drenched arm was stretched towards the kitchen, as if something had tried dragging it out to the garden. Despite its mutilations, Rebecca knew the man immediately, and alongside her revulsion she felt ecstatic relief.

Henry Borders' blubbery lips hung from his face in shreds, and his once-flaring nostrils were now a single, ragged hole. His eyes were gone and one socket trailed a thin cord across his cheek. Of the ten fingers that had once manhandled Rebecca, only the left pinkie and the right middle finger remained; the others lay scattered across the bare boards of the corridor. The legs of Henry's ludicrous white suit bore the red-stained marks of a vicious mauling.

The false king's reign was over.

Raymond, who Rebecca had assumed dead, mewled. The high sound jolted her, drawing her attention, and she saw that both of the boy's cheeks had been sliced neatly open. If he lived, his bewitching face would be scarred forever. She felt profound regret - this should never have happened to one so young, so special – but no matter how great an impact their meeting had made upon her, he was not Rebecca's responsibility, and Rebecca was almost certainly in danger. Once she was a safe distance away, she would anonymously call an ambulance.

It seemed that, somehow, Gary's shop robbery had resulted in a massacre. Now was not the time to question how or why, because thoughts of all that had happened before she had awoken on the doorstep were threatening to breach her mental barriers. If that were to happen, all would be lost, so she focused on her present task.

She could reach into the house and pat Fred's pockets, searching for a gun with which to break into the rental car. The idea of extending even a single limb through the doorway made the hairs on her arms and neck stand upright in protest, but she could not deny a contrasting sense of curiosity.

A thought struck her - had the cab driver seen something amiss, driven away and contacted the police? Were they on their way already? If so, maybe it would be safer for her to stay in the house. She could look around. She could find the precious little thing that she had expelled from her womb and...

No. That never happened.

The house seemed to be watching her, intrigued. Something here felt vulnerable. It wanted her to stay - or needed her to. Could it be that the house itself was responsible for these horrors? Even so, would there be any harm in slipping back inside, just for a peek?

yes yes yes, come back, yes yes yes

She ignored a tug of protectiveness in her chest, certain that stepping over the threshold would be... inadvisable. She crouched, held her breath and strained a hand through the entranceway. She could not quite reach Fred's trousers from where she perched, so she hobbled closer, treading her feet into the blood and exposing her lack of underwear. Thankfully, Raymond was not watching, lost as he was in apparent delirium.

"Mummy..." he muttered, eyes unfocused.

Reluctantly, she lay her knees down onto the step, ignoring the warmth of Fred's blood, and strained her arm, her fingers passing over the dead man's head but reaching no farther than the slope of his shoulders. She felt certain that he *would be carrying a gun and that he would have the keys to one of the cars in his pockets. She remained on her knees at the doorstep, stretching frustratedly into the shadows.*

She scolded herself. To reach Fred's pockets, all it would take would be five or so steps; she could dash in and out within thirty seconds.

Fine. That's what she would do: she would go to Fred's body. Yes,

yes yes yes

surely that was right. Then she would check upstairs for anything unusual, just to prove to herself that the residue on her thighs and the wracking of her pelvis signified nothing important. After all, would she ever be able to sleep again if she remained uncertain? She simply wanted to put her mind at rest.

Rebecca rose, bracing herself against the stench of the blood, training her eyes to avoid the lurid details of the cadavers. It was fine, though. Everything was fine, because the corpses were only empty shells. Even young Raymond, unconscious again or dead on his back, evoked less misery when she lifted one bare foot in preparation to enter.

Her concern evaporated when her foot –

- touches the viscera-strewn floorboards.

She now knows that her beautiful, fearsome offspring is waiting for her in the garden.

In the Garden.

The Gardden.

yes mummy, I'm here, we're all here, we knew you would come back

"Of course, dear," she hears as she sleepwalks

three steps forwards, raising a foot up and over one of Fred's sprawled arms. The certainty of her biology fills her; she had been wrong to fight and flail against it for so long. She is a nurturer, a hole that must be filled and that must care for all she has conceived. Her child – her children – wait for her beneath the leaves out back, under the soil, overseen by the two sightless, all-seeing black eyes of the garden

GARDDEN

She will stay. She will shed the skin of the foolish tales she's never truly believed. She will become the mother she should always have been.

yes yes mummy... you can win... you can be the one

JUST ONE JUST ONE JUST ONE

Her feet carry her down the hallway, and the walls seem to shift and contract. Before her, the kitchen window once again reveals the dark yawning maw of the Gardden, inhaling the sour air of the house through the walls and glass, sucking her closer; a whirlpool of liquid night.

we love you so much, mummy, I we it they will kill your cares and fill your fears, we will and always have wanted you here with us, we will never let you go

JUST ONE JUST ONE

yes mummy, you have to be the last

A sound cuts into her brain: young Raymond's tears, dry and heaving. She knows what she has to do, so she turns away from the Gardden's vorticose gullet towards the sleeping young man.

He would not wish to awaken with his

seraphic face turned to wrack and ruin. He would rather sleep soundly here, forever in this perfect home, this wondrous charnel house. Rebecca stands above him, watching the rise and fall of his pigeon chest and the slathered red of his incised cheeks. She has no pillow with which to smother him, no knife to plunge into his heart, but she has thumbs and ten perfectly manicured nails.

She kneels again, feeling the Gardden's eyes observe her with manic, immature, ageless glee.

yes mummy yes mummy yes mummy

She runs a finger across the wound that half-bridges the space between Raymond's mouth and ear, tempted to slip a nail into the bloody groove to test its depth. She resists and hooks her thumbs, places them against the young man's eyelids. The globes beneath feel as yielding as peeled lychees. She presses experimentally and Raymond remains unaware, his lungs expelling air almost meditatively. He must welcome her touch. Two abrupt thrusts is all it will take to propel her thumbs deep into his brain, ending his suffering.

yes mummy yes then you will win The People Game yes yes yes and then you can play and stay forever

At last, Raymond, the young man, the child, responds, his eyelids shivering as softly as butterfly wings. She retracts her thumbs for a moment and the boy's eyes open, two blue and beautiful oases gazing out from the blood-spattered trauma of his face.

yes mummy do it now

YES YES YES MUMMY NOW NOW NOW

"Mum?" Raymond asks. "What are you doing?"

And the boy begins to cry.

At the sound of his sobs, Rebecca becomes aware once more that something has fooled her, has contorted her body and mind to its own will, like her escorting clients, like Henry, and she must not let it continue to happen.

no no no no

NO NO NO

She must take the confused maternal instincts she feels for the house, the children, and the Gardden, and re-direct them. She stands and pounds an unsteady path down the hallway, the breath of the jealous Gardden still

COME BACK MUMMY COME BACK COME BACK COME BACK

tugging her backwards.

When her heels –

- touched the path outside, the release was complete and unmistakable. It, whatever it was, felt weaker when she was outside, but she knew she had to act fast.

"Stop crying," she hissed, still hearing the Gardden's raging voice

NO NO NO NO NO

despite her exit muffling its words. "Please stop crying, Raymond."

The boy did as he was asked, despite continuing to sniffle. He turned his woeful head towards her, and a split in one bloody cheek revealed white teeth.

It was time for Rebecca to embrace her urges.

It was time to give in and play mother.
She said, "I have a deal for you, son."

Ray

Time passed in hops and flashes. Woozy, barely able to see his own hands, Ray had dragged himself up from the ground and discerned the far-off shape of Henry's carcass. He was aware enough to know that, having bled so much, his life was at risk, and the shock of seeing Henry only served to shut his mind down further. He had searched the pockets of Fred's corpse and when he'd found a pistol and the keys to the BMW he'd pulled them free and begun a tiresome, teetering journey to the outside world.

The pain in his head and wrists and dislocated shoulder had been unrelenting. Little else had registered in his mind, aside from a violent buzzing in his head that he had assumed signified a concussion. A couple of feet back from the doorway, he'd seen the glutinous puddle his face let spill across the floor, and he had almost buckled. Groaning, step after step, stride by resistant stride, he had lumbered towards the late Fred Chalmers' BMW.

Ray must have managed to reach the car because his forehead now pressed against a cool window, his jaws held tightly together to avoid disturbing his injuries. Fields sprinkled with four-legged clouds slid across the middle distance. In the midst of his bloodloss and the weakness of his drained limbs, Ray had found calm.

Rebecca lectured him as she drove. "...to listen to me, because if you don't, you'll end up in more trouble than that little mind of yours can imagine. If there's anything I learned during my time with Henry, it's to stay quiet, and that's just what you should do. You were tortured by muggers, unnamed attackers, and you didn't see any of their faces. Perhaps you don't even remember a thing." She tutted. "I imagine the police will be at that farmhouse by now, examining every lump of gristle and drop of blood."

A school of pylons crept across the horizon.

"Do many people know about your involvement with Henry?"

Ray rolled his head to face Rebecca, hardly absorbing her words.

She glanced at him and shook her head. "You're a very foolish boy," she scolded, but gently. "Getting involved in men's games when you've barely mastered puberty."

Ray returned his face to the smeared glass. His body felt hollow, as if he was already dead.

"You're going to get yourself arrested if you aren't very, very careful. You're bleeding again, you know.

Try not to get any more on the seat..."

He must have drifted into unconsciousness because the radio was on when he awoke again. A female newsreader was speaking.

"...following the apparent failed kidnapping of a pregnant Seadon resident. The as-yet-unnamed intruder remains in critical condition at Witcham Hospital. No one has been arrested at this stage, but a police investigation is already underway."

Hills plodded by.

Another leap forward.

"...that I want to; of course I don't," Rebecca muttered as she overtook a green estate car. Its pre-teen, blonde female passenger stared at Ray in horror. "But maybe I should. I can't stop thinking about it. It's like it's been planted in my head and now it won't leave, as if it's the *whole point*, the whole meaning behind it all. I know that I was ... under stress, and that the whole thing's impossible, so could it really hurt?" She made a scoffing sound. "Users and the used - do you really believe that? Oh, you're no good..."

The next time Ray awoke, the car had stopped. Light-headed, he stared out at a quiet car park. It was raining. Rebecca was patting his breast and he turned to her, exhausted.

"If you don't want it, dispose of it before you go inside." She sounded stern and her face was unclear.

As she leaned over and opened Ray's door he caught a waft of something sweet, and for a second her lips remained just an inch away from his raw face. Looking into his eyes, she breathed, "I hope that we meet under better circumstances next time, young man." She remained within kissing distance for a moment longer, and then said, "Come on, out you get."

He shifted his feet and tried to stand, but his legs crumpled and he collapsed onto the tarmac.

From behind, Rebecca added sadly, "Take care, Raymond."

He heard the door close and, with one injured cheek flat against the ground, watched the BMW pull away.

The last thing Ray saw before blackness enveloped him was the sideways-on face of an elderly woman wearing a purple hat. She looked revolted.

"Don't try to speak."

He was standing bare-footed on the shore of a rose-red beach, pounding a waist-high rock into wet sand with a rubber-topped mallet. The tool was hardly up to the task, but he had to do it now or it would never be finished before the tide was in.

"Can you hear me?"

Maybe he should use a stone instead of the mallet. He might chip the carved edges though, and that wouldn't do. He looked towards the distant end of the shoreline. Rows of suited figures cheered for him soundlessly, waving their arms. Someone fired a pistol silently into the air.

"Sir?"

Ray opened his eyes and winced against a blazing strip of light.

A woman in white sat posture-straight on a chair beside him. A semi-circle of curtains surrounded them. Ray was in bed, propped up by pillows, wearing only his underwear. His cheeks were unnaturally stiff and the world felt like a cotton-wrapped dream.

Ray assumed that his nurse was approaching thirty. Her blonde hair was a whipped ice cream and she had vibrant green eyes that glowed with intelligence. A blue nametag on her full left bosom read 'Lynne'. "Do you want some water?" she said.

Ray's mouth tasted medicinal and his throat was arid. He nodded.

Nurse Lynne rose from her seat and picked up a glass of water from the bedside table. "Only open wide enough to take the straw."

He drank gratefully.

"Don't make any quick movements. You've been given morphine. Do you think you can speak?"

In spite of the warm comfort of the morphine, the thought of opening his lips to talk made him envision the state of his face. He felt his lips tremble and tears welled up in his eyes.

"It's okay, it's okay," Nurse Lynne said, raising a hand and smiling kindly. "Maybe you would prefer to write, for the moment?"

He raised his thumb and wiped his eyes, embarrassed.

Nurse Lynne leaned forwards and placed a notepad and biro onto his lap. Even in his delicate condition, Ray noticed a flash of cleavage at the top of her shirt. She seemed to notice the direction of his gaze. "You can't be *too* sad, then," she grinned, then reached over and ruffled his hair. "Is there someone we should contact?"

Without thinking, he scrawled in unfamiliar, atrocious handwriting, "*rose atticus my mummy.*" He followed this with her phone number.

Nurse Lynne nodded. "I'll call her right away. For now, you just sit tight." She rose to her feet and asked, "Do you remember what happened?"

Ray shook his head, wishing it were the truth.

Nurse Lynne swept a curtain back. Ray's bed was one of many in a ward divided into cubicles by thin sheets of fabric.

When she had gone, questions came in profusion.

Was he going to be arrested? Where was Thomas? Why had Rebecca come to the house? He tried to thrust further enquiries to the back of his mind but they barged through uninvited. What had killed Henry and Fred? What had happened in the garden? What had hauled Percy Locker up into the trees and stripped him of flesh like a joint of meat? What had the twitching, undulating shapes in the undergrowth been, bellowing with such force that Ray's ears still rang, even now?

And what of the voices, that tittering, conspiratory choir, telling him stories and imploring him to stay?

He shrank back into the pillow.

Each of his business associates was dead, and the man who had wrongly believed that he was Ray's father was among them. Ray closed his eyes as an image of his late boss slipped into his thoughts: Henry lying in an angular heap, his plotting, manipulative brain brought to a gruesome standstill by an unknown assailant. Ray tensed. To his surprise, hidden amongst the disturbance was a sense of release. He'd spent weeks wrestling with his conscience, but now the reins had been snatched from his hands. He no longer had a choice to make; all he could do was wait to find out if the police wanted to speak with him. If they did, he would confess to all he knew, including Robbie's murder. Deception hurt his head too much.

He wondered whether Thomas would contact the authorities. It seemed unlikely, given Thomas's own secrets, and his decision to leave Ray at the mercy of the garden.

The Gardden.

Ray shivered, imagining the Gardden's grasping green darkness.

Playful and hateful.

Fatherly and childish.

Ray would need time before he was willing to consider it again, so instead he focused on the future.

If the murder investigation, somewhat implausibly, failed to lead to him, or if Thomas somehow managed to conceal the bodies and vehicles that littered his property, could Ray still vacate Seadon? Travel the world as a form of therapy? Before this day he'd thought he had lost his wanderlust, fearing that he would crumble beneath a surge of panic attacks if he were to leave, but now, injured in hospital, morphined up, freshly scarred and almost certainly in shock, thoughts of departure returned.

From somewhere deep inside him, an unbidden fancy arose: he could choose a route to Asia that would first take him to the north of England, so that he could visit the place where his father Bernard was buried. He could even ask his mother to join him for the initial trip, and during their journey he could insist that she told him everything that she remembered about Ray's real father. Surely she owed him that.

But what of the money? The tough period following Robbie's death had been defined by litres of vintage spirits in expensive wine bars, top-quality coke, hotel stays because he couldn't face his mother, and weeks of needlessly extravagant meals that he had often left uneaten. His savings were not what they had once been, and it would be an age before he could gather the same amount again, if he took on a legitimate job.

He supposed that, given the choice, he would have to stay with his mother. It wasn't so bad in Seadon, after all. There was the sea, there were nightclubs, and there were plenty of potential sex partners – as long as he found a new fanbase that considered facial scars appealing. He was still young, and there was no need to rush things.

Noticing that his clothes had been folded up and placed on the back of Nurse Lynne's chair, Ray remembered Rebecca's parting words.

If you don't want it, dispose of it before you go inside.

Trying not to strain himself, he reached for the suit jacket with his good arm. When it was on his lap he tentatively dipped his fingers into the inner pocket. There, wrapped in neatly taped packages, Ray found two thick bundles of fifty pound notes.

Jesus.

Ten thousand pounds.

If he escaped imprisonment, there would still be a decision for him to make. The whole world would still be out there, waiting to meet him as a boy or as a real man - or perhaps something in between.

Slipping the two bundles beneath the mattress, thinking of dim silver linings, concocting a story, and imagining Nurse Lynne invading him with a rectal thermometer, Raymond Atticus leant back into his pillow to wait for his mother.

EPILOGUE
"The winner"

Rebecca

Rebecca had sat in the BMW for more than half an hour now, parked in the shadows of the empty dirt track. Night had fallen and the moon cast skeletal silhouettes across the walls of the ancient farmhouse.

To Rebecca's astonishment, there had been no police tape blocking her path to the road. Even more curious, the vehicles were gone and the corpses nowhere to be seen. With hundreds of thousands of pounds lying on the seat behind her, Rebecca could have already been on a boat or a plane, travelling across the sea to begin life somewhere new. But there she was.

here you are

The house stood tall and silent. The front door was now closed but she was sure that if she gave it just a gentle push it would swing backwards and invite her inside, an honoured guest. She only wanted to take a quick look around.

She drummed her nails on the wheel, toying with the idea of starting the ignition.

but you're the winner, mummy

Something shifted in an upstairs window; the reflection of a leafy branch or the drifting of a cloud. Or perhaps the movement of a mischievous, misshapen infant, ducking just out of sight.

She glanced back at the bag, filled with its riches. She drummed the wheel harder. With her other hand, she stroked her lower belly, feeling the absence of something sleeping calmly inside her. If there had ever truly been a form nestled there, it was now waiting for her behind the house, encircled by the hungry, playful darkness of the garden.

The Gardden.

Sighing, she took her fingers off the wheel and reached for the car door handle.

Other titles by
Jonathan Butcher

The Chocolateman: a short story by Jonathan Butcher

"There was a rhyme that some of them said the Chocolateman had whispered to them through the pipes: I'm the one who eats your food, after you've digested it …"

"Please stop."

"My aim is never to be rude – just to eat your rich chocolate …"

"Please, I don't like it."

"I'm the Chocolateman, you know, I take my time but I'm never slow…"

"That's enough!"

"Kreb's the name, called one, two, three. Take a dump and there I'll be."

The Sinister Horror Company invites you to wade through the filth of this short story as Jonathan Butcher introduces us to the foulest, most perverse horror villain of the modern age.

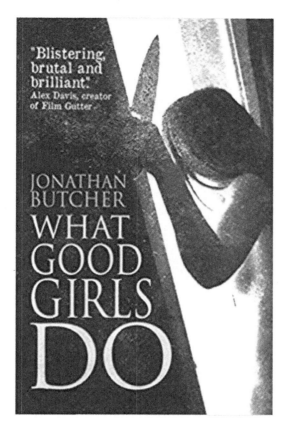

She lives with no name.
She has never left her room.
All she has ever known is pain and abuse.
Until now.
Today, she will breathe fresh air for the first time, feel sunshine against her skin and even witness human kindness.
But she has a point to make – a bleak, violent point – and when she meets her neighbour, Serenity, she finds the perfect pupil.
Forced to endure a lesson distilled from a nightmarish existence, Serenity must face unflinching evil, witness the unspeakable, and question her most deeply-held views, until at last she has no choice but to fight for her family's survival.

ThIs Is NoT a NoRmAl AnThOlOgY...
If you are expecting a neat, predictable set of stories,
THIS IS NOT FOR YOU
If you want horror but hate bizarro or getting "the feels",
STEP AWAY
This collection of tales is what happens when one man's art meets
12 authors fiction, and when writers are free to ignore their genre
of choice and typical story conventions.
12 eye-challenging op-art designs were used to inspire these 12
mind-bending stories, which contain everything from futuristic sci-
fi to fantastical comedy, and heartfelt life musings to near-cosmic
nihilism.
This is VISIONS FROM THE VOID.

Made in the USA
Las Vegas, NV
18 March 2022